FOSSIL HUNTER

Books by Robert J. Sawyer

NOVELS

*Golden Fleece**
*End of an Era**
The Terminal Experiment
Starplex
*Frameshift**
Illegal Alien
*Factoring Humanity**
*Flashforward**
*Calculating God**
*Mindscan**

THE NEANDERTHAL PARALLAX

*Hominids**
*Humans**
*Hybrids**

THE QUINTAGLIO ASCENSION

*Far-Seer**
*Fossil Hunter**
*Foreigner**

SHORT-STORY COLLECTION

Iterations

ANTHOLOGIES

Tesseracts 6 (with Carolyn Clink)
Crossing the Line (with David Skene-Melvin)
Over the Edge (with Peter Sellers)

*Published by Tor Books

(Readers' group guides available at www.sfwriter.com)

FOSSIL HUNTER

Book Two of The Quintaglio Ascension

Robert J. Sawyer

A Tom Doherty Associates Book
New York

FOSSIL HUNTER

Copyright © 1993, 2005 by Robert J. Sawyer

This book was previously published by Ace Books, May 1993.

Edited by David G. Hartwell

Map by Dave Dow

A Tor Book
Published by Tom Doherty Associates, LLC
175 Fifth Avenue
New York, NY 10010

www.tor.com

Tor® is a registered trademark of Tom Doherty Associates, LLC.

ISBN 0-765-30973-4

EAN 978-0765-30973-0

First Tor Paperback Edition: March 2005

Printed in the United States of America

0 9 8 7 6 5 4 3 2 1

For my brothers,

Alan B. Sawyer
and
Peter D. Sawyer

The Quintaglios don't know what they're missing.

ACKNOWLEDGMENTS

This book evolved with the advice of family members Carolyn Clink, David Livingstone Clink, and Alan B. Sawyer; friends Ted Bleaney and Laurie Lupton; agent Richard Curtis; editors Peter Heck and Susan Allison; and fellow writers Barbara Delaplace, Cory Doctorow, Terence M. Green, Garfield Reeves-Stevens, and Andrew Weiner. The map is by Dave Dow. This new edition owes its existence to David G. Hartwell, Moshe Feder, and Ralph Vicinanza.

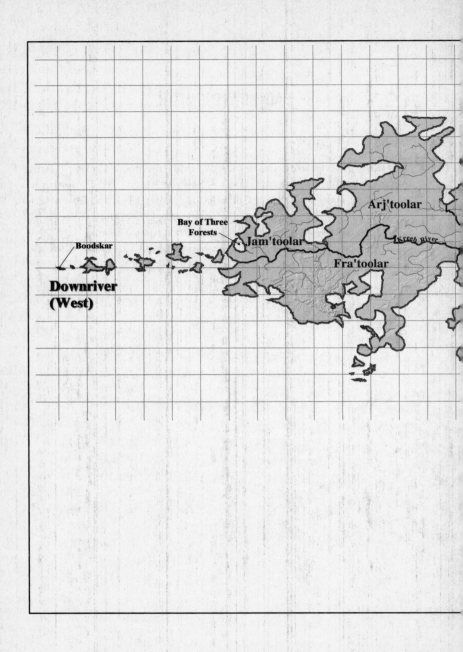

Arj'toolar

Kreeb River

Bay of Three
Forests

Jam'toolar

Boodskar

Fra'toolar

**Downriver
(West)**

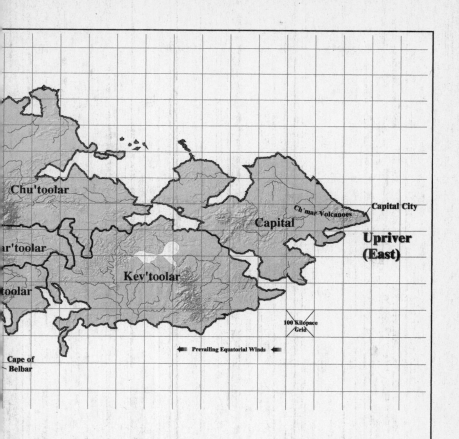

Chu'toolar

ar'toolar

toolar

Kev'toolar

Capital

Ch'mar Volcanoes

Capital City

Upriver
(East)

100 Kilopace
Grid

◄|||| Prevailing Equatorial Winds ◄||||

Cape of
Belbar

-Land-
The Single Continent of the
Quintaglio Home World

N

100	0	100	200	300	400	Kilometers

50	0	50	100	150	200	250	300	350	Miles

Dave Dow
Land - 8/11/03

DRAMATIS PERSONAE

Capital City

Afsan (Sal-Afsan)	advisor to Dy-Dybo
Bogkash (Det-Bogkash)	Master of the Faith
Cadool (Pal-Cadool)	aide to Afsan
Drawtood	dockworker, Afsan's son
Dybo (Dy-Dybo)	Emperor
Galpook (Lub-Galpook)	hunt leader, Afsan's daughter
Gathgol (Var-Gathgol)	undertaker
Maliden (Mek-Maliden)	imperial bloodpriest
Novato (Wab-Novato)	leader of the exodus project

Geological Survey of Land

Babnol (Wab-Babnol)	team member
Biltog (Mar-Biltog)	mate aboard the *Dasheter*
Delplas (Bar-Delplas)	team member
Keenir (Var-Keenir)	captain of the *Dasheter*
Toroca (Kee-Toroca)	leader, Afsan's son

Edz'toolar Province

Rodlox (Dy-Rodlox)	governor

FOSSIL HUNTER

Prologue

The First Sacred Scroll

Five thousand kilodays ago, God laid the eight eggs of creation. When they hatched, the world was born.

From the *first* egg came all the water. God let it run in a vast circular path and it became the Great River.

From the *second* egg came Land itself, and God set Land floating down the River.

From the *third* egg came the air, and God allowed it to flow everywhere that was not the River and not the Land.

From the *fourth* egg came the sun, source of light and heat.

From the *fifth* egg came the stars, planets, and moons, and God raised them high above.

From the *sixth* egg came all the flowers and trees and vegetables and roots and every other thing that is a plant.

From the *seventh* egg came those lesser beasts that eat the plants, including the shovelmouths and thunderbeasts and hornfaces and armorbacks. Also from the seventh egg came the fish and lizards and shelled creatures of the water.

And from the *eighth* and final egg came the greater creatures that dine on flesh, the terrorclaws and blackdeaths and runningbeasts and fangjaws and more.

But even with all eight eggs hatched, God was not pleased. She wanted something else, something that would think and pray. So, after much contemplation, She bit off Her own left arm and let it fall to Land. The blood flowing from the stump of Her arm made the soil rich. The fingers of Her hand detached, and each became one of the five original great and proud hunters: Lubal, Mekt, Katoon, Hoog, and Belbar, five females of strength and courage and acumen. And the five hunters pleased God and She watched them hunt throughout Land.

But the hunters themselves were not pleased, and so they prayed to God. "You have laid the Eggs of Creation," they said, "but we, too, wish to lay eggs and have creations of our own."

For the first time, the Land quaked, for God was angered by the impudence of the Original Five. But then God relented. "Only I may create on my own," She said, "but I will give you the power to create jointly." And God sacrificed of Herself again, biting off Her right arm. It, too, fell to Land, and blood from it made the soil even richer. Its five fingers became five more Quintaglios, and these Quintaglios were the same and yet different, for they were male. They each began a different task: Varkev was the first explorer; Dargo, the original healer; Takood, the first scholar; and Jostark, the craftsperson before all others. And, to keep the rest properly obedient to God, the fifth finger became Detoon the Righteous, first of all priests.

The ten who had been the fingers of God came together and produced five clutches of eight eggs. But God said soon all of Land would be overrun with Quintaglios if all those egglings were allowed to live. Therefore, She charged Mekt with devouring seven out of every eight hatchlings, and Mekt was thus the first bloodpriest.

But then Lubal declared that this portion of Land was hers; and Katoon said, and *this* portion is mine; and Mekt delineated a territory she called her own; and Hoog likewise claimed exclusive dominion over a part of Land; and Belbar asserted a territory, too. And the males, in a similar fashion, divided up the remaining parts of Land.

God was angry, for this was not what She had intended. But She had sacrificed Her arms to make five females and five males and until Her hands regenerated there was nothing that She could do.

Chapter 1

Fra'toolar

One of them was going to die.

Toroca, leader of the Geological Survey of Land, caught sight of the confrontation purely by accident.

He was working nine-tenths of the way up the cliff face, just below the Bookmark layer, looking for fossils.

As usual, Toroca wasn't finding anything. He'd dug his pick countless times into the gray shale just below the chalk stratum, and each time he'd found nothing but plain rock. It was tiring work, so he decided to take a break. He braced himself firmly in a cleft in the rocks, then gulped water from the shovelmouth bladder he used as a canteen. He half-turned to look out. The cliff face dropped for more than a hundred vertical paces directly below him. Still, it bowed out enough that it wasn't a difficult climb in most places, and in those spots where the rocks themselves did not afford adequate purchase, his surveyors had set up webs of climbing ropes.

The cliff ended in a narrow expanse of sandy beach and beyond that there were choppy gray waves leading out to the horizon. Above the waves, far, far out, he could see a large wingfinger circling, its furry, copper-colored wings bright against the purple sky, a sky that today was free of cloud. The sun was a tiny white disk about halfway up the bowl of the sky. Three pale daytime moons were visible.

Toroca's eyes fell back on the beach.

His survey team consisted of eight Quintaglios. Two of them were visible far below and some distance up the beach. They were almost too small to identify, although their green skin stood out well against the beige sands. On the one nearest to him, he could just make out all four limbs and the tail; on the other one, he couldn't even make out that much detail.

They were standing awfully close to each other, only five or six paces between them.

Toroca brought up a hand to shield his eyes. Something funny in the way they were moving—

Bobbing up and down—

Toroca's claws jumped out in shock. He brought his hands to the sides of his muzzle and yelled, "No!"

They couldn't hear him. The wind tore away his words. He began to scramble down the cliff face. Doing so meant turning his back to them so that he could see the rocks, find the footholds.

Where were the other members of the survey team? Either off exploring elsewhere, or else when they'd seen the territorial challenge display, they'd run away, lest they succumb to the sight of bobbing torsos, rhythmically moving up and down, up and down . . .

Toroca's claws were chipping against the rock as he continued his rapid descent. He came to a little fissure in the rocks and turned to climb down the web of thick ropes that covered it. He was about halfway down the cliff now and could see the other two better.

The closer one was Delplas, a middle-aged female. She was still too tiny to recognize by her features, but her distinctive blue and orange sash gave her away. Her torso was tipped right over now, the tail lifted clear off the ground, her body rising and falling over and over again, pivoting at the hips.

Got to hurry. They'd be at each other's throats any moment. Toroca paused in his descent long enough to shout "No!" again, but either the wind was still preventing them from hearing him, or else they were too deep in the madness of *dagamant* to listen.

He'd reached the bottom of the ropes now and turned back to the rocks, the giant claws on his three-toed feet finding purchase in cracks between the strata. His tail hung behind him, a heavy weight. Hurrying, not taking the care he should—

Toroca slipped. The cliff face curved out enough that he didn't fall right off, but he did skid down several paces on his belly, the rocks badly scraping the lighter-colored skin of his front and tearing open two of the many pockets that ran the length of his leather geologist's sash. He clawed frantically for purchase, but the slide continued, down, down, belly over rocks, skin tearing—

More climbing ropes. He shot out his left hand, the five fingers seizing the web. His arm felt like it was going to tear from its socket as he suddenly braked to a halt. He looked briefly at his belly: it was badly scraped but was only bleeding lightly in a couple of places. Too bad: it probably would have been a lot more sanitary to actually have the scrapes flush themselves clean.

Madly, he hurried down the ropes, feet finding homes in the large squares made between intersections of the braided beige fiber. He looked again at the two surveyors, just in time to see it happen.

Delplas lunged, her whole body darting forward, her jaws split wide, showing the serrated white teeth that lined them—

The other Quintaglio—Toroca was now low enough to see that it was Spalton, a male surveyor a bit younger than Delplas—tried to avoid the bite, but Delplas had no trouble connecting, her jaws slamming shut on his shoulder, scooping out bloody red meat . . .

Toroca turned again and hurried down the remaining height of the cliff face, the sound of waves pounding against the shore counterpointing the pounding of his own heart and the roar of the wind no match for his own labored panting.

Finally, he made it to ground level. He ran toward the fighting Quintaglios, now locked in a great ball of green extremities, tails and limbs sticking out every which way. Toroca's own tail was flying behind him as his feet pounded the sand, sand wet enough from rain and spray to make running difficult.

The coppery wingfinger he'd seen before, or one just like it, was now circling high above the two Quintaglios, waiting patiently for fresh meat to dine on. Toroca thundered on.

"Stop!"

It was the word Toroca would have called if he could have found the breath to do so, but it hadn't come from him. No, there, nestled in the rocks at the base of the cliff, back to the fighting Quintaglios, was giant Greeblo, another member of the survey team. "Don't go any closer!" she shouted. "You'll be drawn into the frenzy!"

Toroca ignored her and ran on, his chest aching from without and within as he struggled to continue. Another forty paces to go . . .

Spalton had the advantage now, having slammed Delplas onto the ground. He was coming in to bite down on the back of her neck, a sure way to make the kill—

Territoriality. Toroca cursed it as he closed the remaining distance. The madness of territoriality. Delplas and Spalton had worked together for kilodays now, and yet, somehow, one of them had moved too close, encroaching on the other's territory, and instincts ancient and savage had come into play. The bobbing; the showing of teeth; perhaps for the male, Spalton, the inflation of the dewlap sack on the neck into a ruby-red ball; and then—

The veneer of civilization gone, melted away under the fires of instinct. Claws would have popped from their sheaths, vision clouded over, rational thought drowned out by the rage boiling up within—

They wouldn't last much longer. Delplas had rolled onto her belly, just in time to avoid Spalton's scooping bite, and she'd smashed him in the side of the head, right over his earhole, with a vicious swipe of her tail. Spalton now had tumbled onto his side, muzzle hitting the wet sand hard. Delplas pushed up with her arms, regaining her feet, and once again her jaws opened wide, wider still, the sharp white teeth slick with crimson, her dexterous neck bending down, muscles bulging, readying for the kill—

"No!" shouted Toroca, finally reaching them, the sands beneath them already a slurry of quartz grains and blood. Delplas looked up. She seemed momentarily confused, startled for an instant out of the madness of *dagamant,* but then she turned back to the prone Spalton, her jaws gaping—

Toroca reached out, grabbed her shoulder. *"Stop it!"* The touch shocked her—he could see her inner lids flutter across her obsidian black eyes. He yanked her aside, and brought his other arm up to her other shoulder, shaking her violently. "Stop it!"

Her jaws were still split wide, her whole muzzle a killing maw filled with white daggers. She faced Toroca and turned her head sideways, ready now to bite down on his muzzle or neck, tearing him open—

"No!" shouted Toroca.

Behind them, Spalton was getting up. His left arm hung loosely from his shoulder, half-severed by one of Delplas's great bites. He opened his jaws, ready to take out Delplas from behind, but then he staggered from side to side, and his jaw went slack, half closing, his eyelids likewise shutting partway, and he fell onto his side in a heap behind Delplas.

Delplas, oblivious to all this, snapped her jaws shut, but Toroca did the unthinkable in a territorial battle. He stepped *backward,* dancing out of her way. Her massive head failing to connect, she lost balance and tipped way, way forward. Toroca moved in from the side. He interlocked the fingers of his hands to form a massive club, like the tail knob of an armorback, and pounded down on her shoulders. She lost her footing and slammed down onto the sand. Overhead, the wingfinger let out a shriek, but the only sound Delplas made was a soft *oomph.*

Toroca leapt onto her back, pinning her. He was taking a big chance that Spalton wouldn't recover enough to attack him from behind, but he couldn't let them fight like this.

Delplas tried to push up off the beach, but she was near exhaustion. Toroca continued to hold her down.

He couldn't release her, not until he was sure the madness had passed. At last she spoke, her voice hoarse. "How . . ."

Come on, Delplas, Toroca thought. *Give me a coherent sentence. Let it be over.*

"How," she began again, and a moment later, the rest of it came, "did you do that?" He got off her. She tried to rise, but was too tired or too injured to do so. Her inner eyelids were fluttering in astonishment, but as Toroca moved away from her, he saw her claws slip back into their sheaths.

"How did you do that?" she said again.

He moved over to Spalton, still lying on his side, the vessels in his arm having mostly sealed, but some blood still seeping out. His breathing was shallow but even, the respiration of unconsciousness, not the frantic gulping of air that comes with the territorial madness of *dagamant.*

"How?" said Delplas again, still too weak to get up. "How did you avoid getting drawn into the territorial battle? How could you *touch* me without your claws coming out?"

Toroca bent over to minister to Spalton's wounds. He'd kept it a secret this long; he had no intention of offering an explanation now.

Chapter 2

Universes come and go.

I am the sole survivor of the previous cycle of creation, of the universe that existed prior to this one. My body had ceased to have material substance countless millennia before the end of the old universe, but with forethought and determination and not a small amount of luck my consciousness managed to survive reasonably intact through that universe's contraction into a cosmic egg and the subsequent Big Bang that gave rise to this latest iteration of everything.

It had been an impudent move, for who has the right to outlast the universe? And my impudence, apparently, was to be punished.

I thought I had ended up in hell.

The universe I had evolved in was quite unlike this new one. Mine had teemed with life. Physical laws were different, making almost every world fecund. Innumerable biologies and countless sentient forms arose.

But this current universe is brutally harsh. I found myself apparently alone in it. I'd expected that, of course, at first. After all, life surely would take some time to arise. But the universe expanded and cooled and galaxies formed and spun through dozens of rotations, and still no life emerged.

I spread myself thin, examining billions of galaxies, scanning each star for planets. On those rare occasions that I did find planets, I scrutinized each for signs of life, or even hints that life might someday develop.

Nothing.

For eighty percent of the present age of this universe I looked and looked and looked, disappointed at every turn.

Hell, indeed. I thought perhaps I would go mad; think perhaps that I did.

But then, at long, long last, in a midsized spiral galaxy, on the inner edge of one arm, I found a remarkable yellow star. At that time, it had a cometary halo, an asteroid belt, and eight planets—although it looked as though the outermost of these would eventually lose its large moon to a wildly eccentric orbit of its own.

The third planet was just the right distance from its sun to have substantial amounts of liquid water on its surface. And it had a giant moon—indeed, the pair was a freak double world. Tides from that moon pulled water on and off coastal clays, alternately exposing them to and shielding them from the sun's radiation.

And from these, and a thousand other factors that had come together in just the right way, life had arisen.

A Crucible—of all the worlds in all the galaxies in this vast and infertile cycle of creation, I had found a single Crucible of life.

It soon became apparent that the Crucible was destined to be a battleground. Many creatures would arise, but only a few would survive. This was as much a world of death as of life.

At the outset, it was clear that amino acids would form the basis for biology here. But amino acids come in two orientations, left-handed and right-handed. Separate forms of life—true self-replicating strains—began using each orientation, but it was soon obvious that only the left-handed ones would survive.

All the universe except this one orb was vacant. I couldn't let one of the two lifepaths be snuffed out so early on. I had to find a way to save the right-handed forms, to . . . to . . . to *transplant* them somewhere else.

But how? I had an intellect that could span the galaxies, but I had no way to exert physical force. Unless—unless I adopted a body for myself.

The universe was permeated by dark matter; indeed, such matter comprised most of its bulk. Its presence was what guaranteed that this universe, like those before it, would eventually stop expanding and contract down, down, down into a primordial atom from which the next cycle would burst forth.

Dark matter is everywhere, both in intergalactic space and wending its way through the galaxies themselves. It made the ideal medium for one such as me. I joined with dense streamers of it that stretched through space near the Crucible's sun. The union gave me mass and, therefore, a subtle but inexorable gravitational influence.

The Crucible's solar system was still young. Although most of the planetesimals had been swept up already by the orbiting worlds, enough debris still littered the system to make impacts commonplace. When a piece of stone or metal slammed into the Crucible, it was not unusual for hunks of the Crucible planet itself to be tossed up with sufficient force to reach escape velocity.

At this early stage of development, life on the Crucible was little more than hardy chemicals and self-replicating crystals of acid. From those pieces of the planet that had been thrown into space, I selected the ones containing a preponderance of the right-handed acid forms. Exerting my gravitational influence, I sent them on a long, gentle voyage to another star where a planet awaited covered with oceans of sterile water. Only a small fraction of the amino acids would survive the long voyage— mostly those buried deep within the ejecta—but it would be enough, I hoped, to establish a second living world, this one for right-handed amino forms.

The process had begun. This universe may have only given rise to life in one place, but I would see to it that as much of the potential of that life would be realized across as many worlds as possible.

Chapter 3

Toroca, who had recently become leader of the Geological Survey of Land at the young age of sixteen kilodays, knew he was different.

In part, it was because he actually knew who his parents were, something almost no other Quintaglio did. Toroca's father was the blind sage Sal-Afsan. Seventeen kilodays ago, Afsan had sailed around the world aboard the mighty vessel *Dasheter*, had gazed upon what was called the Face of God, and had determined that it was, in fact, not the countenance of the creator at all, but rather the giant banded planet around which the tiny moon they lived on orbited.

Toroca's mother, equally renowned, was Wab-Novato, inventor of the far-seer which had aided Afsan in his research. Novato and Afsan together had taken the truth about the Face of God one step further, determining that their world orbited much too closely to the Face to be stable, and that it would disintegrate in only a few hundred kilodays into a ring of rubble, just like those around the neighboring planets of Kevpel and Bripel. Shortly after Toroca had hatched, Emperor Dybo had named Novato director of the exodus project: the all-consuming effort to get the Quintaglio people off their world prior to its destruction.

Yes, knowing who his parents were was a difference, but it wasn't the major one.

Toroca also had brothers and sisters. Since the dawn of time, the bloodpriests had devoured seven out of every eight hatchlings, leaving only the fastest one alive. But Toroca's father, Afsan, had been taken to be The One foretold by Lubal—the hunter who would lead the Quintaglios on the greatest hunt of all. And the bloodpriests, an order closely allied with the Lubalites, made a special dispensation for the children of The One, allowing all eight of them to live.

Knowing his parents; knowing his siblings: these indeed made Toroca different.

But beyond that, he was different in a more fundamental way, different to the core of his being.

A crowded street. A room with ten or more people in it. A ship full of other travelers. None of it bothered him. If another Quintaglio accidentally stepped on his tail, Toroca's claws remained sheathed. When from his vantage point high up the cliffs of Fra'toolar he'd seen Delplas and Spalton bobbing up and down from the waist on the verge of *dagamant*, Toroca had felt no need to reply in kind, had no difficulty turning away from the sight as he scaled his way down the cliff. Indeed, he'd been able to rush into the battle and literally pull them apart, all the while keeping his claws sheathed, his rationality at the fore.

Toroca seemed to lack the instinct for territoriality, lack the urge that drove other Quintaglios apart.

He'd never told anyone. Never said a word. It was liberating, this difference. Empowering.

And more than just a little bit frightening.

Toroca had left the other surveyors back at the great cliffs on the storm-swept coast, looking for any fossils at all from below the Bookmark layer, and cataloging the myriad forms they found above it. Rather than talk at length about how he'd managed to intervene rationally in the territorial battle between Delplas and Spalton, he'd simply left, hiking north toward the port town of Otok. This trip had been planned for some time, after all, and it afforded an ideal excuse to avoid conversation on this topic. It was a three-day hike into the town, where he was to rendezvous with Dak-Forgool, an eminent geologist from Arj'toolar newly assigned to the Geological Survey.

Otok was a pleasant enough little town. It consisted mostly of amorphous adobe buildings, the kind easily repairable after a landquake. The streets were simply dirt, pounded down by the caravans of hornfaces. The town square, the only part paved with cobblestones, contained only two statues: there was one of God, Her arms ending in stumps below Her shoulders, and another of Dy-Dybo, the Emperor, who in naked white marble looked even rounder and fatter than he did in the flesh.

Toroca had arranged to meet this Forgool at the foot of Dybo's statue. He was looking forward to the encounter; Forgool had written much of value about the erosion of uprocks into downrocks. Toroca glanced at the sun, tiny, blazingly white, sliding down the purple bowl of the sky. It looked to be about the fourth daytenth, but—

Bells from the Hall of Worship. One. Two. Three. Four. Yes, Toroca was bang on time. But where was Forgool?

Toroca was wearing his geologist's sash—he'd brought along needle and gut ties and had sewn the two ripped pockets during a break in his long hike. A geologist's sash was quite distinctive, what with its twelve pockets running down its length. Forgool should recognize it immediately, and therefore have no trouble spotting Toroca, standing now in the considerable shade afforded by the statue of Dybo.

Toroca scanned the square. It was almost empty, of course. He saw one old Quintaglio crossing from the right, his tail dragging across the stones. A younger Quintaglio approaching from the left changed course to give the oldster wide clearance, and she nodded territorial concession at him as she did so.

Neither of them seemed the least bit interested in Toroca, though. He watched as a large wingfinger alighted on Dybo's statue. The flyer's reptilian head looked down at Toroca briefly, then it pushed off and glided away, its furry white coat shimmering in the afternoon sunlight, the pointed crest off the back of its head acting as a rudder to help it steer in flight. Toroca turned back and looked around the square again.

Ah, someone was coming.

But it wasn't Forgool. It couldn't be.

Forgool was said to be around thirty kilodays old, almost twice Toroca's own age. But this person was no bigger than Toroca himself. Still, whoever it was was crossing the square with purposeful strides, heading straight for Toroca.

As the Quintaglio came closer, Toroca took note of two features simultaneously.

One was startling only in that it again diverged from what he'd been expecting. Forgool was a male, but this person was a female: the front of her neck lacked the loose folds of a dewlap sack.

But the second feature would have been startling under any circumstances. She had a horn growing out of her muzzle. Toroca's inner eyelids batted across his black orbs. He'd never seen the like before on an adult.

When she got within about twenty paces, the female stopped. "Permission to enter your territory?" she said, her voice a bit anxious.

"*Hahat dan,*" said Toroca, with a little bow of concession.

"You are Kee-Toroca, leader of the Geological Survey?"

Toroca nodded.

"I know you were expecting Dak-Forgool," she said. "I am from his Pack, Pack Vando. It is my sad duty to report to you that Forgool is dead. He succumbed to a fever."

Toroca dipped his muzzle. "I'm very sorry. I'd always wanted to meet him. My condolences to your Pack."

"Thank you."

There was a silence between them for several moments, then Toroca said, "I *am* sorry to hear this, and I thank you for bringing me word—I know it was a long journey for you. But I must head back and join my survey team now. It is too bad. We could have used another geologist." Toroca bowed and began to move away.

"Wait," said the female. "Take me with you."

Toroca leaned back on his tail. "What?"

"Take me with you. I've come in Forgool's place."

"Were you his apprentice?"

The female looked at the cobblestones. "No."

"Who did you study under?"

"Hoo-Tendron."

"I've never heard of him. Is he a geologist?"

"No. Ah, he's, um, a merchant."

"A merchant?"

"Yes, with my Pack of Vando. But he trades in gemstones and fossils, and I've been his apprentice for many kilodays."

"The Geological Survey is a scientific undertaking. We have no need of traders."

"Nor do I wish to be a trader anymore." She raised a hand. "It's true I've had no formal training in geology, but I've dealt with fossils and gems for most of my life. Our Pack roams along the Passalat sandstones." The Passalats were the finest-grained stones in all of Land, known for their magnificent fossils. "I've excavated every kind of fossil, even delicate ones like those strange winged things that aren't wingfingers."

"Birds?" said Toroca. "You've personally found bird fossils?"

"Yes."

He nodded, impressed. "They're the rarest find of all. No one knows exactly what birds were."

"Indeed," said the female.

"But you know no geology?" said Toroca.

"I know what I've taught myself. And I can read, Toroca—I'm one of the very few from my Pack that can make that claim. I'm willing to learn, but I've already got skills that your project can use."

Toroca considered. At the very least, they could use another pair of hands. "What's your name?"

"Babnol. Wab-Babnol."

Toroca bowed. "I cast a shadow in your presence, Babnol. You have the same praenomen as—" He stopped himself before he said *my mother.* "As a good friend of mine, Wab-Novato."

But Babnol apparently already knew the story. "She's your mother, isn't she? A great Quintaglio."

Toroca nodded. "That she is." He looked up at the purple sky. "We work in rough conditions, Babnol. And we're about to head south—"

"I've heard all about it," she said. "Forgool was so looking forward to it. A voyage to the south pole!"

"The work is not at all glamorous. You'll be expected to labor hard, to do repetitive and meticulous tasks."

"I'm prepared for all of that, good Toroca. Please: there's nothing for me in Pack Vando. I know you need someone, and it will take many dekadays for any other geologist to get here. Let me join your team. I promise you won't be sorry."

Toroca considered, looking her up and down. She was in fine physical shape: well muscled; her belly so light green as to be almost yellow, her shoulders and arms a darker shade freckled with brown; her eyes, solid black, wide and intelligent.

And the horn.

Bizarre. Bright in the sunlight.

She held her head high, almost haughtily, Toroca thought, but she didn't seem haughty in any other part of her manner. Indeed, she seemed to have a commendable enthusiasm.

"Very well," he said at last. "Welcome to the Geological Survey of Land."

She bowed deep concession. "Thank you, Toroca. Thank you very much. You won't be sorry, I promise you."

"It's a three-day hike down to where the rest of the survey team is working. We should get going. We've found some fascinating downrock beds there. They present quite a puzzle."

"A puzzle?" said Babnol with glee. "I love puzzles."

Toroca clicked his teeth. "I have a feeling this is going to work out very well," he said. "Shall we go?"

Chapter 4

Time was a funny thing, thought Emperor Dy-Dybo, resting his enormous belly on the ruling slab in his rebuilt palace in Capital City. His childhood had seemed as though it would never end. As a member of The Family—the direct descendants of the Prophet Larsk, who had been first to gaze upon the Face of God—Dybo had lived a life of leisure, while his mother, Len-Lends, had ruled with an iron hand.

But then, when Dybo was just twelve kilodays old, all of that had come to an end. A landquake, a collapsing roof, his mother dead, and suddenly he was lying on the ruling slab himself, he, no longer Dybo, but now *Dy-Dybo*, the Emperor of all the Fifty Packs and every one of the eight provinces.

Dybo was twenty-eight kilodays old—even to a pessimist, which Dybo most assuredly was not, still hardly even early middle age. And yet he was feeling old. He looked across the ruling room at the white marble statue of his mother, Lends, with her stern visage. Government had always moved in generations. His mother, in addition to being Empress, was also governor of Capital province, and she had been about the same age as the governors of the other provinces. Throughout his adolescence, while Dybo was being groomed for the Emperorship, seven other children about his age were likewise serving as apprentice governors in Jam'toolar, Fra'toolar, Arj'toolar, Chu'toolar, Mar'toolar, Edz'toolar, and Kev'toolar.

But because of Lends's early death, Dybo had ascended ahead of his time. He'd always thought of himself as a young Emperor, because no one else of his generation had yet become a governor.

That had changed now.

A newsrider brought word this morning.

Len-Ganloor, a contemporary of his mother and the governor of Edz'-toolar, harshest and most isolated of the provinces, had been killed. An accident on a ceremonial hunt, apparently. Ganloor and her senior advisors had gone after a shovelmouth—such an easy kill—but a hornface herd was panicked into a stampede by their arrival. Ganloor and the rest of her party were trampled to death.

Ganloor's apprentice, Rodlox, Dybo's contemporary, was now governor of Edz'toolar.

Rodlox. He'd met him not too long ago, the last time Ganloor had come through the Capital, but Dybo couldn't really recall him at all. Just another of the endless parade of faces that went through his court. Of course, his name no longer would be just Rodlox, but rather now must be Dy-Rodlox, the long-established custom being that governors affirmed their loyalty to the Emperor by taking a praenomen derived from his name. Dybo would have to remember to send appropriate condolences about Len-Ganloor and congratulations about Dy-Rodlox to Edz'toolar.

Rodlox was also twenty-eight kilodays old, the same as Dybo, so the newsrider had said. Dybo was no longer the only one of his generation to hold high office.

And that made him feel older than he was. Old and weary. There was so much yet to do, and, it seemed, so little time.

There was a saying attributed to the ancient philosopher Keladax: time crawls for a child, walks for an adolescent, and runs for an adult. Dybo thought, yes, there was much truth in that.

Time was indeed running.

But more important, time was running *out*.

Dybo's advisor, Afsan, had only a rough idea of how long it would be before the world disintegrated. His best guess had been perhaps three hundred kilodays. But since he'd made that prediction, some sixteen of those kilodays had already gone by.

Still, thought Dybo, a good start had been made. Early on, he had appointed Wab-Novato, inventor of the far-seer, as director of the effort to find a way to get the Quintaglios off their doomed world before it broke apart. And Novato had immediately set to work.

Dybo thought back to the day, long ago, when she had come to see him in his temporary ruling room, a vestibule in one of Capital City's many temples. He had used it until the replacement for his old palace, leveled in one of the great landquakes, had been built.

Novato was a few kilodays older than Dybo, with a mind as sharp as a hunter's polished claw. Dybo had been surprised by the new sash she had worn that day, although now it had become famous throughout Land. The sash crossed from her left shoulder to her right hip, and consisted of two parallel strips of dyed leather, the lower one green, the upper black. Dybo had later learned that these colors symbolized the exodus project, representing the move from verdant Land into the darkness of the night sky.

On that day, back in the temporary ruling room, Novato had begun by saying, "We need to take stock of our resources."

Dybo liked Novato a lot but often couldn't see what she was getting at. "What?" he had replied.

She leaned back on her tail. "We need a complete catalog of raw materials, a list of everything that we've got to work with."

Dybo spread his arms. "But I've already said that you may use anything anywhere on Land, if it will help the exodus project. You've got access to everything already."

Novato bowed deeply. "And I thank you for that, Your Luminance, but, forgive me, you are missing my point. I need to know exactly what's out there: exactly what rocks and ore and crystals and types of wood and so on are available, where they are found, and how easy they will be to collect and use."

"You mean a—what is the word?—an inventory? Of all of Land?"

"An inventory, yes, and a survey. There are so many parts that have never been really explored. Much of the southern region of Edz'toolar province remains unmapped. Most of the great plains of Mar'toolar are barren of life, but may be rich in metals. Some of the small islands in the Downriver Archipelago have never even been visited."

"But such a survey would take kilodays."

"Aye, it would. But we need that information."

"So you'll know what rocks are available?"

"Exactly."

"And who would be in charge of this survey?" asked Dybo.

"I imagine there would be several teams," said Novato, "but Irb-Falpom, the palace land surveyor, seems the right choice for leading the principal expedition."

"A kindly soul, and a keen mind. All right, Falpom it shall be." And indeed, it was Falpom for fifteen kilodays, until she died of old age, and her young apprentice Toroca, one of Afsan and Novato's children, took over. But, back on that long-ago day when he had first approved the Geological Survey, Dybo had commented, "But surely, Novato, you must realize that this survey will take ages to complete."

"I do," she had said.

"So, what, may I ask, will you be doing in the interim?"

"Me?" Novato had replied, a look of utter seriousness on her face. "I'm going to learn how to fly."

Chapter 5

Fra'toolar

As Babnol and Toroca hiked along, heading south to join up with the Geological Survey team, Toroca quietly contemplated Babnol's nose horn.

All Quintaglio children were born with horns on their muzzles—birthing horns, they were called—to help them break out of their shells. But these were always lost within a few days of hatching. Babnol's, for some reason, had not been. Instead, she'd retained the horn into adulthood. It wasn't unattractive, just startling, a fluted cone of yellow-white bone projecting up. It must interfere with Babnol's field of vision, Toroca thought, but then so did his own muzzle—one gets used to the parts of one's face that block vision.

Perhaps Babnol had tried to have it removed, and maybe it regenerated, just like other body parts. Complex structures such as eyes and organs couldn't regenerate, but a simple bony growth like that might very well come back.

It was funny, in a way. Although Toroca had never regenerated any body part, it had always been comforting to know that should he lose a finger or toe or piece of his tail, it would regrow. But how frustrating to have an outlandish protuberance coming out of one's face and not even be able to hack it off. The thing would just keep coming back, time and again.

Toroca would have thought that a facial horn would make Babnol look docile. After all, only hornfaces had such things, and they were dull-witted plant-eaters. But a horn on the muzzle of a carnivore had an entirely different effect. It made Babnol look formidable. And, indeed, the way she carried herself, with her muzzle often tipped up in a haughty fashion, gave her quite an air of power and authority.

Toroca wondered what would cause a growth such as this horn. He'd heard of birth defects, but rarely saw them. The culling by the bloodpriest tended to eliminate those, but Babnol's affliction was one that wouldn't have been apparent at that time, since all egglings have a birthing horn.

A birthing horn on an adult. How bizarre! Toroca's mother, Novato, had told him that when she had lived with Pack Gelbo, she had worked in the same abandoned temple building that housed two young savants who had bred thousands upon thousands of little lizards, studying the inheritance of traits. They'd proven that offspring often have essentially the same characteristics as their parents. Although there was no way to determine who Babnol's parents actually were, Toroca probably would have heard stories or gossip about other adults who had such a horn.

But that meant—

No, ridiculous.

And yet . . .

Could Babnol have a characteristic that wasn't present in her parents? How could that be? A spontaneous appearance of some new quality, some novelty? What would give rise to such novelties?

The hike was long, the terrain rocky. Babnol would come close to Toroca for a while, they'd talk a bit, then territoriality would get the better of her, and she'd fall off to the rear or speed up to put some distance between her and him. Toroca usually looked forward to the times when she was willing to talk; it made the trip go more quickly. On one such occasion, though, she startled him with her boldness. "Forgive my impertinence for asking," she said, "but it's well-known that you are Afsan's . . ."

"Son," said Toroca. "The word is 'son.' "

"Afsan's son, yes. And Novato's, too."

"That's right."

Babnol looked fascinated. "I don't mean to pry, but what's it like, knowing your parents?"

Toroca was a bit taken aback at this, but he was going to spend much time with Babnol, so he decided to answer her question. "It's interesting. Strange. All things being equal, I think I'd prefer not to know who they are."

"Oh?" She seemed surprised. "I've spent some time idly wondering who my parents might have been. I've got the father narrowed down to three possibilities, I think, back in Pack Vando. The mother's more elusive. I'm not obsessed with knowing, you understand. But I'd think it would be satisfying to know."

"It's . . . it's not. Not really."

She turned her muzzle to face him. "I don't understand."

"Well, perhaps it would be different for you," said Toroca. "Forgive me; this is going to sound callous. You see, my parents aren't just any two people. They are Sal-Afsan and Wab-Novato, the one who discovered the nature of the world and the one who invented the far-seer and now leads the exodus. Great people, famous throughout Land."

"They are indeed."

"You know the old greeting, 'I cast a shadow in your presence'?"

"Sure."

"Afsan is blind; I doubt he's aware of how luminous he is. I'm—I'm washed out, lost in his glare. And in my mother's. People judge me differently. They know where I came from, and they expect great things from me. It's . . . it's a burden."

"Oh, I'm sure no one gives it any thought."

"You do, Babnol. You asked me what it was like knowing my parents. In fact, one could take that question two ways: what's it like knowing who your parents are? Or what's it like knowing Afsan and Novato? I do know them both, you know. Indeed, Novato is my overseer on this survey project. It's not just in the eyes of strangers that I see the implied message that, oh, he's Afsan and Novato's child; he must do great things. I see it from them—from my mother and father. *They* expect much of me. It's not like I have just duty to the Emperor and duty to my Pack and duty to my profession. It's as though I have an additional duty to them, to live up to their expectations."

Babnol scratched the side of her neck. "I hadn't thought of it that way."

"So you can see that it is a burden, this knowledge of one's personal ancestors."

"But you will do great things . . . ," began Babnol.

Toroca grunted. "That's exactly what I mean."

Musings of the Watcher

Life seemed to be taking hold on the Crucible. For an eternity, it was all unicellular. After that, small groupings of cells began to appear. And then a miracle happened, an explosion of complexity and diversity, with more than fifty different fundamental body plans appearing almost simultaneously. One had five eyes and a flexible trunk.

Another had seven pairs of stilt legs and seven waving arms. A third had a central nervous cord running the length of its tube-like body. A fourth looked like two perpendicular hoops of segmented tissue joined together.

I knew how evolution worked on this world. Only a handful of the forms would survive. This time my task was even harder, for I wanted to seed samples of all these forms on different worlds, hoping that on each one a different body plan would emerge triumphant.

The bombardment of meteors that characterized the early days of this solar system had slowed to almost nothing by now. Even if it hadn't, there's no way such delicate creatures would survive being tossed into the firmament and then sailing unprotected through the cold of space for vast spans of time. No, I needed another approach.

A planet's gravity well is steep, but it's not a real barrier. Although it took me thousands of Crucible years to do it, I extended corkscrew filaments of dark matter into the seas of the Crucible, and then set the filaments to spinning, drawing up into orbit water teeming with tiny lifeforms. Within the screws the water was kept warm, insulated by the dark matter itself, but when it popped out at the top into the vacuum of space, it flash-froze, sealing the life within into tumbling blocks of ice.

Many of the asteroids that had orbits near that of the Crucible were really dead comets, covered with a dusty crust that prevented them from developing tails. I coated the ice arks in the same way and gave them gentle pushes, launching them on million-year-long journeys to other stars, where watery worlds awaited them.

When they at last reached their destinations, their courses having been periodically adjusted by me with gentle gravitational tugs, the blocks were recaptured and slowly lowered on new dark-matter corkscrews into the alien, lifeless seas. The ice melted and the precious cargo within thawed out. Of course, most of the creatures had not survived the freezing, but some specimens did. Since there was as yet little genetic diversity amongst these lifeforms, I needed only a few survivors to make a viable breeding stock.

In the time it had taken for this long journey, most of the fifty-odd body plans had become extinct on the Crucible, the initial shaking-out period there lasting even less time than I'd feared. But here, in alien seas, some of them had another chance at life.

A Quintaglio's Diary

I saw one of my brothers today. It always takes me aback slightly when I run into one of them. Everyone says we look alike, and that does seem to be true. There's a resemblance, a similarity about the face, a likeness of build. It's a bit like seeing oneself in a mirror, or reflected in the still water.

And yet, the resemblance goes beyond the merely physical, of that I'm sure. There was a moment today when I looked at my brother and could tell by the expression on his face that he was thinking the same thing I was. It was an irreverent thought, the kind one normally keeps private: Emperor Dy-Dybo happened to be walking by where the two of us were standing. He was wearing one of those ceremonial robes. I always thought they were dangerous—one's feet could get tangled up in them. Indeed, just as he passed us, Dybo tripped. The robe billowed up around him and he looked like a fat wingfinger, too big to take off. I glanced over at my brother and saw a little bunching of his jaw muscles, a sure sign that, like me, he was making an effort to keep his teeth from clicking together. He tipped his muzzle toward me, and I knew, just as I'm sure he knew, that we were sharing the same thought.

I've had that experience with other people before, too, of course, but never so often nor so intensely as when I'm with one of my siblings.

It's a very strange feeling. Indeed, one might even call it disconcerting.

Fra'toolar

Talking with Babnol about his parents had gotten Toroca thinking about the bloodpriests, and that brought back fears that he'd thought were long buried. Babnol and he still had two more days of hiking until they would join up with the survey team. They slept on high ground, under the dancing moons, the great sky river shimmering overhead. Babnol, a dozen paces away, was fast asleep; Toroca could hear the gentle hissing of her breathing. But Toroca himself could not sleep. He lay awake beneath the stars, thinking about the disciples of Mekt, the bloodpriest who swallowed hatchlings whole.

Most Quintaglios gave the bloodpriests little thought, and their exact role in society was rarely spoken of out loud. But Toroca had become fascinated with them, had been driven to learn all he could about them, precisely because he and his brothers and sisters had *not* had to face them.

Eight eggs to a clutch.

Seven of every eight children devoured within a day or two of hatching, tiny bodies, still brilliant green or yellow, eyes barely opened, sliding down the gullet of a male priest, a comparative giant, clad in purple robes.

The egglings were doubtless horrified, their brief tenures in this life ending in screams of terror.

Except it wouldn't have gone that way for him. He was Toroca. Toroca who didn't fear other people. Toroca who seemed to have no territorial instinct. Toroca who would have sat there, staring in awe, at the apparition of the priest, but who would not have run away.

He would have been the first to have been devoured.

During the long hike back to join his survey team, Toroca and Babnol stopped several times to rest. Babnol had few belongings with her, but one she did have was a sketchbook, containing studies in charcoal and graphite of many of the fossils she'd collected over the kilodays.

"I'm always tempted to keep intriguing pieces for myself," she said, "but my Pack needed many things, and the fossils were always popular in trading. Our sandstones are very, very fine: we get fossils showing all sorts of detail normally not visible." She opened up the little book, its soft leather cover flopping over. "Anyway, I make sketches of the nicest ones before I put them out on the trading tables." She thumbed the pages. "Here," she said, passing the book across to him. "This is the nicest bird I ever found."

Birds. No one knew exactly what they were, since all that remained of them were their tiny, hollow bones preserved in rock. To the untrained eye, they seemed at first glance to be small carnivorous reptiles. But they had beaks and breastbone keels, characteristics associated with wingfingers—although wingfingers had no tails, and bird fossils usually did.

But they couldn't be wingfingers, these birds. A wingfinger's wing was a membrane, supported along its leading edge by the vastly elongated fourth finger. Bird wings, however, were supported by a variety of bones, including the lower arm and the bones that would have comprised the second finger—none of a bird's digits had claws, so it was thought that none of them actually emerged from the wing structure to be true fingers. Birds also lacked the wingfinger's little backward-pointing lifter bone on the wrist, which supported a small leading membrane flap that connected to the torso at the base of the neck.

And occasionally bird fossils, such as the one in this sketch of Babnol's, showed some kind of bizarre frayed body covering, like stiff fern leaves with inflexible spines. This was completely unlike the simple leathery hide or scales or plates of reptiles, and completely unlike the filaments of hair that insulated wingfingers.

Toroca and others guessed that birds might have flown, but no one knew for sure, for no living bird had ever been seen. They were known only from the fossil record.

Toroca studied the sketch minutely. Babnol was talented indeed.

The cliffs along the eastern shore of Fra'toolar were the tallest in all of Land. They rose up out of the great world-spanning body of water like giant brown walls, towering toward the purple sky. A thin beach ran between them and the churning waves. Scattered along the beach were ragged chunks of rock, pebbles, and fine sands.

The entire height of the cliff face was made of thin horizontal bands, almost as if the whole thing were some impossibly thick book, and each band represented a separate page seen edge on. The bands were all brown or brownish-gray until near the top, where some white layers appeared.

Wingfingers nested in crooks in the rocks, their reptilian heads poking out, their membranous wings covered with silky fur wrapped tightly against their bodies to protect against the chill wind. The only thing marring the neat horizontal banding of the rocks was the countless white streaks caused by their droppings. But these were washed away by the frequent storms, leaving the book of stone layers scrubbed clean for a short time.

Toroca and Babnol arrived on the beach shortly after noon. Overhead, the sun, tiny and white, was visible through the silvery clouds, but none of the thirteen moons was bright enough in the daytime to be visible through the haze.

Far up ahead, they could see two other Quintaglios, barely more than green knots against the long expanse of beach, the vast cliffs, and the churning gray waters.

Toroca cupped his hands to his muzzle and called out, "Ho!" There was no response, the wind whisking the word out over the waters. He shrugged, and they trudged on farther. Eventually, Toroca sang out again, and this time the distant figures did hear him. They turned around and waved. Toroca waved back and, although exhausted from days of hiking, picked up his pace, trotting along to join his friends. Babnol followed alongside. She stopped about fifteen paces away from the others, an appropriate distance when approaching individuals one has not met before. Toroca, though, surged in as close as six paces from the nearest of them, a distance too close by anyone's standards. Reflexively, the other Quintaglios backed up a couple of steps.

It was Delplas and Spalton, the madness of *dagamant* long forgotten, Spalton's arm regenerating nicely. "Who's this?" said Delplas. "Surely not Dak-Forgool?"

Toroca shook his head. "Forgool is dead. Wab-Babnol here has come to join us in his place. Babnol, meet two of the best surveyors in all of Land." His voice was full of warmth. "This reprobate is Gan-Spalton. He has a sly sense of humor, so watch yourself when around him—and only listen to him in the light of day."

Babnol bowed. "I cast a shadow in your presence, Gan-Spalton."

Spalton looked as though he was going to make some comment, possibly about Babnol's horn. But, perhaps catching the expression on Toroca's face, he said nothing, and simply bowed deeply.

"And this is Bar-Delplas."

"Greetings," said Babnol.

"What?" said Delplas with a click of her teeth. "No shadow-casting?"

"I'm sorry," said Babnol. "I cast a—"

Delplas held up her hand. "If you really want to cast something near me," she said, "let it be a net. The waters are rough here, but the fishing is excellent nonetheless. Do you like fish, Babnol?"

"I've rarely had any; I'm from an inland Pack."

"Well, then you've only had freshwater fish. Wait till you taste true River fish!"

Babnol dipped her head. "I'm looking forward to it."

The four of them began to amble down the beach. "You'll meet the other four surveyors later," Toroca said to Babnol. Then he turned to face Delplas. "Babnol is an experienced fossil hunter," said Toroca.

"Whom did you study under?" asked Delplas.

"I'm self-taught," said Babnol, her head once again tilted up in that haughty way.

Delplas turned toward Toroca, her face a question.

"She's not a trained geologist," he said, "but she's very experienced. And she's eager to learn."

Delplas considered for a moment, then: "Would that more of our people shared your passion for learning, Babnol." She bowed deeply. "Welcome to the Geological Survey of Land."

"I'm delighted to be a part of it," Babnol replied warmly.

"You'll be even more delighted when you see what wonders we've found," said Toroca. He faced Spalton. "Still nothing below the Bookmark layer?"

"Nothing. We've taken thousands of samples, and still not a single find."

"The Bookmark layer?" said Babnol.

"Come," said Toroca. "We'll show you."

They hiked farther along the beach, a few wingfingers circling overhead, and a crab occasionally scuttling across their path. Streamers of waterweeds were strewn here and there along the sands.

At last they came to a small encampment consisting of a cluster of eleven small tents made out of thunderbeast hide arranged in a loose circle. A semicircular wall of stones had been built to shield them from the wind.

"This is home, at least for the next few dekadays," said Toroca. "After that, we'll be heading to the south pole by sailing ship; we've recently requisitioned one for that journey. I don't know which ship Novato will send, but I'm sure it will be a major vessel."

Babnol nodded.

The cliffs rose up in front of them. Babnol hadn't been aware that her tail had been swishing back and forth to generate heat until they got here, in the lee of the stone crescent, and it suddenly stopped moving. Out of the biting wind, it was actually fairly pleasant. The sun was even peeking out from behind the clouds now.

Toroca gestured at the cliff, and Babnol let her eyes wander over its surface. She was startled to realize that way, way up the face, there were two Quintaglios, looking like tiny green spiders. "Those are two more members of our team," said Toroca. "You'll meet them later."

"What are they doing?" said Babnol.

"Looking for fossils," said Toroca.

"And is the looking good here?"

"Depends," said Toroca, a mischievous tone in his voice. "I can tell you right now that Tralen—that's the fellow higher up the cliff face—will find plenty, but Greeblo, the one lower down, will come up empty-handed."

"I don't understand," said Babnol.

"Do you know what superposition is?" asked Spalton.

Babnol shook her head.

"My predecessor, Irb-Falpom, spent most of her life developing the theory of it," said Toroca. "It seems intuitively obvious once it's explained, but until Falpom, no one had understood it." He gestured at the cliff. "You see the layers of rock?"

"Yes," said Babnol.

"There are two main types of rock: uprock and downrock. Uprock is thrust up from the ground as lava. Basalt is an uprock."

She nodded.

"But rain and wind and the pounding of waves cause uprock to crumble into dust. That dust is carried down to the bottom of rivers and lakes and gets compressed into downrocks, such as shale and sandstone."

"All right."

"Well, Falpom made the great leap: she realized that when you look at downrock layers, like the sandstone of these cliffs, the layers on the bottom are the oldest and the ones on the top are the youngest."

"How can that be?" said Babnol. "I thought all rocks came from the second egg of creation."

"That's right, but they've changed in the time since that egg hatched. The way the rocks look today isn't the way they were when the world was formed."

She looked skeptical, but let him continue.

"It's really very simple," said Toroca. "I don't know whether you're a tidy person or not. I'm a bit of a slob myself, I'm sorry to say. My desk back in Capital City is covered with writing leathers and books. But I know if I'm looking for something I put on my desk recently, it will be near the top of the clutter, whereas something I set down dekadays ago will be near the bottom. It's the same with rock layers."

"All right," said Babnol.

"Well, the rock layers we see here are the finest sequence in all of Land. The height of the cliffs from top to bottom represents an enormous span of kilodays, with the rock layers at the bottom representing truly ancient times."

"Uh-huh."

He pointed again. "You see that all the lower layers are brown or gray. If you look up, way, way up, almost nine-tenths of the way to the top, you'll find the first layer that's white. See it? Just a thin line?"

"Not really."

"We'll climb up tomorrow, and I'll show you. The layer in question is still a good fifteen paces from the top, of course, this being a *big* cliff, but—ah!" Spalton had disappeared a few moments ago into one of the tents and had now emerged holding a brass tube with an ornate crest on one end. "Thank you, Spalton," said Toroca, taking the object.

"A far-seer," said Babnol, her voice full of wonder. "I've heard of them, but never seen one up close."

"Not just any far-seer," said Delplas, jerking her head at the instrument Toroca now held. "That's the one Wab-Novato gave to Sal-Afsan the morning after Toroca was conceived."

Toroca looked embarrassed. "It meant a great deal to my father," he said, "but once he was blinded, he could no longer use it. He wanted it to still be employed in the search for knowledge, and gave it to me when I embarked on my first expedition as leader of the Geological Survey." He proffered the device to Babnol.

She took it reverently, held the cool length in front of her with both hands, felt its weight, the weight of history. "Afsan's far-seer . . . ," she said with awe.

"Go ahead," said Toroca. "Put it to your eye. Look at the cliff."

She raised the tube. "Everything looks tiny!" she said.

Clicking of teeth from Spalton and Delplas. "That's the wrong end," said Toroca gently. "Try it the other way."

She reversed the tube. "Spectacular!" She turned slowly through a half-circle. "That's amazing!"

"You can sharpen the image by rotating the other part," Toroca said.

"Wonderful," breathed Babnol.

"Now, look at the cliff face."

She turned back to the towering wall of layered downrock. "Hey! There's—what did you say his name was?"

"If it's the fellow in the blue sash, it's Tralen."

"Tralen, yes."

"All right. Scan down the cliff face until you come to a layer of white rock. Not light brown, but actual white. You can't miss it."

"I don't—wait a beat! There it is!"

"Right," said Toroca. "That's what we call the Bookmark layer. It's white because it's made of chalk. There are no chalk layers below it because there are no shells of aquatic animals below it."

Babnol lowered the far-seer. "I don't see the connection."

"Chalk is made of fossilized shells," said Delplas. "We often find beautiful shell pieces in chalk layers."

"Oh. We have no chalk in Arj'toolar. Lots of limestone, though— which is also made from shells."

Delplas nodded. "That's right."

"But here," said Toroca, "there are no fossil shells below that first white layer." He leaned forward. "In fact, *there are no fossils of any kind* beneath that first white layer."

Babnol lifted the far-seer again, letting her circular view slide up and down the cliff face. "No fossils below," she said slowly.

"But *plenty* above," said Toroca. "There's nothing gradual about it. Starting with that white layer, and in every subsequent layer, the rock is full of fossils."

"Then the—what did you call it?—the Bookmark layer . . ."

Toroca nodded. "The Bookmark layer marks the point in our world's history at which life was created. Drink in the sight, Babnol. You're seeing the beginning of it all!"

Chapter 6

A Quintaglio's Diary

I get tired of spending time with my siblings. It's strange, because I have no idea how I should react. With others, my territorial instinct seems to operate properly. I know, without thinking, when I should get out of someone's way and when I can reasonably expect someone to yield to me. But with my brothers and sisters, it's different. Sometimes I feel as though their presence, no matter how close, doesn't bother me in the least. At other times, I find myself challenging their territory for no good reason at all. That they are exactly the same age as me—neither younger nor older, neither bigger nor smaller—makes all standard protocols based on age and size meaningless.

It's confusing, so very confusing. I wish I knew how to behave.

Rockscape, near Capital City

It was an eerie place, a place of the dead.

Ancient cathedral, ancient cemetery, ancient calendar—the debates raged on among the academics. All that remained were ninety-four granite boulders, strewn—or so it seemed at first glance—across a field of tall grasses, a field that ended in a sheer drop, edged with crumbling marl, plummeting to the great world-spanning body of water far below.

But the boulders, as one could clearly see when their positions were plotted, were *not* strewn. They were *arranged*, laid out in geometric patterns, lines drawn between them forming hexagons and pentagons, triangles, and perfect squares.

Rockscape, it was called: a minor tourist attraction, a site that most first-time visitors to Capital City made sure to see, proof that long before the current city had been built, Quintaglios had inhabited this area. Some claimed the rocks represented sacrificial altars on which the earliest Lubalites had practiced their cannibalistic ways. That was an easy theory to believe. The wind sometimes shrieked across the field like the doleful wails of those offered up to placate a God who was making the land tremble.

Afsan often came here, straddling a particular boulder, the one the historians referred to as Sun/Swift-Runner/4 but that everyone else had come to call simply Afsan's rock. This was his place, a place for quiet contemplation, introspection, and deep thought.

Afsan could find his way here as easily at night as in the day, but he never did so. Indeed, he rarely came out at all after sunset. It was unbearable for him. To know that the stars—the glorious, glorious stars—were arching overhead was too much. Of all the sights he would never see again, Afsan missed the night sky most.

The great landquake of kiloday 7110 had left much of Capital City in ruins. In its aftermath, most of the Lubalites had gone into hiding again. Officially, no record was kept of who had been identified as a member of that ancient sect, and even unofficially little concern was paid to it. Oh, there were those who called for retribution, but Dybo declared an amnesty. After all, when he made the public announcement that he agreed with Afsan that Larsk was a false prophet, he couldn't very well penalize those who had refused to worship Larsk earlier. Jal-Tetex was permitted to remain on as imperial hunt leader, although she died eventually, in exactly the way she would have liked to—on the hunt. The lanky Pal-Cadool stayed in favor with the palace, although he was reassigned from being chief butcher to personal assistant to Afsan, a role he had unofficially held anyway since the blinded Afsan had been released from prison.

Afsan, whom some had called The One, the hunter foretold by Lubal, who would lead the Quintaglios on the greatest hunt of all.

Some still believed Afsan to be this—and, indeed, some took the exodus to be the hunt Lubal had spoken of. Others who had believed it once, had grown less and less convinced of it as time went by. Afsan, after all, had not hunted in kilodays. And others still, of course, had always scoffed at the suggestion that Afsan was The One.

Cadool did his best to make Afsan's life comfortable. Afsan often sent Cadool to run errands or do things that he could not himself, and that meant that Afsan was often alone.

Alone, that is, except for Gork.

"It'll help look after you," Cadool had said. Afsan had been dubious. As a youngster with Pack Carno, he had kept pet lizards, but Gork was awfully big to be considered a pet. It was about half Afsan's own size. Afsan had never seen such a creature before he had been blinded, so he really had only an approximate idea of what Gork looked like. Its hide was dark gray, like slate, according to Cadool, and it constantly tasted the air with a flicking bifurcated tongue. Gork was quite tame, and Afsan had petted it up and down its leathery hide. The reptile's limbs sprawled out in a push-up posture. Its head was flat and elongated. Its tail was thick and flattened, and it worked from side to side as Gork walked.

Gork gladly wore a leather harness and led Afsan around, always choosing a safe path for its master, avoiding rocks and gutters and dung. Afsan found himself growing inordinately fond of the beast and ascribed to it all sorts of advanced qualities, including at least a rudimentary intelligence.

He was surprised that such pets weren't more common. It was in some ways pleasant to spend time with another living, breathing creature that didn't trigger the territorial instinct. Although Gork was cold-blooded, and therefore not very energetic, it was still fast enough as a guide for Afsan, given how slowly Afsan walked most of the time, nervous about tripping.

Afsan and Gork, alone, out among the ancient boulders, wind whipping over them, until—

"Eggling!" A deep and gravelly voice.

Afsan lifted his head up and turned his empty eye sockets toward the sound. It couldn't be . . .

"Eggling!" the voice called again, closer now.

Afsan got up off his rock and began to walk toward the approaching visitor. "That's a voice I haven't heard in kilodays," he said, surprise and warmth in his tone. "Var-Keenir, is that you?"

"Aye."

They approached each other as closely as territoriality would allow. "I cast a shadow in your presence," said Keenir.

Afsan clicked his teeth. "I'll have to take your word for that. Keenir, it's grand to hear your voice!"

"And it's wonderful to see you, good thighbone," said Keenir, his rough tones like pebbles chafing together. "You're still a scrawny thing, though."

"I don't anticipate that changing," said Afsan, with another clicking of teeth.

"Aye, it must be in your nature, since I'm sure that at Emperor Dybo's table there's always plenty of food."

"That there is. Tell me how you've been."

The old mariner's words were so low they were difficult to make out over the wind, even for Afsan, whose hearing had grown very acute since the loss of his sight. "I'm fine," said Keenir. "Oh, I begin to feel my age, and, except for my regenerated tail, my skin is showing a lot of mottling, but that's to be expected."

Indeed, thought Afsan, for Keenir had now outlived his creche-mate, Tak-Saleed, by some sixteen kilodays. "What brings you to the Capital?"

"The *Dasheter*."

Afsan clicked his teeth politely. "Everyone's a comedian. I mean, what business are you up to?"

"Word went out that a ship was needed for a major voyage. I've come to get the job."

"You want to sail to the south pole?"

"Aye, why not? I've been close enough to see the ice before, but we never had the equipment for a landing. The *Dasheter* is still the finest ship in the world, eggling. It's had a complete overhaul. And, if you'll forgive an oldster a spot of immodesty, you won't find a more experienced captain."

"That much is certain. You know that it is my son Toroca who will be leading the Antarctic expedition?"

"No, I did not know that. But it's even more fitting. His very first water voyage was aboard the *Dasheter*, when we brought Novato and your children to Capital City all those kilodays ago. And Toroca took his pilgrimage with me three or four kilodays ago."

"We don't call it a pilgrimage anymore."

"Aye, but I'm set in my ways. Still, not having to bring along that bombastic priest, Bleen, does make the voyage more pleasant."

Afsan actually thought that Bleen wasn't a bad sort, as priests went. He said nothing, though.

"Where is Toroca now?" asked Keenir.

"According to his last report, he's finishing up some studies on the eastern shore of Fra'toolar. He's expecting a ship to rendezvous with his team there, near the tip of the Cape of Mekt."

"Very good," said Keenir. "Whom do I see about getting this job?"

"The sailing voyage is part of the Geological Survey of Land. That comes under the authority of Wab-Novato, director of the exodus."

"Novato? I'm certain to get the job, then, I daresay."

Afsan clicked his teeth. "No doubt," and then, in a moment of sudden exuberance, he stepped closer to the old mariner. "By the very fangs of God, Keenir, it's good to be with you again!"

Musings of the Watcher

At last, other intellects! At last, intelligent life native to this iteration of the universe.

It had arisen not on the Crucible, but rather on one of the worlds to which I had transplanted earlier lifeforms. I'd been right: body plans other than those that would have survived the initial weeding of natural selection on the Crucible had the potential for sentience.

They called themselves Jijaki collectively, and each individual was a Jijak.

A Jijak had five phosphorescent eyes, each on a short stalk, arranged in one row of three and a lower row of two. A long flexible trunk depended from the face just below the lower row of eyes. The trunk was made up of hundreds of hard rings held together by tough connective tissue. It ended in a pair of complex cup-shaped manipulators that faced each other. The manipulators could be brought together so that they made one large grasping claw, or they could be spread widely apart, exposing six small appendages within each cup.

The creature's torso, made of fifteen disk-like segments, was held at a forty-five-degree angle. In a dissected creature, the disks could be seen to have complex spokes and buttresses running into their centers, these crosspieces making up the skeletal support for the internal organs. Each of the disks, except the first, had a triangular breathing hole on each side.

The surface of the disks had an opalescent sheen. When a Jijak was moving in the dark, little white sparks, caused by a muscular-chemical reaction, could be seen flashing in the connective tissue exposed as the disks separated.

About halfway down the underside of the torso there was an indentation containing a mouth-sphincter. The trunk was sufficiently long and flexible to easily move food there.

Wrapping around the rear of the torso was a horizontally held U-shaped brace from which six legs—three on each side—angled forward. Only the front pair of legs normally touched the ground. Each of the other two pairs was successively shorter and much less robust. They were used only in mating, in digging holes for depositing eggs, and in certain sporting activities.

I'm surprised at how body plans endure through vast spans of time. Although infinitely more complex and dozens of times bigger than their distant ancestors from the Crucible's early seas, the basic architecture of a Jijak was much the same as that of the creature I had taken from there. Oh, that tiny being had been aquatic, instead of land-living; had compound instead of single-lens eyes, and its eyes were on the opposite side of the head from the trunk; it had had only a simple pincer at the trunk's end; wing-like gills had projected from its body segments; and six paddle-like rudders, instead of articulated legs, made up its tail. But the fundamental architecture of these Jijaki was indeed obviously based on this ancient plan.

It was high time I introduced myself to them.

Chapter 7

Fra'toolar

Toroca had learned to fake the appropriate responses. It was expected behavior, and he had quickly discovered that life was so much easier if one responded as expected. He couldn't remember the last time his claws had distended of their own accord, but, when the situation warranted, he could force them from their sheaths, force the tapered yellow-white points out into the light of day, force himself to look like a hunter, a killer.

But he was neither of those things. Oh, he had gone on his first ritual hunt—and had been amazed at the bloodiness of the affair, the viciousness of the others in his pack—for to be an adult who did not bear the hunter's tattoo over his left earhole would mean he would be shunned by society, reduced to a life of begging.

He didn't want that.

But he didn't want to ever again taste blood that was still warm, either. One hunt had been enough.

Toroca had seen the abandoned stone buildings near the edge of the towering brown cliffs when they'd first arrived here, and his team hiked all the way up to them for shelter when storms made it impossible to camp out on the beach. Today, though, the weather was fine. Toroca and Babnol had simply come up to the old buildings to fetch the equipment they had stored there, as they prepared for the rendezvous with the sailing ship that would take them to the south pole.

The buildings were made out of stone blocks. Doubtless the walls had originally been straight, but over the kilodays landquakes or other forces had caused them to bulge here, to buckle there. Some of the walls had faint paintings on them, primitive in style, showing Quintaglios solely in profile, backs held halfway between horizontal and vertical, two arms dangling down, looking like they were mounted on the body one atop the other—the attempt at perspective was crude, and the "upper" arm was always in exactly the same position as the "lower" one. Tails were long and impossibly straight, and faces showed one black Quintaglio eye staring out from the side of the head, instead of facing forward. Toroca noted that the Quintaglios in the frescoes were wearing broad belts, but no sashes. He wondered how old the paintings were.

A guttural scream split the air.

Toroca and Babnol ran for the doorway of the building they'd been in, and came out into the light of day. Toroca scanned all around, looking for the source of the sound, but—

"There!" shouted Babnol.

Toroca wheeled. Off toward the north, a group of Quintaglio hunters had descended on a hornface. The four-footed beast had its head tipped low, the massive frill of bone at the back of its skull rising up like a shield, the two horns above the eyes thrusting out like lances, the shorter, slightly curved horn above the nose sticking proudly up.

The animal screamed again as a midsized Quintaglio female leapt onto its back and, holding on to the edge of the neck frill for balance, dug her jaws into the bunching muscles of the shoulder. The ground was now slick with blood.

The hunters made short work of the hornface. In a matter of moments, it was dead, the corpse teetering for a moment, then falling onto its left side with a great leathery slapping sound.

It was wise to wait until hunters were satiated before approaching them. Toroca and Babnol did just that, watching long muzzles scoop out great hunks of meat. A flock of wingfingers circled over the kill. They, too, were waiting. Once the hunters had begun to collapse onto their bellies, Toroca moved out of the doorway and ambled over to them. "Permission to enter your territory?" he called out.

An elderly female looked up. "*Hahat dan,*" she replied. "But, you are right—this is indeed our territory. What are you doing here?"

Toroca stopped well short of the site of the kill and bowed. "I am Kee-Toroca," he said. "Leader of the Geological Survey of Land."

The female gestured to her hunting partners. "Get up, friends. We have an imperial emissary amongst us." The others staggered to their feet, then leaned back on their tails for balance. "I'm Fas-Jodor," she said, "and these are the best hunters of Pack Derrilo."

"Greetings," said Toroca. He indicated Babnol. "This is Wab-Babnol, a trader in fossils."

"You'll have to collect old Jodor before you go," said one of the hunters, and the others clicked teeth at the jest. Babnol nodded good-naturedly.

"Pack Derrilo is returning to this area," said Jodor.

"This is part of your normal range?" said Toroca.

"It is, and of Packs Horbo and Quebelmo. Horbo vacated here about five kilodays ago, heading west along the bottom of the Cape of Mekt, then back up the west side. We've been working our way down the east side from the north." Packs roamed, moving from place to place, lest an area be overhunted. It was not unusual for ancient settlements such as this one to play host to several Packs in rotation, with long periods of vacancy in between. "The hunting had gotten quite sparse by the time Pack Horbo cleared out," said Jodor. "But, as you can see, things seem to have improved in the interim." She slapped her belly.

Toroca nodded. It was normal ritual for a hunting party to precede the caravans with the rest of the Pack's people and goods, and for the hunters to consecrate the ground with a traditional kill as a way of reclaiming the vacant territory.

"We're just leaving ourselves," said Toroca, "by sailing ship."

"Surely you'll stay until the rest of our Pack arrives," said Jodor. "They'd like to see people from the Capital."

"We'd enjoy that, but I'm afraid we're on a tight schedule. We have a rendezvous to make on a specific date."

Jodor nodded. "Unfortunate. But walk with me now, Toroca. There's one more ritual I have to perform. Babnol, you can join us, or partake of some of the kill, whichever you prefer."

Babnol looked at the hornface carcass. "Thank you, no. That particular kind is not to my taste. I'll walk with you."

Jodor began walking, and Babnol and Toroca, spread out in a line with five paces between each of them, followed.

" 'Geological Survey,' " said Jodor. "What's that mean, exactly?"

"Geology is the study of the history and structure of our world," said Toroca.

"Hmm," said Jodor. "Seems a rather frivolous task, if you don't mind me saying so. I thought all scientific efforts were being bent toward the exodus."

"Oh, this survey is indeed in support of getting us off this moon," Toroca said. "I report directly to Wab-Novato, leader of that effort. Our goal is to find and catalog all the resources that Land—and indeed this entire world—has to offer. We have to know exactly what's available to work with."

"Ah," said Jodor. "That makes sense. So you're strictly looking for minerals—coal, metals, and the like."

They were getting close to the edge of the cliff now. "Well, that's the main task, but while we're at it, we're indulging our curiosity in other matters. I'm particularly interested in fossils myself."

"Fossils?"

"Remains of ancient life. Stone bones and shells and such."

"Oh, so that's what Gatabor meant a moment ago," said Jodor. "Funny guy."

Before them was an ancient *salabaja* tree, its trunk as wide as Toroca was tall, its branches thick and gnarled, its dark brown bark massively corrugated. Jodor extended a claw and walked right up to the tree. She began to carve something into the bark, the movements of her finger digging out little pieces. There were several designs already carved into the tree's trunk.

Toroca, hands on hips, looked out over the edge of the cliff. The tree was right on the lip; in fact, some of its roots were exposed at the edge. As far out as he could see, there was only choppy gray water, and yet, he knew, somewhere far, far to the south, there was the icy polar cap. Looking straight down, he almost succumbed to vertigo. The massive cliff face dropped away from him, curving out slightly, several chalk layers visible here, near the top, including the Bookmark layer, and then, continuing on down, down to the beach far below, barren layer after layer of brown sandstone. On the beach, he could see Spalton and Tralen dismantling the tents—he could only tell who it was because those were the people he'd assigned that task to; the Quintaglios looked like nothing more than green specks from this dizzying height.

Toroca turned back to Jodor. Babnol was watching her intently. "What are you doing?" she said at last.

Jodor had almost finished a complex design in the bark. It was the same as one of the designs that were already present; in fact, looking more closely, Toroca saw that there were only three designs in total, but each one appeared in several different places.

"This is the emblem of my Pack," said Jodor. "Upon returning to this area, I always make our symbol here, in this old *salabaja*, then mark the date. The other two are the emblems of Packs Horbo and Quebelmo."

Toroca counted. There seemed to be about ten of each symbol. "You'll have to find a new tree soon enough," said Toroca absently. "This one's almost over the edge."

Jodor looked up. "It's always been like that."

"But the cliff face is eroding away . . . ," said Toroca.

"Eroding?"

"Crumbling to sand. That's what the beach is made of: sand that weathered out of the rocks of the cliff face."

Jodor looked impressed. "Is that a fact?"

"So this tree must have been farther back from the edge originally," said Babnol.

"Not that I can recall," said Jodor.

"Oh, it's a gradual process, to be sure," said Toroca.

Jodor shook her head. "See that branch there? See the way it sticks out over the cliff face?"

Toroca nodded.

"When I was a youngster, that used to be the great stunt: climb up the tree, then crawl out along that branch, so that there was nothing except it between you and the sheer drop down to the beach."

Toroca's inner eyelids fluttered. "It was that close to the edge when you were a child?"

"Uh-huh. And I'll save you the trouble of asking. Yes, I'm as old as I look. I hatched forty-seven kilodays ago."

"And you're sure that the branch stuck over the edge even when you were very young?"

"Oh, yes, indeed," said Jodor, pleased to be dumbfounding the fellow from the big city. "In fact, my old creche master caught me crawling out onto that branch once. He gave me a stern talking-to, I'll tell you, but then he had to admit that he'd done the same thing back when he'd been a boy. He was almost as old then as I am now, so that means it's been right up at the edge for at least a hundred kilodays."

"A hundred kilodays," said Toroca. He held out an arm to steady himself against the massive, ancient tree trunk.

Babnol looked startled, too. "But the first sacred scroll says the world is only five thousand kilodays old. If a hundred kilodays can pass with next to no visible retreating of the cliff edge, Toroca, how long would it take to erode enough rock to make all the sand on that beach?"

Toroca looked back over the edge, as if some trick must be involved that proper scrutiny would reveal. "During our stay here, we dug very deep indeed on the beach," he said. "We must have gone down ten paces, and the bottom of the sand was nowhere in sight."

He looked again at the tree, gnarled, proud. "A hundred kilodays, and no visible progress." He turned to Jodor. "A hundred kilodays is about two percent of the age of the world," he said, "according to the scrolls."

Jodor seemed unconcerned. She was just finishing chiseling today's date into the bark beneath the emblem she'd carved. "So?"

"So if the erosion is that slow, it would take more than five thousand kilodays to accumulate that much sand."

Jodor clicked her teeth. "I see the mistake you're making," she said. "The first sacred scroll was written over two thousand kilodays ago. That means there have been seven thousand, not five thousand, kilodays since the world was created."

Toroca shook his head. "It's not enough. It's off by—by orders of magnitude."

"What are 'orders of magnitude'?" asked Jodor.

"Powers of ten. Seven thousand kilodays wouldn't be enough. Tubers, *seventy* thousand kilodays wouldn't be enough, either."

Jodor still seemed to be unconcerned. "If this wasn't stormy Fra'-toolar, I'd say you'd been out in the sun too long, Toroca. We know the world is seven thousand kilodays old; therefore, whatever process you're concerned about could not have taken longer than seven thousand kilo-days to occur."

Toroca dipped his head. "I'm sure you're right," he said. But then he swung around, looking out over the panorama visible from the top of the cliff, before Jodor could see his muzzle turn blue with the liar's tint.

Chapter 8

Capital City: The Avenue of Traders

It was well-known that Emperor Dy-Dybo didn't care much for parades, but this was Jostark's Day, in honor of craftspeople. The parade was important to Capital City's economy, launching the ten-day festival that brought skilled workers from all over the province to trade their wares in the central marketplace.

The day was sunny, the sky a pristine, cloudless mauve. Four pale moons were visible despite the daylight, two of them on either side of the brilliant sun, crescents bowing away from the tiny white disk. The constant east-west breeze blew harbor air over the city, but the usual background sound of ships' bells and drums coming up from the docks was gone. All work had suspended so that everyone could attend the parade.

In addition to all the city folk and the many tourists, there were two unexpected spectators. One was Rodlox, the governor of Edz'toolar province, about the same height as Dybo, but trim and well-muscled. Yes, strictly speaking, his name was now "Dy-Rodlox," he having recently ascended to the governorship upon the death of his predecessor, Len-Ganloor, but he suffered the use of the praenomen that honored Dybo only on the most formal of occasions. At all other times, he was merely "Rodlox." He stood, arms folded in front of his chest, leaning back on his tail, waiting. Next to him was his aide, Pod-Oro, about twice Rodlox's age.

Governor Rodlox and Pod-Oro would be missed today in Edz'toolar, for a corresponding but much less elaborate parade was being held in that province's capital to mark Jostark's Day there. But they had come here, to the Capital, precisely to see the Emperor, chubby Dybo himself, march down the public streets.

Rodlox and Oro watched from the side of the Avenue of Traders, one of Capital City's widest thoroughfares, as the procession approached. At the front of the marching group was Lub-Galpook, daughter to Afsan and Novato, who, since the death of Jal-Tetex, had become the new imperial hunt leader. She moved with stealth, as if stalking prey. Behind her, fanned out in a traditional pattern, were nine of the town's best hunters. As Galpook continued forward, she would periodically hold up her hands in the hunter's sign language, redeploying her pack. The nine would silently take on new configurations.

The governor of Edz'toolar paid little attention. His mind was on other matters, weightier matters. He couldn't stand the name "Dy-Rodlox," but thought that "Rod-Rodlox" had quite an attractive ring to it . . .

And then, at last, Dybo was visible, there, in the distance, at the very end of the parade.

The Emperor. The mad Emperor who wanted to take them to the stars.

Dybo was almost exactly the same height as Rodlox, but the Emperor's girth . . . Rodlox thought it was like seeing himself stretched wide, reflected in some distorted mirror. Still, that he saw any of Dybo in himself was disturbing. It robbed him of some of his individuality. Did Dybo have the same fears as he did? The same weaknesses? One's innermost self should be private. But here, waddling toward him, was another iteration, a caricature, a mockery of himself.

The crowd lining the road was sparse. Even to see the Emperor, Quintaglios would not pack themselves tightly together. The parade would continue for a distance of many kilopaces so that everyone would have a chance to see it.

Crafters—in whose honor this march was held, after all—were passing by now, each holding a sample of his or her wares: a tall, thin Quintaglio with tanned leathers draped over his snake-like arms; a stouter fellow with brown and yellow freckles on his muzzle holding two complex metal instruments; a slim female, apparently one of Novato's students, carrying a brass far-seer, sunlight glinting off its metal tube and glass lenses; a vastly old giant, skin so dark green as to be almost black, bearing books bound in hornface hide; many tens more.

Rodlox kept his eye on the approaching Dybo. *Soon*, he thought. *Soon*.

The imperial staff was now abreast of Rodlox and Oro. Leading the way were two burly imperial guards, the kind that warded off animals that might wander into the city. They held ceremonial staffs high, each with a red banner showing Dybo's cartouche.

Next came Det-Bogkash, the Master of the Faith, followed by several other holy people. Rodlox remembered the days when priests wore flowing, banded robes, imitating the Face of God's roiling cloud patterns. The new robes, pristine white, seemed bland in comparison. Perhaps that could be changed . . .

After the priests came senior palace advisors: Nom-Lirpan, in charge of provincial relations; Wab-Novato, leader of this crazed exodus; Afsan, the blind sage, with a large, ugly reptile on a leash leading him in the correct path.

And then, Dy-Dybo himself, the Emperor of the Fifty Packs, ruler of the eight provinces, sovereign of all of Land, the great-great-great-great-grandson of Larsk.

Dybo's hand was raised in a traditional hunter's sign, a calling together of the pack, simultaneously a gesture reinforcing his leadership and the assembled group's sense of community.

Suddenly Rodlox stepped away from the curb, moved into the center of the roadway, and stood directly in Dybo's path. There were five paces between them. Spectators gasped.

Dybo looked up, startled.

"Get out of the way!" shouted someone from the roadside.

Rodlox spoke firmly. "No."

"You're blocking the path of the Emperor," said another spectator. The procession came to a complete halt.

"I know exactly what I'm doing," said Rodlox, glancing once at Oro, standing at the roadside, the aide's muzzle scrunched in a satisfied expression.

Dybo himself spoke now, his smooth voice the most remarkable of all his musical instruments. "Please step aside, friend." His words were fluid, warm, a spoken song.

Friend, thought Rodlox. *He doesn't even recognize me!*

"No," Rodlox said again.

Dybo's face twisted in concern. "You're not injured, are you?" His muzzle tipped up and down as he appraised Rodlox. "Are you unable to move?"

"I can move," said Rodlox, his tone steady, controlled, "but I will not."

"Why not?" said a calm voice from behind him. Rodlox turned to see the blind one, Afsan, facing in his direction. It was disconcerting to have those empty sockets, covered by caved-in, wrinkled lids, staring at him. At his side, Afsan's reptile hissed softly at Rodlox.

"That is no concern of yours."

"You interfere with a procession of which I am part," said Afsan, spreading his hands. "You block the path of my friend and ruler, Dy-Dybo. Yes, Rodlox, it is a concern of mine."

Rodlox felt his heart flutter. How did the blind one know who he was? "You called me by name."

"I recognize your voice. We met once shortly before your ascension, when Len-Ganloor brought you to the Capital. What, I wonder, is the new governor of Edz'toolar doing here so soon after his last visit to this province?"

This Afsan . . . a most disconcerting individual. Rodlox had heard tales of his facility with arguments. Best not to engage him further. He turned instead to look defiantly at Dybo.

For his part, Dybo seemed unperturbed, as if such a thing as a recalcitrant pedestrian was a matter of no import next to the issues of state. "I ask you again," said the Emperor politely, each word flowing into the next like water into a goblet, "please step aside."

"And I say again: I refuse."

"Very well," said Dybo, with a tilt of the head which reaffirmed that the whole matter was of little consequence to him. "Then I shall go around you." Dybo moved diagonally toward the curb, but Rodlox again stepped in his path. The crowd was silent.

"A real leader would not concede territory to another so easily."

"A real leader," said Dybo in a congenial tone, "knows what is worth arguing over and what is not." Again, the Emperor stepped aside, but once more Rodlox blocked his path. Dybo then moved to the left, and Rodlox did likewise. The imperial guards had stepped back to stand on either side of Dybo, their banners snapping in the breeze. Their eyes were locked on the Emperor, looking for any sign from him that they should intervene. The whole procession was breaking up now. Everyone had turned around to see what the delay was, and some, including several crafters and members of Galpook's hunting pack, had moved near.

Dybo let out a sigh, a long affected hiss indicating that he'd grown tired of this game. He took a bold step forward. Rodlox reached out a stiff arm and pushed it into the Emperor's shoulder.

A murmur went through the crowd. To touch another—*especially* the Emperor!

"Do not do that again," said Dybo quietly.

But Rodlox tipped from the waist, his tail lifting from the ground, and in a slow, deliberate gesture, too choreographed and extended to be instinct, he bobbed his torso up and down, up and down. A display of territorial challenge.

Silence, save for some whispering behind him. Rodlox realized that Novato had stepped over to Afsan and was giving him a running description.

"I challenge you," Rodlox said, his voice loud and firm.

Dybo spread his arms. "Challenge me for what? This is a street of the people; all streets in Capital City are so designated. I don't claim it as my territory; you, Rodlox, and all others are free to use it."

Rodlox bobbed again. "It's not the street I challenge you for," he said. "I challenge your right to rule. I challenge your right to be Emperor."

"I am of The Family," said Dybo. "I am the son of the daughter of the daughter of the son of the daughter of the son of Larsk, the prophet."

"And," said Rodlox, "I, Rodlox, governor of Edz'toolar, am also"—he had rehearsed the litany—"the son of the daughter of the daughter of the son of the daughter of the son of Larsk, the prophet."

"The fellow's mad," said a voice from the curbside. "Thinks he's the Emperor."

Rodlox wheeled to face the speaker. "No, I do not think I am the Emperor, citizen, and I assure you I am not mad." He turned again to Dybo. "Am I, *brother?*"

"Brother?" said Dybo, his mouth remaining agape after speaking the word.

Rodlox heard what sounded like a sharp inhalation of breath from behind him. Was it Afsan? "Yes, *brother*: male child of the same parents." He pointed to the one who'd called him mad. "You! Come here!" The citizen—a maker of pottery, judging by the symbols on her blue sash—seemed afraid. "Come here, I said. I'll not hurt you."

Rodlox's muzzle didn't flush blue, but then if the citizen really did think him insane, she might not give that much credence. A couple of those standing near the citizen urged her on, and she took a hesitant step forward.

"Come closer," snapped Rodlox.

"I—I do not wish to invade your territory," said the citizen.

"*Hahat dan*, for God's sake!" said Rodlox. "I grant you permission. Come stand right next to me, right here." He pointed at the ground beside him. The citizen looked back at the crowd.

"Go ahead!" shouted an onlooker. Others made encouraging gestures. The potmaker slowly stepped up to Rodlox. "Now, look at my earholes." Rodlox swiveled his neck so that the citizen could see first one, then the other.

The citizen's expression was blank. "Yes?"

"*Look* at them. What do you notice about them?"

"I don't know what you want me to say—"

"The shape, fool. The shape! What shape are they?"

"Oval, I guess."

"Oval. Unusual, isn't that?"

"Well, I suppose. But, umm, I mean no offense by that."

"None taken. Go look at the Emperor's earholes."

The citizen stood there. "Your Luminance?"

"Hahat dan," said Dybo, with a slight concessional nod. "Feel free."

The citizen peered at the sides of Dybo's head.

"Well?" snapped Rodlox.

"His are oval, too."

"Louder. Shout it. I want everyone to hear."

The citizen's voice cracked slightly, but she did manage a more robust volume. "I said, his are oval, too."

Rodlox bowed full concession at the citizen. "Thank you. You may return to the side of the road." The citizen hastened to do just that. Rodlox shouted so all could hear: "My associates and I have cataloged fourteen distinctive physical features that Dybo and I have in common. Fourteen!" He turned through a slow circle, facing members of the public, the procession, spectators on the far curb, and then Dybo again. "The earholes are an obvious example." He tipped forward, lifting his tail from the paving stones. "The mottling on the undersides of our tails is the same." He pointed at his own feet, then at Dybo's. "Instead of our middle toeclaw being longer than the other two, it's the same length as our inner toeclaw." He looked up. "We both have exceptional vision. Our muzzles are shorter than average. And on and on."

Dybo spoke softly. "I fail to see the significance—"

"We're brothers," said Rodlox flatly. "Brothers."

"How can the two of you be brothers?" shouted another voice from the far curb. "No one has brothers." A pause. "Well, no one except Afsan and Novato's children."

Rodlox spun to face the speaker. "No one *should* have brothers, or sisters for that matter," he said. "But I do, and he does. In fact, there are eight of us, siblings all. Every one of Lends's eight egglings has lived to adulthood. And of the eight, I'm sure that I, Rodlox, am the strongest, for if I were not, I would not have been sent to Edz'toolar, the most barren and isolated part of Land. I am the rightful leader of the Fifty Packs."

"But that's impossible!" said a voice, an old fellow standing near Oro. "The bloodpriest—"

Rodlox nodded, as if pleased by the question. "Ah, yes. The imperial bloodpriest. He did not devour seven of the eight hatchlings. Rather, I'm convinced that seven of the eight were sent out to be apprentice governors in the outlying provinces, and the eighth remained in the Capital, to be groomed for Emperorship."

Dy-Dybo looked as though he'd had quite enough. "Ridiculous!" he said, his voice for the first time sharp. He turned his muzzle toward his blind sage. "Afsan, you're a clear thinker. Explain the folly of his logic to this fellow."

Rodlox spun around, looked at Afsan. And he saw in Afsan's face something—

Rodlox narrowed his eyes. "You—you know of this!"

Afsan said nothing.

"Speak, blind one. You *do* know of this, don't you?"

"I—" began Afsan, but he did not continue. His pet reptile hissed quietly at his side.

"Speak! If what I say isn't true, tell me now."

"You've presented no irrefutable proof of your extraordinary claim," said Afsan slowly.

"I can prove it," said Rodlox. "But you—I see it in your expression. You have known of this!"

"Everything you've said is just circumstantial evidence, or could be explained as mere coincidence," said Afsan.

"Then deny it directly, sightless one. Say it out loud for all to hear! Declare publicly that what I've said is not true."

There was a long silence, every set of eyes locked on Afsan. "What you say," said Afsan at last, spacing the words out, "is not true."

"By the fangs of God—" said Dybo wanly, as he watched Afsan's face.

"See!" shouted Rodlox, spinning again to look at everyone in turn. "See! The blind one's muzzle turns blue. His words are a lie!"

Afsan dipped his head.

"Afsan?" said Dybo, a note of desperation in his voice.

Even though they were sightless, Afsan apparently could not lift his eyes to meet the Emperor's. "I'm sorry," he said, very softly.

Dybo's inner eyelids were snapping up and down spasmodically, no doubt turning his vision into a strobing display. "Are you sure?" he said.

"He's sure!" shouted Rodlox. "He knows I am right."

Afsan rallied some strength. "No," he said. "I don't know that what you say is true, Rodlox. I can't see the evidence of physical similarity you are apparently presenting."

"No, you can't," said Rodlox. "But you believe me. I see that in your face. Admit it. Admit the truth."

Afsan was silent. Dybo spoke at last, "Afsan, is it true?"

"I am not positive," Afsan said quietly, "but . . . yes. I've long suspected that what Rodlox has suggested is true." Afsan looked slightly
defensive. "I *did* mention the possibility to you once, long ago."

Dybo leaned back on his tail for support.

"The bloodpriests have lied!" shouted Rodlox. "Not only have they
betrayed the people, they've betrayed the very Emperorship itself." He
faced the spectators lining the near curb now. "Surely the imperial bloodpriest should have chosen the best and fastest of the egglings to become
Emperor. Look at him!" He jabbed a finger at Dybo. "Look at him! Fat,
dull-witted, lazy." The crowd hissed at the insults, but Rodlox pressed on.
"And look at me: lean and muscular, and sharp of mind. The bloodpriests
wanted someone on the ruling slab that they could easily manipulate, so
they sent the rightful heir away. I'm the one who should be Emperor." He
turned directly toward Dybo. "With me in the palace, our people will get
on with the business of living, not be mired in your mad dream of leaving our home."

Rodlox bobbed his torso up and down. "I challenge you, Dybo, here
and now, in front of these hundred witnesses—

"I challenge your authority to lead—

"I challenge your right to the throne—

"I challenge your very right to be alive."

Emperor Dy-Dybo stood motionless, mouth agape.

Chapter 9

A Quintaglio's Diary

So we children of Afsan and Novato are no longer unique. Emperor Dybo, being of The Family, has, of course, always known who his parents were, but now it seems that he, too, also has living siblings.

I guess no one had ever noticed the resemblance between Dybo and his brothers and sisters. After all, the apprentice governors are scattered across Land, and I doubt two of them have often been seen side by side. And, of course, Dybo is quite portly, making comparisons between him and the others less obvious.

I wonder how Dybo is dealing with the knowledge that he has siblings. It's different for him than it is for me, I'm sure. To begin with, apparently he's only just discovered this fact (if it is a fact—there seems to be some doubt still). He didn't grow up with them, doesn't know them at all, except in a perfunctory and official way. It's too bad: I'd be grateful to discuss what I'm going through with someone older and more experienced. But my role is minor. The Emperor, I'm sure, would never find time in his day to talk with me.

Fra'toolar

Toroca was poised in a little cleft, nine-tenths of the way up the cliff side, working along the Bookmark layer, the chalky seam marking the first rocks containing evidence of life. He kept hoping to unearth one of the shards of the eggs of creation. What a find that would be! An actual shell piece from an egg laid by God! So far, though, he'd found nothing like that. In fact, this layer was remarkably similar to all the layers above it: rich with shells, with bones of fish, and even with occasional pieces of the skeletons of great water serpents, similar to the famed Kal-ta-goot that Afsan had killed aboard the sailing ship *Dasheter*.

A great fissure ran through the rocks here, the handiwork of a landquake, no doubt. At this little perch, one could reach into the side of the cliff and simply pull out chunks of rock. The material here, just below the Bookmark layer, was a gray shale. It split cleanly along bedding planes, and Toroca opened slab after slab of it. Every piece was pristine, not marred by the fossils that were shot through the rocks from higher up.

Toroca whacked the flat end of his hammer against the chisel again, and another slab split cleanly open. Nothing. He tried again with a different piece, a surprisingly heavy piece, but accidentally smashed his thumb instead. Occupational hazard: he didn't even really feel the pain anymore. He repositioned the chisel and tried once more. This slab, for a change, did not split cleanly. The upper layers started to separate, but ceased to split off about halfway across. Curious. Toroca used his fingers to pry the slab apart. A large hunk snapped off, exposing a small rounded bit of something strange.

Something blue.

There were blue gemstones, of course, and a couple of blue minerals, but they were not normally found in downrocks such as these. But this thing, whatever it was, was definitely blue, a light shade, like that of certain wingfinger eggshells.

There was only a tiny piece of it visible, jutting from the bedding plane. Toroca turned the slab over and positioned his chisel on the opposite side, then tapped his hammer lightly against it. The stone began to split, and once again he pried with his fingers to separate the rock. It took a great effort, but at last the upper layers broke free in sharp-edged flat pieces. He let them slide away, tumbling down the cliff face. There, just about in the middle of the slab, was a blue hemisphere with a diameter the length of Toroca's longest finger.

Toroca was normally excited by every discovery, for each new one advanced his knowledge. But with this one, he simply felt puzzled and confused. After all, he had thought these rocks were old, coming from just below the first layer in which remnants of life were found. But this was clearly a manufactured object, meaning that it couldn't be very old at all: perhaps a few hundred kilodays, although its smooth surface made even that much of a pedigree doubtful.

And then it hit him, causing his heart to flutter. The theory of superposition, carefully worked out by the late Irb-Falpom, might be destroyed by this find. Falpom's theory had seemed so elegant, so simple: the older rocks were on the bottom. Such a revolution that had made in geology! But Toroca's survey was the first one extensive enough to really prove or disprove the theory, although it had been accepted as fact for several kilodays now. Everything found to date had seemed to coincide with superposition, but now this, whatever it was, destroyed all that. A theory was only as good as the data that supported it, and superposition couldn't explain a contemporary artifact buried deep within ancient rock.

For one brief moment, Toroca thought about tossing aside the find, never showing it to anyone. The theory was so good, after all, and it was the one great claim to fame of his mentor and friend, Falpom. But of course he couldn't do that. He was a scholar, and this blue dome was a fact, a fact that had to be accounted for.

It was surprising that the object, whatever it was, had survived burial so well. Regardless of what theory would eventually replace superposition, this blue thingamajig had been here for some time, in these rock layers, with the weight of all the cliff above pressing down on it. That it wasn't crushed, or even scratched, fascinated Toroca.

He extended a claw and tapped the hard surface. The thing sounded slightly hollow. Toroca retracted the claw and ran his finger over the object. It was very smooth, but felt warmer than glass. Presumably there was more of it still buried in the slab. Perhaps the object was some sort of game ball.

Toroca tried to chisel into the rock along another bedding plane, but it didn't seem to want to split. After several failed attempts, he used the brute-force method. Balancing the slab on another piece of rock, with an edge of the slab overhanging, he pressed down upon the overhang until it broke off, right at the leading edge of the blue object. The object popped out of the matrix and went rolling down the embankment.

Toroca scrambled down, loose stones clacking together underfoot. It was easy to spot the blue artifact against the brown sandstone. It teetered for a moment at the edge of another fissure. If it fell in there, the object would be lost for good. But it rolled the other way, catching on some jutting layers. Toroca scraped his knees and tail going after it, but finally got close enough to pick it up. It was surprisingly heavy, especially for something that might be hollow.

It was not a ball.

Rather it was some sort of complex device. The upper surface was indeed a smooth hemisphere, but the lower half was sculpted in a strange fluid shape, and had a row of hollow blue rings depending from it. The pattern of rings made Toroca think of finger holes, and indeed, he tried slipping the device onto his left hand—

—and immediately realized that the rings could not be finger holes, because there were *six* of them instead of five.

Still, if he balled his fist, the device, although apparently not built for a hand as large as his, did seem designed to be worn that way, as a rounded extension of the knuckles. It could have been some kind of inflexible glove, perhaps to protect the fingers when rock climbing, or to prevent one from doing damage with one's claws. Toroca had heard of unfortunate fellows inflicted with a condition that caused their claws to extend and retract uncontrollably.

But it couldn't be that, because of the six finger holes.

Unless, of course, it was ambidextrous, designed for use on either hand. The first five holes would be used when worn on the left; the second through sixth holes would be used when worn on the right. But that wouldn't work; the first and sixth holes were not mirror images of each other. Instead, the holes got progressively bigger.

What could it be?

He wiggled his fingers to try to get them to sit better in the rings. His middle finger seemed to press up and into the hemisphere. Toroca removed the object, turned it over, and looked at the rings. The construction was much more complex than he'd first thought. The rings seemed to contain little movable parts that could push into the main body of the object. The others were clogged with dirt, but the third clicked in and out of its indentation easily. If the device was cleaned, one could probably click each ring up and down separately. Toroca wondered if it was a musical instrument of some sort, but he couldn't find an aperture either for breathing into or for sound to emerge.

He knew he'd regret it as the afternoon sun grew hotter, but he used the water in his canteen to wash off the object. Two more of the finger rings loosened up after having been flushed with water; the others seemed permanently seized.

The material had warmed to be about the same temperature as Toroca's hand. It definitely wasn't glass or crystal: there didn't seem to be any fragility about it. It wasn't metal either, although it seemed heavier than lead. Not only was the color wrong for metal, it didn't conduct heat the way metal did, and, despite having been buried, there was no sign of corrosion.

Toroca extended a fingerclaw again and tapped the surface. There was definitely a hollow space within. He brought the object up to his earhole and shook it. No rattling; nothing was loose. He drew his fingerclaw across the curve of the hemisphere, first gently, then applying great pressure. Not a scratch. The thing was dirty, but otherwise completely undamaged. Toroca had no idea how old the object was: it looked freshly made, but he knew that no one besides his surveyors and the recently arrived Pack Derrilo had been in this remote part of Land for ages. And yet, it had to be recent: it was so smooth and lacked the ornate adornments found on artifacts from an earlier age.

Or *did* it have to be recent?

The stratigraphy of the rocks said no. They said it was ancient, predating all life.

Yet it was clearly manufactured.

Or was it? It bore no cartouches, no glyphs. There were only a couple of simple geometric markings on the underside of it. Could it be a fancy shell? Many of them were made of a lustrous material that looked manufactured.

He tried to scratch it again. Nothing. Well, it was hollow; if it was a shell, there might be some sign within of the creature that had inhabited it.

He balanced the object on a rock, held it firmly with his right hand, and brought down the pointed end of his hammer with his left. The hammer bounced right back up, almost hitting Toroca in the muzzle. He tried again, smashing harder. Nothing—not the slightest crack or scratch. He tried a third time, pounding the hammer with all his might. The point simply skidded across the curving surface, and Toroca pitched forward, losing his balance.

He scrambled for purchase and steadied himself. He'd been so wrapped up in the puzzling object, he'd all but forgotten he was still way up the side of a cliff. He moved back up the precipice a bit until he found a place with firmer footing.

The object was amazing. Toroca was a geologist; he knew about forged metals and alloys and every type of mineral and volcanic glass. There was nothing—nothing—like this material.

Who could have built such a thing?

And when?

The builder—or, at least, the thing that it had been built for—apparently had six fingers, not five.

Six.

Toroca was wearing a geologist's sash, with pockets running up its entire length. One of them contained his kit of ten numbered mineralogical samples used for determining the relative hardness of materials. He fished it out.

The softest specimen, number 1, was a piece of graphite. The hardest, number 10, was a brilliant diamond crystal. During fieldwork, an unknown specimen would be rubbed against the samples in turn. The specimen would scratch some of the lower-numbered samples, meaning it was harder than those, but would be scratched by all the remaining higher-numbered samples. A piece of cinnabar, for instance, would scratch graphite (#1) and gypsum (#2) but would be scratched by a piece of copper (#3), meaning that cinnabar had a hardness rating of 2 and a bit. The hardness value was often diagnostic, distinguishing, for instance, pyrite from gold.

There was a rectangular projection on the undersurface of the artifact, just past the last of the six finger rings. The blue material was obviously very hard, so he decided to skip samples 1 through 6. He started with number 7, a common hexagonal quartz crystal. Holding the quartz piece firmly, he dragged it across one of the pointed corners of the rectangular projection. White powder appeared at the corner's vertex. Powdered quartz; the blue stuff was harder than the seventh sample.

He tried the same thing with sample number 8. Yellow powder collected on the point, and a short straight scratch appeared in the sample crystal. Harder than topaz. Sample number 9 was a star sapphire, a worthless specimen damaged by a lapidary. Toroca pressed it hard against the blue point on the surface of the object and worked the gem back and forth. When he pulled it away, he could see a deep scratch marring the six-pointed star image across the stone's face.

Hard, indeed. He got out his final sample. The diamond glinted in the bright sunlight. This, at least, should scratch the strange object. Toroca grunted. A part of him would take a perverse pleasure in blemishing the blue surface.

He worked the diamond back and forth across a corner point of the rectangular projection, making five or six good, firm scrapes. He then pulled the diamond away. White dust covered the point. He rubbed his finger over the tip to clear it away.

The point was undamaged.

He looked at the diamond.

A deep scratch had been cut into it.

Harder than specimen #10.

Harder than the hardest-known substance.

Harder than diamond.

Toroca almost lost his footing again.

Chapter 10

Musings of the Watcher

The Jijaki did not react the way I had expected.

What do I know of psychology—especially the psychology of primitive races? I'd been alone for eons.

Although I could always observe them, the Jijaki became most accessible to me once they started broadcasting electromagnetic signals. It took me several of their years to sort through the vast amount of material that leaked from their world, but without a key I could not unlock their language. And then, at last, a key was laid before me. One of their audiovisual programs was an educational series aimed at young Jijaki—the demographics of those on it were highly skewed from the population norm, concentrating on juvenile forms. Much of it was presented in two-dimensional animation, and a great deal was, I eventually realized, song, although Jijaki singing, made by holding the manipulators at the end of the trunk over the triangular breathing holes while breath was forced out, was not sufficiently complex to really interest me.

The program, identified as *Kijititatak Gikta* at the start of each installment, was broadcast once each planetary day, except that every fourth day was skipped. Each installment lasted a fraction under one-twentieth of one day. The program provided the rudimentary sort of introduction I needed to at last decipher the language of their broadcasts (or at least one of their languages, for the form used seemed to vary with geographic location on the planet), introducing not only the characters of the Jijaki alphabet but also the sounds associated with each character, and giving pictorial representations of the objects that individual words described.

The direct approach seemed the best. I manipulated hydrogen gas in the space between the Jijak star and its nearest neighbor, blocked out portions with streamers of dark matter, and arranged for the whole thing to glow. On *Kijititatak Gikta*, there was an animated character apparently named Tilk. Tilk was bright pink in color, unlike the muted opalescence of real Jijaki, and had eye stalks that could extend to enormous distances and waggle about in wild patterns. No such creature actually existed in the fauna of this world, as far as I could tell. In any event, Tilk began each of his appearances on the show with a simple, apparently colloquial greeting. I lit up those same words in the sky: "Howdy, girls and boys and little neuters!"

The words were invisible to those on the surface. But I knew the Jijaki had optical telescopes, so I waited patiently for my greeting to be found. The planet completed about three-quarters of an orbit before it was, and then suddenly the broadcasts were full of it. They even interrupted *Kijititatak Gikta* for an announcement about my greeting.

It became apparent that the Jijaki thought this was a deliberate trick on the part of one of their own, but astronomers across their planet soon confirmed that the words were really there, floating in space. Jijaki had only just begun suborbital flights, so they knew there was no way any of their people could have been responsible.

Suddenly all broadcasts, except for a furtive few, stopped. I was shocked. It seemed the Jijaki had figured out that I'd been listening in, and wanted nothing to do with me.

To have waited since the dawn of the universe for these creatures to emerge, and then to be shunned—it was more than I could bear. For a brief time, I thought to hurtle asteroids at their world, for it was only because of my intervention that they existed at all. But that thought passed, and instead I formulated another sentence. It took me close to a Jijaki year to do it, and doing it that quickly taxed my powers to the utmost. "Please talk to me," was all I said.

And, at last, they did. The broadcasts resumed, with major transmitters on all landmasses sending up a message. Most replied in the same language form I had used, but a few, apparently partisans of another form, and feeling it deserved equal consideration, replied in one of the geographic variants. "Who are you?" they said.

I told them. Reaction was mixed, and it took me some time to figure it all out. One broadcast frequency was given over to what I eventually realized was a religion, in worship of me. Others engaged me in dialog, showing me how to send visual signals in a more efficient method, using a simple binary code that I could blink out much more quickly than I could form letters in the sky. Eventually the normal cacophony of broadcasts resumed, including even *Kijititatak Gikta*. Within a short time, the general populace had largely lost interest in me.

But I soon had work for my Jijaki to do.

Fra'toolar

Back at the base camp, Toroca thoroughly washed the strange blue artifact in the waters crashing against the beach. It became clear that there was a seam running around the object's widest part. At four places, little gray tabs seemed to be protruding through slots, as if the two halves of the unit were held together by the pressure they exerted. Toroca extended his fingerclaws and used them to depress the tabs one at a time. They did indeed give a bit, but as soon as he stopped pressing upon them, they popped back out. Next he tried to depress them all simultaneously. It was difficult to do so, and one of the tabs resisted his pressure, but at last the casing popped open.

Toroca was disappointed. He'd expected to see enormously complex gearworks within the thing's smooth blue shell. Instead it seemed to contain no moving parts at all: a tight packing of solid cubes, a cylinder of some kind of metal, and two mutually perpendicular flat boards covered with geometric patterns in red and black and gold. Connecting the crammed components were flexible strands of some material as clear as glass.

But no moving parts.

What the object had been used for remained a mystery. How it worked was also elusive. But slowly it dawned on Toroca that this was not a disappointing discovery—not at all. Rather, he'd learned something that had never occurred to him, or, he was sure, to anyone else: it was possible to build devices that surely did complex work without resorting to mechanics. Solid blocks could do—what, he did not know. But they could do something. And Quintaglio engineers would eventually be able to figure out what they did, and how they did it. And knowing that such devices were possible—laying the egg of that idea in their heads—might let them develop similar devices themselves kilodays before they would have stumbled on the concept on their own.

Layers.

Layers of rock.

Layers of mystery.

Standing on the beach at sunset, Toroca's eye roamed over the cliff face, searching.

The sacred scrolls were written two thousand kilodays ago.

And they said the world was created five thousand kilodays before that.

But the erosion here and, now that he thought about it, almost every-where in Land that he'd been, would have taken more than seven thou-sand kilodays to happen. *Much* more. Jodor's tree, clinging to the precipice—

—like Toroca's preconceptions.

A Quintaglio might live for seventy kilodays or so. But it would have taken far, far more than one hundred lifetimes to deposit the layers he was now looking at. Indeed, just to accumulate the fifteen vertical paces of rock between the Bookmark layer and the top of the cliff would take far longer than that—

—and add to that whatever amount of time it took for those layers to get pushed up into the sky, until they towered overhead as they did now . . .

Staring up at the cliff face, Toroca felt a wave of vertigo.

The world was *old*, inconceivably ancient.

And even life, although it had appeared very recently in the overall geologic record, must have arisen much more than seven thousand kilo-days ago.

Layers of mystery. Toroca exhaled noisily.

The sacred scrolls described a gradual unfolding. *First* plants, *then* plant-eaters, *then* carnivores.

The rocks showed nothing like that. In them, all forms of life appeared simultaneously.

All.

The sacred scrolls must be wrong, not just about the age of the world, but about the sequence of events.

Toroca was reminded again of how the layers of sediment that made up this towering cliff looked like the pages of a massive book seen edge-on. If only he could open that book, browse through the pages, see, *really see*, what had happened.

And, in his hand, heavy, indestructible . . . the blue object, the six-fingered artifact, the *thing*.

He knew where it fit in: right near the top, just below the Bookmark layer.

What he didn't know yet was *how* it fit in.

But he would figure it out, he would peel back the layers, he would uncover the truth.

The chill wind cut him. As always, darkness came quickly.

But it would not last for long.

Chapter 11

A Quintaglio's Diary

I felt some odd stirrings today, a kind of excitement I hadn't really known before. That I was reacting to some pheromones, as when on the hunt, seemed obvious, but we were not hunting. No, I was simply waiting in an anteroom for an appointment. The only other person in the room was my sister, Haldan.

It was she. I was reacting to her.

She must be coming into receptivity. I'd have thought her too young—she was just sixteen, after all, and estrus normally began in one's eighteenth kiloday, but, then again, these things were not written in stone.

My reaction was slight, as if she was not yet fully in heat, but rather was just beginning to be open. Perhaps she herself wasn't yet aware of it.

I didn't like the effect it had on me. There was something inappropriate about it. Yes, I was eager to mate myself, but, somehow, to mate with my sister seemed wrong.

Without a word, I got up and hurried from the room, terrified that my dewlap would puff in front of her.

With Pack Tablo on the Outskirts of Edz'toolar

In the last moments of his life, the irony was not lost on Mek-Lastoon, the bloodpriest of Pack Tablo. Oh, the circumstances were not quite reversed. Here, it was a mob of adults chasing a single other adult—him—instead of him, the purple robe of his priesthood swirling about his body, chasing squealing egglings.

But the ending would be the same.

Lastoon's triple-clawed feet threw up globs of mud as he continued to run, his back held almost parallel to the ground, his thick, muscular tail outstretched behind him.

He was surprised that he could still think clearly. Surely those pursuing him were now deep in *dagamant*, the killing rage clouding their thoughts. But all Lastoon felt was fear, naked and raw.

They'd come for him at the creche shortly after the sun, a sharp white disk not much wider than a point, had risen above the volcanic cones to the east. Lastoon had immediately been wary—their pheromones were all wrong—but had hid his hands in the folds of his robe. A priest should never show outstretched claws to any member of the Pack.

Eight adults had formed a semicircle around him, like the crescent shape of one of the many moons. "How are the hatchlings?" Jal-Garsub had asked him abruptly, with no ceremonial bow of greeting. A female of middle age, she was the Pack's hunt leader. The respect she commanded was equal to that accorded a bloodpriest.

"Good Garsub," Lastoon had replied, tipping from his waist. "I cast a shadow in your presence." He looked into her solid black eyes, seeking any reason for this rude intrusion. "The hatchlings are fine. They're eating fresh meat now, instead of regurgitated flesh."

"And how many are there?" asked Bon-Cartark, standing on Garsub's right, massive green arms crossed over his torso.

"How many?" Lastoon repeated. "Why, six—one from each clutch of eggs laid this kiloday."

"And how many were there?" said hunt leader Garsub.

"How many were there when?" asked Lastoon.

"How many were there originally? How many children stumbled out of eggs onto the birthing sands?"

Lastoon dipped his head in puzzlement. "One does not speak of those who were dispatched, Garsub. The Eighteenth Scroll says—"

"I know what the scrolls say, priest." Garsub brought her right hand into plain view. Her claws were unsheathed.

Lastoon was silent for a moment, watching the polished talons glint in the morning sun. "There were six clutches of eight eggs apiece," he said at last. "One of the eggs never hatched; that's not an uncommon occurrence. So, there were forty-seven hatchlings originally."

"And now there are six," said Garsub.

"Now there are six."

"What happened to the other forty-one?"

"Why, what always happens," said Lastoon. "I dispatched them."

"You *ate* them."

Lastoon did not like Garsub's tone. "Good hunter, you use such a harsh turn of phrase. Perhaps next time the chief provincial priest visits our Pack, you can discuss the theology with her. I think she's due back in less than a kiloday—"

"You ate them," Garsub said again.

Lastoon turned his head so that all would know that he was looking away. "That is the prescribed rite, yes."

"You ate forty-one of the Pack's children."

"Hatchlings are not children of the Pack until after the culling; I dispatched the excess spawn." He paused briefly. "It's my job."

"You dispatch seven out of every eight hatchlings?" said Garsub.

"Of course."

"And in all of the Fifty Packs there are bloodpriests such as yourself."

"One per Pack, yes, plus one apprentice to take my place when I am gone." Lastoon looked up. "I haven't seen Cafeed yet this morning. He's usually not this late."

"Young Cafeed will not be coming to the creche today," said one of the others, Cat-Madool, his voice soft, almost a hiss.

"Oh?" said Lastoon.

"You dispatch seven out of every eight," repeated Garsub.

"That's right."

"Your counterparts do the same elsewhere."

"Indeed. In each of the Fifty Packs, across all eight provinces of Land."

"There are no exceptions?" asked Garsub, her voice talon-sharp.

"Of course not."

"*No* exceptions?"

"Good Garsub, I don't see what you're getting at."

"Who is governor of this province?" asked Garsub.

"Why, Dy-Rodlox, of course," said Lastoon.

"And who is his brother?" demanded Garsub.

Lastoon felt a tingling in his muzzle. "I don't—"

"*Who is his brother?*"

"Why would I know the answer to such a question?"

"But you *do* know," said Garsub. "Answer!"

"I don't—"

"*Answer!* Answer, or feel my claws!"

"Good Garsub, surely you wouldn't strike a member of your own Pack?"

Garsub surged closer. "Answer! Who is Rodlox's brother?"

The bloodpriest was silent.

Garsub raised her hand. "*Answer!*"

Lastoon looked from face to face, seeking a way out. At last, his voice very small indeed, he said, "He doesn't have a brother."

Cartark pointed directly at Lastoon, fingerclaw extended. "His muzzle flushes blue."

"You're lying," said Garsub.

"Please, hunt leader, there are some things best left unknown. Surely you appreciate that—"

"Who is Governor Rodlox's brother?"

Lastoon crossed his arms over his chest, robes dangling from them. "I cannot answer that."

"It is Emperor Dybo," said Garsub. "Isn't it?"

"Garsub, please—"

"If it is not true, bloodpriest, then deny it, here and now. Deny it while the sun shines on your muzzle. *Deny it.*"

It was pointless, of course. His muzzle would show the liar's tint if he tried to do as Garsub asked. He looked at the ground, damp soil compacted by his own footprints and swept by his own tail.

"Forty-one babies killed this kiloday by you," said Garsub. "Perhaps as many last kiloday. And as many again the kiloday before that."

"It's necessary," said Lastoon softly. "The population must be kept in check. It is the sacred role of the bloodpriest. My holy order—"

"Your order is corrupt!" snapped Garsub. "You swallow our children whole, but you all have complicity in a fraud against our entire race. The Emperor's children live, do they not?"

"Where did you hear this?"

"A newsrider from Capital City," said Garsub. "She brought news of Governor Rodlox having declared this for all to hear. You bloodpriests deceive us common people. You enshrine the power of The Family. But the truth is out now. Dy-Rodlox here in Edz'toolar, and the apprentice governors in all the other provinces, are brothers and sisters to fat Dybo, who lies in the Capital on the ruling throne, a throne he did not earn, a throne he does not deserve."

Cartark spoke again: "Why should all the children of The Family live when our own do not?"

"You're mistaken, Cartark. It's just that—"

"Your muzzle betrays you, priest."

"No, please, you don't understand. Mine is a holy duty."

"Yours is a lie," said Garsub, "an attempt to keep the Fifty Packs under control, control that dates back to the false prophet Larsk, control that should be in the hands of the people."

"But the population—it must be kept in check."

"Then," said Garsub, her voice a hiss, "we shall start by eliminating one worthless mouth to feed."

It was all a blur. Garsub sprang forward, but Lastoon was already in motion, running as fast as his legs could carry him. He was much older than the hunt leader, perhaps half again her bulk. It was a lot more mass to move, but he had a correspondingly longer stride. Still, Garsub and her hunting parties brought down thunderbeasts and hornfaces and armorbacks and shovelmouths. His greater speed would postpone the inevitable, nothing more.

The creche was in the center of the tiny town; Lastoon bolted for the town's northern periphery, hoping to make it into the *galamaja* forest.

The others gave chase. They started as a wall of eight Quintaglios, but it was only a matter of heartbeats before they fell into a single file behind Lastoon, arranged in descending order of age/size/stride. Lastoon felt his heart pounding as he ran on.

It had rained the previous night, and the ground was still dotted with puddles. Lastoon's feet made great sucking sounds as they pulled out of the mud. Behind him, he could hear the others splashing along. The footing was treacherous. Lastoon's robe was ruined, sodden at its base, the purple cloth now dappled brown with muck.

Where were the others? Granted, it was still early, and last night had been odd-night, when most people slept, but some Quintaglios should have been up and about by now. Or had Garsub and the rest kept them away, just as they'd kept his apprentice Cafeed away?

Lastoon rounded a bend, his thundering, splashing arrival startling a small clutch of wingfingers into flight, their chorus of screams a substitute for the ones Lastoon would have made if he could have caught the breath to do so.

Footfalls pounding the ground, mud flying everywhere, the trees still fifty paces or so away—

—and then—

—stumbling, falling, flailing in the filth, a great splash of water, the underside of his muzzle plowing a swath—

—a mad scramble to get back to his feet, toeclaws slipping and sliding in the brown ooze, unable to find purchase—

—at last righting himself, lunging forward.

But it was too late.

Pain shot up his spine. Lastoon looked back. Right behind him was Garsub, something big in her mouth.

The end of Lastoon's tail.

Sheared off in one massive bite.

Lastoon tried to run on, but he felt nauseous, and his stride was thrown off by the change in balance.

The others were fast approaching.

Garsub lunged forward again, and again Lastoon found himself sliding headfirst across the mud. The hunt leader was upon him. Lastoon rolled his eyes to look up at her. Garsub's left arm came swiping down, claws extended. Lastoon felt a sharp pain in his side, and then an incredible cold. He struggled to roll her off and in the process saw that his intestines were spilling out onto the mud.

The others reached him now, great jaws lined with sharp curved teeth snapping shut on his arm, his leg, his tail, his rump. Lastoon watched in a final, almost detached, moment as Cartark's gullet extended, gulping a hunk out of Lastoon.

Blood was everywhere, and then, soon, there was darkness.

As his life ebbed from him, flowing into the muddy water, Lastoon thought his last thought:

At least I had the decency to swallow the children whole.

Chapter 12

Rockscape

Huffing and puffing, Dybo made his way up the sloping path to Afsan's rock. Normally the Emperor didn't like coming out here: the trip made his dewlap waggle in an effort to dissipate heat. But today he welcomed it, for his meeting with Afsan required absolute privacy. No one could approach within a hundred paces without being heard or seen.

There was Afsan, up ahead, straddling the granite boulder, his tail hanging over the back. Snoozing quietly beside the rock was Afsan's pet lizard, Gork, its lithe body curved into a crescent shape. Afsan was sometimes accompanied by Cadool, or a scribe, or someone who could read to him from books, or by students who had come to ask him about the moons and planets and the Face of God. But today he was alone, just sitting on his rock.

Thinking.

That Afsan thought great thoughts Dybo already knew, though the idea of just staring out into space and thinking for daytenths on end was something he could not fathom. But, of course, that wasn't right, either. Afsan was not staring out into space. Rather, he was in perpetual darkness, seeing only those images his mind provided. It had been sixteen kilodays since Afsan's blinding, and, although Det-Yenalb, the one who had actually pierced Afsan's eyes with an obsidian dagger, was long dead, Dybo still felt guilt each time he saw his friend, each time he realized yet again that his friend could not see him.

Did Afsan still think in pictures? Still remember the things he'd seen when he'd had eyes? Still cherish, say, the sight of a flower or a marble sculpture? Dybo tried briefly to remember what, for instance, the tapestries that hung in his own ruling room looked like. Colorful, of course, and ornate. But the details? Dybo couldn't conjure them up. Would Afsan's memories of vision be like that, only even more attenuated, having faded over time?

And yet, it was apparent that Afsan's mind was as sharp as ever, indeed possibly even more keen than it had been when he was sighted. Perhaps the lack of distractions enabled him to more fully concentrate, to give over his thought processes to whatever problem he sought to solve. It staggered Dybo, his friend's intellect, and sometimes it frightened him a bit. But he also knew that Afsan's counsel was the sagest and most logical and purest of heart of any that he might receive.

Dybo saw Afsan's head snap up. "Who's approaching?" Afsan said into the air.

Dybo sang out, "It's me, Dybo." He was still many paces from Afsan, but, once the gap had narrowed, he said, "I cast a shadow in your presence, Afsan. May I enter your territory?"

Afsan made a concessional bow without getting up from his rock, and said, "*Hahat dan.*" At his feet, the giant lizard stirred, opened an eye, looked at Dybo, and, apparently recognizing him, closed the lid and went back to sleep.

Dybo found another rock to sit upon. The stone had warmed nicely in the sun. "It *is* peaceful here," said Dybo at last, looking around at the grasses, the trees, and the great water visible beyond the cliff's edge.

"More peaceful than the palace, I'm sure," Afsan said quietly.

Dybo nodded, then, remembering Afsan's condition, said, "Yes."

Afsan's muzzle turned toward Dybo. "You've come about Rodlox's challenge, haven't you?"

Dybo was quiet for a time. Afsan had known him so long; knew him so well. "Yes," the Emperor said at last.

"What do you intend to do?" asked Afsan.

"I don't know. My constitutional advisor tells me I need not respond at all."

Afsan's head turned slowly to follow the sound of a wingfinger making its way across the sky. "What you must do legally and what is wise to do are often different things," he said.

Dybo sighed, long and loud. "Indeed. My authority is already diminished, they tell me, for the people know that my ancestor, Larsk, was not a divinely inspired prophet." Dybo was surprised at the sudden bitterness he felt toward Afsan. After all, it was through Afsan's efforts that Larsk had been reduced. *But then,* he thought, *what Afsan did to me and The Family was done without malice. Can I honestly say the same about what I did to him?* Dybo pressed on. "I am the first Emperor to not rule by divine right."

Afsan's reply came quickly, perhaps too quickly. "You rule because the people respect your judgment." A pat answer, soothing to hear.

Dybo nodded. "Some of the people do. But there are dissenters." And again he surprised himself with his anger, for it was Afsan who had burdened Dybo with the task of getting the Quintaglios off their world before it disintegrated. "There are many who feel I am pushing us in the wrong direction."

"You are pushing us in the only direction that will ensure the survival of our people. No other choice is possible."

"You *know* that. That is, you understand the reasoning. I *accept* that. That is, I trust your judgment. But there are others who neither understand nor accept the necessity of the exodus."

Afsan's turn to sigh. "Yes, there are such people."

"Those against the exodus oppose not just it, but me personally. Those who believe The Family no longer has a right to rule also oppose me. And Rodlox, who apparently is my brother, he opposes me, too." A pause. "You knew about my brothers and sisters?"

"I suspected it," said Afsan softly.

"Why?"

Afsan said nothing.

"You suspected it because you could not see how one such as me could be the best of a clutch of hatchlings," Dybo said flatly.

In the light of day, there was nothing for Afsan to say.

"I may not be physically strong, Afsan, but I try as best I can. I put the interests of the people before my own interests, and it's not every leader who can say that when the sun is shining."

"That is true."

"But there was a time when even you wished for a different ruler?"

"There was a time," Afsan said softly, "when I had eyes."

Dybo was silent awhile. "I'm sorry."

"I know." The silence between them protracted to an awkward length. Afsan pressed on. "You cannot rule under these conditions. We don't have time for dissent." He gestured expansively, taking in all of Rockscape and everything beyond. "The world is coming to an end. We must have unchallenged leadership. We must have an Emperor who can take us to the stars."

"But it's not just me personally who's being challenged," said Dybo.

"Oh?"

"The newsriders and sailing ships are carrying Rodlox's story to all points of Land."

"So I would imagine."

"Bloodpriests are being banished from their Packs. In some instances, they're even being killed."

Afsan's voice was soft. "That is unfortunate."

"I have reports that in many Packs all egglings are being allowed to live."

Afsan looked thoughtful. "I suspect the people feel it's unfair for only the egglings of The Family to go unculled."

"But the population—?"

"Will swell. By eightfold."

"We are creatures of instinct, Afsan. Even you, even the most rational of us. I remember Nor-Gampar, the way you tore his throat out aboard the *Dasheter*—"

"Yes," said Afsan sadly. "We are creatures of instinct."

"Right now, with the egglings confined to the creches, the matter is in hand. But when they venture out into the world—"

"They will seek to establish their own territories. And there won't be enough space for each of them. The territorial imperative will drive them, and everyone, into *dagamant*."

"That is my fear, too." Dybo spread his arms. "What can I do?"

Afsan tilted his head slightly upward, thinking. "It's difficult. Obviously we as a people simply can't allow all of our offspring to live—we're much too fecund for that. Since the hatching of time, the bloodpriests have taken care of weeding the population. But now those priests are in disrepute. Their respectability must be restored."

"How?" Dybo got up off the rock he had been straddling and began to pace. "When I father hatchlings, I will gladly submit them to dispatch."

Afsan shook his head. "You will not be believed."

"But they'll know I'm not lying."

"Not intentionally, no. But you might be misinformed or misled by your advisors, as, apparently, you and perhaps your predecessors have been in the past."

"I'll submit my egglings to public dispatch, then, so that there can be no doubt."

"*Public dispatch,*" said Afsan, the idea evidently intriguing him. "You know, I once saw a litter dispatched."

"What—when?"

"When I stopped in my home Pack of Carno, venturing back from the *Dasheter*'s landing after we circumnavigated the world. I stumbled into the creche at the wrong time. It's a sight I've never forgotten. Public dispatch—yes, people would flock to watch that." He scratched the underside of his muzzle. "But even that would leave all eight of your mother's children alive."

Dybo flicked his tail. "There's nothing I can do about that."

"Perhaps there is," said Afsan slowly.

Dybo stopped pacing directly abreast of Afsan. "What do you mean?"

"You have been challenged by your brother. He claims he would have been chosen as best, had the imperial bloodpriest performed his job properly."

"That's what he says."

"What has become of that bloodpriest?"

"You mean the one who held the job when I hatched?" said Dybo. "Mek-Maliden is his name. He's still alive. He's very old, of course, but in theory he's still the imperial bloodpriest."

"Have you asked this Maliden whether Rodlox's claim is true?"

Dybo looked away. "Maliden has gone missing. No one has seen him since the day Rodlox made his challenge."

"Are you sure that he, too, as a bloodpriest, hasn't fallen prey to an angry mob?"

Dybo shook his head. "I don't think so. Maliden's personal effects are missing, too."

Afsan nodded slowly. "That he's run away is strong evidence that Rodlox's claim is true, I'm afraid. Have you searched the documents at the imperial Hall of Worship?"

"Not personally, of course. But I've ordered it done. Nothing has been found to either corroborate or refute Rodlox's claim." Dybo sighed. "Of course, if I were involved in such a monumental deception, I doubt I'd write anything down, either."

"No. Nor would I. So the truth has fled the city with Maliden."

"Apparently."

Silence, except for the calls of wingfingers and the drums and bells from a ship sailing by far below. Then: "There are two thrusts to Rodlox's claim," said Afsan. "The first, that all eight of Lends's children got to live, seems verified, if we take Maliden's disappearance as an admission of guilt. But that, in and of itself, is not so damaging. After all, all eight of Novato's and my children were allowed to live, too."

"Indeed."

"But the second part of the claim, that the wrong eggling was designated as Emperor-to-be, is very bad indeed, and it hasn't been proven. Maliden could tell us."

"If we could find him," said the Emperor. "I've sent out riders with orders for his arrest."

"I doubt you'll locate him soon enough," said Afsan.

"Frankly, I doubt it, too," agreed Dybo. "If the other bloodpriests are in cahoots with him, he'll have an ally in every Pack. Without Maliden, there's no one who can categorically refute Rodlox." Dybo slapped his tail against the ground in frustration. "Regardless, the people have made up their minds already. They believe that everything Rodlox said is true."

"And that hampers your ability to lead," said Afsan.

"Yes."

"The question of who rightfully belongs on the ruling slab must be resolved."

"But how? I suppose, if the overwhelming opinion is that I'm not the rightful heir, then I could step down and let Rodlox take my place."

"No!" said Afsan. "No. You can't do that. Rodlox would abandon the exodus. No, a way must be found to prove that you are the correct leader."

"And how can we do that?"

Wingfingers careened overhead. Nearby, insects buzzed in low shrubs.

"A replay," said Afsan simply. "You and your siblings must face the culling of the bloodpriest again."

Dybo was silent for a long time, then his teeth began to click. "Afsan, you're yanking my tail. Do you know who becomes imperial bloodpriest in Maliden's absence? His apprentice, Dagtool. He's not that formidable. Chances are I could take him in a fight, and if I couldn't alone, certainly my siblings and I together could."

"Of course," said Afsan. "To set eight adults against one would be silly. When the bloodpriest does his culling, it's eight tiny hatchlings he must deal with." He looked up, blind eyes on Dybo. "What we need is an appropriately scaled-up bloodpriest."

Dybo stared at his friend. "What do you mean?"

"We need something as formidable to you as an adult Quintaglio is to an eggling. Something that will have no trouble going against eight adult Quintaglios. Something ten times your size."

"Afsan, you're gibbering. There's nothing that meets your description."

"Yes, there is."

"Oh, come on. The only thing that even remotely sounds like that is . . ."

"Yes?"

"Oh, Afsan, be serious."

"I *am* serious. You and your siblings should publicly replay the culling of the bloodpriest against a blackdeath."

"A blackdeath? Afsan, those creatures are dangerous!"

"So is a Quintaglio bloodpriest to a newly hatched infant."

"But a blackdeath!"

"It's an elegant solution. We will end up with the rightful Emperor. Plus, by having you and your siblings—members of The Family—submitting to such a public culling, the role of the bloodpriest will be re-established, and the population will return to its traditional controls."

"But, Afsan, umm, there's no way that I could survive against a blackdeath—no way any Quintaglio could."

Afsan's teeth touched together gently. "I'm sure your first point is the one that really concerns you, my friend. You're afraid that in such a test, you would not be the winner."

"Well," said Dybo, "even if the odds were even, I'd only have a one-in-eight chance of survival—assuming, that is, that the blackdeath could be stopped somehow before it devoured all of us, not to mention everyone else in the vicinity."

"A one-in-eight chance is all a newborn Quintaglio gets."

"Yes, but—"

"The species grows strong because only the best survive."

"I know that, but—"

"But you doubt that your odds are even one in eight? You are not in the best of shape."

"Thank you."

"I know only what they tell me. I haven't seen you in kilodays."

"Frankly," said Dybo, "I came to you hoping for a solution that would leave me in power."

"I, too, would like to see you remain Emperor."

Dybo was bitter. "It doesn't sound that way."

"Dybo, I fought long and hard to convince you of the truth about our world." Afsan clicked his teeth. "It's not easy breaking in a new Emperor."

Dybo spread his hands. "But if I were to go up against a blackdeath, I wouldn't survive."

"Perhaps. Perhaps not."

"I'd prefer to hear something a bit more definite than that."

Afsan slid from his rock and stood over the sleeping Gork, who was hissing softly in the boulder's shade. "You're missing the obvious, Dybo. An eggling's only hope of surviving the culling is to run the fastest and thus avoid being gulped down by the bloodpriest. But you are an adult. You have your intellect to aid you." He reached down and stroked the sleeping lizard's hide. "Remember Lubal's dictum: 'A great hunter has not only sharp tooth and polished claw but a keen mind as well, for it is cunning that will save all when the predator becomes the prey.'"

"Meaning?"

"Meaning, I will be your trainer."

"Just what I need. A blind person telling me how to fight."

Gork awoke and pushed its belly up off the grass. "Have you forgotten who I am?" said Afsan. "The best hunters in all of Land called me *The One* in my youth. Was it not I who felled the largest thunderbeast ever seen? Was it not I who dispatched the water serpent Kal-ta-goot?"

Dybo bowed and then, feeling silly doing so but doing it nonetheless, said out loud, "I am bowing." He added a moment later: "You are indeed a great hunter."

Afsan returned the bow. "There is a way for one Quintaglio to survive against a blackdeath."

"And that is?"

He shook his head. "I don't know. I haven't figured it out yet. But I'm confident that I can find a way."

"Confident enough to bet my life on it?"

"I'll do the best I am able," said Afsan.

"It's more than just my life, Afsan. You enjoy the support of the Emperor. You want for nothing under my leadership, and your dream of getting us off this world is pursued because of me. If I lose, you lose."

"I know that. But, forgive me, it seems as though your reign will soon abruptly end unless you consolidate your power, unless a stop is put to this challenge to your right to rule. We are a hunting society; no one knows better than I how strongly our people revere those with skill at the hunt." Gork rubbed gently against Afsan's legs. "If you could survive against a blackdeath, you would by definition be the greatest hunter in all of Land. That, in and of itself, would be enough to make most people willing to accept your right—your *earned* right—to rule."

"I am Emperor now," said Dybo, "because my mother died young. And Rodlox is a governor, because his predecessor likewise met an unexpected death. The rest of my putative siblings are merely apprentice governors."

"True."

"But the governors they are apprenticed to are also my relatives, if one believes Rodlox. They are my mother's brothers and sisters."

"And they are old," said Afsan simply.

"So?"

"So, respect for elders runs deep. People may grumble about their right to hold high office in light of what Rodlox has said, but I doubt anyone will seriously call for their replacement. First, to be blunt, they'll all die of old age soon enough anyway. And most of them have governed since long before you or I were born. In those many kilodays they've earned the right to continue administering their provinces, earned it by deeds. If the question of rightful Emperorship is solved, I suspect the issue of who should be governing the outlying provinces will fade into the background."

"Very well," said Dybo. "But members of The Family are not the only ones to have avoided the test of the bloodpriest. You and Novato had eight children, and all of them, except poor Helbark, are still alive." Helbark had succumbed to fever shortly after his birth.

Afsan shook his head. "My children lived because of the wishes of the people, not despite them. I knew nothing about them being alive until the *Dasheter* returned to Capital City sixteen kilodays ago. The bloodpriests and the people chose to make a special dispensation."

"Because they thought you were The One, the great hunter foretold by Lubal."

"Indeed."

"But you are not The One. You may indeed be a great hunter, but you are not The One."

"Perhaps not."

"I know you are not."

"I have never made a claim either way."

"*You* know you are not."

Afsan made a dismissive gesture with his hand. "I don't play up the suggestion, but if some support the exodus because they feel that it is the great hunt foretold by Lubal, I do nothing to dissuade them. Regardless, my children were a special case, made with full public knowledge. The deceit practiced by The Family was something quite different: an attempt to control all of Land. But the circumstances were reversed. The palace advisors deceived The Family, in an attempt to wrest control from Larsk's descendants and vest it in themselves. You now have a chance to rectify that: to put an end to the deceit, to eliminate the advisors who have corrupted the government, to establish once and for all your right to lead."

"What you suggest is radical."

"This is not the first time I've made a radical suggestion."

"No, no, I suppose not." Dybo leaned against one of the boulders, weary. "There is no other way?"

"The only alternative is the one you've already mentioned. You could abdicate. Let Rodlox take over. It would mean the end of our people, though—the death of our race."

Dybo looked thoughtful. "I try to keep the welfare of all Quintaglios in mind, of course," he said quickly, "but, um, what do you suppose would become of me if I did choose to abdicate?"

"You'd be sent into exile, I'd imagine," said Afsan. "There's plenty of land on the southern shore of Edz'toolar where you could hunt and live and study in absolute peace." A pause. "Or so High Priest Det-Yenalb once told me."

"What?"

"Kilodays ago, when you had me held prisoner in the palace basement, Yenalb came to visit me. He offered me safe passage from the Capital, under his protection, if only I would disappear and never again speak my so-called heresies."

"I didn't know about that. And you turned him down?"

"Yes."

"This was before . . . ?"

"Before my eyes were put out? Yes."

"You turned down a safe way out?"

"I had no choice. The world's survival depended on making the people understand what I'd come to know."

"Yenalb's offer must have tempted you."

"More than you know. But one must not shirk responsibilities, Dybo, especially if one is to lead."

"If I don't answer Rodlox's challenge, continued infighting will distract us from the task at hand."

"Yes."

"And if I do answer the challenge, and Rodlox wins, he will cancel the exodus attempt."

"Yes."

"And our people will die."

"Yes."

"Then I must not only accept the challenge, I must win it," said Dybo. "I have no choice, do I?"

Afsan turned his blind eyes on his friend. "That's the funny thing about being a leader, Dybo: you rarely do."

Chapter 13

Fra'toolar

Babnol kept watching the horizon. The sun had long since risen from it and was now making its usual fast progress across the bowl of the purple sky. The waves were choppy, as always, and as gray as stone.

Toroca came near her. "Looking for our ship?"

Babnol nodded.

"It could show up anytime today, or tomorrow for that matter."

"I know."

"But you're anxious to leave this place?"

"Since Pack Derrilo returned, it has been awfully crowded around here."

"It will be even more crowded aboard whatever ship they send for us."

"I suppose . . . but at least it will be a *different* crowd. That will help."

Toroca understood none of this, but nodded anyway. "The voyage should be quite exciting," he said.

Babnol scanned the horizon again. "I suppose. It depends—Look!"

She pointed. Out where the sky met the waves there was something. "It's a ship," said Toroca, squinting.

"*Our* ship," said Babnol. She had the far-seer with her and brought it to her eye. "It's a big one."

"The sails look red," said Toroca.

"Yes," she said, squinting. "Four great red sails. And two hulls, connected by a joining piece, it looks like."

"May I see?" asked Toroca.

Babnol handed him the brass tube.

"I know that ship!" said Toroca. "Babnol, this is going to be a very interesting voyage indeed. We're about to sail on a piece of history."

Var-Keenir anchored the mighty *Dasheter* offshore, and small landing boats were used to transfer Toroca, Babnol, and the rest of the surveyors on board.

It hadn't been that long since Toroca had taken his pilgrimage aboard this ship. He had hoped that this voyage would go more easily than the last, but he found the ship's rolling from side to side no less disconcerting than it had been on his trip to gaze upon the Face of God. And the stench! He knew the sources of each smell—wet wood and tree sap and salt and musty fabric—but they were no more welcoming than they'd been the last time. Likewise he was getting a headache from the constant barrage of sounds: slapping of waves, snapping of sails, groaning of wooden planks, footsteps on the deck above.

On his previous voyage, Toroca had been one of fourteen pilgrims and therefore had had no special status. But this time out, he was the expedition leader. He could have claimed the grandest guest cabin aboard, but he opted instead for a small one on the port side of the topmost of the aft decks, the same cabin Afsan had used, seventeen kilodays ago, when he had embarked on his pilgrimage aboard the *Dasheter*.

The door to the cabin was carved in an intricate relief of the original five hunters. The wood was dark with age and splitting in several places, but the carving was still stunning. Toroca had no trouble telling the five apart. That was Lubal running; Hoog with her mouth open, teeth exposed; Belbar leaping, claws unsheathed; Katoon bending over a carcass, picking it clean; and Mekt, the first bloodpriest, head tipped back, a Quintaglio hatchling sliding down her throat. Katoon and Lubal had their hands held in the Lubalite salute: claws out on their second and third fingers, the fourth and fifth splayed, the thumb held against the palm.

Although it was not as ornate, Toroca was more impressed by the bronze plaque placed next to the door. It said, "In this cabin, 150 kilodays after Larsk made his first voyage to gaze upon the Face of God, Sal-Afsan, the astrologer who discovered the true nature of the Face, began his pilgrimage. It was in this room that he first realized that our world is a moon revolving around a giant planet."

The plaque wasn't entirely accurate. Afsan hadn't yet taken his praenomen syllable at the time he first sailed aboard the *Dasheter*, and he'd never held the position of astrologer, although he had been an apprentice in that profession back then.

Toroca wondered if his father knew of this plaque, and, if so, what he felt about it. Afsan had always struck Toroca as modest.

He pushed the door open and entered. The room was hot, its last occupant having left the leather curtain drawn back from the single porthole, letting the afternoon sun beat in. The floor, although sanded periodically, showed myriad claw tickmarks. As he settled in for the long voyage, Toroca wondered if any of them were Afsan's own.

On dry land, almost all adults slept on odd-nights. Toroca had often wondered about that: it seemed to make sense that one should sleep every night, not every other night. After all, flowers open and close each day, and small animals certainly slept every night (or every day, if they were nocturnal). But Quintaglios and many large animals did indeed sleep only on alternate nights. Actually, they would go to sleep at sunset on an odd-day, but usually not wake up until close to noon the following even-day, meaning each Quintaglio spent about a third of his adult life asleep.

Toroca sometimes speculated about why God had designed it this way. It occurred to him, although, of course, he never spoke such thoughts aloud, that it might have been more efficient to make the day longer, dispensing with the need for some to be called "even-days" and others to be called "odd-days." If the day was twice its current length, and the night correspondingly longer, one could easily fall into the habit of simply always sleeping when it was dark and always being awake when it was light. Far be it from Toroca to criticize God, but that might have eliminated "liar's night," the term sometimes used for even-night, when most Quintaglios were awake but it was still dark, and therefore the color of one's muzzle could not be easily seen. A different length of day would make a lot of sense . . .

But aboard a ship, such as the *Dasheter*, the normal practice of everyone sleeping on odd-nights had to be modified anyway. Only half of the passengers and crew were to sleep on that night. Those in the other half were asked to readjust their rhythms and sleep instead on even-night. The point, of course, was to minimize the number of awake Quintaglios milling about, and thereby take the edge off the collective sense of territoriality.

Keenir couldn't gather everyone together to announce who should sleep when, since bringing all those aboard out onto deck simultaneously would have fanned the flames of the very problem he was trying to avoid. Instead, a list was posted on the base of the leading foremast.

Toroca waited patiently for the others to look at it, then he ambled over. He'd had no concerns about which group he might end up in. Indeed, part of him hoped he'd be assigned to the group that would have to change its habits. His father, Afsan, had been notorious for being awake when everyone else was asleep, and Toroca had often wondered what it would be like to alter one's sleeping schedule.

The list was written on leather in Keenir's own bold style of glyphs and protected from the wind and rain by a thin sheet of glass. Toroca stood at the base of the mast, and the flapping of the great red sail above him was deafening. He knew that when Afsan had taken his first voyage aboard the *Dasheter*, each of the sails had sported an emblem of Larsk, but this one now had a more politically neutral design: the cartouche of Vek-Inlee, famed explorer of the past.

Toroca was listed as one of those who would sleep, as usual, on odd-night. Oh, well. But then his heart sank: Babnol had been put in the even-night column—

His immediate thought was to object, to rush to Keenir and have him change the designation, but . . . but . . . but . . .

But how could he? On what grounds?

Toroca felt himself trembling slightly. Embarrassment?

Why did he care when Babnol slept?

Does she care when I sleep?

No. Madness.

But he enjoyed spending time with her.

Enjoyed it.

And more.

More?

Yes, there was more. He enjoyed it, he looked forward to it.

He wanted to do it as much as possible.

To be with her.

To *be* with her.

Such thoughts. Such strange thoughts for a Quintaglio.

But not for me.

He scurried away from the mast. For once, he really did want to be alone.

Chapter 14

The *Dasheter*

The *year* was a unit of time little used, although since Afsan's discovery that the world was the moon of a large planet, the concept at least now had a meaningful definition. A year was the time it took for the Face of God—the planet around which the Quintaglio moon orbited—to complete one of its own orbits about the sun.

Astrologers had always been vaguely aware of the year, for that was the length of time it took for the pattern of constellations viewed at, say, the seventh daytenth, to cycle through a complete circle. But the year was such an impossibly long span that people paid little attention to it. The average Quintaglio would see only four years completed during his or her lifetime. Still, those who wished to be perceived as fashionable might now say, "It's been years since I did thus and so," whereas before the Afsanian revolution they would have remarked that it had been kilodays.

Not that a year and a kiloday were anywhere close to being equal in length. A kiloday was one thousand days, but a year was—opinions varied—somewhere between 18,310 and 18,335 days.

Still, there were subtle changes besides the constellations during the course of a year. The reproductive cycle of Quintaglios as well as some animals seemed to be tied to it. A female Quintaglio would normally be receptive for the first time eighteen kilodays—one year—after hatching, and become receptive again at an age of thirty-six kilodays and perhaps once more at fifty-four or fifty-five kilodays, producing, therefore, two or three clutches of eggs during her lifetime. A few females were constantly receptive, although, ironically, usually they were also barren. They tended to become hunt leaders.

Hereditary rulers were always taken from the first clutch of eggs. Dybo had been one of Len-Lends's first clutch; she had not lived long enough to lay another. Even if she had, the second round of egglings would have been accorded little status. Dybo was male and therefore had some say in when he reproduced. He had been expected to do so when he reached the age of eighteen kilodays, but now, at twenty-eight, had still not called for a mate.

Even for females, the once-a-year mating cycle was only a loose corre-
lation. They could be moved to estrus at different times, as, for instance,
Wab-Novato had been, leading to her union with Afsan and the birth of
Toroca and his siblings.

No one knew for sure how many years the world had left, but it was
thought to be no more than ten or twenty. Novato decided therefore that
the Geological Survey—which, after all, was only a preliminary stage in
the exodus project—must be completed in a single year. That was a substantial amount of time—Toroca would be twenty kilodays old by the
time the survey was finished, and Novato would be well into middle
age—but the world was a big place, and there really wasn't much time in
that schedule to spare.

And because of that, Toroca hated how time-consuming this voyage
would be. It was now understood that Land was an equatorial body,
halfway between the world's poles. The journey to the south pole, then,
would be equivalent to sailing halfway around the world—the length of
one leg of a pilgrimage voyage. And yet, to Toroca's relief, the time
passed reasonably quickly, for throughout this voyage, there were wonders to behold.

"My God!" Toroca exclaimed to himself one morning, standing on
the *Dasheter*'s foredeck.

Keenir happened to be passing by. "What?" he said in his gravelly
voice.

"My breath," said Toroca, his eyes wide. "I can see my breath!"

Keenir clicked his teeth. "You've never been on a voyage to southern
waters before, eh? Well, look at this." The captain opened his mouth
wide, gulped air, then moved his jaws together so that only a thin slit separated them. He exhaled, and a flat disk of whitish fog appeared around
his muzzle.

"That's incredible." Toroca mimicked Keenir's trick. He blinked in
surprise. "What causes it?"

"The cold, lad. The air you breathe in is warmed in your lungs, so they
tell me, then, when you expel it, it hits the cold air outside and condensation occurs. Just like fogging a piece of glass by breathing on it."

"It's amazing."

Keenir ground his teeth in a chuckle. "You'll get used to it."

Toroca puffed air out again, white fog dissipating rapidly.

Some of Keenir's crew had been with the *Dasheter* long enough to remember when the captain had been obsessed with having the lookout's bucket, high atop the foremast, constantly occupied. He'd been mad to find Kal-ta-goot, the giant water reptile that had torn off his tail and scarred his face. But after Kal had been slain, Keenir had become less rigorous about having someone scanning the horizons. Now, though, with the *Dasheter* journeying ever southward, he insisted that the bucket always have an occupant.

His prudence paid off. Shortly after they passed the two-thirds mark in their voyage, a shout went up from old Mar-Biltog, the officer doing the watch.

Another officer scurried off to alert Keenir, running down the ramp that led to the lower decks. A moment later the captain thundered up onto the damp wooden planks. He glanced up at the lookout's bucket to see which direction Biltog was indicating, then moved to the railing around the port leading edge of the ship's fore hull. Keenir had his far-seer in hand, and he brought the brass tube to his eye.

"That's a huge one," said Keenir softly. Then, shouting: "It'll be breaking up, this far north. Watch for fragments!"

Toroca, now wearing a light cloak—such a strange feeling for a non-priest to have clothes on!—had come up on deck to see what all the shouting was about. He moved as close to Keenir as protocol would allow and looked out in the direction Keenir's far-seer was pointed. There was indeed something there, brilliant in the sunlight, completely white. An island, perhaps? That would be fascinating! No islands were known this far from the mainland. "What is it?" Toroca asked.

Keenir stepped close enough to Toroca to hand him the far-seer, then moved back to a more appropriate separation. "Have a look. It's called an iceberg."

"An iceberg!" Toroca rotated the tube, bringing the object into focus for his younger eyes. "I've heard of them. Frozen water, right?"

"Right."

"I never knew they could be so huge."

"That's a small one, actually."

"It's white," said Toroca. "Water is clear."

"Not when frozen. And not when there's that much of it. It's white, or bluish-white."

"An iceberg. I've always wanted to see one of those. Captain, we must go closer!"

"No. It's a hazard to navigation. The part you're seeing above the waves is only a tenth of the whole thing; most of it is submerged. These icebergs drift north and melt. And they don't just grow smaller and smaller until they disappear. Hunks drop off. If we hit one, it could rip our hull open. We'll give it wide clearance; treat it as if it were a member of The Family—just get out of its way."

"But I'd love to see so much ice up close."

"You will. You'll see more ice than you can possibly imagine. You'll grow sick of it, I promise you." Keenir lifted his head and shouted to his crew, "Hard to starboard!"

The night sky danced.

A curtain of diaphanous green fluttered across the firmament, now rippling, now waving. Its reflection could be seen on the water. Moments later, streamers of yellow grew upward from the horizon, twisting and intertwining as they did so, growing taller with each passing moment. Vertical bands of deeper green, pulsating as if alive, appeared across the sky, counterpointing the yellow.

Toroca thought he could hear, just below the threshold of certainty, a hissing sound, punctuated by occasional crackles, like a fire spitting its last.

The display was awe-inspiring, gorgeous—

—and fleeting. Already, it had started to fade.

Toroca shook his head in wonderment. He'd thought, perhaps, that his father had unraveled all the secrets of the skies, but it was clear that they still contained many new mysteries.

Chapter 15

The old imperial palace had been destroyed in the great landquake that occurred shortly after Dybo and Afsan had returned from their pilgrimage voyage to gaze upon the Face of God. The new palace, built not far from the ruins of the old, was less ornate, more modern in design, simpler and cleaner. After all, it would not do for resources to be lavished on the Emperor's home when all on Land were being asked to make sacrifices to speed the exodus project.

Rodlox was brought by imperial guards to the palace's ruling room. He wasn't wearing his gubernatorial sash, perhaps a sign that he no longer considered that office a sufficient honor. No, the sash he wore, crossing from his left shoulder to his right hip, tapering as it did so, sported no decorations at all. But it was red, the color traditionally reserved for members of The Family. He was making clear to all that he claimed his place amongst the ruling dynasty.

Rodlox was furious that Dybo was not yet here. A deliberate slight, no doubt, this keeping him waiting. He fought to prevent his anger from showing. He would not let the guards report to Dybo that this insult had been effective.

At last the Emperor waddled in. His sash—made of perhaps twice as much material as Rodlox's, to accommodate Dybo's greater circumference—was also red, a true blood red, a hunter's color, made with the finest and rarest dyes. In comparison to the royal livery, Rodlox's looked too light, too pink, quite literally a pale imitation of Dybo's own. Rodlox clenched his fists.

Dybo looked Rodlox up and down, an appraisal made clear by the tipping of his muzzle. At last the Emperor said, without preamble or traditional bow, "Why have you challenged me?"

Rodlox folded his arms across his muscular chest. "You are not the rightful Emperor."

Dybo, in turn, spread his arms. "You cannot be sure of that. Without conclusive evidence, it's a hollow claim."

Rodlox's tone was firm. "I am sure of it, sure in my very bones."

Dybo stepped up to the marble platform that supported the ruling slab and the *katadu* benches for imperial advisors. He lowered himself belly-first onto the angled slab and looked down upon Rodlox.

Rodlox refused to be victim of such a transparent ploy. Rather than look up at the Emperor, he simply turned sideways and gave the appearance of examining the tapestries on the far wall, although in fact his black eyes were locked on his rival. "It's true," he said. "I know it's true."

The ruling slab creaked slightly under Dybo's weight; that amused Rodlox, but the Emperor went on, oblivious. "Dy-Rodlox, look at me. Look at my muzzle." Rodlox turned to face him. "I tell you, I have no direct reason to believe what you say is true."

Rodlox shrugged. "That your muzzle hasn't turned blue doesn't surprise me. It means only that those who perpetrated this fraud did not confide in you."

"Are you saying they did confide in you, Dy-Rodlox? Did someone tell you this, someone who would know?"

"No, but it doesn't matter. Consider this, *brother*: not one of the provincial governors has risen up to challenge your authority to rule, authority based solely on the fact that you are a descendant of the now-discredited Larsk. Not one of them. Why is that?"

"Satisfaction with my administration?" Dybo said innocently.

"You know full well that many people object to the exodus project, think it a mad obsession on your part, an obsession driving us to ruin."

Dybo dipped his muzzle in mild concession. "Some say that, yes."

"And yet, despite the opposition to the exodus, not one of the other governors has risen against you."

An insect had somehow made it into the room and was buzzing above Dybo's back. He flicked his tail, trying to shoo it away. "So you're saying the reason they haven't challenged me is that the other governors are also party to this conspiracy."

"I think they are," said Rodlox, "except for myself."

"If such a conspiracy involved all governors, why are you exempt?"

"Both the previous incumbent in your office of Emperor and the previous incumbent in my office of governor of Edz'toolar died prematurely. I know my predecessor told me nothing about this before she died; perhaps Lends had said nothing to you before that roof collapsed on her."

"I tell you, she did not."

"I must accept that," said Rodlox, "but I suspect at least some of your advisors know. Mek-Maliden, the imperial bloodpriest, for one. Have you asked him?"

"No."

"Why not? If my claim is absurd, he could prove that. Ask him."

"I cannot."

"Why not?"

"He's gone missing."

"You've had him locked away, I'd warrant."

"I've done no such thing. He's left town, apparently of his own volition."

"Regardless," said Rodlox, "his absence bolsters my claim."

"If this is true, surely Maliden isn't the only one who knows."

"That's right. I'm confident the other provincial governors know. Again, that's why they continue to support you, despite your delusions. To expose your secret would be to expose their secret: that they were illegally exempted from the culling of the bloodpriest."

"What about your advisors, Dy-Rodlox? Surely Len-Ganloor told some of them before she died?"

"An unusual situation," said Rodlox with a shrug. "Those who would have been my two most-senior aides, Cat-Makdon and Pal-Haskan, were part of that same ill-fated hunting party on which Governor Len-Ganloor died." Rodlox shook his head. "It should have been an easy kill, a concession to ceremony, really. Ganloor, Makdon, and Haskan were all trampled to death in the stampede."

"And you think the secret about your siblings died with them?"

"Yes. I don't think there's anyone left in my province who knows the truth," said Rodlox. "But once you fight me, they will. The entire world will."

Dybo waved his hand. "Even if, as you claim, I was not the strongest eggling of Lends's clutch, that does not necessarily mean that you were the strongest. There would have been six others, besides you and me."

"The six who now serve as apprentice governors in the other provinces." Rodlox nodded. "But the same logic that says keep the weakest here at the imperial court also says send the strongest to the most isolated province. Edz'toolar isn't the farthest of the *toolars* from the Capital, but it is the harshest and most difficult to get into, requiring the climbing of many mountains if approaching by land, and weathering its stormswept shores if arriving by water."

"But there's no guarantee that the winner of a battle between just the two of us now would indeed be the same one of the eight who would have best eluded the bloodpriest twenty-eight kilodays ago."

Rodlox grunted. "True. But in the absence of any alternative method of making the determination, it must suffice. I can prove I am of the imperial line, prove that I am Larsk's descendant."

"Proof is an elusive thing—"

"I can demonstrate it to the reasonable satisfaction of the public. And that, fat one, is all that counts."

A moment later, Dybo's claws slipped out, and it seemed to Rodlox that it was perhaps a deliberate gesture rather than an instinctive response. "You will not address me that way. My name is Dy-Dybo, and I grant you permission to use it. If you prefer to call me by title, you will use 'Your Luminance' or 'Emperor.'"

"I will call you what I wish."

Dybo raised his hand. "Then this conversation is at an end. I have granted you no special privileges, beyond the right to call me directly by name. *I* rule, Dy-Rodlox. Acknowledge that."

"For the time being, Dybo." That Rodlox had chosen the familiar form of his name visibly irritated Dybo, for it was clearly done not from affection but out of defiance. "But you must answer my challenge."

Still, Dybo adopted a slightly mollified tone. "I see that you are a person of strong will, and I grant that your intellect is keen." He scratched his belly, which was spilling over the side of the polished stone slab. "Perhaps Edz'toolar is too barren and isolated a prize for one such as you. I offer an accommodation, a middle ground: a senior official's role, with whatever portfolio you desire. Public works? The judiciary? Name it, and it is yours. You will move here to the Capital and enjoy all the benefits of life at the imperial court."

Rodlox scraped his teeth together, a deliberate mockery of laughter. "You are transparent, Dybo. You perceive me as a threat, so you would have me underfoot where I could be watched at all times. I reject your offer. You will fight me in single combat. And I shall win."

Dybo spoke now as one might speak to a child. "Single combat has been barred since ancient times. You know that. There is no way to begin a battle without having it continue until one participant is dead."

"That is true."

"You threaten me with death? There are prescribed penalties for such treason."

"I make no threat. I simply note the probable outcome of a battle between us."

"I concede that I am perhaps not your physical match—"

"Indeed you are not."

"But being Emperor is not about physical prowess. It's about fairness and progress and clarity of vision."

"Which is why the most appropriate person—the rightful heir—must, *must*, lie upon that ruling slab that now strains to support you."

Dybo spread his arms, looking to Rodlox like a monster wingfinger, suspended in air by the slab. "All the Packs are prosperous. We're making great strides toward the stars. What quarrel do you have with me?"

"I hate you." The words were unexpectedly harsh.

Dybo's inner eyelids blinked. "I do not hate you, Rodlox."

"You should. For I am your downfall personified. I will push and push and push until I am in your place."

"I could have you banished."

"To where? Edz'toolar?" Rodlox clicked his teeth. "I am *lord* of Edz'-toolar already."

"I could have you executed."

"And violate the ancient laws? I think not. There are those who would not stand for that; you would destroy what's left of your own authority if you flouted our laws so. No, Dybo, you have only three choices. One,"—and here Rodlox raised a finger, claw extended—"you can accept my challenge. Two,"—a second finger erect, its claw likewise unsheathed—"you can abdicate your role, acknowledge my claim, and let me assume the Emperorship. I will allow you to live. Or, three," and a third clawed finger was held up, "you can take the coward's route and wait until the people force you to respond to my challenge."

Dybo regarded Rodlox's raised hand. The ticking off of points with clawed fingers was so like his mother's way. For the first time, Dybo realized that, without a doubt, this was his brother. It was a tragedy, this conflict, for surely in cooperation they could accomplish so much more than they individually would through a rivalry.

Dybo shook his head. "You are wrong, Rodlox. There is a fourth alternative, and one that is more appropriate than any of your choices. Hear me describe it, and then we shall see which of us is the coward."

A Quintaglio's Diary

I wish I didn't have siblings. I try not to compare myself to them, but it's futile. I can't help myself. Am I as proficient as they? As keen of mind? Is my pilgrimage tattoo as intricate and well-balanced as that sported by Yabool? And which of us does Novato and Afsan favor? Surely they've thought that if things had gone differently, only one of their children would have lived. Which would they have preferred it to be?

I was thinking these thoughts today as I ate in one of the communal dining halls when Haldan walked in. She passed nowhere near me on her way to fetch a piece of meat, so she didn't bother to bow concession in my direction. She simply settled herself in at a bench on the opposite side of the room and began to gnaw at her meal.

I watched her. Of course I was careful not to swing my muzzle in her direction; she couldn't tell where I was looking. But it came to me, as I worried out the final bits of meat adhering to the bone in front of me, that I couldn't tell where she was looking, either. Her eyes, solid black, could have been focused on the flesh in front of her.

Or they could have been focused on me.

On me.

We'd often thought the same thoughts before; I'd seen it in her expression.

Were we thinking the same thing now?

And suddenly I realized exactly what it was that I was thinking at that moment, a ripple that wouldn't die down, a thought dark and dangerous and persistent.

I wished she was dead.

I stopped picking over my meat and, at the same moment, she stopped picking over hers.

I wondered if she was thinking the same thing about me.

Chapter 16

Toroca was up on deck. On board a sailing ship, everyone had chores to perform, and Babnol knew she could count on him being occupied for at least a couple of daytenths. She went down the ramp, its timbers groaning not under her weight but rather under the buffeting of the ship, and came to Toroca's cabin.

She paused briefly to reread the plaque about Afsan and to admire the carving of the five hunters in the dark wood of the door. There was a copper signaling plate adjacent to the doorjamb, but she didn't drum her claws against it. Instead, she stole a furtive glance over her shoulder, then opened the door, the squeaking of its hinges making her even more nervous. As soon as she was inside Toroca's cabin, she swung the door shut.

Her claws were exposed. Invading another's territory was uncomfortable. Although she knew Toroca wouldn't be back for some time, she couldn't tarry here. It was too upsetting.

Although there was a desk with a small bench in front of it—space aboard a sailing ship was at too much of a premium to allow for a dayslab—Toroca had wisely placed all fragile objects directly on the floor, lest the pitching of waves knock them off the desk. No lamps were lit, of course; it was far too dangerous to leave a flame unattended. But the leather curtain was drawn back from the porthole, and, indeed, the little window had been swung open, letting the cold, salty air from outside pour in. In the harsh sunlight coming from the porthole, she could see the hinged wooden case that held the far-seer Afsan had given to Toroca. But that was not what she had come for, nor was the object of her quest plainly visible.

Even more distasteful: she would have to rummage through Toroca's things. Such a breach of protocol! Still, it had to be done. She moved over to the storage trough and gingerly picked up sashes and backpacks and pieces of the specially designed arctic clothing, carefully stacking each piece on the floor so that she could put them back exactly the way they had been. There were several books amongst Toroca's effects, including one written by his father and, to her surprise, a well-thumbed copy of the book of Lubalite prayer.

At last she found what she was looking for: the object, the strange blue hemisphere with the vexing six-fingered handle attached. She picked it up and, cradling it in both hands, held it in front of her. She was always surprised by its weight and the way the material warmed so quickly in her hands. She looked at the strange geometric carvings—little strings of symbols—at several places on its lower surface, and wondered for the thousandth time what they meant.

The object's color bespoke evil. Blue. An unholy color; the color of lies, of deceit.

No Quintaglio made this object, of that she was sure. The strange material—harder than diamond!—couldn't be worked by any tool, and that grip wasn't made for a hunter's hand.

But if not a Quintaglio, then who?

Quintaglios had five fingers.

God had five fingers.

The sixth finger hole made this an unholy device. Not of Quintaglio. Not of God.

There was goodness in God, goodness in God's creations.

This—*thing*—lacked goodness. And, therefore, it was dangerous. She had seen how Toroca had spent endless daytenths staring at it, turning it over and over again in his hands, clicking the rings up and down, up and down . . .

Six fingers.

And yet—perhaps the user of this device had been like her: different from most. A facial horn; a sixth finger. Did one or the other make you lack goodness?

Of course not.

But this was an ancient artifact, dating from the very beginning of life.

Things do occasionally hatch from eggs that are so horrible, so deformed, that the bloodpriests dispatch them immediately, without waiting for the formal culling.

There were no bloodpriests at the beginning, none until God bit off Her own arms, and Mekt formed from one of Her fingers.

So a horrible thing that hatched from one of the eggs of creation wouldn't have been dispatched, since there was no one to do the dispatching.

She turned the device over in her hands.

It lacked goodness. She was convinced of that.

It had been dead and buried for thousands of kilodays, sealed in a tomb of solid rock. It was only by sheer accident that Toroca had released it.

Time, now, to correct that.

She walked over to the porthole, felt the chill wind on her muzzle, heard the slapping of waves against the hull, the snapping of sails, the calls of distant wingfingers.

Toroca would hate her for this.

But she was only thinking of him, of his safety, of his soul.

She tossed the object out the porthole. It hit the gray waves with a splash and sank immediately from sight, gone forevermore.

Chapter 17

Arj'toolar

Arj'toolar, in northwestern Land, is a province known for its shel-
tered ports and hospitable inns, its metalworkers who turn copper
and brass into complex instruments, its weavers who make fishing nets
used throughout the world, its large holy sector, and its vast herds of
orange-and-blue-striped shovelmouths, a peculiar breed with meat considered the tastiest of all.

Its governor was Len-Haktood, a hoary fellow who had survived to
old age despite his quick temper only because his office shielded him
from the kinds of attacks such a temper would normally engender. He
was a meaner, pettier version of his sister, the late empress Len-Lends.
Apprenticed to Haktood was Kroy, sister of the current Emperor, Dybo.

Haktood looked out the window. An ugly mob had gathered outside—fully ten people, standing far too close to each other. They were
chanting slogans: "Truth in government!" "No special deals!" "A rightful
leader for the people!" Five burly imperial guards, sent by Dybo, stood
mutely along the far wall of Haktood's office.

Haktood summoned Kroy, who did indeed look a lot like Dybo,
although she lacked his plumpness, and handed her the scroll that the
imperial guards had brought with them.

Kroy saw that the seal on the scroll was that of the Emperor. It had
already been broken. She unfurled the leather sheet. At the top was
Dybo's cartouche, tooled in exquisite detail. Beneath it in bold, black
glyphs, was a memorandum:

From: *Dy-Dybo, Emperor of Land, Leader of the Fifty*
            Packs, Head of The Family, Descendant of Larsk

To: *Governors of the provinces of Jam'toolar, Fra'toolar,*
            Arj'toolar, Chu'toolar, Mar'toolar, and Kev'toolar

It has come to be commonly believed that the governors of the
seven outlying provinces are also members of The Family, being

the siblings of the late Empress Len-Lends, and that their apprentices are the siblings of myself, the current Emperor.

Dy-Rodlox, who, since the untimely death of Len-Ganloor, has been governor of Edz'toolar, claims that he, not I, is rightful heir to the ruling slab. The accompanying documents give more details about his assertions.

The culling of the bloodpriest must be replayed, this time in full public view. You are ordered to send your apprentice governor, as well as at least three official observers, to Capital City by the 666th day of kiloday 7128, wherein each of the apprentices will have a fair chance of becoming Emperor. My imperial guards will escort your delegation here.

Kroy looked up. "Who does Dybo think he is, summoning me this way?"

Haktood was terse. "He thinks he is the Emperor. And he is correct—at least for the time being."

"Surely you will decline."

Haktood looked out the window. "I haven't the power to do that."

"But you're a provincial governor!"

"There are forces at work greater than any authority I might have. The people are demanding this."

"Someday, I will be governor of this province," said Kroy.

Haktood's tone was sly. "But why be content with governing a single province when you could be Emperor of all of Land?"

"No. I won't go. Let the other apprentice governors play this foolish game. I'll stay here."

"I am your master, Kroy. I am governor of Arj'toolar; you are simply my apprentice. You will do as I say."

"But to replay the culling. What does that mean?"

"I'm not sure. But you are strong; whatever the test, I'm sure you will be the victor."

"I am strong," said Kroy, "but you, Haktood, you are weak. You urge me to go to the Capital solely so that Arj'toolar will be seen to have dealt with the scandal of the imperial children. You divert attention from yourself, for you, as much as me, are the product of the bloodpriests' deception. Your right to be alive is as questionable as my own."

"I have earned the respect of the people, Kroy. You are still an apprentice; you have earned nothing."

Kroy bared her fangs at Haktood. "Pray that I do not win. Under normal circumstances, an apprentice, such as myself, would have had no power until you passed on. But if I become Emperor, I shall be your superior, Haktood. Our positions will be reversed; I will be the master—not just of you, but of all of Land. You will regret not supporting me now, that I promise you."

From outside came the cries of the mob.

"You'll have a one-in-eight chance, Kroy. Do you fancy your odds are better against that mob?"

The lead imperial guard stepped forward. "I will guarantee your safe passage to the Capital."

Kroy looked the burly fellow up and down. "And what about my safety once I'm there?"

The guard was silent.

Chapter 18

Special cold-weather clothing had been made for the sailors. Toroca wasn't used to wearing any clothing, except his sash, and the concept of garments that would cover him almost completely was not appealing.

The clothing was well-designed. Most of it was made out of an inner and outer layer of thick leather, stuffed in between with wingfinger hair. The jacket had a long hood that tied down around the muzzle, leaving only a slit for the eyes and a small opening at the tip for breathing.

The lower part consisted of three tubes, two open-ended ones for the legs and a third, tapered one, closed at the end for the tail. Getting the lower part on was awkward: Toroca seemed to always end up with one extremity left over that hadn't made it into its appropriate tube, or else with it on backward so that the tail's part faced off the front.

Once the two parts—bottom and jacket—were on, the wearer then tied on a thick, padded waistband, lined right around with pockets. The waistband protected the parts that would otherwise become exposed when tipping over caused the jacket to separate from the bottom. There were also thick boots of thunderbeast leather, lined inside with wingfinger hair, and silly things that weren't quite gloves, since all the fingers save the thumb went into the same amorphous, hair-lined pocket.

The problem, of course, was that these costumes were almost too efficient to test. During the early part of the voyage, Toroca could stand wearing his complete snowsuit for only a few centidays before he began to overheat, his dewlap waggling. But soon he would be glad to have such warm clothing.

Very soon.

Toroca watched Babnol constantly, his eyes following the way she moved, the way she gestured, the way she leaned back on her tail, the way her muzzle crinkled when she was amused, the way her eyes narrowed to slits when she was concentrating.

The way she breathed.

The way she existed.

He longed to reach out, to touch her, to feel the rough texture of her skin, the tiny bumps of her tattoos, the warmth of her flesh. Every time she stepped back from him, opening a territorial buffer between them, it hurt.

It hurt.

The sun sat low on the horizon. It never rose far here in the southern latitudes. A day was brief enough as it was; that the sun never reached the zenith, so that long shadows were cast even at noon, was downright depressing.

It really wasn't *that* cold, Toroca realized. Var-Osfik, the Arbiter of the Sequence, had recently approved a new scale of temperature, devised by one of the contemplatives of the holy land of Arj'toolar. On it, the freezing and boiling points of water were separated by one hundred degrees, and the freezing point was designated as zero. Keenir had an elaborate blown-glass tube, filled with colored liquid, that was supposed to indicate the temperature on this scale. No one knew how accurate it was, since it had obviously never been tested at temperatures much below ten degrees—the coldest it normally got even at night on Land. Here it was indicating about twelve degrees below zero at noon, and temperatures of perhaps twenty below at night. (It was hard to get a good reading at night, since the device couldn't be read in the dark, and the colored liquid began to rise as soon as one brought a lamp flame close to it.) Cold, yes, but not so cold as Toroca had feared. In fact, he was getting quite used to the bracing nature of the air here, and even found it invigorating at times.

Still, the darkness was dispiriting. Toroca understood why the sun never seemed to rise very high in the sky, but that didn't make it any less dreary. More and more people had taken to being up on deck at noon, to enjoy what little brightness and warmth there was. Conditions were crowded, but everyone strove to keep the mood light. Toward that end, the noontime swapping of jokes on the *Dasheter*'s foredeck had quickly become a tradition. Since people's teeth were often chattering from the cold anyway, every joke, even the lamest, got a good reception.

"That's awful," groaned Toroca in good humor to Biltog, a ship's mate who had known his father. Biltog had just told the old groaner about the traveling doctor and the shovelmouth, which somehow Toroca had avoided hearing—mercifully, many would say—until now.

Surveyor Bar-Delplas was making a face. "Now, listen to a *real* joke, Biltog," she said. She saw Babnol coming toward them. "Hey, Babnol!" she called. "What do you call a hornface that's had too much to eat?"

Babnol looked in her direction briefly, but continued on without a word.

"What's with her?" Delplas asked Toroca.

"You swished your tail right into it, I'm afraid," said Toroca. "Babnol doesn't like the word 'hornface.' "

"Why not?"

Toroca tilted his head in the direction of the departing Babnol. "They called her that when she was a child."

Delplas shrugged, then went on with her joke. But Toroca paid no attention to the punch line, and instead stared after Babnol, all glee gone from him.

"Land ho!"

The shout went up from Biltog, once again up in the lookout bucket.

Except it wasn't land that was ho. Toroca, Keenir, Babnol, and many others hurried up onto the *Dasheter*'s foredeck. Biltog's greater elevation gave him a substantial advantage; it took some time for what he'd spotted to come into view.

For dekadays, the horizon had been nothing but gray water touching mauve sky. But at last there was a line, a bright white line, scintillating in the blazing sun.

As the *Dasheter* sailed closer, the line expanded into cliffs of bluish-white ice and hard-packed snow. Fissures cut through the ice at places, showing a cool blue interior.

Toroca watched in amazement as a great wall of ice fell away into the water, splashing up giant waves. As they came closer, he could see cracked sheets of ice jostling together along the rim of the solid snow-packed ice cap. He'd had no ideas what he might find here that could be useful for the exodus project, but, at first assessment, it looked like nothing at all was here except ice and snow.

Keenir wouldn't bring the *Dasheter* any closer, lest one of the floating pieces of ice pierce its hull. Unfortunately the water here was too deep for the anchor. They sailed along, parallel to the ice edge, searching.

But then Keenir, who had been scanning the ice with his far-seer, motioned for Toroca to come close. He handed him the instrument. The brass tube was bitterly cold; Toroca was indeed thankful now for the strange handgear he'd been given to wear. He rotated the tube to bring the image into focus, then staggered back on his tail.

Something was moving around on the ice.

Chapter 19

Musings of the Watcher

During the 460 million Crucible years it took for the Jijaki to evolve sentience on their world, a lot happened on the Crucible itself. Of those body plans that had originally appeared in that great, explosive diversification, one became predominant—the tube with a head at one end, a spinal cord, and, eventually, paired limbs. Soon the spinal cord was encased in a backbone—an interesting solution, so unlike that of my own ancestors. An age of fishes gave way to an age of amphibians, then one of reptiles.

Brain-body ratios increased as time went by. It seemed clear that eventually, joyously, intelligence would arise on the Crucible as well.

Before it did, though, a new form appeared, living in the shadows of the reptiles: tiny furred creatures that nursed their young.

It was wonderfully, terribly clear what was happening. Both the reptiles and the mammals were on their way to intelligence, and at about the same rate, too—the ratio of brain size to body size was increasing on a simple curve through time, and the scale-clad and fur-bearing creatures were both at the same point on that curve. The brightest of the reptiles and the brightest of the mammals soon had brains of equal, if as yet insignificant, power.

It would still take a long time for real intelligence to develop on this world—some 60 or 70 million Crucible years, I judged. But the mammals had already come up against a dead end. Intelligence, at least in the way these beings were trying to express it, required physical bulk—large, centralized, convoluted brains. The reptiles had long dominated every ecological niche for big animals; the rise of mammalian intelligence had ground to a halt.

Not one, but two potential paths to sentience. Yet only one of them, it seemed, could make it on this world.

I summoned the Jijaki.

The South Pole

Toroca, Babnol, and Keenir headed toward the ice in a shore boat. It took Keenir a while to find a suitable place to land. Even so, he wasn't able to anchor the boat properly, so he had to stay with it to keep it from drifting away and stranding them. Toroca and Babnol, clad from muzzle to tail in their strange, bulky garments, headed out onto the ice pack. The surface was covered with hard snow that cracked or squeaked when they stepped on it. Toroca was amazed at its texture, like frozen waves.

And the brightness! Glaring white, everywhere he looked. He found himself shielding his face with his arm. Even with his eyes narrowed to slits, it was still difficult to see.

As his eyes adjusted to the glare, Toroca was surpriseed to see that there were insects here: little black things that hopped across the snow. But it wasn't those that had caught his attention from the deck of the *Dasheter*, but, rather, the strange creatures visible just ahead.

"Why don't they run?" Babnol's words were all but stolen away on the shrieking wind.

"What?" called Toroca.

"Why don't they run from us?" she said again. "Aren't they afraid?"

There were thousands, perhaps tens of thousands, of the creatures covering the ice, each one like a drop of quicksilver in the low Antarctic sun.

"They don't seem to be."

"How can they not be afraid of animals bigger than they are? Certainly, they have no way to defend themselves."

Toroca and Babnol stepped closer, the snow so hard that they left no footprints in it. "And look at the way they crowd together!" said Babnol. "They could touch each other without moving, if they wanted to. Have they no notion of territoriality?"

"Lots of herbivores herd."

"Excuse me, Toroca, you are the scholar, but, umm, there are no plants around, in case you hadn't noticed. These creatures must be fish-eaters."

The creatures had little round bodies and strange heads that were drawn out into long points both off the front of the face and at the back of the head. There was no doubt that they had seen the approaching Quintaglios. Many had swiveled their heads toward Toroca and Babnol. But they seemed not in the least alarmed by the intruders. Toroca saw one slide lazily off the ice into the water. Others were preening themselves with their long prows.

For want of a better name, Toroca thought of these creatures as *divers*. They seemed to have no qualms about slipping into the freezing water, and when they went beneath the surface, Toroca lost all track of them. They were presumably diving deep.

There were only about twenty paces between Toroca and the closest of the divers now. Most of the divers were flopped on their bellies, but some stood fully erect, with thick flippers hanging at their sides. There was something red about halfway down the leading edge of each flipper, but Toroca couldn't yet make out what it was.

As if the complacency of the divers wasn't baffling enough, one of the larger divers began waddling *toward* Toroca and Babnol. The thing's gait was awkward, its short legs not allowing very fast movement. As it approached, Toroca saw that its prow—more of a beak, really—had interlocking pointed sides, but whether these were protruding teeth or simply a saw-toothed edge to the horny sheath, he couldn't say. Still, although the sharp edges were doubtless effective against fish, they didn't look like they could do much to a Quintaglio. Pointing in exactly the opposite direction of the beak was a similarly tapered crest off the back of the head.

Low on the far horizon, Toroca could see two crescent moons, almost lost in the glare from the ice. Given the position of the sun, Toroca and Babnol should have been casting long shadows in front of themselves, but the ice and snow were so reflective that ambient light bounced in to banish them.

The big diver continued to come closer, seeming to take five or six left-right waddles to cover the distance Toroca traveled in a single step. Toroca could see the animal's flippers better now. The red growths in the middle of the flippers' front edges were claws—three small, curved claws. Toroca couldn't imagine what use they were to the animal there, although perhaps they could act as brakes should the diver's waddling gait fail and it found itself facedown sliding across the ice.

There was now just a semi-ten of paces between him and the vanguard diver. Other divers were watching with perhaps growing interest, but no real sign of concern. Suddenly Toroca got the feeling that perhaps he was being set up. The long forward-facing tunnel of his snow jacket kept his muzzle warm at the expense of eliminating peripheral vision. Toroca swung his head in a wide arc and then turned around, almost slipping on the ice as he did so, to check behind him. Nothing, except Babnol, looking as surprised as Toroca felt.

In some ways, it didn't seem sporting. Toroca was no fan of the hunt, but he understood that part of the excitement was the pursuit. He'd never had an animal walk up to him before. For one brief moment he thought that perhaps this meant the diver wasn't an animal. But that was silly. Besides, the diver had a tiny head, and the pointed projection off the top, apparently counterbalancing the beak, seemed to be a rudder-like crest, not an enlarged braincase.

That the animal was completely without fear was puzzling. And yet, it had never seen a Quintaglio before (and really wasn't seeing one now, Toroca thought, since the thick winter vestments hid all of his body except for the tip of his face). Perhaps the beasts had no predators here. Certainly that would explain their vast numbers.

Toroca took another step forward and was now close enough to the diver to touch it. Its little streamlined body was covered with short silver fur that seemed to glisten, as though slicked down with oil. He could see it breathing in and out, its rounded torso expanding and contracting. Although walking seemed to be something of an effort for it, the diver had by no means been really exerting itself. The fast pace of its breathing therefore must mean that it was indeed warm-blooded, something the insulating fur had suggested anyway.

Toroca simply wanted a specimen for study, of course. He reached down with both arms and, using a scalpel, its metal bitterly cold, its surface frosted, he slit the diver's throat.

As soon as the knife touched its skin, the diver let out a call like wooden boards clacking together. That evidently meant something to the other divers, because they started making the same call.

The tableau held for several beats, the only sound the washboard calls of the divers, the only movement their pointed beaks and the flow of blood onto the ice from the dead diver, the red liquid already thick and sluggish in the cold.

And then, as one, the thousands upon thousands of divers moved.

And Toroca suddenly realized that he hadn't thought things through as well as he should have . . .

For the divers, rather than running away from him and Babnol, were waddling as fast as they could toward him, ragged-edged beaks snapping open and closed.

Toroca wheeled around and began to hurry across the ice, his wide shoes slipping and sliding as he did so. He threw his momentum forward, lifting his tail to balance himself, still clutching the dead diver in his left hand. It wouldn't do to fall down here, for the little silver creatures would be all over him, and although individually they were no match for a grown Quintaglio, thousands of them swarming over his body was probably an ignominious way to die . . .

But his footing held, as did Babnol's, and soon it became apparent even to the divers that the Quintaglios were going to easily outdistance them. The silver creatures quit their running, although their wood-on-wood calls persisted for some time.

Keenir was rowing the shore boat toward Toroca and Babnol, trying to hasten their rendezvous. The two surveyors made it aboard . . .

. . . and realized that the divers were doing just what their name implied: diving into the icy water and paddling like silver meteors beneath the surface toward the little wooden boat. Keenir was already rowing like a demon, and Toroca and Babnol found their oars as well, but the boat was not nearly as maneuverable or fast as the divers. Looking over the gunwales, Toroca could see hundreds of them swarming beneath the gray, chilled surface.

The boat buffeted as beaks beat against the underside of its hull. The clattering of the impacts was deafening. Toroca pulled his oar from the water and smashed it against the surface with a great splashing sound. That startled the divers, and their assault of beaks stopped—but only briefly. Soon it renewed in earnest. The boat was rocking enough that Toroca feared it would capsize. He thought for an instant of throwing back the dead diver, in hopes that that might appease its avengers.

Toroca and Babnol smashed their paddles into the surface again, and this time, against his intentions, Toroca felt his oar connect with something hard and pointed. He imagined he had just brained a diver.

Chilled water was splashing everywhere. Toroca could feel the arm of his jacket stiffening as it began to freeze up, presumably soaked on the outside.

Fortunately, though, the divers didn't have the energy or attention span to keep at it. After a short period of time, they stopped their attack and swam off beneath the cold surface. Looking back, Toroca could see them clambering up onto the ice, shaking their little bodies violently to fling off water droplets.

The three of them continued to row out toward the *Dasheter*. Toroca glanced down at the corpse of the diver, with its pointed head and funny little claws along its flippers. It was an odd anatomical mix, and yet, somehow, it was strangely familiar.

He looked forward to getting back aboard ship and studying the body in detail.

Chapter 20

The tip of Afsan's tail beat up and down impatiently. It wasn't like Haldan to be late. They had arranged to meet here, in the Plaza of Belkom, at the fourth daytenth, and Afsan had arrived in plenty of time to hear the four bells from the Hall of Worship. But those bells had rung long ago and still Haldan hadn't shown up.

Gork was growing restive. Afsan could feel the lizard's thick tail slapping against his legs. Gork had been trained to do that when they were stationary so that Afsan would know precisely where the lizard was, lest he start to walk and trip over it. But when impatient, Gork's slapping would become more frequent, and it had now reached a violent rhythm. Afsan stooped over and stroked the beast's flank.

Afsan and his daughter had agreed to meet here simply to spare Afsan the difficulty of negotiating his way without a guide down the bending corridors of her apartment building.

"What do you think, Gork?" said Afsan. "Think we can find her?" He'd been to his daughter's home often enough that he thought he knew the way. "Let's try." He pulled up on Gork's harness and pointed his arm in the direction he wanted to go. Gork let out a pleased grunt of acknowledgment and they set out.

Although Gork did a fine job keeping Afsan from stepping in front of caravans or walking off a cliff, Afsan still used his cane to feel the terrain in front of him, so as to keep his footing sure. The original stick that Pal-Cadool had first fashioned for him had been lost kilodays ago in the great landquake. This intricately carved pole had been a gift long ago from mariner Var-Keenir, who had used it himself while his tail, chomped off by the great serpent Kal-ta-goot, had been regenerating.

Gork and Afsan made slow but steady progress. At one point, Afsan heard the clacking of claws on stone paving and asked the unknown passerby to confirm that he was going in the right direction. At last they entered the lobby of Haldan's building, Afsan recognizing the way the ticks of his cane echoed off the stone walls. Gork seemed to remember the place too, for it picked up the pace a bit as they headed down the correct corridor, which made the traditional zigzag bends that kept other users out of sight. Afsan tucked his cane under his arm and held one hand out toward the wall, letting it bounce lightly off the wooden jambs as he counted doorways.

He tugged on Gork's harness to stop the animal. "It's this one," he said. With a little groping, he found the brass signaling plate next to the door and drummed his claws on it. There was no answer. Afsan leaned in toward the wood and ran his hand over the cartouche carved into it, confirming that these were indeed the symbols associated with his daughter, a naturalist who studied animal populations. "Haldan," he called out, "it's me, Afsan."

Still no answer.

He bent to stroke Gork's side again. "She must have been detained," he said soothingly. "Well, she's bound to come here sooner or later. Shall we go in and sit down?"

Gork hissed softly. Afsan reached down, operated the brass bar that controlled the door mechanism, and stepped into the room. He left the door open so that Haldan would see him as soon as she approached: bad things could happen when one Quintaglio startled another in what might be construed as a territorial invasion.

As soon as they were fully within the room, Gork began to hiss violently. "What is it?" said Afsan, crouching next to the beast. But then Afsan himself smelled it: fresh meat, the gentle tinge of blood in the air.

"Ah, hungry, are you?" said Afsan to the lizard, scratching its neck gently. "Well, perhaps Haldan won't mind if I give you a gobbet." Afsan flared his nostrils. The inviting smell was coming from across the room. He paused for a moment, recalling the arrangement of furniture from the last time he'd been here, then let go of Gork's harness and, guiding himself with his cane, began toward the source of the smell. It was slightly unusual; Afsan could normally recognize any type of meat by a single whiff, but this one, although not completely unfamiliar, was something he couldn't immediately place.

He remembered there being a table against a wall at the point the smell was coming from, but it wasn't a table Haldan normally would use for food. Rather, it was more of a work space. As Afsan got closer, the smell of blood became more pronounced. Unusual, he thought, since she'd hardly have killed or butchered something right in her own home, and any haunch brought from the market would have been well-drained.

Afsan felt a slapping against his legs. Gork had come alongside. The lizard was hissing loudly, almost spitting—a strange, unpleasant sound, one Afsan had never heard his companion make before.

He arrived at the table and bent from the waist, one arm outstretched to feel. At once he connected with something large and wet. He yanked his hand away, brought his fingers to his nostrils, inhaled the blood.

He reached down again, tentatively, and felt the object. It was warm. Heavy. Rounded. Covered with rough skin. He ran his fingertips over it. No scales, no scutes, just rough hide. Except here—little raised dots. Strange . . . they seemed to form a pattern.

A tattoo. A hunting tattoo.

Afsan staggered back, leaning against his tail.

It was a head. A Quintaglio head.

Sleeping, then, surely—

But it was wet. Wet with blood.

Afsan struggled to control the fear rising within him, and leaned in closer. He touched the back of the head, ran his fingers lightly down the bulbous braincase, over the thick neck muscles, their corded construction obvious even through the skin, and onto the broad shoulders.

The torso did not rise and fall with breathing.

He slid his hand around the shoulder, feeling the articulation between it and the upper arm.

Suddenly his hand was wet again. Just as suddenly, his fingers were *inside*—there was a fleshy shelf, and he felt soft tissue.

The mouth? Surely not so soon. And yet, it gaped like a toothless maw. Afsan's heart pounded as he moved his hand along the soft, slippery surface, farther and farther and even farther still . . .

The throat had been slit wide open across its entire breadth. The head was propped forward, the length of its muzzle resting against the table-top, leaving the cut yawning wide. As he touched it, the delicate balance was disturbed and the body slumped farther forward, the severed carotid arteries, too thick to simply crust over, spilling a torrent of new blood over Afsan's hand and arm.

Revolted, Afsan yanked his arm away, but he realized, almost as an afterthought, that there had been no signs of the remains of a dewlap sack around the cut. A female.

He used his other hand—the dry one—to feel the leather of the sash crossing over the female's chest. It was stiff with drying blood, but he easily found what he'd been afraid to find, the sculpted metal pin of a naturalist. It was Haldan.

Afsan reached out to the table to steady himself and felt his own hand slice open. He pulled it back instantly. The cut wasn't very deep, but it stung. His claws, unnoticed, had extended on their own. Afsan tapped them against the wooden tabletop and found many sharp flat pieces of broken glass.

Afsan became aware of a sound: Gork lapping at the blood that had spilled on the floor. He groped for the lizard's harness and yanked the beast away from the body.

For a moment, Afsan thought to run, to try to find help, but his mental picture of the room dissolved into a swirling nothingness, a panicked abyss. He forced himself to think, to reason. Any attempt at hurrying would just result in him tripping. If he could just—

But reason lasted only a few fleeting moments and without further thought, Afsan found himself leaning back on his tail and yelling and yelling and yelling until, after an eternity, help finally arrived.

Chapter 21

In his cabin, the one that had been his father's all those kilodays ago, Toroca examined the body of the diver by lamplight, the flame dancing to and fro as the *Dasheter* pitched on the waves.

The diver was an exquisite animal, about the length of Toroca's arm and covered in fine silver fur. At first he didn't know what to make of it. Fur was sometimes seen on certain plants, especially fungi and molds, and on the bodies of those flying reptiles known as wingfingers. Toroca had never heard of any land-dwelling or aquatic creature having it. Yet this one did: a good, thick coat of the stuff. He stroked it, saw that it had a nap, saw how it appeared to change color from a dark silver to almost white depending on which way the individual strands were deployed. It had an oddly revolting feel, this fur: thousands upon thousands of tiny fibers, moving back and forth almost like plants swaying in a breeze. He had to fight down the sensation that the filaments might pierce his skin, or fly loose to enter his nostrils or eyes. That the fur was oily just made the sensation even more unpleasant.

Although the body covering was disgusting, the creature's head was fascinating. As he'd observed on the ice, it tapered to a pointed, toothed beak. Counterbalancing the beak was a long crest off the back of the skull, pointed in the opposite direction.

The diver had flippers held, in death, tightly against its side. Rigor hadn't set in yet, although everything was a bit stiff in these cold temperatures. Toroca gently pulled the left flipper away from the body. He was surprised to find that it was rigid only along its leading edge. The rest of the flipper consisted of a thick mass of tissue, but seemed to be completely unreinforced by bone. In the middle of the flipper's leading edge were three small red claws.

That was unusual. Five was the normal number of digits, of course. Some creatures, Quintaglios and blackdeaths among them, had fewer on their feet, and blackdeaths had only two on their hands. But three on the forelimbs was a rare number. Toroca took out his scalpel and sliced into the flipper, gently exposing the inner flesh.

Dark blood spilled out onto the worktable. He carved further into the flipper and saw that it was well padded with yellow fat. But it was the leading edge that he really wanted to see. He made an incision along the entire length of the flipper's anterior margin, then used his hands to pull back the clammy flesh. It took a little twisting and yanking, but he soon had the bones that made up the front of the flipper exposed.

From the shoulder to the claws, there were two long bones, obviously the humerus and the radius—the upper and lower arm bones. At the end of the radius, there were the phalangeal bones of the three red-clawed fingers that protruded from the flipper, and then running along the remaining length of the flipper, from this tiny hand to its outermost tip, four long bones.

Four extraordinarily long phalangeal bones.

The bones of a fourth, vastly extended finger.

It was the same structure as in a wingfinger's wing, the structure that gave those flying reptiles their name.

Toroca rolled the corpse over and pressed his own fingers into the corpse's belly. They came up against a hard plate of bone.

A breastplate.

Suddenly the head crest made sense. Just like those in some flying reptiles.

This beast *was* a wingfinger.

A water-going wingfinger.

A wingfinger that swam through the cold waters the way its equatorial cousins flew through the air.

Toroca staggered back on his tail, the lamp flickering, the timbers of the ship groaning.

How does a wingfinger come to be a swimmer? How does a flyer take to the water?

What caprice of God was this?

Chapter 22

Var-Gathgol, the undertaker, felt out of his depth. It was bad enough that blind Afsan was here. Senior palace officials always were difficult to deal with. But now the Emperor himself had arrived. Gathgol had no idea how to behave in front of such important people.

Dybo was standing near Afsan—altogether too near, really; such easy proximity was uncomfortable even to watch. Gathgol had hoped to simply slip in, bundle up the body, and take it away in the wagon he had left outside the apartment block. But someone—Gathgol thought perhaps it was the building's administrator—had told him not to touch the corpse.

It was, indeed, an unusual set of circumstances.

Suddenly Gathgol felt a frightened rippling at the tips of his fingers. The Emperor himself was gesturing at him. At first Gathgol froze, but the waving of the Emperor's arm became impatient and that spurred him into motion. He hurried across the room, taking care to avoid the pieces of broken glass on the floor.

"You're the undertaker?" said the Emperor.

Gathgol bowed rapidly. "Yes, umm, Your, Your . . ."

"Luminance," said Dybo absently.

"Yes, Your Luminance. I cast a shadow in your presence."

"Do you know Sal-Afsan, a savant and my advisor?"

"By reputation, of course," stammered Gathgol. He tipped his body toward the blind one, then after a moment said, "I'm, uh, bowing at you." Afsan's muzzle swiveled toward him, but that was his only response. Gathgol felt like a fool.

"And you?" said Dybo.

Gathgol was now completely confused. "I'm, uh, the undertaker. I'm sorry. I thought you wanted—"

Dybo made an exasperated sound. "I know what you do. What's your name?"

"Oh. Gathgol. Var-Gathgol."

Dybo nodded. "How exactly did Haldan die?"

Gathgol gestured at the table. "Her throat was cut open by a jagged piece of mirror."

Afsan's head snapped up. "Mirror? Is that what it is?"

Gathgol nodded. "Yes, mirror. That's, um, glass with a silvered backing. You can, ah, see your reflection in it."

Afsan's tone was neutral, perhaps that of one accustomed to such gaffes. "I appreciate your explanation, Gathgol, but I've not been blind my whole life. I know what a mirror is."

"My apologies," Gathgol said.

"How could a mirror cut one's neck open?" asked Afsan.

"Well, the glass is broken," said Gathgol. "The pieces have a sharp edge—beveled, almost. A large section was drawn across her neck, quite rapidly, I should think."

"I don't understand," said Afsan. "Did she trip somehow? I've felt with my walking stick for an obstacle but can't find one."

"Trip, savant? No, she didn't trip. She was probably seated on that stool when it happened."

"Did the mirror fall off the wall, then? Had it been mounted poorly? Was there a little landquake today?"

Gathgol shook his head. "A piece of art hangs on the wall above the table, savant. It's still there now. A still life of some sort."

"A still life." Afsan nodded. "But then how did the accident happen?"

Gathgol felt his nictitating membranes fluttering. "It was not an accident, savant."

"What do you mean?"

Could a genius of Afsan's rank be so thick? "Good Sal-Afsan, Haldan was killed. Deliberately. By an intruder, most likely."

"Killed," said Afsan slowly, as if he'd never heard the word, moving it around inside his mouth like an odd-tasting piece of meat. "You mean murdered?"

"Yes."

"Murdered. Somebody took her life?"

"Yes, savant."

"But surely it was *dagamant*, then—a territorial challenge of some sort, an instinctive reaction."

Gathgol shook his head. "No. This was planned, savant. We've gathered up all the shards of the mirror. They don't form a complete rectangle. Somebody brought a large jagged piece of mirrored glass here, probably approached Haldan from behind, and, with a quick movement, slit her throat. The mirror was still partly in a wooden frame, and that gave it rigidity, as well as something for the assailant to hold on to without risking cutting his or her hands."

"Murder," said Dybo, who was looking quite queasy. "I've never heard of such a thing."

"I haven't heard of one in modern times," said Gathgol, "but when I was apprenticing to be an undertaker, my master taught me a little about such things. Of course, she said I would never need to know this, that the knowledge was only for historical overview, but . . . yes, there are stories of murder from the past. Myths about the Lubalites and so on."

"Murder," said Afsan softly. And then, a few beats later: "But how? Surely the demon responsible, whoever it was, couldn't have opened the door and sneaked up on Haldan. She doubtless would have heard the approach and turned to face her attacker."

"It is puzzling," said Gathgol. "But I'm sure of the cause of death. I mean, it's obvious."

"Well," said Dybo, "what do we do now?"

"We find the person who did this," said Afsan flatly.

Dybo nodded slowly. "But how? I don't know anyone who has experience with such matters." He turned toward Gathgol. "Do you know how to do it, undertaker?"

"Me? I don't have the slightest idea."

Afsan spoke softly. "I'll do it."

Dybo's voice was equally soft. "My friend, even you—"

Afsan's claws peeked out. "I will do it. She was my daughter, Dybo. If not me, who?"

"But Afsan, friend, you are . . . without sight. I will assign another to the task."

"To another, it would be exactly that: a task. I—I can't explain my feelings in this matter. We were related, she and I. I've never known what import, if any, that had, whether she and I would have been friends regardless of the odd circumstances that led to her knowing that I was indeed her father, she in truth my daughter. But I feel it now, Dybo, a—a special obligation to her."

Dybo nodded; Gathgol saw that he and the savant were old friends, that Dybo knew when to give up arguing with Afsan. "Very well," said the Emperor. "I know that once you sink your teeth into a problem, you do not let go."

Afsan took the comment easily, Gathgol saw—a simple statement of fact, something both Afsan and Dybo knew to be true. But then the savant's face hardened. "I swear," he said, "I will not give up until I have found her killer."

Rockscape

Rockscape at sunset. Pal-Cadool, straddling one of the ancient boulders, his long legs dangling to the ground, loved the sight: it was one of the rare times when he still pitied Afsan. The sun was no longer a tiny blazingly white disk; it had swollen and grown purple. From here amongst the ancient boulders the sun would set behind the Ch'mar volcanoes to the west. Their caps, some pointed, some ragged calderas, were stained dark blue. Above the sun, along the ecliptic—a word Afsan had taught Cadool—three crescent moons were visible, their illuminated limbs curving up like drinking bowls.

The lizard Gork needed no more cue than this that night was coming. It had already curled up at Afsan's feet, sleeping, its body pressed against the savant's legs so that he would know where the lizard was. Afsan was perched on his usual rock, his face, coincidentally, turned toward the glorious sunset spectacle that he could not see. It would soon be time for him to go back indoors.

"I don't understand," said Afsan slowly, interrupting Cadool's reverie.

Something Afsan didn't understand? Surely, Cadool thought, there was nothing he could do to help in such a circumstance. Still, he asked, "What is it?"

Afsan's head was tilted at an odd angle. "Who," he said at last, "would want to kill Haldan?"

Cadool wished Afsan would let go of this problem. It pained him to see Afsan so distraught. "I don't know who would want to kill *anyone*," said Cadool, spreading his arms. "I mean, I get angry from time to time, angry at other people. But the hunt is supposed to purge those emotions. It certainly does that for me."

"Indeed," said Afsan. "But someone had enough fury to kill my daughter."

The darkness was gathering rapidly, as it always did. Stars were becoming visible overhead.

"I've never known anyone who has killed," said Cadool.

"Yes, you do."

"Who?"

"Me," said Afsan softly. "I killed a person once. Nor-Gampar was his name. He was crazed, in full *dagamant*. It happened sixteen kilodays ago, during my pilgrimage voyage aboard the *Dasheter*."

"*Dagamant* doesn't count," said Cadool quickly. "You had no choice."

"I know that. But not a day goes by that I don't think of it. It is not an easy burden to carry."

"You bear it well."

"Do I?" Afsan sounded surprised. "Perhaps." He fell silent for several heartbeats. "Perhaps, indeed, some small good came of it. I will never completely forgive Emperor Dybo for allowing my blinding, but I know he feels great guilt and sadness over it. Just as I feel guilt and sadness over the death of Gampar. I can't forgive Dybo—I try to, but I can't. But I do understand that if he could do it over differently, he would. Just as I would." Afsan's muzzle creased. "I'm sorry, Cadool. I didn't mean to burden you with stories of my past."

Cadool bowed. "It is an honor for me to hear them . . . friend."

" 'Friend,' " repeated Afsan, surprised. "We've known each other an awfully long time, Cadool—I count anyone whose appearance I actually know as a long acquaintance—but in all that time, you've never called me friend."

Cadool looked at Afsan, almost a silhouette now in the gathering darkness. "It was not for lack of affection, Afsan. You know that. You have always been special to me. But you are a savant, you can read—" He stopped himself. "I'm sorry; you used to be able to read. We are not of equal stations in life."

"We *are* friends, Cadool."

"Yes."

They were both quiet for a time.

"Are you sure," Cadool said at last, "that Haldan's death was murder? Could she not have taken her own life? Again, I don't know anyone who has ever contemplated that, but—"

"Yes, you do, my friend. I thought about it once, when I saw what my discoveries about the Face of God would do to our people. I was atop the foremast of the *Dasheter*, doing a turn as lookout. I thought about jumping to the deck below."

"Oh." Cadool's voice was thin.

"But, no, Gathgol has described the way in which the mirror was drawn across the throat. It could only have been done by someone standing behind Haldan while she was seated on a bench in front of her worktable. It was not suicide."

Cadool said nothing. After a time, Afsan spoke again. "I've disturbed you with my own tale of pondered suicide, haven't I?"

Cadool could have lied, of course, since Afsan couldn't see his muzzle, but he did not. He never did. "Yes."

"I'm sorry. I didn't mean to upset you."

"There's much I didn't know about you, I guess."

"Friends should share, Cadool." In the darkness, Afsan's torso tipped in Cadool's direction. "I'm sorry to have not told you before."

"Your secret is safe with me."

"I know it is, Cadool. We've been through much together; I trust you completely."

"I'm bowing."

"I need someone I can trust, Cadool. I need someone to help me."

"I am always there for you."

"Yes, you always are. And although I may not say it often, I am grateful. It—I'm sorry, it's just that, even though I prize your company greatly, I feel some resentment that I can't always get along on my own. I do appreciate your help."

"I know you do. The words aren't necessary."

"Sometimes," Afsan said slowly, "I do wonder *why*, though. Why you give so much of your time to helping me. Early on, I could understand it. You thought I was The One foretold by Lubal. I rarely speak about claims that I'm The One, but, down deep, Cadool, you must know that it's not true."

"I know it. It doesn't matter. You are trying to save our people. I have no skills, except butchery and animal handling—and those are hardly rare vocations. Helping you out is the way I play my part in saving the Quintaglio race."

Afsan nodded. "You are a good person, Cadool."

"Thank you—but it is my pleasure to help, for you, Afsan, you are a *great* person."

"Some might say that, I suppose, but like you, I have but a single talent. I can solve puzzles; it's all I've ever been really good at."

"Except the hunt."

Afsan nodded again. "Except the hunt." The moons blazed overhead. "And now, Cadool, I have a difficult puzzle indeed to solve. I have sworn to find out who is responsible for the murder of Haldan. This puzzle will depend upon hearing the testimony of many people. People can lie to me, Cadool. I can't see their muzzles. I need someone whom I trust absolutely to tell me if what I'm hearing is said honestly. I ask you now to accompany me on my quest, to be my arbiter of honesty. There is no one else I trust so completely."

Cadool was silent for a few beats. Then: "Exactly what oath did you swear?"

"To not rest until I'd found the killer of Haldan."

Cadool stood up. "Come with me now to the Hall of Worship, Afsan. I shall stand before the statue of Lubal and swear the same thing."

Chapter 23

The *Dasheter*

Babnol had known this moment had to come, and she had been dreading it for days. She was up on the foredeck of the *Dasheter*, clad in the jacket of her snowsuit, performing one of the jobs that had been assigned to her: tightening the many knots that anchored the web of climbing ropes to the boom.

Toroca was approaching now from the rear deck, having just come up the ramp that led from his quarters. As he headed across the little connecting piece that joined the *Dasheter*'s two diamond-shaped hulls, Babnol wondered how long ago Toroca had noticed the blue artifact was missing. Had he mulled for days over what to do about it? Or had he only now noticed its absence? Had he questioned anyone else? Or did he immediately suspect Babnol?

She bent to the task of retying knots, pretending to take no notice of his approach. Overhead, towering gray clouds marred the purple bowl of the sky.

"Greetings," said Toroca, stopping about ten paces short of her, the word appearing as a puff of condensation.

Babnol pulled tightly on the ropes, but didn't look up. *"Hahat dan."*

"There's something I want to talk to you about," Toroca said.

She gestured at the climbing web. "I've got a lot of work left to do still. Perhaps we can speak later?"

"No, I think now would be best. This task can wait."

"Keenir needs it done."

"Keenir works for me on this voyage," said Toroca with uncharacteristic firmness. "My needs outweigh his."

She stopped working on the knots and straightened. "Of course."

"The object is missing from my cabin," said Toroca.

"Object?" repeated Babnol innocently.

"The artifact from Fra'toolar. The blue hemisphere with the strange handgrip."

"Ah," said Babnol. "And you say it is missing?"

Toroca's fingers flexed, a reaction of shock, an instinctive prelude to the unsheathing of claws. He recognized what was happening here, saw that Babnol had moved from him questioning her to her questioning him. It was the first step in the dance, the social custom of avoiding direct questions in uncomfortable areas. At that moment, he knew that Babnol was involved, his worst fears confirmed.

"Yes," said Toroca, willing to play on a step or two further. "I say that object is missing."

"You must have been surprised," said Babnol.

"Yes."

"Have you asked Keenir if he knows——?"

"*Babnol.*" Toroca spoke the name sharply. "*I* will ask the questions, please."

To force direct responses was the height of bad manners. "Why would you want to question me?" she said.

Toroca ignored that. "*I,*" he said again, with heavy emphasis, "will ask the questions."

"I really must get back to my work," said Babnol, grabbing the climbing ropes, yanking them, looking for another loose knot.

"Did you take the object?" asked Toroca firmly.

There was a moment, a pause, a break in the dance. A Quintaglio could not get away with a lie in the light of day. And yet, although direct confrontations such as this rarely occurred, for one did not want to force another to feel he or she had no territory left to retreat into, there was often a final step to the dance, one last, brief movement in which the party wishing to avoid answering would spout a lie in the forlorn hope that his or her muzzle miraculously would not change color.

Toroca waited patiently, and, at last, Babnol dipped her head. "Yes," she said. "I took the object."

Toroca turned and looked out over the gray waves. "Thank you," he said at last, "for not lying to me." His heart was aching. He cared so much for Babnol, and yet this breach, this violation, cut him to the bone. Toroca had no interest in territoriality but he valued his privacy, which was quite a different thing. "You could have asked me if you wanted to borrow the object," he said, trying to put his words in a light tone. "I was given quite a start when I realized it was gone."

"I'm sorry," said Babnol, and Toroca was relieved to see that her muzzle did not flush blue as she said it.

"I'm certain you are," he said. "Where is the object now?"

"Toroca—"

"Babnol, where is it? In your quarters?"

"Not in my quarters."

"Then where?"

"Toroca, I did it for you."

Toroca's claws did slip out. *"Where?"*

"It's gone, Toroca. For good. Overboard."

Toroca closed his eyes and exhaled noisily. "Oh, Babnol." He shook his head. "How could you be so careless?"

"I was not careless," she said. "I threw it overboard on purpose, out the porthole in your cabin."

Toroca staggered back on his tail. Had she struck him, he'd have felt no less shocked. *"Threw* it overboard? But, Babnol, why? Why?"

"It was not a proper thing. It—lacked goodness." She turned her muzzle directly toward him. There could be no doubt that her obsidian eyes were meeting his. "God must have intended it to remain buried." Her voice was defiant. "That's why She had sealed it in rock."

"Oh, Babnol." Toroca's voice was heavy. "Babnol, you . . ." He hesitated, as if unsure whether to complete the sentence, but at last, with a simple shrug, he did, ". . . you fool." For the first time in his memory, he found himself stepping back from her, instead of toward her. "You promised me when you came to me, looking to join the Geological Survey, that I wouldn't be sorry if I let you do so. Well, I'm sorry now." He shook his head. "Do you know what that object was, Babnol? It was our salvation. It was a *gift* from God. She put it exactly where I would find it; you credit me far too much if you think my random opening of rocks could find something She wanted hidden. Babnol, that object was a clue, a hint, a suggestion—a whole new way of building machines. Solid blocks that somehow performed work! Flexible clear strands, unlike anything we've ever imagined! That object could have been the key to getting us off this doomed moon in time. You didn't just throw it overboard, you threw our best chance of survival overboard, too."

Babnol was defensive now. "But you yourself said we didn't understand the object . . ."

"*I* didn't understand it. *You* didn't. But others might. After we finish this voyage, we are returning to Capital City. There I was going to turn the object over to Novato. She and the other finest minds would examine it, and they, or the finest minds of the next generation, or of the generation after that, would have fathomed the object, would have understood the principles it employed."

Toroca was now furious with himself. He could have sent the object back to Capital City with someone else instead of bringing it on this voyage, but he'd wanted to spend more time with it, and most of all, he'd wanted to be there personally to see his mother's face when he presented it to her. Such vanity! Such arrogance. He slapped his tail against the deck, and with words that were talon-sharp, took all that fury out on Babnol. "By the very claws of Lubal, herbivore, how could you do this?"

She looked at the wooden deck, splintering here and there where claws had dug into it. "I did it for you. I—I saw the way it obsessed you, the way it was drawing you in. It was like a whirlpool, Toroca, sucking the goodness out of you, sucking it into an empty, spiritless abyss." She looked up. "I did it for you," she said again.

"I see that you're telling the truth, Babnol, but—" He sighed, a long, whispery exhalation, a whitish cloud of expelled air appearing around his muzzle. He tried again. "The whole point of the Geological Survey is to learn things. We cannot be afraid to look."

"But some things are best left unknown," she said.

"*Nothing* is best left unknown," said Toroca. "*Nothing*. We're trying to save our entire race! It's only knowledge that will let us do that. We have to shed our superstitions and fears the way a snake sheds its skin. We can't cower in the face of what we might discover. Look at Afsan! Others cowered and trembled at the sight of the Face of God, but he reasoned. Aboard this very boat, he reasoned it out! We cannot—we *must* not—do any less than what he did. We cannot be afraid, for if we are afraid, then we—all our people—will die."

Babnol was trembling slightly. "I'm sorry," she said. "I'm very sorry."

Toroca saw how upset she was, and how very afraid. He wanted to move closer, to comfort her, but knew that that would frighten her even more. Finally, softly, he said, "I know."

She lifted her muzzle, tried to meet his eyes. "And what happens now?"

"When this Antarctic expedition is over, we will return briefly to Capital City for provisions and so that I can report to Novato. After that, we will go back to the shore of Fra'toolar."

"But I thought we were finished there?"

"We *were* finished," spat Toroca, but he immediately reigned in his tone. "We were. But now we have to go back and search and search and search until we find another artifact. And you, Babnol, here, with the sun burning above your head, you must now pledge your loyalty to the cause, your loyalty to the Geological Survey, your loyalty to *me*, or I will have no choice but to have you left behind in Capital City. I need you, Babnol, and I—I want you, to be part of my team. But there must be no repetition of this. We're growing up fast, Babnol—as a race, I mean. We have to leave behind the fears of our childhood. Pledge your loyalty."

She lifted her left hand, claws extended on her second and third finger, fingers four and five spread out, her thumb pressed against her palm: the ancient Lubalite salute of loyalty.

"I see," said Toroca, his voice not bitter, "that you noticed more than just the object when you searched my quarters." He nodded after a moment. "I accept your pledge of loyalty." A pause. "Back to your knot-tying, Babnol, but while you do it, pray."

"Pray?" she said.

He nodded. "Pray that the object was not one of a kind."

Being cooped up on a ship was enough to make almost any Quintaglio edgy. Except on pilgrimage voyages, ships rarely sailed far from the coastline of Land, and they would put in to shore every few days so that those aboard could hunt.

The journey to the south polar cap had been a long one, with no stopovers. It was time to release the energy and emotions that had built up during the voyage. It was time for a hunt.

The divers were by far the most common lifeform on the cap, but they were by no means the only one. Several other creatures had been glimpsed through the far-seer. That was fortunate, for a diver was much too small to make a proper meal for one Quintaglio, let alone a hungry pack.

Delplas's tail was swishing over the *Dasheter*'s deck in anticipation. "Ah, to hunt again," said the surveyor. "At last! My claws have been itching for dekadays." Each word appeared as a puff of white vapor. She turned to Toroca, who was leaning against the railing around the edge of the ship. "Surely you'll join us on this hunt, Toroca. Even you must be ready for one now."

Toroca looked down over the edge, watched tiny pieces of ice bumping together in the gray water. "No, thank you."

"But it's been ages! It's high time for a hunt."

"I wish you every success," said Toroca, turning to face Delplas.

"We've known each other for kilodays," said Delplas, "and still I don't understand you."

Toroca was thinking of Babnol. "Does one ever really understand another?"

Delplas shook her head. "You know what I mean." She turned her muzzle to directly face Toroca. "You'll kill an animal whose anatomy you're curious about, but you hate to kill your own food."

"I kill the specimens as painlessly as possible," Toroca replied. "In the hunt, animals die in agony."

"It doesn't make any sense," said Delplas. "After all, your father is Afsan."

"Yes."

"The greatest hunter of all time."

Toroca turned back to looking over the ship's railing. "Afsan hasn't hunted for—what?—sixteen kilodays," he said softly.

"Well, *of course*," replied Delplas, exasperated. "He's blind."

Toroca shrugged. "Even before that, he only hunted once or twice."

"But what hunts! The biggest thunderbeast ever known. Aboard this very ship, that serpent, Kal-ta-goot! And even a fangjaw. They talk about his kills still."

"Yes," said Toroca. "Still."

"He was The One: the hunter foretold by Lubal."

"Perhaps."

"By not hunting, you dishonor your father."

Toroca swung around, leveling a steady gaze at Delplas. "Don't talk to me about duty to my father. Duty to one's parents is a subject about which you and everyone else know *nothing*."

Toroca strode away, his feet, clad in insulated shoes, slapping the deck like thunderclaps. Delplas simply stood there, inner eyelids batting up and down.

Chapter 24

The Jijaki traveled along my star lanes.

Not only is this particular iteration of the universe unwelcoming of life, it's also rigidly opposed to high-speed travel. I tried to predict what forms of interstellar voyaging would be possible for whatever lifeforms arose here. The kinds of nuclear reactions that occur in this universe seemed to hold possible answers. Still, carrying fuel over long distances is always a problem. It would be so much easier if the fuel could be collected along the way.

A ramjet could use an electromagnetic field to gather up interstellar hydrogen to be burned in a nuclear-fusion reactor. In theory, a ship so propelled could reach velocities near that of light, the speed cap in this creation. Unfortunately, for it to work one would need an average density of usable hydrogen particles about ten thousand times greater than what existed in normal space. And, as if that weren't bad enough, the majority of the interstellar hydrogen in this universe was in the form of protium, an isotope that can undergo fusion only through a nuclear catalytic cycle within the core of stars.

However, having bound my being to the dark matter, I had some trifling control over gravity. Over a period of millions of years, I attracted more hydrogen into corridors connecting the Crucible's sun and the Jijaki sun, and between the Crucible's sun and stars that I had selected as transplantation targets. I built up ribbons of suitable density. Along these paths, and these paths alone, would hydrogen-ramscoop fusion starships be able to travel.

A ramscoop needs to be very strong. The strength of the electromagnetic field used to attract the interstellar hydrogen would cause even a starship made of diamond to collapse, and the hull must be immune to erosion by interstellar dust grains. Ah, but once I'd spelled out the problems for them, my Jijaki proved clever, devising a blue material they called *kiit* that exceeded by a hundred times the strength of diamond. *Kiit*, which could be injection-molded like plastic until it crystallized, became a common building material.

Was I unfair to the Jijaki, paving roads only where I wanted them to go? I don't think so. They wished to find other life, and I rolled out a pathway for them. They longed to travel to the stars, and I made that possible for them, with journeys lasting only a single one of their infinitesimal lifetimes.

The Crucible was a glorious world, green and blue, with stunning white clouds and vast oceans. At the time I plucked the ancestors of the Jijaki from here, all the land was concentrated into a single mass. Now it had broken up, and separate continents had begun to drift apart.

The dinosaurs had been around now for 130 million Crucible years. Unfortunately, their diversity had recently begun to decrease. Only about fifty or so genera were left. Among them were great bipedal carnivores, horned dinosaurs, a few types with armored carapaces, hadrosaurs with ornate headcrests and bills resembling those of aquatic birds, gracile types that resembled flightless birds, great four-footed beasts with endless tapering tails and endless tapering necks, and small crepuscular hunters with giant eyes and grasping hands.

In some ways it was fortunate that there were so few kinds of dinosaurs left. Gathering up a goodly sample of each type was not too difficult for my Jijaki. They also collected some of the great seagoing reptiles and the flying reptiles, too. And, of course, enough of the rest of the biota to keep the food chain intact.

A fleet of arks was dispatched from the Crucible to the target world. Some arks—those carrying basic anaerobic life, such as blue-green algae—went as fast as possible by ramship, and began preparing the new world. Others climbed out of the solar system, then locked their interiors into stasis and let me slowly nudge them across the starscape, tugging them on gentle leashes of dark matter, taking millennia to make the voyage. The Jijaki crews knew I was going to do this, knew that they would, in essence, be transported eons into the future. But the cult of my worship that began as soon as my first message had been received persisted to this day, and I had no lack of volunteers.

The target star was a young white giant—far younger than the Crucible's own yellow sun. It was circled by eight planets. The three innermost and the two outermost were small, rocky bodies. The remaining three, Planets 4, 5, and 6, were similar to the largest planets in the Crucible's own system: gas-giant worlds with many moons.

Planet 5 was striped with roiling bands of methane and ammonia, whirlpool storms of white cloud raging here and there. It was somewhat flattened by its rapid rotation, and its equator was dotted by a few black circles, the shadows cast by some of the fourteen moons that careened around it. This system's mother star appeared as nothing more than a tiny intense disk at this distance.

Each of the giant planet's fourteen moons had its own personality. One was shrouded in pink cloud. Another was cracked by deep fissures. A third had active volcanoes spewing sulfur into space. Another was just a ball of rock.

But the one that interested me was, then, the third moon. It was almost exactly the same size as the Crucible. Over ninety percent of its surface was covered by water, mostly liquid, but frozen into caps at either pole. Like the Crucible's own single moon, this one was tidally locked so that the same side always faced the planet it orbited. There were two continents, both straddling the equator, and both located on the moon's far side, so the gas-giant planet was never visible from them.

Not a perfect fit for my needs, you understand, but, in this sterile and bland universe, the best I had been able to find.

Before the arrival of the first ark, with the blue-green algae, the moon's atmosphere was heavy in carbon dioxide and water vapor, with almost no free oxygen. The algae did its work, and subsequent arks created soil by blasting mountains from orbit, and transplanted mosses and lichens and mushrooms and trees and those newcomers to the Crucible's botanic riches, flowering plants and the first proto-grasses. Eventually the air hummed with insects. Frogs, salamanders, lizards, snakes, and turtles were soon established. The world-spanning ocean teemed with plankton and seaweed and fish and ammonites.

It took only a few short years for these creatures to overrun the world, and, at last, the final arks began to arrive, bringing dinosaurs, pterosaurs, mosasaurs, plesiosaurs, and birds.

Their new world was ready for them, and the Jijaki began to let them loose.

Chapter 25

The Temple of Lubal

The hunters of Capital City claimed to be the most efficient killers in all of Land. But they knew that wasn't true. Not really. The most efficient killer in all of Land was the blackdeath. From snout to tip of its tail, the length of six middle-aged Quintaglios. Its hind legs, which pounded the ground like pillars when it charged, were taller than the oldest adult. Each leg ended in a three-toed foot, with claws that would slice through the thickest hide the way a stone drops through water.

The head bulged with bunched jaw muscles—a blackdeath could chomp through iron bars. Its teeth were like the teeth of a Quintaglio, but magnified many times in size. The longest were a handspan from gum to tip, with serrated edges. Discarded ones were prized tools used by leather workers.

A blackdeath's skin was indeed solid black, darker than the darkest night, accented only by the white flashes of claw and teeth and the deep bloody red of the inside of the mouth. The hide was pebbly and rough. A row of tiny projections ran down the monster's back, right to the tip of the tail, giving its profile a ragged stair-step edge.

Its eyes were likewise black, like Quintaglio eyes, pools of ink amidst the dull ebony of the head, visible only in the way the sun glinted off them. The neck was dexterous, powerful. On the males, a coal-dark dewlap sack hung against the throat. Blackdeath breath was stomach-turning, acrid, like rotted meat.

If there was anything puny about a blackdeath, it was the forearms, tiny and delicate, with two small curving claws. The creature didn't use them much. It killed with its teeth, tore flesh from bone with its mouth.

All in all, not the sort of creature one normally likes to run into. But this day, under imperial hunt leader Lub-Galpook, a large pack had departed Capital City specifically to hunt down a blackdeath. No neophytes were allowed on this expedition; Galpook had brought with her only the most experienced hunters. Galpook herself, daughter of Afsan, whom some still called The One, had much of the same skill on the hunt that had made her father so famous.

Blackdeaths were rare, and even more territorial than Quintaglios. Hundreds of days could go by without one being sighted anywhere near the Capital. Galpook had selected her team dekadays ago, and they had been training together regularly, waiting, waiting.

And then, finally, a merchant caravan had lumbered into town saying that they'd seen a blackdeath in the distance as they'd passed the ruins of the Temple of Lubal on the far side of the Ch'mar volcanoes.

Galpook assembled her team immediately. A creature the size of a blackdeath could travel many kilopaces in a day. Their best hope would be that the animal had eaten recently and would therefore be gorged and torpid after the kill. (Indeed, one of Galpook's hunters had to drop out of the pack, for he himself was torpid following a large meal.)

The quickest way to get to the Temple of Lubal would be atop runningbeasts, but the pack had too much equipment to carry. Such a hunt had only rarely been mounted. Not only was it considered folly to go up against a blackdeath, but no Quintaglio could bring one down without the aid of tools, and the sacred scrolls banned both the eating of food that had been felled with implements and the killing of animals that were not going to be eaten—taken together, strictures that seemed to make blackdeath hunting an impossible proposition.

But today's hunt was different. Galpook wanted to take a blackdeath *alive*.

The pack's equipment was loaded onto long wagons, and these were pulled by bossnosed hornfaces. *Hornface* was a misnomer, really, since these four-footed creatures, although in all other ways resembling that class of animals, had no facial horns. Rather, they had a thick boss, a knob-like protuberance, on the ends of their snouts. Great shields of bone still protected their necks, and their sharp beaks could inflict nasty bites, but without horns there was no chance that they could kill the blackdeath. Galpook was more than willing to sacrifice a few domesticated beasts in order to bring down the mighty hunter. In fact, as her final task before departing, she had had to sacrifice a small shovelmouth.

The beast, a juvenile not much bigger than Galpook herself, was let out of the stockyards. It ambled out stupidly on all fours, then tipped back on its thick, flattened tail to sniff the air. On its head was a semicircular crest of bone. Its face was long and drawn-out, ending in a flat, toothless prow. The thing's flatulence, like that of many herbivores, was constant, and the thick methane smell made Galpook woozy.

She walked over to the creature, patted its rough gray hide, and, in one fluid motion, moved beneath the beast and closed her jaws in a swift chomp on the underside of its neck.

As it died, the shoveler let out a massive scream, pumped through its head crest, reverberating, the sound almost deafening Galpook. Blood poured as though through a sluice. The taste of blood helped to heighten Galpook's senses. She thought in passing that perhaps such a kill might be a good prelude to future hunts.

Then she and her assistant set to work practicing a skill she'd learned from her father's companion, Cadool: butchery. With long, sharp knives they flayed the beast, removing its skin from the base of the neck to the tip of the tail in one neat, thick, fat-layered sheet, gray on the outside, blue, white, red, and yellow with membranes, connective tissue, blood, and fat on the inside. The ground was soaked, a mud of blood and dirt squishing underfoot. The skin was carried quickly to one of the equipment carts. Other carts were already loaded, including one with a massive spherical object covered by a sheet of leather.

Egglings—some fifty or sixty, for none had been culled from the most recent hatchings—had been brought by their creche master to watch the great hunting pack depart. Galpook motioned for them to come close and eat of the shovelmouth. Timidly, they did so, waddling up to its now-hideless carcass. "Go ahead," said Galpook. "Dig in." First one, then another, then, finally, all of them set to work on the corpse. Galpook always found it cute, watching little children claw and tear at massive bones, trying to get their muzzles around, say, a thick femur. She clicked her teeth in satisfaction, then walked over to the caravan. Using the foothold pockets hanging from the saddle—designed to prevent her toe-claws from piercing the bossnosed brute's hide—she scrambled up into her seat, and with a loud cry of *"Latark!"* urged her beast into motion.

Although a hornface could easily accommodate four large riders, Galpook's primary group consisted of ten animals with but one rider each. They headed off in single file to the west. The sun, a fierce white point, was about halfway up the purple sky. Wisps of white cloud were visible, as were three pale daytime moons, two crescent and one almost full.

Off in the distance, Galpook thought she saw a giant wingfinger, rising and falling in the sky. Such giants mostly fed on fish and aquatic lizards, but there were a few who would simply follow a blackdeath for days, waiting for it to make a kill, knowing that even the most famished of the dark horrors would leave huge amounts of meat on a carcass. Perhaps this one, far away, was indeed following the blackdeath Galpook and her team were now pursuing.

Like shovelmouths, lumbering hornfaces were also known for their pungent flatulence. Galpook, in the lead, was taking the full brunt of the excesses of ten beasts, for the steady daytime wind was blowing from behind. Conversely, her own pheromones—Galpook had been named hunt leader because she was one of those rare females who were in perpetual heat—were being blown ahead of the pack, instead of back on the hunters. It was too bad: exposure to such smells honed the senses.

The Ch'mar peaks made a ragged line ahead, like torn paper. Galpook had seen drawings of how they had looked before the great eruption of sixteen kilodays ago, but this is how she'd always known them: the cone of the leftmost caved in on one side, one of the mountains in the middle half again the height it had once been, a third burst open like a puckered sore.

Galpook didn't really like riding. The constant up-and-down heaving of the hornface's flanks was uncomfortable. But she needed to save her strength for what was ahead. She looked over her shoulder. Behind her, nine more hornfaces lumbered along, each with a Quintaglio rider. Four of the brutes hauled wagons. And behind them, mostly on foot, the secondary team.

The sun was rising with not-quite-visible speed. Insects buzzed. The hunting party continued on. The Ch'mar peaks grew closer, closer still, until at last they loomed before the caravan, black and gray bulks, their stony perfection marred by some scraggly vegetation here and there. At intervals, little waterfalls trickled down the tortuous rock faces, black sands accumulating around the bases of the mountains. The pounding of the hornfaces' round feet kicked up gray clouds of rock dust. The great wingfinger Galpook had spotted earlier continued to glide high above in vast, leisurely circles. Occasionally it cut loose its call, a high-pitched keening that also seemed to waft on the hot currents of air.

Night fell. They continued on. As they passed the foothills, early the next day, the members of the secondary team stopped, waiting until they were needed, but Galpook's primary team forged ahead. At last they came to the ruins of the Temple of Lubal, one of the five original hunters.

Much damage had been done to the temple grounds in the last great series of landquakes, sixteen kilodays ago. Dybo's mother, Lends, had been contemplating ordering excavations here shortly before her death, but the latest lava flows had plugged up the ruins so severely that no practical digging was possible, and Dybo had abandoned the idea. There was a smooth gray plain of stone, looking like a calm lake on a leaden morn, stretching out before them. The tops of buildings poked through, like half-sunk ships, but they were strangely twisted, as if in the heat of the eruption they had partially melted, flowing into malformed shapes. Of the Spires of the Original Five, representing the upward-stretched fingers of the Hand of God from which Lubal, Katoon, Belbar, Mekt, and Hoog had sprung, only two were still intact, poking like lances out of the basalt plain. The other three had tumbled, breaking into the tapering stone disks from which they'd been assembled, like chains of vertebrae half-caught in the volcanic rock.

Everything was still, frozen in congealed lava, a tableau, the aftermath of the volcanic fury that once had come close to destroying the Capital. From here, three days ago, a blackdeath had been sighted. But where was the beast now? Where?

Galpook looked up. The center point of the wingfinger's circular gliding was almost directly overhead. If it had been following the blackdeath, then that creature must be nearby. But perhaps the giant flyer had given up on the blackdeath, and had decided instead that the hunting party itself represented the most likely source of its next meal. Galpook wondered idly what defense she'd employ against the beast should it swoop down upon her, its great hairy wings flapping, its long, pointed prow snapping open and closed.

Galpook swung slowly off the shoulders of her bossnosed mount and lowered herself to the ground. Her toeclaws ticked against the gray basalt, but the underside of her tail, callused though it was, slid smoothly over the flat, dry rock. She walked back to the first of the hornfaces that was pulling a wagon and motioned for her assistant, Foss, who was riding that creature, to help her. He slid down to the ground and came over to join Galpook. Together, they clambered into the wagon and uncovered the device Gan-Pradak, the chief palace engineer, had built for them. At its heart was the skull of a tube-crested shovelmouth, glaring white in the sun, which was now well past the zenith. The skull, including the giant backward-pointing crest, was longer than Galpook's arm span. The engineer had plugged the pre-orbital fenestrae and eye sockets with clay and had attached a great bellows supported by a wooden brace to the back of the skull.

Galpook and Foss grabbed the upper arm of the bellows and pulled down with all their weight. The bellows pumped air into the crest and a great thundering noise emanated from the skull's nostril holes. Galpook and Foss pumped the bellows again and again. The other hunters covered their ears and the hornfaces made low sounds of pain. After ten repetitions, they were tired and stopped, but for several moments the ersatz shovelmouth call continued to echo off the mountainsides. Galpook lifted her tail to dissipate heat; Foss's dewlap waggled in the breeze.

The ruse was working on the wingfinger, at least. It had dropped to a much lower altitude, evidently assuming the repetitious bellowing signified a shovelmouth in great distress.

Having recuperated, Foss and Galpook operated the bellows again, pumping air through the shoveler's skull, forcing out the great cries the skull's original owner had once made in life. Again and again and—

There it was.

Lumbering around from the south.

Blackdeath.

It stood there, perfectly framed between the two intact hunters' spires, its whole body so dark that it looked like a silhouette against the purple sky even though it was fully lit.

Galpook heard Foss suck in his breath.

The monster stood, head cocked, eyeing the scene before it. It seemed confused, perhaps indeed having expected a shovelmouth. But these puny Quintaglios probably looked like tasty morsels, and the bossnosed hornfaces were surely easy pickings. Perhaps the same thought occurred to the bossnoses themselves, for they immediately started jostling each other. Galpook motioned to the riders, and they touched the beasts behind the neck frills in ways meant to calm them.

Of course, all that presupposed that the blackdeath was hungry—which perhaps it was not. The monster tilted its head back and forth, appraising, it seemed, each member of the hunting party, but then after a few beats, it half turned as if to go, as if the Quintaglios and their mounts didn't sufficiently amuse it.

Galpook leaned back on her tail and yelled.

It was a loud, long shriek, much higher pitched and much sharper than the reverberating call made by the shovelmouth skull. That did the trick: the blackdeath turned back to face Galpook, staring down at her. Without looking back, Galpook held up her hands, two fingers extended on each, to show in the hunter's sign language that she wanted half her team deployed. She then spread her arms wide, and the four hunters represented by those four stretched-out fingers spread out in a line, with Galpook in the center.

Galpook marveled at how much the great black monster looked like a Quintaglio. Oh, the color was all wrong, of course, and the muzzle sloped back into the head, instead of the head bulging up into an expanded braincase. Further, the arms were tiny in comparison to the body (although in real terms about the same size as Galpook's own), and they terminated in two tiny fingers instead of five. The eyes, all but invisible against the midnight skin, were proportionately smaller than those of Quintaglios, although the monster's did indeed face forward in overlapping fields of vision. But the overall appearance and proportions of the blackdeath were not that much different from those of Galpook herself. That made sense to her, for in both creatures had not God designed efficient hunters?

The blackdeath still hadn't charged. It did indeed seem that it wasn't hungry—but, then, why had it come at the fake call of a shovelmouth? Or perhaps it had been craving shovelmouth in particular: a hunter so powerful could certainly be picky about what it wished to eat.

The monster was still some fifty paces away. Behind her, Galpook could hear the remaining hunters speaking softly in soothing tones to their hornface mounts. She turned and motioned to them to go to work on the bait. They scrambled up onto one of the wagons and went under the sheets of leather, out of view. It was doubtless stifling under there.

Galpook started walking slowly, brazenly, toward the blackdeath. With a gesture of her hand, she had the pair of hunters on either side of her begin to do the same. Would the stupid beast never charge?

There were now but thirty paces between the Quintaglios and the black behemoth. It galled Galpook that the blackdeath was content just to watch her approach, didn't think her worthy of any response. Closer she continued, and closer still, but the beast seemed indifferent to her presence. Indeed, its eyes, so hard to make out against the ebony hide, perhaps weren't even looking at her. She was near enough now to see the blackdeath's torso expanding and contracting with each breath. The sun was sliding down behind the beast now, and its black bulk was hard to distinguish from the shadow it was casting on the gray basalt plain in front of it.

In frustration, Galpook clapped her hands together, but the report was soon gone on the breeze. She bent low and picked up a rock, whether a piece of volcanic ejecta or a rounded bit from the ruined temple, she couldn't tell. She heaved it at the blackdeath, and it arced through the air, bouncing off its belly. The creature tipped its muzzle down, as if puzzled, then lightly rubbed the spot where the stone had hit with its tiny left forearm.

She was now a mere twenty paces from the huge creature. It loomed up in front of her, a dark mountain like a dormant volcano. If only it would erupt . . .

Another shadow moved across the scene, and Galpook looked up. Low in the sky, directly overhead, was the giant wingfinger, its long snake-like neck weaving slightly as it glided by.

Galpook turned around briefly and spread her arms in a gesture of frustration. She saw that all five of the remaining primary hunters were out in plain sight now, meaning the work beneath the leather sheets had been completed. She decided to take yet another step forward, in case, perhaps, the blackdeath had not yet felt that its territory had been challenged. She brought her foot down, toeclaws clicking lightly against the basalt, and then—

—the beast charging—

—the land shaking—

It shouldered its way through the two intact hunters' spires, and, as its massive hips scraped past, the one on the right tottered and split along the lines where its constituent segments had been joined thousands of kilodays ago. It fell to the ground, crashing apart, shards of stone flying up in a volley, and a great gray cloud of dust rising into the sky. The hunters farthest to Galpook's left and right ran in semicircular paths toward the beast, while Galpook herself faced the creature, running backward, taking care not to trip over her own tail, clapping her palms together to keep the monster's attention.

But in a flash, the blackdeath was almost upon her, its great legs having covered the distance separating them with two massive strides. Galpook turned tail and ran as fast as she could toward the caravan. The other hunters were ready. The two who earlier had gone under the leather sheet on one of the wagons now pulled that sheet back to reveal the prize: the flayed shovelmouth hide, inside out, still somewhat bloody and now redolent in the heat, wrapped over a great ball, the ball's yellowish-white substance visible here and there through gaps in the hide. The sphere came up to the shoulders of the Quintaglio standing nearest to it. The flayed skin was held onto the ball by its limbs and tail, which had been tied together in knots, making it look like a tight-fitting garment.

The bossnosed hornfaces panicked—as well they should—at the sight of the barreling blackdeath. Their harnesses had been undone, and the hunters let them go. But the other Quintaglios copied Galpook's actions, jumping up and down, whooping and clapping to keep the black killer's attention. They all moved behind the wagon containing the great ball, interposing it between themselves and the charging predator.

The blackdeath bent low, its head barely clearing the ground, its massive jaws snapping together with a sound like cracking thunder. Galpook was only just managing to stay out of the creature's reach.

The jaws snapped again.

Galpook managed to scramble through some ruins that the giant would have to negotiate around and thus renewed her lead.

The wooden wagon holding the great ball was only a couple of body-lengths away now. Galpook leapt up onto the wagon, its planks creaking in protest under her impact. The smell of shovelmouth hide was strong, and the wooden boards were gummy with old blood. Galpook dug in her footclaws to hold her balance, but she tumbled forward, slamming prone against the wood.

Pain sliced through her and thunder rang in her ears. She dared not halt even to look back, but it was clear to her that the blackdeath's jaws had closed on her tail, nipping off the last couple of hand spans of it. She literally leapt up from the position she had fallen in and sailed over the far side of the wagon, where most of the other Quintaglios were.

The bossnoses were scattered now. Two had gone clear into a ragged copse of trees, others were cowering behind the parts of ruined buildings that poked up from the vast flat basalt plain.

The blackdeath let out a loud sticky roar, and, the final indignity, Galpook saw it spit aside as not worth swallowing the hunk it had taken out of her tail. Between them and it lay the wagon, with the giant ball covered with glistening hide. The inside of the blackdeath's mouth, flashing red with flesh and white with teeth, seemed almost to float disembodied in the black space made by its massive form. Galpook made a sharp gesture with her hands, and the others froze, save for Foss, whose tail was swishing back and forth in unconcealed fear.

The blackdeath was close enough that Galpook could feel the hot wind of its breath. It tipped its head to one side; it could clearly smell the hide of the shovelmouth.

The situation could not hold for long. Even a creature as dumb as the blackdeath would soon realize that it could simply walk around the caravan of wagons to get at the hunters—or, for that matter, could burst through the caravan, crushing the vehicles as it went. It brought its muzzle in low to sniff the ball, then nudged the skin, its face coming away freckled with dried blood.

Galpook nodded slightly to a hunter on her right. He swiftly brought his own jaws together on a thick rope. The cord snapped, and the floor of the wagon's carriage compartment, spring loaded from beneath and hinged along the side facing the blackdeath, shot up with a *whoomp*, tossing the giant ball into the air, hitting the blackdeath in the throat. It bounced off and fell to the ground.

The blackdeath was outraged. Its maw split wide, wider still, to its maximum extent, showing bluish membranes at the corners and massive white curved teeth, teeth that were to daggers what boulders were to pebbles. The stench of the creature's openmouthed exhalations washed over everyone, and then, and then, and then—

—the blackdeath chomped down on the bloody giant ball, teeth slicing the hide with ease, sinking and sinking and sinking into the soft material of the sphere, a collection of gums and saps and rubber gathered from hundreds of trees and plants, glue-like, adhesive. The giant attempted to roar, but its teeth were firmly lodged in the ball. Its tiny hands worked in a frenzy, but could not grab the sphere firmly enough to dislodge it. The more the massive jaws worked, the more firmly they became mired.

"Now!" shouted Galpook, negotiating her way around the wagons. The hunters she'd originally called upon burst toward the blackdeath's rear and immediately leapt on the beast's back. Galpook followed suit. There were six, now seven, now eight, now ten Quintaglios leaping onto the blackdeath's spine, pummeling it with clenched fists, trying to drive the beast to its knees. The giant humped its backbone, trying to buck the Quintaglios, and one indeed did go flying, ending up lying dazed some distance away. But after a moment she got back to her feet and leapt again onto the back of the blackdeath. The giant staggered under the weight of ten adult Quintaglios. It moved in broad circles, stooped from the waist. The hunters continued to ride it, the setting sun glaring into their eyes each time the beast swung around. The blackdeath tottered, lurched, its torso heaving raggedly.

Its head swung left and right, but the great sticky ball in its mouth was vexing it more than the members of the hunting pack, for it interfered with the beast's breathing and was depriving it of its best weapon. At last it tipped forward, bringing its right leg up, in hopes of using footclaws to clear away the gunky sphere. Galpook and her team slammed their bodies against the great blackdeath in unison, and, at last, it flopped to the ground, a cloud of dust choking them all as it hit.

The secondary team now swarmed in from its hiding place in the foothills, some fifty Quintaglio engineers and builders, a vast green tide flowing over the ruins of the temple, brandishing block and tackle. They threw nets laced with interlocking hooks that came together into a continuous web, half covering the monster.

One of the Quintaglios forgot that the blackdeath's arm was puny only in comparison to its body, and Galpook watched in horror as the limb swung out, opening up the belly of a male engineer, his guts spilling like a sacrifice onto the stones of the Temple of Lubal.

But the weight of the rest of the Quintaglios was enough to keep the blackdeath from regaining its feet. The Quintaglios were risking a territorial frenzy of their own, but naked fear of the giant hunter was enough to keep that in check for a short time. Soon the blackdeath was trussed up, its legs bound, thick leather cord wrapped around its arms and tail.

Galpook herself stood in front of the beast's muzzle: a blocky black shape, warty this close up, the size of Galpook's own torso. She signaled for a pair of gloves to be brought to her, and when they arrived she put them on. They had holes at the fingertips allowing her claws to poke through.

Terrified, she furtively brought her hands in toward the creature's face, carefully pulling on the rounded edge of the sticky sap, which had oozed up and around the tip of the muzzle. She drew the sap away from the blackdeath's giant, flaring nostrils, ensuring that it could breathe well for the long trip back to Capital City. The thing's great black eyes stared at Galpook, and it made snorting sounds around the sticky gum.

Although it took well into the night, illuminated by five bright, dancing moons, the blackdeath was eventually transferred onto a massive cart. Galpook's people were able to round up three of their bossnoses to pull the cart; the others were long gone.

Most of the secondary team had to disperse as soon as they were no longer needed, for such prolonged close contact was putting nerves on edge. Many went off with some of Galpook's hunters to try their hand at nocturnal tracking. Others simply chose their own paths back to the Capital.

In the light of the semi-ten of moons, Galpook walked slowly beside the captured killer, its mountainous hide heaving as it breathed.

She did not envy Dybo and the others. Not at all.

Chapter 26

My time sense is malleable. If I scatter myself widely, signals between parts of myself take longer to travel. The delays are completely undetectable to me, of course. It simply seems as though the external universe has speeded up, since my senses are sampling it less frequently. Likewise, if I collapse myself into a smaller area, my thoughts are processed more quickly, and I see the external universe move by at a slower rate.

I extruded a portion of my presence into the outer periphery of the Crucible system's cometary halo, about one-fifth of a Crucible light-year from its sun. Mustering my gravitational influence, I nudged a cometary nucleus. It began to fall toward the inner solar system.

The pace was indolent. It took 350,000 Crucible years for the comet to traverse the distance to the ninth planet's orbit (that moon of the eighth planet had indeed broken free by now, as I'd thought it might). I spread myself thin, letting the years pass quickly.

A short time into that long span, a sad although not unpredictable thing happened. The Jijaki, my only companions in a vast and empty universe, discovered energy sources they'd never dreamed of before. A war broke out. I called to them, begging them to stop, but a crazed individual in the principal language group launched a massive attack against those speaking a less common tongue, and, despite my entreaties from the sky, in a very short time the Jijaki had destroyed themselves, leveling their home world and their colonies. I mourn them to this day.

From the orbit of the ninth planet, it would only take twenty-six years for the comet nucleus to reach the Crucible. By now, the comet was moving at a speed of about five kilometers per second. I contracted myself, slowing the apparent pace of time.

With only forty percent of a single year left until the impact, the comet—now whipping along at eighteen kilometers per second—passed through the system's asteroid belt.

It crossed the orbit of the fourth planet. Just nine percent of a year until impact. The reptiles and mammals on the Crucible doubtless saw it in the night sky, for its head now glowed and a diaphanous tail stretched behind it.

I contracted, partly to savor every detail, partly to concentrate my meager gravitational influence to effect the required course corrections. The comet passed the orbit of the Crucible's moon. Its speed was now thirty kilometers per second. Time to impact: one-eighth of one day.

And then, and then, and then . . .

Traveling at sixty-seven kilometers per second, it drilled through the Crucible's atmosphere in less than two seconds, leaving a vacuum hole behind it.

On impact, a lethal shock wave spread for twelve hundred kilometers from the crash site. The comet and much of the target material vaporized completely, electron shells stripped off to form a super-heated plasma. Much of it blew out the hole in the atmosphere, and, in a fraction of a day, enveloped the world above the stratosphere. The planet was plunged into darkness.

In the atmosphere, nitrogen ignited, leading to strong nitric-acid rains.

Forest fires raged across all the continents.

Plant life died on land; photosynthetic plankton expired throughout the seas.

The food chains collapsed.

And, just as I had planned, in a very short time every land animal massing over twenty-five kilograms died, including every single one of the dinosaurs.

The way was paved on the Crucible for the mammals.

Capital City: Office of the Undertaker

Gathgol was used to solitude. After all, he was an undertaker.

People didn't fear death—not exactly—but neither did they like to contemplate it. Being undertaker was a pretty good job. There were only seven thousand Quintaglios in all of Capital province, fully half of them here in Capital City. Gathgol's services were rarely called for, although he did travel to wherever a death had occurred. More often than not, a death would happen on the hunt—a pack had foolishly gone after a meat eater instead of a herbivore, or attacked a hornface from the front instead of the rear. In those cases, assuming the surviving hunters had been successful, Gathgol would get to dine on fresh meat before he bundled up the body for the trip to Prath.

These days, though, Gathgol was not getting much solitude. Since the murder of Haldan, he had had many visitors to his small establishment in the holy quarter of town. Today, Sal-Afsan himself had come, along with his assistant, the lanky Pal-Cadool.

"I believe we can determine several things about the person who did the killing," said Afsan without preamble. He groped for a stool. "For instance, to cut Haldan's neck at the angle he or she did, he or she would have to be of a certain height. Isn't that right, Gathgol?"

There was no response.

"Gathgol? Are you still here?"

The undertaker found his voice. "Forgive me, Sal-Afsan. Yes, I'm still here. I'm sorry, it's just I'm flabbergasted that a savant such as yourself would ask questions of me."

Afsan waved a hand in the direction Gathgol's voice had come from. "You are the expert in matters of death, Gathgol. I am no savant in this area."

"Yes. No. I mean—"

Afsan held up his palm. "Just answer the question as if it were posed by a child, a student. And call me 'Afsan,' please. The formal name is just adding to your discomfort, I'm sure."

"'Afsan.' But that's what your intimates call you."

"Some of them call me 'fathead,'" said Afsan, with a disarming wrinkle of his muzzle, "but the ones who like me call me 'Afsan,' yes."

"Afsan," said Gathgol, trying the name on for size. Then, again, "Afsan." There was wonder in Gathgol's voice; evidently the undertaker had never expected such informality.

"Yes, Gathgol. Now, if you could perhaps answer my question?"

"I'm sorry. Of course. No one could do this while balancing on tippy-toe. Assuming the mirror was held like this—"

"I can't see you, Gathgol. Please describe what you mean."

"Sorry. I assume the mirror was held in both hands, outstretched. Doubtless the murderer was holding it by the intact part of the wooden frame, one hand on either side. The mirror was a heavy piece, and one hand would have been inadequate to steady it. The murderer must have lifted it over Haldan's head, the broken, sharp edge facing in, then brought it down below her muzzle and sliced up into the neck. To do all that, and carve at the angle that was used, the murderer would have to be at least one hundred and eighty centipaces tall."

"At least sixteen kilodays old, then."

"Yes, although perhaps a kiloday younger if a female. Don't put too much credence on that, though—these are rough estimates."

"Sixteen kilodays is pretty young."

"It's a pretty young age to die at, too," said Gathgol, but he instantly regretted speaking the observation out loud. "I'm sorry, forgive me. But that was Haldan's age, wasn't it?"

"Yes."

"A young adult," said Gathgol. "More than old enough to have taken the pilgrimage, though."

"Would someone that age have enough arm reach to bring the glass over Haldan's head?" asked Afsan.

"Arm reach varies from individual to individual, of course. Um, if you'll forgive my impudence of making an example of you, good Cadool, I'll point out that you have a much greater reach than is normal for one your age. Your limbs are quite long. Could a person one hundred eighty centipaces tall have managed it if he or she was of average build? Yes, but there wouldn't have been much clearance. Still, I found no cuts on the upper surface of Haldan's muzzle, so it must have happened cleanly. And, of course, the killer could have been taller than one hundred eighty centipaces, and, therefore, older. One-eighty is simply the bottom end of the range."

"Wouldn't Haldan have seen the glass passing in front of her eyes?" asked Afsan.

"Of course," said Gathgol. "And she probably swung her head around to look at the murderer. In fact, the swinging of her head, as much as the murderer's swiping, would have been what carved the neck open. But as she was dying, Haldan would have seen the person who killed her."

They were silent for a moment.

"What about the glass?" said Afsan.

"As I said before, it was a mirror. Not a great one—the optical qualities weren't all that good, judging by the fragments, and the metallic backing was uneven. Still, they don't make mirrors here in Capital City; too much basalt, not enough quartz-rich sand. One that big would have likely been made in Chu'toolar, but merchants distribute many of them each kiloday."

"There's no way to be more specific about where it came from?"

"Not really," said Gathgol. "At least, I can't think of a way. The frame is unadorned; just plain wood."

"What kind of wood?"

"It looks like *hamadaja* to me."

"Thunderbeast fodder," observed Afsan. "Found in all eight provinces."

"Exactly."

"What about a manufacturer's mark?"

"If there was one on the glass or the frame, it's not on any of the fragments we have."

"Perhaps Novato will have an idea," offered Cadool. He turned to Gathgol and added, "She used to deal with glassworkers in making her far-seers."

"Of course," said Gathgol. "The mirror was incomplete. A large hunk was used to do the killing, and after the deed was done it was dropped on the tabletop, and shattered, but the whole thing wasn't brought to Haldan's apartment."

"And no one heard the sound of breaking glass?" asked Afsan.

"The walls of Haldan's apartment were thick, of course," said Gathgol. "You couldn't have noise leaking from one apartment to the next without creating territorial tensions. Forgive me, but even your own calls for help wouldn't have been heard if you hadn't left the main door open behind you. And, of course, the crime took place during the middle of the day; very few people would have been home then, I'd warrant."

Afsan nodded. "Do you know how much of the mirror is missing?"

"Well, if it were just squared off, not that much. But most household mirrors are twice as tall as they are long. I'd suspect there's at least as much missing as we have here. The wooden frame was cut with a saw, but the glass was broken more roughly."

"All we have to do, then, is find a person who remembers seeing someone carrying a mirror that day," said Cadool. "Or better yet, half a mirror."

"I wish it were that simple," said Gathgol. "But we also found a leather drop-sheet in Haldan's apartment. It's creased and scored in such a way that it's pretty clear that the mirror was wrapped in it when brought into the apartment. The sight of someone carrying something wrapped in dark leather is not at all uncommon, I'm afraid. I'd doubt if anyone would have noticed."

"That is unfortunate," said Afsan.

They were all silent for a time.

"Afsan," said Gathgol at last, still sounding a bit uncomfortable with the short name.

"Yes?"

"Forgive me, but it seems the most likely method for finding the murderer is to figure out who would want to kill Haldan."

"Indeed," said Afsan. "But why would anyone kill another person?"

"You really don't know, do you?" said Gathgol.

"No, I don't."

"There have been murders in the past," said Gathgol. "They're not common, not at all, but they do happen. And the killer always has a reason."

"What sort of reason?"

"Well, in the old accounts, the reasons are usually pretty much the same. One kills another to possess something the other has, to prevent the other from revealing something the first one wants to remain secret, or out of fear."

"Fear?"

"Yes," said Gathgol. "One kills someone because one is afraid of that someone; afraid that that someone might kill or otherwise harm them."

Afsan's tail swished left and right. "Who could possibly fear my daughter?"

"Who indeed?" said Gathgol.

Chapter 27

The South Pole

Two shore boats were lowered from the side of the *Dasheter* and rowed in toward the ice. One carried Delplas, Biltog, and giant Var-Keenir; the other, Babnol, Spalton, and Toroca. Although Toroca wasn't actually going to take part in the hunt, he had decided to come along to observe whatever animal the others tracked down.

Between the first excursion onto the cap and this one, special anchors had been fashioned for the shore boats: metal hooks on long tethers that could be sunk into the ice. The ships were anchored and the six Quintaglios disembarked.

The temperature was about fourteen degrees below zero, according to Keenir. The snow covering the ice was hard and crisp. No one quite knew how snow was formed. It melted into what seemed to be ordinary water if you held it in your hands, but it was different in texture from the clear ice that underlay it, and, in places, it was loose enough to blow like powder in the air.

All six were wearing their stuffed leather jackets and snow pants, plus wide-soled shoes. Captain Keenir himself was going to lead the hunt. In the hunter's sign language, each finger represented a different member of the team. So that he could communicate with his pack, Keenir took off his left mitten and tossed it into a shore boat, bobbing in the chilled gray water.

They'd waited until late afternoon before coming here. The sun was low enough that the glare of its light off the snow wasn't quite blinding now.

Keenir gestured with his naked hand and the six of them began walking in from the shore. Where the ground was covered with snow, traction was reasonably good, although the going was slow because here their feet sank in. But where the ground was icy, walking was treacherous, and Toroca found his legs going out from underneath him on several occasions.

The white ground undulated—not so much so that one would refer to the terrain as having hills and valleys, but enough that whatever was up ahead was often invisible until they were almost upon it. The pack came across a hole in the ice, with perhaps a hundred divers lounging around it. The sight of the hole, with water visible through it, gave Toroca pause. There wasn't solid ground beneath them, just a layer of ice that varied wildly in thickness from place to place. Here it was perhaps thick enough to support the weight of divers, but possibly not strong enough in all places to hold up adult Quintaglios. Although the air itself wasn't devastatingly cold, the water was so icy as to be dangerous indeed. Two days before, Spalton had slipped when getting into a shore boat and fallen into the water. He'd turned white from head to tail; Toroca had thought he was going to die.

The divers had apparently learned something from their previous encounter with Quintaglios. They immediately began slipping into the water—it apparently wasn't too cold for them—their rounded silver bodies looking like drops of mercury running down a drain.

The wind had a bite to it. They continued on. Toroca could see the irritation in Keenir's movements, the impatience. There must be something worth killing, his body language seemed to scream. There must be.

And then they suddenly came upon it in a small valley: a giant creature flopped on the ice. It was unlike anything Toroca had ever seen: three or four times the size of a middle-aged Quintaglio, with a great rounded torso covered in white fur. Short legs were splayed out behind it, and it had very long, almost delicate arms resting against its sides. Its rounded head, ending in a fleshy muzzle, was lying on the ice.

The whistling wind was loud enough that the creature hadn't heard them approach, and Toroca found his sense of smell all but gone in the frozen air, the membranes inside his nostrils seemingly deadened by the cold. Perhaps the creature had the same handicap, for it seemed completely oblivious to the hunters, even though it was downwind of them.

In fact, for one brief moment, Toroca thought this was a corpse, but then, through the glare of reflected sunlight, he noticed its bone-colored torso expanding and contracting—quite rapidly, actually; a sure sign of an energetic, warm-blooded beast.

Keenir raised his left hand, all fingers splayed, to get the team's attention. He then used gestures to deploy the hunters in a line along the edge of a small ridge of ice: Babnol and Spalton to his left, Biltog and Delplas on his right. Toroca hung back, his eyes glued to the creature.

Keenir made two rapid chops with his hand, signaling the attack. All five of the hunters sprang into action. The creature had apparently been asleep, for it was slow in reacting, but soon its head lifted from the ground, and eyelids peeled back to reveal two golden forward-facing orbs above the fleshy muzzle.

The creature opened its mouth. There was something very unusual about its sharp teeth, but Toroca couldn't quite make it out from this distance. Babnol lost her footing and fell backward onto the icy incline leading down to the creature. Her limbs were flailing about, desperately trying to halt her slide toward the animal. It would take the others, moving very slowly as they negotiated their way down the incline, much, much longer to reach the beast.

Keenir sized up the situation in an instant and dived onto his belly, sliding headfirst down the icy grade. With a whoop, Spalton followed suit, and the three of them—giant Keenir, much younger Spalton, and the flailing Babnol—rushed toward the creature. Keenir, who had the muzzle guard on his snowsuit undone, opened his jaws wide. He clearly intended to arrive biting.

But then the creature rose up on its short hind legs, its torso bigger than Keenir's own barrel-chested frame, and then—

The whole scene became a strobing display for Toroca as his nictitating membranes batted up and down in wonder—

The creature's long, gangly forearms were *unfolding*, first one long segment and then another, the pieces having been folded back upon themselves like the rulers Toroca had seen architects use that hinged together for compact storage—

The long, narrow arms, almost insectile in their proportions, were now three times the length of the torso—

Keenir and Babnol and Spalton were still sliding toward it, only ten or so paces separating them from it—

The long arms swung down, in great sweeping movements, now touching the ground. At their tips where hands should have been were wide flat pads that seemed to sink only slightly into the snow—

And then the beast rose up, up, up into the air, its feet lifting off the ground to dangle freely beneath its torso, as the multi-jointed arms carried it higher and higher.

Keenir, heaviest of all the hunters, arrived first, skidding between the two articulated arms and continuing to slide along the ice past where the creature had been. The old mariner was flailing now, like Babnol, trying to halt his slide.

Babnol slid in next, seemingly about to crash into one of the insectile limbs—limbs that looked so delicate, Toroca expected them to shatter like icicles upon the impact—when the creature simply lifted its arm up, out of Babnol's path, balancing for a moment on a single lanky appendage, and she, too, skidded on, ending up in a heap with Keenir against a bank of snow.

The other hunters had now made it to the bottom, sliding Spalton having managed to halt his headlong rush, and Biltog and Delplas still on their feet. They were all staring up at this snow beast, jaws hanging open not to attack, but rather in amazement.

The creature's dangling legs then reached out, grasping the long arms about halfway down their length, the legs forming little diagonal struts, the feet, ending in five prehensile toes, wrapping around the thin arms, and then—

The creature began to walk, its short legs controlling the elongated arms, the arms acting like stilts, its strides giant, carrying it far away over the white, windswept landscape . . .

Keenir, clearly indignant at having ended up in a snowbank, rose to his feet and began to run after the beast, his tail, wrapped in a tapered extension of his snowsuit, flying out behind him, his footfalls making *kaflumping* sounds, clouds of white powder rising in his wake.

It took the others a few beats to react, but then they, too, took off after the rapidly receding arm-walker.

The chase seemed hopeless. Quintaglios were used to running on hard ground or over rocks, not on yielding snow or slippery ice. Indeed, they soon came to a fissure in the ground. The creature—a *stilt*, Toroca had dubbed it in his mind—had no trouble stepping over it, but Keenir, his longer legs putting him by far in the lead over the other hunters, hadn't seen it until he was almost upon it. He skidded, desperately trying to avoid slipping down it, to keep from breaking his neck on the hard blue ice far below, down in the crevice. That they no longer had to worry about the thinness of the ice was small consolation . . .

Keenir was slipping, slipping, slipping, his tail and right leg already hanging over the precipice. The stilt had stopped running, and, realizing that it was now apparently safe, turned to watch Keenir with interest. The captain was still sliding forward, his shod feet finding no purchase.

Toroca and the others had arrived now, but the ice on the perimeter of the crevice was too slippery to venture onto. All that was saving Keenir were the claws from his one ungloved hand, digging into the ice, white shavings piling up in trails behind them as he continued a slow, inexorable slide toward the opening.

Toroca came up right beside Babnol. "Give me your hand," he demanded, his words all but lost on the wind. She looked at him, not understanding. He reached out, seized her arm at the wrist, then, with a hand on her shoulder, pushed her to the ground, so that they were both lying in the snow. He then stretched toward Keenir.

Babnol finally caught the idea and gestured wildly for Delplas to take her other hand. Toroca looked back at Delplas, just standing there, and for the thousandth time cursed the incredible territoriality of his brethren, the stupid instinct that kept them from reaching out to each other, even when a life was at stake . . .

"Take Babnol's hand, you vegetable!" he shouted, the insult snapping Delplas out of her stupor. She threw off her own mitten and grabbed Babnol's hand firmly, then fell to the ice herself. Biltog and Spalton lined up behind her, at last completing the living chain.

Toroca's tail was close enough that Keenir could grab it, if the captain dared to lift his one naked hand off the ice, but that would have been suicide. Under sufficient stress, a tail would simply detach from the body, and Keenir, clutching the thing, would have sailed over the edge of the crevice to his death. Toroca spun his body around on the ice and reached out with his free arm. He was moving toward the old mariner at about the same rate as Keenir was slipping down toward the fissure. Babnol must have realized that, because, with a burst of strength, she pushed herself closer to the edge, dragging the other four Quintaglios behind her.

Close. Very close.

Got him!

Toroca's hand clasped Keenir's, and the six-person chain pulled itself back up away from the adamantine edge.

The stilt on the other side of the fissure must have still thought it was safe, for it stood there, its torso high atop long, thin arms, looking down on the Quintaglios, who were now whooping with joy at the rescue of Keenir.

But then Keenir saw that the fissure began only ten or so paces away from where he'd almost fallen down into it, and he took off again, running along its length until he could cross without difficulty to where the stilt was. The stilt realized it was in trouble again, and took off, its vast strides its ticket to safety—

Except that *another* fissure split the ice some twenty paces farther along, and this one yawned far too wide for the stilt to cross it, even with its long arms.

And so at last, Keenir was upon it, followed moments later by Babnol and Delplas and Spalton and Biltog, while Toroca averted his eyes from the kill, from the snapping of jaws, from the slicking of the ice with dark red blood . . .

But once the stilt was dead, Toroca bounded in toward it, the others scooping hunks of flesh, already stiffening in the cold, out of the corpse.

Delplas paused, tilted her head back, and bolted down the flesh she'd torn free. Shouting to be heard above the whipping wind, she called to Toroca, "Can't resist fresh meat after all, eh?"

"I don't want to eat it," Toroca called back. "I want to look at the arms."

Keenir stopped bolting long enough to shout, "Not much meat on those, Toroca. After what you did, you're entitled to the choicest hunks. Dig in!"

But Toroca ignored him, and instead brought his scalpel out of a pocket on his snowsuit, and slit the stilt's left arm along its entire length, exposing the bones within.

It was not an arm. Or, at least, the actual arm ended at the first articulation point. The rest of the incredibly long walking appendage was made of four super-elongated finger bones.

Toroca sagged down against the snow.

Finger bones!

He tried to crack one of the phalangeal bones open with his hands, but found he could not. At last he held the limb in place with his feet and pulled up with all his strength. The bone broke. It was mostly solid, but with a narrow hollow core that betrayed its origins, the central hollow packed with dense brown meat or marrow to give it further strength.

And the head? That fleshy muzzle? Babnol was now splitting the beast's skull open, looking for the hopefully tasty brain within. The muzzle was just an overlay on top of a horny sheath, and the teeth weren't teeth at all, just the ragged edges of that sheath: a making-do with what was available by a creature that had come from toothless stock.

Everyone reacted with surprise, and Keenir with delight, as Toroca, a look of disgust on his face, got up and dipped his muzzle into the thing's torso, tearing out a small hunk of flesh.

It tasted as he expected it would.

Just like a wingfinger.

Chapter 28

The Emperor headed into the palace dining hall, passing through the public areas, nodding acknowledgment at the senior advisors present, and entered the private rear section.

Much to his surprise, scrawny Afsan, no devotee of any dining establishment, was there.

"Ho, Afsan," said Dybo, lowering his weight onto a dayslab on the opposite side of the table. "It's good to see you."

"You won't think so when I tell you why I'm here," said Afsan.

"Oh?"

At that moment, a butcher came in, wearing a red smock. She was carrying a silver platter on which rested the leg of a juvenile shovelmouth.

Dybo looked up at her. "That's enough for Afsan, I'd warrant, but you'd best slay an adult for me."

Afsan inhaled deeply and turned his blind eyes up at the butcher. "It's as I requested?" he asked.

"Yes," she replied, sounding, to Dybo's ear, somewhat nervous.

"Then you are dismissed, Fetarb. You may spend the rest of the day in leisure activities."

She nodded quickly and scurried away.

"Wait a beat," said Dybo to Afsan. "What about me?"

"This is for you."

"It's hardly enough. And what will you eat?"

"This is for me, too. We're going to share it."

"Share *this*? It's barely a snack."

"It's more than enough for two, Dybo. From now on, until the battle, you will eat your meals with me, taking only as much as I do."

"I am the Emperor!"

"You are also, old friend, quite fat. We'll get you in shape for the battle yet, starting with putting you on a diet."

"You cannot give me orders," said Dybo.

Afsan spread his arms. "No, of course not. I am only an advisor. But I do strongly give you this advice. Eat less. You'll need to be fleet of foot if you are to survive."

Dybo eyed the leg suspiciously. "It's not very meaty."

"It will do just fine."

"But, Afsan, you are notorious for your thinness, for how little you eat. Couldn't I match the consumption of, say, Pal-Cadool, or Det-Bogkash?"

"They're both much older than you. I'm your age, I'm the same height as you. Come, I've been generous. Even half of this is a much bigger meal than I normally take."

"But what if I feel hungry later?"

"Perhaps you will. And you can eat as much as you like then."

"Ah, that's better."

"So long as you hunt it down and kill it yourself. A healthy chase through tall grass will do you good."

"Afsan, you are a hard taskmaster."

"No," said Afsan. "I'm simply your friend. And I want you to win."

Dybo grunted, then dipped his muzzle toward the meat.

Dybo spent three daytenths every second odd-day at court, lying on the ruling slab, with his chief aides seated on *katadu* benches to his left and right. Any citizen could make an appointment to see Dybo, this being one of Dybo's chief reforms, replacing the isolated and autocratic style of his mother and predecessor, Len-Lends.

Sometimes people came to appeal rulings made by the legal system. Dybo, of course, could overturn any judgment, and he had a reputation as something of a softy. On other occasions, scholars and inventors would come, looking for imperial support. Here, Dybo was more pragmatic: if the proposal would aid the exodus, even peripherally, its sponsor usually walked away with a document bearing Dybo's cartouche. Any other project had a tough time getting his interest, although occasionally he showered support on musicians, music having been the Emperor's first love. Dybo required no direct tribute, never having been a materialist. However, those who brought toys for the children in the creche were often favored.

Just now he was hearing the complaint of a young female who had traveled from Chu'toolar. She felt the profession selected for her was inappropriate. But the proceedings were interrupted by Withool, a junior page, bursting into the ruling room.

Dybo knew his staff would not disturb him without good cause. He looked expectantly at Withool.

"There's been another one," said the page. "Another murder."

"Where?" Dybo pushed off his ruling slab and stepped down from the pedestal.

"Again, in an apartment complex, this time by the Pakta tannery."

"Who was the victim?"

"Yabool, a mathematician and naturalist."

"Haldan's brother," said Dybo.

"Haldan's what?"

"Brother," said Dybo, irritated. "Male sibling."

"Oh. I thought—"

"How did it happen?"

"As before," said Withool, "Yabool's throat was slit, quite nastily, apparently by a broken mirror. Pieces of shattered mirror were found all around the body."

"I see," said Dybo.

"Someone should tell the newsriders," proffered one of Dybo's aides.

"Not yet."

"As you say, Your Luminance."

Dybo said, "There are others who should be informed directly. His supervisor, for instance."

"Of course," said Withool. "I'll attend to that."

"And his parents."

"I beg your pardon?"

"His parents, Afsan and Novato."

"Oh, he's one of *those*, was he?" said Withool. "Well, I'll attend to that, too, Emperor."

"No. I'll do it myself."

Withool bowed. "Surely the Emperor should be spared such a task."

"I said I'll do it." Dybo looked up at the statue of Lends standing on the far side of the room. "I'm the only one who understands what it's like to lose a member of your . . . family."

The *Dasheter*

The divers and stilts weren't the only vertebrates down here at the bottom of the world. Toroca and Babnol managed to collect many specimens as the days went on.

They were all different.

But they all had one thing in common.

They were all—every last one of them—based on the wingfinger body plan.

It was even-night; the night Toroca was supposed to be awake. But it was far, far too cold to go on deck after dark. He sat in his cabin, lamp spluttering, going over his notes and the intricate sketches he'd made.

Scooters had all but lost their wings. They shot around the ice surface, using their powerful hind feet to propel themselves.

Shawls were tall and thin and stood like trees rooted in the ice, wrapping their bodies in cloaks made of their thick rubbery wings.

Skimmers used their wings to glide over the ice. They never rose more than a tiny distance off its surface, but carried by the wind they managed to cover huge distances, their broad mouths hanging wide open, gulping down insects that hopped along the snow.

Lancers had only the incredibly elongated fingers, with no wing membranes attached. The final finger bone was tapered to a sharp point. In lightning movements, lancers used these to spear fish swimming near the surface. Toroca had even seen one lancer simultaneously spear separate fish on both its left and right fingers, then nibble the still thrashing meals off the skewers, alternating bites between them.

Anchors—so named because their beaks and skull crests gave them the appearance of a sailing ship's holdfast—had lost their arms altogether but still had the breastbones that betrayed their wingfinger affinities.

Wingfingers. Every single one.

How they got here was obvious . . .

. . . unless you thought about it.

After all, wingfingers could fly, so they'd simply come here from Land, perhaps thousands of kilodays ago.

Except.

Except that many of *these* wingfingers could not fly. Anchors had no wings; divers had flippers instead of wings; stilts and shawls and scooters had forelimbs useless for flight.

All right, then. They swam here from Land.

But the stilts couldn't do that; as far as Toroca could tell, they could barely swim at all. And, besides, if these creatures could swim that great distance, why did none of them ever come back *to* Land? Why was every one of these animals completely unknown?

They must have flown here.

They *must* have.

And then—

Changed.

Changed!

Toroca shook his head. Madness! An animal cannot change from one thing to another . . .

And yet. And yet. And yet.

Apparently they *had*.

It baffled him, but he *would* figure it out. He would.

He looked out the single porthole, patterns of frost crisscrossing its surface, the leather curtain folded back like a flying reptile's wing.

A new day was dawning.

Capital City

Dybo found himself making the hike out to Rockscape for the second time recently. It was a warm day, insects buzzing, wingfingers wheeling overhead, a silvery haze turning the sky almost blue. As he approached the arrayed boulders, Dybo's claws leapt out.

Afsan, Cadool, and even Gork were prone on the ground. For one horrible moment, Dybo thought that they, too, had been murdered, but at last Gork, ever vigilant, lifted its head and tasted the air with its forked tongue. Cadool awoke a moment later, with a yawn. He clamped the side of his muzzle to indicate silence, and walked with his loping gate to join the Emperor, several tens of paces from where Afsan lay.

"He's sleeping," whispered Cadool. "It's the first time in many days that he's slept so soundly."

Dybo bent his neck to look up at the lanky Cadool. "There's been another murder," he said simply.

Cadool's tail swished. "Who?"

"Yabool."

"I'll wake him," said Cadool.

"No, perhaps he should sleep. There's nothing he can do."

Cadool shook his head. "Forgive me, Your Luminance, but it's like the hunt. The quarry will get away if the trail grows cold. I know Afsan will be angry if he's not told at once."

It was not wise to be too close to one who was waking up. Standing where he was, Cadool shouted out, "Afsan!"

A threat, a challenge. Even from here, Dybo and Cadool could see Afsan's claws leap out. The savant lifted his head, opened his jaws to show sharp teeth. And then it passed. Claws slid back into their sheaths. "Cadool?"

"Afsan, Emperor Dy-Dybo is here. He needs to speak to you."

Afsan pushed up off the ground. Still slightly groggy, he leaned back on his tail for a moment to steady himself, then walked in the direction he'd thought Cadool's voice had come from. Normally, Afsan had impeccable hearing, but having just awoken he was heading at a tangent to the course he should have taken. Cadool and Dybo walked over to intercept him, although, of course, each came no closer than about five paces from the other.

"Ho, Afsan," said Dybo. "I cast a shadow in your presence."

"And I in yours. You need to see me?"

"Yes, my friend. Lean back on your tail, please."

Afsan did so, a stable tripod stance.

"Afsan, there's been another murder. Your son Yabool is dead."

Afsan did stagger visibly, but his tail held him upright. "Yabool . . . ," he said. "The same way?"

Dybo nodded. "The same."

"I must examine the place where it occurred."

"Of course," said Dybo. "Are you ready?"

"I'll never be ready," said Afsan softly. "But this must be done."

The three of them walked silently back to the city, Gork padding along behind.

The details differed, of course, but the overall picture was the same. Yabool had been lying on a dayslab, the angled piece of marble overhanging a worktable. The slab had supported his torso as he'd worked, but his neck and head had extended past the end of the stone pallet. His neck had been cut from the side, and a deluge of blood had completely covered the top of the desk. The mirror fragment was smaller this time, but although it had cracked, it was still in one piece, lying on the tabletop, fused to it by a crust of dried, flaking blood. A piece of wooden frame ran along two adjacent sides of the fragment. The wood, as before, looked like *hamadaja*.

Yabool had been killed some time ago—perhaps yesterday, perhaps even the day before. The crust of blood on the floor showed a couple of footprints, but they'd been badly distorted by the swishing of a tail through the mess.

On the way to Yabool's apartment, Afsan, Cadool, and Dybo had had to pass near Gathgol's establishment, so they had brought him along as well.

Gathgol used his claws to pry the mirror out of the crust of blood.

"We're in luck," he said, holding the mirror up to a lamp flame. "There is a maker's mark this time. 'Hoo-Noltith, Chu.' "

"Chu'toolar," said Afsan.

"That's right," said Gathgol. "As I'd suspected."

Cadool, Gathgol, and Dybo scoured the scene for further clues, while Afsan stood by, listening intently to their running commentaries.

"This one would be a lot harder to pull off than the last," said Gathgol.

"How do you mean?" said Afsan.

"Well, Haldan had been seated on a stool, facing a wall, her back to the room. It would not have been too difficult to approach her from the rear. But this dayslab is quite central in the room, and so Yabool would have had quite a wide field of view. Either he was very absorbed in what he was writing—his left middle claw is covered with ink, so that is doubtless what he was doing—or else his assailant approached with great stealth."

"What had Yabool been writing?" asked Afsan.

"I'm afraid we may never know," said Gathgol. "His piece of writing leather was completely covered with blood, and, as if that weren't bad enough, his pots of ink and solvent have been knocked over and spilled upon the sheet. He might have been quite intent on the work, but there's no way to tell."

"And if he was not intent, then the killer approached—"

"With stealth," said Gathgol. "You know, like a hunter."

"A hunter," repeated Afsan.

"That's right."

"I can't imagine a hunter committing murder," said Cadool. "The hunt purges feelings of violence and aggression."

"Usually," said Afsan, perhaps remembering his own few, spectacular hunts. He looked in the direction of Gathgol's voice. "A hunter, you say?"

Gathgol nodded. "It's a possibility."

"A hunter," Afsan said again, filing away the idea in a corner of his mind. "Any other possibilities?"

"Not that I can think of."

"He's—" began Cadool.

"Yes, I was lying," said Gathgol. "I'm sorry, it's just that, well, I'm afraid to mention this suggestion out loud." He looked nervously in the direction of Dybo, who was leaning back on his tail, listening intently.

"What you say will go no farther than this room," said Afsan, "and, believe me, I'm the last person who would punish someone for expressing an unpopular thought."

"Well," said Gathgol, "have you considered the possibility that the murderer might be a disgruntled bloodpriest?"

"No," said Afsan, "I have not. What makes you think that?"

"Well, forgive me," said Gathgol, "but, umm, I've heard the tale of how your eight children came to be allowed to live. The bloodpriests thought you were The One foretold by Lubal. Perhaps now, ah, some bloodpriest feels that judgment was a mistake, and a renegade may have tried to set the matter straight, so to speak."

"And kill my children?"

"It's a thought."

"A disgruntled bloodpriest," said Afsan, thinking. "But the current imperial bloodpriest is missing—"

"In the historical records, murderers often disappear," said Gathgol. "The imperial bloodpriest is Mek-Maliden, isn't it?"

"Yes," said Dybo from across the room. "But Maliden is out of town."

"Oh. You've sent him away on a mission, then?"

"No," said Dybo. "It's just that his bags are missing."

Gathgol nodded. "Forgive me, Your Luminance, but, ah, that doesn't necessarily mean he's left Capital City. Perhaps he only wants to give the *appearance* of having done so."

Dybo turned to Afsan. "Maliden is a criminal once already, in many people's eyes," he said, "if he in fact was responsible for a deception involving the hatching of myself and the other imperial egglings. If he's committed one crime, why not another?"

Afsan appeared to consider this. "Mek-Maliden," he said softly. "Perhaps." He looked at Gathgol. "Any other thoughts?"

"No," said the undertaker.

"Your muzzle . . . ," said Cadool.

"I cannot speak this one," said Gathgol.

"Come on," said Dybo. "Whatever it is, go ahead."

Gathgol shook his head.

"You have nothing to fear simply by stating an idea," said Afsan. "Speak up."

"I can't. Not with—"

"Not with what?" said Afsan. "Not with—not with the Emperor here, is that it?"

"You can say anything you like in front of me, Gathgol," said Dybo. "I give you leave to do so."

"But you will be angry . . ."

"Perhaps. But I will not punish you for your words."

"It's all right," said Afsan. "Tell us."

Gathgol swallowed. His tail swished back and forth. "Well, until your children came along, Afsan, The Family was the only group that knew who its relatives were."

"Yes."

"Forgive me, Your Luminance, but that was a very special privilege. Perhaps some member of The Family objected to the same privilege being accorded to someone else." He looked briefly at Dybo, then dropped his head.

"That's all right, undertaker," said Dybo. "It's a valid thought." The Emperor turned to face Cadool and Afsan. "I did not commit the murders," he said out loud, and turned his head from side to side so that all of them could see his muzzle. "What about those who are said to be my siblings?"

"They've been showing up for the challenge battle with the black-death," said Afsan. "Several have already arrived."

Dybo nodded. "They don't have to be here until the 666th day of this kiloday, but, yes, Dedprod and Spenress are already here."

"Spenress," said Afsan. "She's the apprentice governor from Chu'-toolar, isn't she?"

"Yes," said Dybo.

"And the mirror used for the killings came from Chu'toolar."

"Indeed," said Cadool. "But, of course, Chu'toolar is very close to Capital province, especially if she came by boat. It's not surprising that she's arrived early."

"None of the others are here yet?" said Afsan.

"Well, Rodlox, of course," said Dybo, "who started all this challenge nonsense."

"Yes," said Afsan. "He certainly has enough anger in him."

"And he has flouted our laws already in defying the Emperor," said Cadool.

"Yes," said Afsan. He was silent for a time. "First Haldan, then Yabool," he said.

"That suggests," said Gathgol slowly, "that, whoever the killer might be, your other children are perhaps at risk."

"I'll order imperial guards to accompany them," said Dybo.

Afsan nodded. "Thank you."

Cadool's tail swished. "It's all so insane."

"Yes," said Afsan. "Insane."

Chapter 29

She had come to his quarters—come of her own volition, come without him having to seek her out.

Unlike other Quintaglios, Toroca was never startled by the sounds of claws on a signaling plate, and the little ticking noises from outside his cabin door this morning were no exception. Still, his heart did leap slightly. There were so few possibilities of who it might be. One of the other surveyors, perhaps, yes. Maybe Keenir. Maybe Biltog.

Maybe Babnol.

He called out, *"Hahat dan"*—a little too eagerly, a little too loudly.

But it was she.

The door swung open, the squeaking hinges a counterpoint for the creaking of the ship's wooden hull. "Good morning, Toroca," she said.

"And good morning to you, Babnol. Did you sleep well?"

"No. I was up half the night, thinking."

"About?"

"About the creatures we've found here. The divers and shawls and stilts."

Toroca was beaming. "We're two of a kind, then, good Babnol. I have spent the last several nights—and days—thinking about the very same things." He gestured at the sketches and notes that covered his desk.

She came a pace into the room, turned, closed the door behind her, and leaned back on her tail. "They're all wingfingers," she said.

Toroca nodded.

"And yet—I'm not a savant, Toroca. Explain it to me. Why should they all be wingfingers? Why are there no other kinds of animal here?" It was fairly cramped in this room that used to be Afsan's quarters. Babnol had been standing as far away from Toroca as possible. Indeed, after a moment, she turned away, a common response to a feeling of crowding. She looked at the knotty planks making up the cabin wall.

"All right," said Toroca, "I'll try—but I'm not yet completely sure myself. Consider this: our world has one landmass, Land. It happens to be on the equator, which is the warmest part of the world. Most of the lifeforms that live there, regardless of whether they are warm-blooded or cold-blooded, have either scales or naked skin. In other words, next to no bodily insulation."

"Insulation?"

"An external covering to keep heat in or the cold out. Like the thick snowsuits we wear here. But, of course, we don't really need insulation back on Land. The climate there is always warm, and most of the warm-blooded animals are quite large."

"I'm not following you, Toroca."

"The larger you are, the less skin you have per unit volume. Since it's through the skin that an animal can lose heat, large size is a good thing to have if you are an uninsulated warm-blooded animal. Body volume increases with the cube; skin surface area increases with the square."

"You've lost me."

"Sorry." Toroca clicked his teeth. "I forget not everyone had my father for a teacher. The physics is not important; simply accept that large animals—and even we Quintaglios are large, compared to lizards and snakes—have less of a need for insulation. The mere fact of our bulk helps us keep a constant body temperature."

"All right."

"But wingfingers tend to be small. Yes, they may have huge wingspans, but the actual wingfinger torso is quite tiny. And wings, because they are almost all surface area and have practically no bulk, radiate heat at a great rate. Although wingfingers are warm-blooded, like us, they'd lose all their heat if they didn't have insulation."

"Fur!"

"Exactly. A wingfinger's fur helps it retain its body heat. Now, consider this. Here at the south pole, it is cold—"

"I'll say."

"Indeed, it's so cold that *no* amphibians or lizards or snakes are found here at all. The only cold-blooded animals are insects and fish in the waters. On the ice cap itself, there is not one single cold-blooded vertebrate. There cannot be, for cold-blooded vertebrates require heat from the sun, of which, as we've observed, there is precious little here."

"I get it!" said Babnol. "Wingfingers have both the means to get from Land to here—by flying—and they have their furry body coverings to keep them warm!"

"Exactly. *Only* wingfingers could survive here. No cold-blooded vertebrate has a chance. No walking vertebrate could get here, and, even if one could, without insulation, it would die from exposure. Of all the animals in the world, only wingfingers are suited for this place."

"But the creatures we've found here aren't simple wingfingers."

"No, they're not." Toroca gestured at the notes on his desk. "This is the part that I'm having difficulty with. The wingfingers that did fly here, no doubt countless kilodays ago—countless *years* ago—found an environment in which no other large animals lived. They had no predators here. Some were able to give up flying altogether and take up life on the ice surface. Others went further and learned to dive into the waters. What must have started out as standard flying wingfingers ended up as the wide range of animals we see here. Roles that would have been played by runningbeasts or blackdeaths back on Land were unfilled here on the southern ice. Wingfingers seized the opportunities and took over those vacant roles, becoming lords not only of the air but of the ground and the waters as well."

Babnol turned her head away from the wall and faced Toroca. Her teeth were clicking.

"Why are you amused?" asked Toroca.

"Well, it's a good story, my friend," she said. "But it can't be true. An animal cannot change from one thing into something else. What nonsense!"

"I am coming to believe that an animal *can* change," said Toroca.

"How? I've never seen an animal change. Well, yes, I've seen tadpoles change into frogs, and larvae into adult insects, but that's not the kind of change you're talking about."

"No, it's not."

"You're talking about changing completely, from one . . . one . . ."

"One species."

"From one species into another."

"That's right."

Babnol's teeth clicked again. "But how could that happen? A wingfinger can no more decide that it will grow swimming paddles than I can decide that I'll grow wings. A thing is what it is."

Toroca's voice was soft. "Forgive me, dear Babnol, but have you looked at yourself in a mirror?"

Babnol's tone suddenly grew as frosty as the air. "What's that supposed to mean?"

"I mean, you have a horn growing from your muzzle."

Defensive: "Yes. So?"

"Have you wondered how it got there?"

Babnol sighed. "Many times."

"It's a change, a novelty, something that's never before existed. You have a characteristic that your parents lacked."

"It was God's will," said Babnol, her muzzle, as usual, tilted haughtily up. "I do my best to accept it."

Toroca thought about telling her how fascinating, how appealing, how *attractive* the growth was, but was afraid of what her reaction might be. Instead: "Don't be angry, Babnol, but I think perhaps it has nothing to do with God. I have begun to suspect that such changes can occur *spontaneously*. Usually such a change would be of no value one way or another: your retention of the birthing horn is neither a hindrance nor a help to you. It just *is*. Sometimes, though, a change might be undesirable. For instance, your horn could have completely obscured your vision. That would have been a terrible disadvantage. On the other hand, rarely, a change might be advantageous. If your horn were longer and perhaps placed slightly differently, it might make a formidable hunting aid."

"It is just what it is," said Babnol, still defensive. "No more, no less. You are making me uncomfortable talking about my deformity." She turned back to face the wall.

Toroca instantly regretted using her as an example. "I'm sorry," he said, wanting to reach out, to touch her, to soothe her hurt. "Let's—let's talk only of wingfingers, then. Consider one that arrived here, but had a thicker coat of fur than its companions. It would have an advantage over them. Likewise, a wingfinger with thick stubby wings—perhaps of little use for flying—might find they made very serviceable swimming paddles."

Still facing the wall: "I suppose."

"So you can see that the creatures here might have arisen from normal wingfingers."

"Or," said Babnol, "perhaps God just made them this way from the start."

"But why on the body plan of a wingfinger?" asked Toroca.

"Why not?"

"Well, because it's not efficient."

Babnol's tone showed she was still upset. "Using a tried-and-true design seems efficient to me. Our shipwrights do that, for instance."

"But the wingfinger design is *not* efficient for anything *except* flying. Look at the paddles of a diver; they're not nearly as effective as, say, the fins of a fish."

Babnol had brought a hand up to cover her horn. "The handiwork of God is perfection—by definition."

"But the creatures here are *not* perfect," said Toroca. "It's in the imperfections, the making-do with what's available, that we see evidence for a mechanism of creating new species other than God's own hand."

Babnol turned now to face him, the ship swaying back and forth beneath her. "Changing from one thing to something else?" she said. "Toroca, all my life I've tried to fit in, despite this deformity." Her voice was edged like a hunter's claw. "And now you're saying it means I'm less of a Quintaglio than you are."

Toroca immediately rose to his feet. "No, I'm not saying that at all—" But it was too late.

Babnol stormed out the cabin door.

Capital City: The Hall of Worship

The new Hall of Worship was different from its predecessor. The old one had reflected Larsk's worldview. It was bisected by a channel of water, representing what was once thought to be a vast river down which the rocky island of Land floated, and its roof was a high dome, painted in roiling bands, representing the Face of God.

That Hall had been damaged beyond repair in the last great landquake. This one, at the order of Dybo, had been built with no reference to the outdated view of creation. It was vital that everyone accept and understand that the world was a water-covered moon, companion to a giant, gas-shrouded planet. Henceforth, Halls of Worship would not contradict that truth.

Fortunately there was much more to Quintaglio religion than just the relatively recent prophecies of Larsk. This new Hall resurrected much of the ancient imagery. Central was a giant sculpture of God Herself, a preLarskian rendition, looking every bit like a regal and serene Quintaglio. God's arms were gone, chewed off between the shoulder and the elbow.

The circular chamber had ten niches built into its perimeter, and each niche contained a sculpture of one of the ten original Quintaglios, hunters alternating with mates. No direct worship of the original five hunters was practiced here, but they, and the five males that came after them, were still revered as the first children of God, born from Her very fingers. The niches were just out of reach, for a channel of water ran around the circumference of the room. Ceremonies involving marching through water still figured prominently in Quintaglio worship, but the water was no longer thought of as a representation of the great mythical river.

Afsan entered through the secondary doorway, an arch outlined with polished agate tiles, between the niches holding the statue of the hunter Katoon and that of the first-crafter, Jostark.

"Det-Bogkash?" Afsan called into the chamber. The name echoed off the stone walls.

A moment later, from the far side of the circular room, Priest Bogkash appeared. He entered through a hidden doorway, sculpted to look like part of the ornate bas-relief that covered the curving walls, a portal to his inner sanctum nestled between the statues of Mekt, hunter and original bloodpriest, and Detoon the Righteous, first member of the clergy.

"Permission to enter your territory?" called Afsan.

"*Hahat dan*," said Bogkash, peering in Afsan's direction. "Is that you, Sal-Afsan? I can barely see you in this light."

"You still have me at an advantage," said Afsan, teeth clicking in forced good humor as he stepped farther into the room. "Yes, it's me."

Bogkash closed the gap between them, but only slightly—a gesture of peace that did not arouse territoriality. "It's rare to see the palace's chief savant at the Hall of Worship."

Afsan accepted the gibe stoically.

"You need perhaps some comforting?" offered Bogkash. "I heard, of course, about Haldan and Yabool. I didn't know them well, but I understand they were friends of yours."

"They were my children," said Afsan simply.

"So it is said. Frankly, I don't know what that means. I don't understand these matters at all. But I do know what it is to lose a friend, and I take it, child or not, that Haldan and Yabool were indeed your friends."

"Yes. Yes, they were."

"Then accept my condolences. I've been to Prath for Haldan, and plan to make it out there again to say a prayer over Yabool's body."

"That would be most welcome," said Afsan. "They had each taken both rites of passage, but, well, the circumstances of their deaths were not normal—"

"Oh, their acceptance into heaven is not in danger, Afsan, if that's what's worrying you."

"I'm pleased to hear it. But, no, that's not what's worrying me, not exactly."

"Well?" Bogkash said.

"I've come to ask you if you know anything about the disappearance of Mek-Maliden."

"Afsan, I am a priest in the order of Detoon the Righteous. Maliden is a bloodpriest in the order of Mekt. These are entirely different categories of the ministry."

"Maliden is *imperial* bloodpriest," said Afsan, "and you are Master of the Faith, and, therefore, primary priest to the Emperor. Surely you and Maliden must have interacted often and known each other well."

"Afsan, you were training to be an astrologer; that was a science. Do you therefore automatically know Pas-Harnal, a metallurgist who lives in this city? He is a scientist, too. All holy people no more make up a single community than do all savants."

"In point of fact, I do know Harnal, although not well." Afsan's tail swished. "Surely you must know something of the bloodpriest?"

"Yes, of course, I know Maliden, but we rarely had contact, and no, I do not know where he's gone, although I must say that if I had done what he is accused of—tampering with imperial succession—I'd have left town, too."

"We have reason to suspect that Maliden has not left town."

"What? Why?"

In the flickering light, Afsan couldn't avoid a direct question. "We think he may have had something to do with the murders."

Bogkash's teeth clicked derisively. "Maliden? A murderer? Afsan, first, he's very, very old. Second, he's gentle to a fault."

"Well," said Afsan, "I'm open to other suggestions. Do you know anything that might help identify the killer or killers? Anything you might have learned in your professional capacity?"

There was a moment's silence. Perhaps Bogkash was thinking. "Why, no, Afsan, not a thing."

Pal-Cadool moved out of the shadows.

"He's lying."

Suddenly the priest wheeled, his white robe flowing around him, claws glinting in the wan torchlight. "What is this impudence?" said Bogkash.

"Forgive me," said Afsan, "but my associate says you are not telling the truth."

"I am. He's the one who is lying."

"Cadool would not lie to me."

"Cadool, is it? A butcher? You take the word of a butcher over a priest?"

"Cadool is no longer a butcher. He is my assistant. And I take his word over anyone's."

"But I'm telling the truth," said Bogkash.

"You thought to lie to me," said Afsan simply. "A blind person can't see if you are lying. But Cadool is my eyes in these matters. Now, I ask you again, do you have any knowledge of the death of my daughter and my son?"

Bogkash looked at Afsan, then Cadool. "Surely what happens here, in the Hall of Worship, is private."

"Is it? Whenever I had to do penance here as an apprentice, your predecessor, Det-Yenalb, would later discuss it with my master, Tak-Saleed."

"Saleed and Yenalb died ages ago. You must have been just a child then."

"Shy of my first hunt. That makes a difference?"

"Well, of course."

"Haldan is—was—little older now than I was then. She'd only taken her pilgrimage three kilodays ago. And Yabool, of course, was the same age as Haldan." A pause. "Regardless, I have imperial authority for this investigation." Afsan had no need of a document bearing Dybo's cartouche to assert this; his muzzle declared that the stated authority was genuine. "Answer my questions."

Bogkash appeared to consider. At last he said, "About Haldan and Yabool, I know little. But another of your children—the one who works on the docks . . ."

"Drawtood."

"Yes, Drawtood. He has been here often of late, walking the sinner's march, circling the Hall over and over again."

"Have you asked him about it?"

"An unburdening of guilt must be freely offered. I note which individuals enter and leave the Hall at times other than normal services, but I don't normally engage them in conversation. Even here, the rules of territoriality apply most of the time."

"But you know nothing about Haldan or Yabool, only Drawtood?"

"That's right."

"Why bring it up, then?" asked Afsan. "What's he got to do with them?"

Bogkash shrugged. "You tell me."

Chapter 30

The surveying of the polar cap required sailing right around it. Fortunately it was quite small, so its circumnavigation only took a few dekadays.

Still, sailing east meant that the *Dasheter* was soon on the side of the world that looked upon the Face of God.

Everybody aboard had seen the Face at least once, when they took their pilgrimage voyage at the passage into adulthood. But the spectacle from here at the bottom of the world was shockingly different from the one they had beheld in equatorial waters.

At the equator, the Face went through phases from top to bottom. Here it waxed from side to side. On pilgrimage voyages, the yellow and brown and white bands of cloud striped the Face vertically. Here they roiled across it horizontally. When seen from warm waters, the Face was squished so that it appeared taller than it was wide. Here, in the Antarctic, it was oblate, apparently compressed vertically.

It all made sense when one looked at that newest of fads—a globe of the world—for a Quintaglio standing at the south pole was indeed perpendicular to one at the equator, therefore rotating the frame of reference through a quarter of a circle. Indeed, after seeing the Face both ways— waxing like a winking eye at the latitudes of Land; waning like a rounded door down here at the southern ice cap—one could no longer doubt that the world was indeed a sphere.

From this far south, though, much of the Face was always below the horizon, because, as Toroca understood, the plane of the world's orbit around the Face was through the world's equator, so that here, near the pole, they were looking down upon the Face from a height equal to the radius of their world. It meant that when the Face was crescent, it appeared as a great curving horn rising up from the horizon, stretching toward the zenith, as though some great beast lurked just beyond the edge of the world.

But when the curtains of aurora danced around it, nothing was more beautiful than the Face of God. Toroca, who'd been anxious to leave, to get back to warmer climes, and to speak to other scholars about his theory, could have tarried here forever, drinking in the sight of that wonderful, spellbinding planet.

The *Dasheter* had begun its long voyage home. The ice had disappeared over the southern horizon, and each night more of the old familiar stars became visible. Toroca took note of the position of the constellation of the Hunter—known for a time, but no more, as the constellation of the Prophet. It was hugging the northern horizon, but as the *Dasheter* pressed on toward Land, it would move higher and higher with each passing night.

Toroca and Babnol were supposed to still be on opposite sleeping schedules, but he had stayed up tonight to speak with her. She had come up on deck after sunset to enjoy the stars. Temperatures still plummeted too much at night to be on deck for more than about a daytenth after the sun had slipped below the waves. Toroca saw her, leaning against the railing that ran around the edge of the ship's aft diamond-shaped hull. He moved over to her, the splashing of waves against the ship masking his footsteps.

"I'm sorry," he said at once, before any ritual exchange of greetings, before she had a chance to get away.

She looked up, startled. She was wearing her snowsuit, but had the hood unstrapped, so he could clearly see her black, intelligent eyes; her graceful, almost tapered muzzle; and her horn, the yellowish-white cone that had hurt them both.

"I'm sorry, too," she said at last. He moved over to the railing and leaned on it as well. Together, they watched the beauty of the night, the air somehow not seeming cold at all.

There was a shout from the lookout bucket.

Surely not land so soon? Toroca looked up. Biltog, who seemed to be making a career of sitting in the bucket atop the foremast, was scrambling frantically out of that bucket and down the web of ropes. He was yelling something, but Toroca couldn't make it—

"—deck!" shouted Biltog. "Clear the deck!"

Toroca spun around and looked over the little railing around the edge of the *Dasheter*'s foredeck. He couldn't see—oh, God . . .

A giant wave was barreling toward the *Dasheter*, its crest a wild, roiling white, its body a wall of blue-gray fury.

"Clear the deck!" shouted Biltog again. "Get below!"

Toroca needed no further prodding. He ran for the nearest accessway leading down. Others were doing the same. Crew members were furiously locking down the hatches over the entrances—

And then it hit.

The ship rolled far to starboard. Toroca, on the little stepladder just below deck, held on for his life, his claws digging into the wood. Little lizards went skittering across the floor—he'd heard that the *Dasheter*, like most ships, had a degree of lizard infestation, but this was the first he'd seen of them. The ship's timbers groaned in agony. Toroca felt his stomach turning inside out. Down below, he could see Babnol, prone on the floor.

The *Dasheter* continued to list, farther and farther. One of the boards making up the stepladder splintered in two. The ladder was almost horizontal now, the whole ship practically knocked on its side.

And then—

Swinging back the other way, rolling to port, back, back, farther, Toroca spraining his arm as he tried to hold on, the ship's lumber moaning under the stress.

And then, at last, the ship stabilized.

Captain Keenir was moving up and down the corridors. "That should be it for a few moments," he called in his gravelly voice. "But get to your quarters and lie down on the floor. There'll likely be two or three more."

Toroca made his way down the rest of the stepladder.

Babnol was also gaining her feet. "What is it?" she called to Keenir as he passed. "What's happening?"

"Quake," said the old mariner. "You'll believe the world's coming to an end after you weather a few of those out here in open water. Quickly now, to your cabin. Aftershocks coming!"

During the many days of the return voyage, Toroca paced the decks of the *Dasheter*, back and forth and back again, stem to stern, thinking.

An animal changing from one thing to something else. A flying wingfinger becoming a swimming one.

Change.

Evolution.

The idea needed a name, and that was the best one he could think of. In general use, the word meant "unrolling," or "gradual change." It cer-

196 Robert J. Sawyer

tainly seemed appropriate when applied here, to the changing of one form of life into another.

For the change *must* be gradual, surely. A wingfinger couldn't go in one generation from having a flying membrane attached to its elongated digit to having a swimming paddle. No, rather, it must happen a little at a time, with wingfingers perhaps swimming on the surface of the water, and those with a thicker membrane being the best paddlers, and therefore getting the most fish. A thick membrane would be an advantage, then, over a thin one, in an environment where swimming was more profitable than flying.

And those that had the advantage would live longer and have more children.

And the children would tend to take after the parents, just as, just as, just as . . .

Just as Governor Rodlox and Emperor Dybo took after Empress Lends, or, or, or . . .

Or as I take after Afsan and Novato.

And in each subsequent generation, the favorable trait would become concentrated more and more, until it became the norm.

An entire population of wingfingers with paddles instead of flying membranes.

Or with walking stilts instead of wings.

A selection process, imposed by the environment: a *natural* selection.

Toroca continued to pace.

Babnol was eighteen kilodays old.

Toroca understood this; knew the significance of the figure.

A year was about eighteen thousand days long.

And, therefore, Babnol was now about one year old.

Toroca felt a little tingling as he contemplated what that meant.

Sexual maturity.

The ripening. The receptivity.

Soon, Babnol would call for a mate.

Very soon.

Toroca had longed after Babnol since shortly after they had first met, and at last he could bear it no more. She was coming close now, down the cramped corridor beneath the decks of the *Dasheter*. She'd have to squeeze by him in this narrow space to get where she wanted to go. Of course, as was the custom, she would avert her eyes for the brief time during which she would be invading his territory. He was supposed to do the same.

Closer now. Closer. Just a few paces away.

He could smell her pheromones—the normal scent of all Quintaglios; the undercurrent of her femaleness, growing more pronounced day by day as she moved toward receptivity; the subtle tinge that indicated that she hadn't eaten recently; the slight whiff of abasement at having to encroach on another's territory.

She looked to one side and stepped abreast of him.

Toroca lifted his arm, ever so slightly, so that the back of his hand slid smoothly, gently, across her flank as she passed.

Her claws slipped out into the light of day, but she said not a word. Not a word.

Toroca was pacing the decks of the *Dasheter* again, his theory bothering him.

Yes, evolution explained the bizarre wingfinger-derived life-forms of the south pole. Yes, the mechanism of natural selection could account for their strange adaptations to the aquatic, fish-laden environment there.

But so what?

What relevance did evolution have to life back on Land?

He'd seen in the fossils of the Bookmark layer that all forms of life had emerged simultaneously: reptiles and fish and amphibians and wingfingers. All of them appeared at once.

Evolution had nothing to do with, oh, say, with a fish spontaneously developing a novelty that allowed it to survive for a short time out of water, and that trait being concentrated over the generations, to, for the sake of a wild example, give rise to amphibians.

Oh, it made sense that it *could* have happened that way, but that's not the way it did. Fish and amphibians appeared simultaneously in the fossil record. Evolution had nothing to do with their arrival.

Arrival. Oddly appropriate, that word.

Toroca slapped the deck in frustration. He'd figure it out eventually. He knew he would.

And he knew something else, too: that this, not some silly feat of hunting, was what he owed to his father.

Once again it was Biltog who was doing the watch in the lookout's bucket.

And once again, he let out a shout of "Land ho!"

But this time it was land indeed, not a frozen waste of ice and snow. In fact, it was Land—the word written as a left-facing glyph, instead of a right-facing one, referring specifically to the vast equatorial mass upon which the Fifty Packs roamed.

The *Dasheter*'s sails snapped in the steady east-west wind. Toroca reflected briefly that he'd gotten used to that sound, and to the groaning of the ship's timber, and the scraping of claws on wooden decks, and the slapping of waves against the hull. He was so used to them, in fact, that he barely heard them anymore, but thought that their absence might be almost deafening for his first few days back on solid ground.

Although they had departed from Fra'toolar, they were returning to Capital province, at least for a few days, so that they could take on supplies, and so that Toroca could have meetings with the leader of The Family—a left-facing glyph again—and with members of his own family.

The *Dasheter* continued in toward the shore, the rocky cliffs of Capital province, similar to although not as spectacular as those along the coast of Fra'toolar, towering up ahead of them, and, in the background, the ragged cones of the Ch'mar volcanoes.

The docks were approaching with visible speed.

The *Dasheter* was singing out its identification call: five loud bells and two deafening drumbeats, then the same sounds again, but softer. Then loudly again, then another soft iteration, over and over as the mighty vessel slipped in next to a vacant pier.

Home, thought Toroca.

Home at last.

Chapter 31

Musings of the Watcher

In this universe, intelligent life perhaps needed more of a hand than I'd been providing so far. At least, that's what the Jijaki aboard the arks told me. They had learned to peer intently into the structures of things and could see the intertwining double spiral of the acid molecule that controlled life.

Of the dinosaurs that had existed on the Crucible, there had been several kinds with potential. The Jijaki had particularly liked one smallish type that was bipedal, with a horizontally held torso balanced by a stiff whip of a tail. It had giant yellow eyes with overlapping fields of vision and three-fingered hands each with an opposable digit. I agreed these beings had possibilities and had ordered them shifted to another, less-promising target world. I was dubious of their chances, though, because their numbers were already in sharp decline on the Crucible, hinting that they weren't as ideally suited for the road to sentience as they appeared at first glance.

No, the dinosaurs I had favored most, partly because they'd already had a long and successful history as a group, were tyrannosaurs: large, slope-backed carnivores with great heads and giant teeth. Only one problem: for almost the entire lifetime of this group, their forelimbs had been diminishing until now they were withered and all but useless, with just two clawed fingers on the end of each hand.

The Jijaki read the genetic code of these creatures and found the instructions that had originally produced a third and fourth finger, instructions that now were turned off in the early stages of embryonic development. On some of the individuals being transplanted, the Jijaki edited out the termination sequence.

Jijaki had six little tentacles on the inner surface of each of their cup-shaped manipulators. They believed, therefore, that six was the optimal number of digits. It took much searching, but they finally found buried in the tyrannosaurs' genetic code the long-dormant instruction for the lost fifth finger that their quadrupedal ancestors had possessed. The Jijaki reactivated that as well. They wanted to go further, adding code for a sixth finger, but I forbade that.

Five, and enough time, should be sufficient.

Prath

The *Dasheter* had only just docked at Capital City when Toroca was told about the death of his sister Haldan and his brother Yabool. All other concerns—even unpacking the specimens he had carefully collected in the Antarctic—were put aside, and he immediately set out for Prath.

Prath, a half-day's march southwest of the Capital, was the place of the dead. Here the ground was made up of the tops of lava columns. But the life had gone out of the once-liquid stone, and instead of glowing red, the rock was cool and black. The tops of the columns were each not much bigger than Toroca's foot. They were polygonal, with straight vertical sides. Most were six-sided, though a few were pentagons and some were squares. Each was a slightly different height from those adjacent to it. In places, one low hexagon of basalt was surrounded by six taller ones, and the declivity had filled with rainwater.

At the southern periphery of the field, the columns rose high into the sky, and their bases were littered with the black rubble of pieces that had broken free and crashed down.

At some places, scraggly green and brown vegetation poked through, growing up from cracks between adjacent polygons. Many of the stone columns were covered with lichens, pale blue and pale green and pale pink.

Haldan's body was long gone, dragged away by some predator in the night, no doubt.

Yabool's body had been brought here two days ago.

Wingfingers circled overhead.

They would have their chance, as would the four-footed scavenger lizards that skittered over the black stones. A hunter was part of the food cycle, and Yabool's body would be given back to the environment.

But not yet. Not until all those who wished to had had the chance to say good-bye.

Toroca moved along the rocks, carefully picking the appropriate stones to step upon. It was difficult terrain, but the people of Capital City had used Prath as a funereal site for generations. Even the body of Larsk had been laid out here.

Toroca was not too surprised to find that someone was already standing over the body. He used his hand to shield his eyes from the sun. Why, it was Dynax, one of his two remaining sisters. She must have come in from Chu'toolar upon hearing the news.

The basalt plain dipped so that Toroca was looking down upon his sister and the body of his brother from a slight elevation. Dynax's back was to him, but her unique brown and blue sash, combining the disciplines of *hamrak* and *delbarn*, made her easy to identify. Yabool's body was wrapped tightly in thunderbeast hide, keeping out insects and predators until the five days of mourning were over.

Toroca's eye was caught by movement amongst the rocks on the opposite side of the depression. It was Drawtood, another brother, approaching from the east. Dynax, standing over the body, looked up. Drawtood bowed concession first in Dynax's direction, then at Toroca, acknowledging that the other two had arrived first. Dynax, to this point unaware of Toroca's presence, turned around and, appearing slightly startled, bowed at him in turn.

It was strange, thought Toroca, that the three of us should happen to come here at the same time.

And, yet, is it strange? We're related.

He wondered what his siblings were thinking. They'd all known Yabool, of course, and would have come to pay final tribute, even if he had not shared their parents.

But was the fact that he *was* their blood relation significant? It seemed so, somehow, to Toroca. But territoriality kept Quintaglios apart. Dynax would stand silently over the body, then Toroca would, and, at last, Drawtood would.

Each alone with their thoughts.

Chapter 32

The ground shook slightly. Like all Quintaglios, Toroca reacted with fear, for trembling ground could mean a landquake. He swung his head around, and soon his fear gave way to a soft clicking of teeth. Jogging along, tail flying, gut barely clearing the black soil, was His Luminance himself, the Emperor, Dy-Dybo.

Toroca stepped out of the Emperor's path and watched him, huffing and puffing, make his way around the courtyard.

The arena in which the battle with the blackdeath would occur was modern in construction, of course: few buildings survived more than a generation or two, because of the landquakes. But it was built to the ancient specifications, using the traditional stone-cutting techniques outlined in the scrolls of Jostark.

The playing field was diamond-shaped, like a ship's hull, with the long axis half again the length of the short. The long axis ran north-south. Along the two eastern sides of the diamond were layer upon layer of seating compartments. The two banks of compartments joined in an obtuse angle at the center of the playing field. Each compartment was big enough to hold even the largest adult. The backs of the compartments were open. Not only did this afford access, but, because they opened into the steady wind from the east, they ensured that the pheromones of all the occupants were blown out over the field, instead of back onto the spectators.

Each compartment contained an angled dayslab, set far enough back that the walls between compartments prevented the user from seeing adjacent cells or even the other bank of compartments. From within such a cell, one could comfortably watch a sporting event that lasted many daytenths while maintaining the illusion of splendid, peaceful isolation.

All of this had to be explained to Afsan, who, having come from a small Pack, had never been in an arena before. He ran his hands over an architect's wooden model. And then, once he had a mental picture, he, Pal-Cadool, and Gork walked the length and breadth of the field, and circumnavigated its perimeter over and over again, so that Afsan could better understand the layout, better formulate a strategy for Emperor Dybo.

Governor Rodlox and his aide, Pod-Oro, entered Capital City's town square, where merchants traded their goods. "It sure is crowded here," observed Rodlox.

Oro grunted in reply.

Toroca's briefing with the Emperor took place in Dybo's office in the new palace building, a simple, functional room, devoid of opulence or ostentation. Dybo's desk, cluttered with papers, writing leathers, and scrolls, was situated near one corner. Novato and Afsan attended the meeting, too. They were aware of their kinship with Toroca, of course, but if it carried any special meaning for any of them, there were no outward signs.

"I cast a shadow in your presence," Toroca said to the Emperor. Dybo acknowledged the greeting with a bow. Novato and Afsan were likewise met with the same traditional words, but they, being of lesser station than the Emperor, reciprocated, repeating the same greeting back at Toroca. The four of them slowly drifted to the four corners of the room, maximizing the space between them. Dybo settled onto the dayslab overhanging his cluttered desk. Afsan leaned back on his tail, arms folded across his chest. Novato straddled a small stool.

"What new finds do you have to report?" asked Wab-Novato.

"Well," said Toroca slowly, "the most interesting was an—an artifact, a device made of some incredibly strong material, material that was harder than diamond."

Afsan lifted his muzzle. "There is nothing harder than diamond."

Toroca nodded. "That's what I thought, too. But this—thing—was indeed made out of some blue material that was harder than the diamond in my testing kit. And it had been buried in rock for ages, but showed no signs of crushing or damage. The material was virtually indestructible."

Novato was leaning forward. "Fascinating!" She turned to Dybo. "You see, Your Luminance? This is exactly the sort of thing I was hoping the Geological Survey would turn up: new resources to make our exodus more feasible." She swung her muzzle toward her son. "Toroca, where is this specimen?"

He looked at the floor. "It's lost, I'm afraid. It fell overboard on the *Dasheter*."

"Toroca!" There was shock in Novato's tone. "Your muzzle shows some blue."

"I'm sorry," he said. "I mean, it was *thrown* overboard."

"By whom?"

"My assistant, Babnol." He paused, then, as if the coincidence of praenomens might forestall his mother's wrath, said, "*Wab*-Babnol."

"She's clearly unstable," said Novato. "I'll have her replaced."

"No," said Toroca too loudly, and then once more, "No. She and I have discussed the incident. There won't be a repetition; that I guarantee."

Novato looked dubious, but nodded. "As you wish." Seeing that she'd clearly swished her tail into something unpleasant, she sought to move the conversation along. "What else did you discover of value?"

"Well, the south polar cap is, as myth had it, nothing but ice and snow. We now have a map of its coastline, but even that's of limited use, since it seems that it will change over time as ice cracks and melts. So, no, there's nothing there, unfortunately, that will be directly useful in getting us off this world. Nothing, that is, except the life-forms that inhabit it."

Toroca waited for that to sink in.

"Life-forms?" said Novato and Afsan simultaneously, and, a moment later, "Life-forms?" said Dybo.

"Yes."

"What kind of life-forms?" asked Novato.

"Wingfingers," said Toroca. "Except that these wingfingers don't fly."

Dybo, no savant himself, took a certain pleasure in catching his intellectuals in errors. "Then they can't be wingfingers," he said. "By definition, wingfingers fly."

"Umm, forgive me, Your Luminance," said Toroca, "but that's not the definition set out by the Arbiter of the Sequence. A wingfinger is a type of animal, basically reptilian, as we are, but, also as we are, warm-blooded, and, unlike us, with bodies covered with hair. But the diagnostic characteristic—the one thing that determines whether an animal is or is not a wingfinger—is the structure of the hand. If the four bones of the last finger are enormously elongated, as if to support a membrane, then the creature is a wingfinger."

"All right," said Dybo, sounding a little disappointed at Toroca's recovery, "so they *are* wingfingers. But if they can't fly, how did they get to the south pole?"

"That's a very perceptive question, Your Luminance. How indeed? My guess is that they *used* to be able to fly."

"You mean," said Dybo, "that the wingfingers you found are old and feeble?"

"No, no, no. I mean their *ancestors* used to fly, but, over generations, they lost the ability to do so, and instead used their elongated fingers for other functions."

Afsan, rapt, was no longer leaning back on his tail. "Changed over time, you say?"

"Aye," said Toroca.

The blind savant's voice was a whisper. "Fascinating."

Dybo, ever pragmatic, said, "But how does this aid the exodus?"

"It doesn't," said Toroca, "at least not directly. But I've brought back many specimens of the life-forms from down there. The variations in wing architecture and design should help Novato in her studies of flight."

"I'm sure they will," said Novato. "And, I must say, this is all very intriguing."

"Indeed," said Afsan.

"Wait a beat," said Dybo, at last catching up to the meaning of what Toroca had said earlier. "You're saying one kind of animal changed into another?"

"Yes, sir," said Toroca.

"That's not possible."

"Forgive me, Your Luminance, but I believe that it is."

"But that's sacrilege."

Toroca opened his mouth as if to speak, apparently thought better, closed it, and was then silent for several moments. At last, looking at the floor, he said, "Whatever you say, Your Luminance."

Afsan stepped closer. "Don't be afraid, Toroca. Dybo has learned from the past. Haven't you, Dybo? He would not punish one simply for engaging in an intellectual inquiry."

"What?" said Dybo, and then, "Umm, no, of course not. I only suggest you not speak such thoughts around the priests, Toroca."

Toroca was looking now at his blind father, who had lost his eyes at Dybo's order all those kilodays ago. "I'll gladly heed that advice," he said softly.

After the briefing with Toroca, Afsan and Dybo headed off to the dining hall. There was never much meat on the pieces Afsan ordered for his meals with Dybo—at least, not much by Dybo's standards. Today they ate hornface rump, not the best flesh, but not bad, either. Afsan had said it was important that Dybo learn to think of food simply as nutrition and not a sensual experience.

Although perhaps it wasn't the best choice of mealtime topics, their conversation turned, as it often did, to the murders of Haldan and Yabool.

"You have to acknowledge the pattern," said Dybo.

"That both murder victims are children of mine?" said Afsan.

"It can't be coincidence."

"No, I suppose not. Although they're both savants, both—"

"It's possible," said Dybo, "that they were killed by someone wanting to get at you."

Afsan's shriveled eyelids made a strange beating, the closest he could get to the fluttering of nictitating membranes that normally denoted surprise. "At me?"

"You have enemies. More than I have, I daresay. You took God out of the sky. You started the exodus, something not everyone is in favor of. Some Lubalites still see you as The One, but others consider you as false a figure as Larsk."

"I'm a blind person. If someone wanted me dead, it would not be difficult."

"Perhaps. Perhaps someone merely wants to frighten you."

"They've succeeded."

"Or perhaps it has nothing to do with you at all. Perhaps Novato is the key. They are her children as well, and she now leads the exodus project."

"That's true."

Dybo was silent for a long moment. Then, slowly, he said, "How well do you really know Novato?"

Afsan's claws extended. "I do not like the tone of that question, Dybo."

"No doubt you don't, my friend. But it's something I must ask. As you said so eloquently, a leader rarely has any choice in what he or she must do. I ask again, how well do you know Novato?"

"*Very* well. I do not suspect her of the murders. Not at all."

Dybo shrugged. "I don't suspect her in particular, either," he said. "But that means, I think, that I must suspect everyone in general. Certainly she has a connection—indeed, a *relationship*—to the victims."

"She is beyond reproach. You might as well ask me whether *I* was responsible for the crimes."

Dybo spoke softly. "Afsan, if I thought that you were capable— physically, I mean, not emotionally, for who really knows what another thinks?—of such violence, yes, I would ask you, too. I do not underestimate you; I know your hunting prowess. Even now, even as I train to face the blackdeath, I would not favor myself in a contest with you. But you are indeed blind. The method employed in these killings was not one a blind person could successfully manage."

"There is such a thing as *trust*, Dybo. There are individuals whom you do not question, whom you believe in implicitly."

"Oh, indeed, my friend. You are one such for me; I trust you with my life. And I know you likewise trust Cadool, and I like to think myself as well. But, forgive me, old friend, you are, well, *particularly* blind in matters of trust. You've speculated that the killer approached the victims with stealth, but you've missed the most obvious interpretation."

"Oh?"

"Indeed. The most obvious interpretation is that Haldan and Yabool *knew* their killer, and trusted him or her enough to allow the killer to approach them closely." Afsan looked shocked, but whether at the content of Dybo's suggestion or at the realization that he'd foolishly failed to consider this possibility himself, the Emperor couldn't say. Dybo pressed on. "They both apparently let the killer into their homes. They obviously felt no fear in that person's presence; indeed, felt little territoriality even."

"Whom would they trust thus?" said Afsan.

"Ah, now, that's my point!" said Dybo. "Haldan and Yabool might each trust certain of their colleagues. But they had different professions, so there would be no overlap there. They might trust certain of their neighbors. But they lived in different parts of Capital City, so, again, no overlap. But they did both trust their parents, you and Novato."

Afsan was quiet for a time, digesting this. At last he said, "And each other."

"Eh?"

"And they would have trusted each other, Yabool and Haldan. Indeed, all my children would have trusted each other. They were creche-mates, after all. Creche-mates are as one. But why would one relative want to kill another?"

"My brother," said Dybo, "wants to kill me."

Afsan was silent again.

"But there you have it. As much as it pains me to suggest it, in addition to bloodpriest Maliden and the other names that have been put forth, you must consider Wab-Novato and your remaining children as suspects."

"You force me to agree to that which is uncomfortable," said Afsan.

Dybo clicked his teeth. "Then our roles are reversed, friend, for you once forced me, and all Quintaglios, to agree that the Face of God was not the actual deity."

There was another silence. Finally, from Afsan: "I'll consider your suggestion, Dybo, but I prefer still the idea that the killer sneaked up on my children."

"Of course," said Dybo, deciding not to push the matter. "Of course." A pause while he worried a piece of meat from the bone, and then an attempt to change the subject: "By the way, Afsan, did you know that your daughter Dynax is back in Capital City?"

Afsan lifted his head. "No, I hadn't heard that."

"Yes, she's here. Awfully fast trip from Chu'toolar; she must have made very good time."

"Chu'toolar," repeated Afsan.

"Wake up, my friend. That's where Dynax lives, remember?"

"I *know* that," said Afsan. "It's just that mirrors that were used to kill Haldan and Yabool were manufactured in Chu'toolar. And now you say Dynax is here."

"Yes. To pay respects to her dead siblings."

"But here so quickly? I wonder just exactly how long she has been in town . . ."

Toroca was no longer startled when he felt the ground rumble. He, and just about everyone else at the palace, had gotten used to Dybo's exercising. As the Emperor thundered near, Toroca noticed that there was a much greater gap between the ground and Dybo's belly than there used to be. He called out, "How many laps today?"

Dybo's voice came back, ragged with exertion. "Five."

Toroca's eyelids fluttered. He doubted he could do that many himself.

"Cadool," said Afsan as they walked down one of the cobblestone streets of Capital City, adobe buildings to their left and right, "you know my daughter Galpook."

"Yes, indeed. A great hunter! The way her team captured that blackdeath—wonderful."

"Indeed. You have seen her hunt, then?"

"Oh, yes. I was fortunate enough to go on a hunt with her about a kilo-day ago. She has many of your moves, Afsan, and much of the same skill."

"How is she at tracking?"

"Excellent. She spotted the signs of our quarry long before I did."

"And in the tracking, did she ever alert the prey?"

"No. She tracks silently."

"With stealth," said Afsan.

"Pardon me?"

"With stealth. That's the word Gathgol used to describe the way in which the murderer might have sneaked up on Yabool. With stealth."

"Yes, but—" Cadool came to a halt at an intersection. "We'd better not go that way," he said.

Afsan stopped at once, his walking stick swinging in a slow arc across the paving stones in front of him. "Why not? What's wrong?"

"It's too crowded. There must be eight or ten adolescents down there."

"Children?" said Afsan. "I like children."

"But so many!" said Cadool. "They're growing fast; they're up to my waist already."

"Children don't have much scent," said Afsan. "I could probably pass through such a crowd without difficulty."

Cadool was unusually edgy. "But I cannot, Afsan. I can *see* them. And now three other adults have stopped at the next intersection. They, too, don't know which way to go." Cadool slapped his tail against the paving stones. "Roots! This congestion is getting unbearable!"

Chapter 33

Toroca tried to maintain a relationship with each of his siblings. Some of them seemed more interested in acknowledging kinship than others. He never forced the issue, but he did enjoy spending time with those who didn't seem to mind.

There was an exception, though. His brother Drawtood appeared to be uncomfortable around people. In some strange way, that made Toroca even more interested in seeing him, for Drawtood seemed as lonely as Toroca. Toroca's loneliness came from no one sharing his desire for intimacy. Drawtood's, on the other hand, seemed self-imposed, as if he went to special lengths to distance himself from the rest of society.

Beyond that, though, there was another reason for the separation between them. Toroca was a geologist. His sister Dynax, a doctor. Brother Kelboon was an authority on mathematics. But Drawtood had never done well academically. He worked on the docks of Capital City, helping to load and unload boats. If it hadn't been for their shared blood, their lives would probably not intersect at all. Still, each time he came to the Capital, Toroca visited several of his siblings, including, always, Drawtood.

Drawtood's home was so close to the harbor that the sounds of ship's bells and drums and the high-pitched calls of wingfingers circling above the docks were a constant background. Toroca entered the vestibule of the adobe building and drummed his claws on the copper signaling plate. Drawtood answered, expressionless as always, and swung the door aside to let Toroca in.

"I brought you a small gift," said Toroca, fishing in the hip pouch of his sash. "Here."

The proper way to give a gift was to set it on a tabletop or some other piece of furniture, then to back away so that the recipient could easily fetch it. But Toroca simply held the object out in his palm. He did demand a small price for his presents, and that was that the recipient actually take them from his hand. Drawtood shuffled forward, took the object, his fingers briefly touching Toroca's hand as he did so, and then scurried to the opposite side of the room.

It was a gemstone polished in a cabochon shape. The material was golden brown and seemed to have a white four-pointed star embedded in its center. The stone was quite lovely, thought Toroca, and although common at traders' tables in western Land, it was rare here. For Afsan and Novato and his other siblings, he usually brought something that was *interesting*—a curiosity of some sort, an unusual crystal or intriguing fossil. But Toroca reckoned that such things would hold little appeal for Drawtood, although the laborer did seem to enjoy pretty rocks.

"Thank you," said Drawtood, shifting the gem back and forth in his hand, watching the way light played across its surface.

"It's from Arj'toolar," said Toroca. "Not far from where Afsan was born."

"Afsan," repeated Drawtood. By mutual consent, they never referred to him as their father. "I don't see him very often."

"I've just come from a meeting that he was at. An update on the Geological Survey."

Drawtood nodded. "Of course." A pause. "Does he ever mention me?"

"He speaks fondly of all his children," said Toroca.

Drawtood looked at the floor. "I'm sure he does."

Toroca couldn't determine its cause, but there seemed to be a melancholy air about his brother. "Are you well, Drawtood?" he asked at last.

"Fine," he said. "I'm fine."

"And—happy?" Toroca surprised himself with the question.

"I have my job. I have this little place to live in. Why should I not be happy?"

"I don't mean to pry," said Toroca. "It's just that I worry about you."

"And I about you, brother."

Toroca was taken aback. "You do?"

"Of course. Your job takes you far away, to dangerous places."

Toroca looked out the window. "I suppose that's true." A beat, then: "What's new since the last time we met, Drawtood?"

"New with me? Nothing is ever new with me. You're the one who leads the interesting life." There was no trace of malice, or any emotion, in Drawtood's tone. "You tell me what's new with you."

Toroca opened his mouth, but then, after a few moments, closed it without saying a word. What could he talk to Drawtood about? Superposition? Fossils? The strange life-forms of the south polar cap? His new theory of evolution? Drawtood didn't have the schooling to appreciate any of those topics. Finally: "I've made a new friend."

This did seem to interest Drawtood. "Yes?"

"A female. Her name is Wab-Babnol. We work together."

"'Babnol.' An unusual name. It means 'loner,' doesn't it?"

Toroca was surprised. "Does it? I've never encountered the name before."

"Yes, I'm sure—'loner.' Or maybe "outcast." Funny name for the creche masters to have given her."

"In a way," said Toroca, "it's fitting."

Drawtood nodded politely, not understanding.

"You'd like her," said Toroca.

"I'm sure I would," replied Drawtood. "How old is she?"

Toroca felt a slight tinge of embarrassment. "Eighteen kilodays."

Drawtood clicked his teeth. He understood the significance of the figure. "I see."

Toroca thought to feign shock, to take mock offense at the innuendo, but then, after a moment, he clicked his teeth also. "You know me well, Drawtood."

The dockworker nodded. "Of course," he said simply. "We're brothers."

Chapter 34

Capital City

Toroca hadn't seen Babnol for several days. At last, though, he caught sight of her on the grounds of the palace. He jogged over to catch up with her, the late afternoon sun beating down from above. The grass here in the courtyard was kept short by a couple of armorbacks that roamed freely within its confines.

"Babnol!" called Toroca.

She looked up, but the expression on her face was not the one Toroca had hoped to see. "Greetings," she said softly.

"I've been wondering where you've been," he said. "It's as though you've been avoiding me." He clicked his teeth to show the remark was intended as a jest.

"I'm sorry," said Babnol. "Very sorry."

"Well, it's good to see you now," said Toroca. "Are you packed? The *Dasheter* sets sail for Fra'toolar tomorrow."

Babnol turned away and was quiet for several moments. Finally: "I can't go back there with you."

Toroca's voice was full of concern. "Is something wrong?"

A hint of blue on Babnol's muzzle. "It's nothing." She looked away. "Nothing at all."

Toroca longed to move closer to her, to bridge the gap between them, but he stood fast. "It's not because we'll be searching for artifacts again, is it? I thought we now agreed on that—"

"It's nothing to do with that, Toroca," she said, and there was no hint of a blush this time. "It's just . . . just something I prefer not to discuss."

Toroca's tail swished; he was slightly hurt. "Well," he said, "if there's anything I can do—you know I'm not completely without influence."

She bowed slightly. "Indeed. But even Dy-Dybo himself—or whoever succeeds him in this mad challenge—couldn't do anything about what's troubling me, I'm afraid. Don't worry about it. I'll be fine." No blue; Toroca relaxed somewhat. "It's just that I have to be on my own for a bit."

"Where are you going?"

A direct question. Babnol was silent for a few moments, then said, "I don't know. Perhaps the Shanpin foothills."

"The foothills! No Pack roams there; it's all scorched ground and basalt."

"That's right."

"You'll be all alone."

"That's right, too."

"I don't understand," said Toroca faintly.

"No," she said after a few heartbeats. "No, I suppose you don't."

She turned and walked away, tail swishing sadly.

When Afsan and Novato had first met, Novato had worked in a small room in the ruins of an ancient temple to the hunter Hoog. Although Var-Keenir and a few other mariners prized her far-seers, her work had largely been considered unimportant. Novato's home Pack of Gelbo, in distant Fra'toolar, had tolerated her labors, for although her far-seers brought little in trade, the visits from mariners meant great ships came to the tiny port, making available goods that otherwise would have been rare.

Now, though, she lived in the Capital. Here she was director of the exodus, a minister of the throne, and confidante to the Emperor. Instead of one room, she had an entire building and the largest staff of any ministry, a staggering eighteen people.

When she'd become a member of Dybo's court, Novato had been given a new cartouche. It was carved in intricate detail on the door to her workshop. The upper part showed a far-seer tube in profile. Beneath that was a diagram showing the truth about the universe, with Land a single continent on the far side of a moon of a giant planet that was covered with bands of cloud. And beneath that, a sailing ship, with double-diamond hulls, moving freely through space. A cartouche was normally carved with a raised oval lip around it, but for Novato's the artist had left gaps in the border, indicating that Novato's work was not constrained by the traditional borders of the world.

It was bad form to arrive at any confined area in a group. Such an intrusion might trigger the territorial reflex. Afsan therefore went up to Novato's office door alone, scratched on the signaling plate, and was granted permission to enter.

"Greetings, Afsan," said Novato, pushing off her dayslab to stand up.

"Hello, Novato."

On her desk were sketches of wingfinger and insect wings. Little model wingfingers made of wood and bits of leather were everywhere; some seemed quite sophisticated, others, perhaps older attempts, were being used simply as paperweights. One wall was covered with intricate charcoal sketches of fossil birds. On tabletops around the office were mounted specimens and skeletons of the fauna Toroca had brought from the Antarctic.

Novato hurried to move a pile of books that had been sitting in the middle of the floor, lest Afsan trip over them. "What brings you here?" she said, her voice warm. "It's always a pleasure, of course, but I didn't expect you."

Afsan's tone was neutral, perhaps even timid. "I have a question to ask."

"Of course. Anything."

"Cadool must join us."

"Cadly is here, too?" "Cadly" was Novato's nickname for Cadool. "Cadool" meant "hunter of runningbeasts," but "Cadly" meant "long of leg," something Cadool definitely was. "I've missed him. By all means, bring him in."

Afsan went to the door and called for Cadool. A few moments later, he appeared.

"Cadly!" declared Novato.

Cadool nodded concession. "It is good to see you, Novato."

"I'm so glad the two of you have come," said Novato. "Coordinating the exodus keeps me very busy, I'm afraid. I'm sorry I haven't called on either of you lately."

"It *is* good to see you," said Afsan.

"I'm sorry, Afsan," said Novato. "I've been babbling. You said you had a question for me?"

"That's right."

There was silence for a time. Novato's teeth touched in laughter. "That silence you're hearing is me looking at you expectantly, my dear."

"I'm sorry. The question is . . ." Afsan hesitated, his tail swishing back and forth nervously. "The question is, did you kill Yabool or Haldan?"

"And this silence," said Novato, no levity in her tone at all, "is me glaring at you. What moves you to ask such a thing?"

"What always moves me," said Afsan. "The need to expose the truth."

"And what is Cadool"—no friendly sobriquets now—"doing here?"

Afsan's voice was small. "He is here to see whether you are lying."

Novato's voice had a tone Afsan had never heard in it, the sharp edge of anger. "Why are you doing this?"

Afsan thought. Finally: "I do it out of . . . out of *affection* for our children."

"And what about affection for me?"

Afsan's voice carried a note of surprise. "That is a given."

"A given? Then why treat me this way?"

Afsan paused. "Cadool, perhaps you would leave us?"

"No," said Novato sarcastically. "Stay. It's obvious why you've brought him along, Afsan: to assure you that my words are honest."

Afsan nodded, then swiveled his muzzle toward his assistant. "Stay, Cadool. But not for that reason. Rather, stay because we agreed that friends should share. I make no secret of my feelings for Novato." He paused, as if seeking the right words, then turned back toward where he'd heard Novato's voice coming from. "Novato, I abjure pity, but I suspect you know it's not easy being blind." His tail swished back and forth slowly. "Falling asleep is—is *strange* for me." He gestured in her direction. "For you, and for Cadool, it's a slipping from light into darkness; you close your eyes, shut out the world, and drift into unconsciousness."

He paused again, phrasing what he was about to say in his mind. "But I am always in darkness. When I change from being awake to being asleep, there is no real sensory change, no shutting out. I—I need something else, some substitute for the drawing of eyelids over orbs, for changing from day to night. For me, every night that I do sleep, I do so thinking of you, Novato."

Afsan's voice was warm, but with a melancholy tinge to the words. "As I lie on my belly, wishing to sleep, I recall your face. Oh, I know it's your face of sixteen kilodays ago, the one and only time I ever saw you, a younger, less interesting face than I'm sure you have now, but it's you nonetheless." He paused. "I can still describe it in detail, Novato. Other images I have trouble recalling, but not you, not your face, not the line of your muzzle, the shape of your eyes, the delicate curve of your earholes. It's that face that calms me each night, that helps me let go of the burdens of the day, and, for just a little while, forget that I cannot see."

He dipped his torso in a concessional bow. "You are special to me, Novato, more special than I can say, and that time we spent together, discovering truths both about ourselves and about the universe, was the happiest, indeed, the only truly happy, time of my life."

He shook his head. "To hurt you is to hurt myself. It pains me to ask the question I have asked, but suspicion *has* fallen on you. It was not I who thought of you, and I tell you that I reacted with indignation, too, when your name was suggested. I came to you first, before any others, not because I see any possibility of you being the perpetrator, but because I couldn't bear, even for a few days, that others might think you capable of such crimes. So I ask the question to exonerate you, and Cadool's declarations about your reply—not to me, for I need no proof of your honesty, but to others—will clear you of suspicion for all time."

Novato's breath came out in a long, whispery sigh. "And you, Afsan? Surely if I'm suspected, so are you."

"Doubtless this is true, although there are those who say a blind person couldn't have killed in the way that was used. On the other hand, although no one has raised the point, I have not hunted for kilodays, and it is, after all, through the hunt that we supposedly purge our emotions of anger. Perhaps one such as myself, a great hunter in his youth but now no longer able to join in a pack, might indeed need another outlet for his hostility."

"Then will you answer the same question, Cadool to be the witness to the answers for both of us?"

"I will. Gladly."

"Very well. Ask your question again."

"Did you, Wab-Novato, kill Haldan or Yabool?"

"No."

"Do you have any knowledge of who did?"

"No."

"Very well."

"Aren't you going to ask Cadool if my muzzle turned blue?"

"I know," said Afsan, "that it did not." A pause. "Now ask me."

Novato's tone was one of appeasement. "I'm sorry, Afsan, I didn't mean to doubt you. You are very special to me as well."

"You should ask the question, though. No one has yet."

"I—"

"Consider it a favor."

Novato swallowed. "Did you, Sal-Afsan, kill Yabool or Haldan?"

"I did not."

There was silence for a time. Finally, Novato exhaled noisily. "Well," she said warmly, "I'm glad that is over."

"I wish it were," said Afsan sadly. "I'm afraid I still have to ask that question of several other people I also care deeply about."

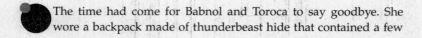 The time had come for Babnol and Toroca to say goodbye. She wore a backpack made of thunderbeast hide that contained a few

things she might need on her journey. Food wouldn't be a problem, though. She would kill what she needed along the way.

The sun, white and fiercely bright, was crawling its way up from the horizon. Babnol bowed. "I'll rendezvous with you at Fra'toolar in a hundred days or so," she said.

Toroca said nothing at first. He watched a golden wingfinger move across the purple sky. Then: "Don't go."

"I have to."

"No," he said. "You don't."

"You don't understand," she said. "I'm . . ." Her voice trailed off.

"You're changing," supplied Toroca. "You're coming into heat."

She swung her muzzle to face him directly. "How do you know that?"

"Your age. Your manner." Toroca shrugged amiably. "Your smell."

Babnol's muzzle tipped down. "Then you can understand why I must go."

"No," said Toroca. "I don't."

She looked off into the distance. "Regardless, the decision is mine. I don't owe you an explanation."

"Yes, you do, Babnol." Toroca's tone was gentle. "I'm your friend."

At last Babnol nodded. "All right. Soon, as you say, I will feel the urge to call for a mate."

"Very soon, I'd warrant," said Toroca.

"Exactly. And I do not want to couple."

Toroca's inner eyelids fluttered. "But why not?"

Babnol spread her arms. "Look at me. *Look at me*. I'm ugly." A pause. "Deformed."

"I don't know what—" But Toroca stopped when he felt the warming that meant his muzzle was flushing blue. He tried again. "I don't consider you ugly."

"I'm a freak," said Babnol. "A freak of nature. This *pastak* nose horn." The swear word was one rarely spoken.

"I find it . . ." Toroca sought the appropriate word. ". . . intriguing."

Babnol lifted her muzzle again, and at last Toroca understood that the gesture was not one of haughty arrogance, but rather a subconscious desire to reduce the apparent size of the horn. "It has not been *intriguing* to go through life with this defect, Toroca."

Toroca nodded. "Of course. I didn't mean to minimize your experience."

"You yourself told me once about the work that was done with lizard breeding," she said. "It demonstrated the inheritance of characteristics."

Toroca looked blank.

"Don't you see? My offspring might indeed be similarly deformed. I can't risk that. I have to go away, to be alone, until after the mating urge passes. Then I can safely return to the company of others for another full year—for eighteen kilodays."

"One is never completely safe. My mother was only sixteen kilodays old—well shy of her first year—when she was moved to mate with Afsan."

"The risk is minimal at other times. It's monumental now." She paused again, then, wistfully: "I must leave right away. Good-bye, Toroca."

"No, wait," he said.

She hesitated, and, for a moment, it seemed as though she really did not want to go.

"You're not a freak," said Toroca. "You're special."

"Special," she repeated, as if trying the word on for size. But then she shook her head.

"Look," he said, "you know about my theory of evolution. It's not the things that make us the same that increase our survivability. It's the differences, the things that make us unique."

"I've listened to you more attentively than that," said Babnol. "A novelty can be either good or bad. A difference is just as likely—more likely—to be a bad thing."

"Any difference that lets an individual survive to breeding age is, by definition, beneficial, or, at the very least, neutral." He adopted a teacher's tone. "To artificially remove yourself from the breeding population is unnatural."

"All of our selection is unnatural, Toroca. The bloodpriests do for us what nature can no longer do: select who should live and who should die. It's only because all egglings have birthing horns that the bloodpriest of my Pack did not realize I was defective. I'm just compensating for the error of that selection process."

"You worry about the bloodpriest's culling?" said Toroca.

"I suspect many people do. Seven died so that I might live. Only you, you who never underwent the culling, are probably immune from the self-doubt engendered by that process. I suspect that that is much more the real reason why people rarely speak of the bloodpriests. We avoid the topic not because it's bloody—we're carnivores, after all!—but rather because it makes us wonder about whether we really were the ones who should have lived."

Toroca said nothing about how he, too, had wondered about the culling of the bloodpriest, how he had suspected that he would have not been allowed to live. He felt closer to Babnol than ever.

"But you're special," he said again. And then, bolder, "Special to me."

She looked up, perplexed.

"I like you, Babnol."

"And I like you, Toroca."

"I mean I like you *a lot*. I was hoping we could spend more time together."

"We already spend a good tenth of each day together, Toroca. That's more than I spend with anyone, and, to be honest, as much as I can take. We need our privacy."

Toroca shook his head. "*Others* need their privacy. I don't."

Her inner eyelids fluttered in puzzlement. "I don't understand."

He shrugged. "I don't feel oppressed when others are around. I don't feel claustrophobic, trapped." He indicated the space between them. "I don't feel territoriality."

Babnol tipped her head to the side. "You don't?"

"Nope. Never have."

"But that's—forgive me—that's sick."

"I feel fine."

"No territoriality, you say?"

"None."

"What's it like?" she said.

"I have nothing to compare it with."

"No, I guess not. But, then, how do you react if other people are around you?"

"If they are people I like, I want them to be closer."

"But they move away."

Wistful: "Yes."

"How does that feel?"

"It hurts," he said softly.

"I can't imagine that," Babnol said.

"No. I don't suppose anyone else can."

"And you want to be close to me?"

"Especially to you." He took a step toward her. "There are perhaps seven paces between us now." He took another step. "And now six." Another. "Five."

Babnol stood up straight, taking her weight off her tail.

"I could come even closer," he said.

"How close?"

He stepped again, and then, boldly, once more. "Very close."

Only three paces between them now. Toroca felt his heart racing. Three paces: much greater proximity than protocol would normally allow, and yet, still a tremendous gulf. He lifted his left foot, moved another pace nearer.

Babnol's claws popped out. "No closer," she said, an edge in her voice. She shook her head. "What you're saying is alien to me. Alien to all of us."

Toroca spoke softly. "I know."

Babnol looked uncomfortable. She backed off two paces. "I have to go."

"No," said Toroca. "Stay."

"Soon," she said, "my body will be crying for a mate. I have to be alone when that happens. I have to go."

"There's nothing wrong with you," said Toroca. "A horn on your face? What significance does that have?" He spread his arms. "And there's nothing wrong with me. I see what territoriality has done to our people. We'd be better off if more of us were free of it."

Babnol said nothing.

"Stay. When it comes time for you to call for a mate, call for me." He looked directly at her. "I would be honored."

More silence from Babnol.

"The bloodpriests are currently in disrepute, so I hear, but even if they are reinstated and only one eggling gets to live from our clutch, I'm sure it would be special. Perhaps it would have a horn throughout life. Perhaps it would be less territorial than most. Those are wonderful things, not things to be avoided."

Babnol's tail swished slightly. "Your words are tempting," she said at last.

"Then stay! Stay here. Stay with me."

There was a long, long moment between them. The sun slid behind a silvery cloud.

"I'm sorry," she said at last. "I have to do what I think is right." She turned and walked away.

Toroca kept her in his sight until she was lost among the folds of the landscape.

For the first time in his life, he felt the urge to go out and hunt.

Chapter 35

Capital City

Afsan lay on the grass outside of the palace, the sun warming his back. Next to him lay Gork, its thick tail touching Afsan's leg. Afsan tried to conjure up a picture of the grounds, but it had been so long. Grass: green, of course. And the sun, brilliant white. The sky, mauve, most likely, and cloudless, judging by how warm the sun felt. Daytime moons? Surely. This was noon on the 590th day of this kiloday. He calculated. The Big One would be high in the sky and waxing. Swift Runner would be much lower and almost full.

Still, it had been so long since he had seen any of these things. The picture still came when he willed it, but how true the colors were, how accurate the details, he could no longer say.

Sound was more real, as was smell, and touch. He could hear the buzzing of insects—a small swarm above his head, larger chirpers over in that direction, the smell of pollens, of grass shorn by domesticated plant eaters that had been tethered near here. And the hard ground beneath his belly, the roughness of the grass blades, a pebble under his thigh, not exactly comfortable, but not irritating enough to warrant changing his position.

And now the ground vibrating slightly. Someone walking toward him. Afsan lifted his head.

"Who's there?"

"It's me, Dybo."

"Dybo." Afsan relaxed again, letting his long jaw rest against the ground. "Your step is lighter than it used to be."

"Yes," said the Emperor, who, judging by the way his voice had shifted location, was crouching a few paces to Afsan's right.

"How do you feel?" asked Afsan.

"To my considerable surprise," said Dybo, "I feel better than I've ever felt before. But I'll tell you: when all this is over, I shall eat an entire hornface as a reward." Dybo paused. "That is, of course, if I win."

Afsan's tail was sticking up in the air. He flicked it absently to disperse insects. "Think positively, my friend. And, by all means, keep thinking of that hornface, if it motivates you."

There was quiet between them. The comfortable quiet of two old friends, a quiet that neither felt a need to fill. The bugs in the distance continued to chirp.

"Afsan?"

"Yes, Dybo?"

"How do you assess me, compared to Rodlox?"

Afsan reached over to Gork, and slid his hand soothingly over the beast's leathery hide. "I have never seen Rodlox."

"No, of course not. But you must have an opinion."

Gork's hide had warmed mightily in the sunlight. If the lizard had been alone, Afsan was sure it would have shuttled into the shade, but Gork was always reluctant to leave its master. Afsan pushed himself up onto his feet and followed the slight swelling in the ground caused by distended roots in toward the trunk of a nearby tree. Gork padded along next to him, hissing contentedly. The shade was cool. "Rodlox is loud and belligerent," Afsan said at last.

"And I am not," said Dybo, as if it were a failing to not be those things.

"You are peaceful and, well, pleasant."

"He's stronger than me, Afsan. Even after all of this training, I'm sure he's still stronger."

Gork nuzzled against Afsan's legs. "Physically, yes."

"And, Afsan, I have lived in awe of your intellect since we first met. I know I'm not the brightest person in the world."

Afsan said nothing.

"If I'm not the strongest, and I'm not the brightest, then perhaps Rodlox is right. Perhaps I should not be the leader."

"There is something else to consider."

"What else can there be, besides intellectual and physical prowess?"

"There's *goodness*, Dybo. There's moral rectitude. There's doing the right thing when the wrong thing would be easier. Those are your strengths, Dybo. And those, more than anything else, are what a good ruler needs."

Dybo was silent for a time. "Thank you," he said, and then: "But those traits sound flimsy against muscle and brains. Do I really have a hope of winning against the blackdeath?"

"If there's a god in heaven, you'll win."

Dybo answered wistfully. "Coming from the person who took God out of the heavens, that does little to comfort me."

Afsan's expression was carefully blank.

————

The blackdeath had been held captive for many dekadays now. Its pen was a giant area just north of the arena, hastily walled off by fences of stone. Indeed, the pen itself was bigger than the actual arena. The blackdeath had tried to scale the stone walls, but could not, and, although it occasionally still tried—perhaps having forgotten its previous attempts—it had mostly settled into its life of captivity.

At the south end, the pen's walls connected with the pointed apex of the walls to the diamond-shaped arena. Through a gate in the arena wall, a shovelmouth was driven into the pen every ten days or so, to provide food for the blackdeath.

Dybo often watched the blackdeath. Ladders had been built up to the top of the stone wall, and Dybo sat for great lengths of time on the edge, his feet dangling down the inside of the wall, his tail dangling off the outside. He observed that the blackdeath only seemed happy when it was stalking and killing the shovelmouths.

It was a horrendous beast even here, even caged, but it had a beauty and a nobility about it. Dybo's observation perch was upwind of the creature, and so long as he sat still, it paid him no attention. Next to him on the wall's upper surface lay a small satchel containing books, papers, and writing leathers.

Dybo was surprised to hear the sound of flexing wood made by someone coming up the ladder he'd leaned against the outer wall. He swiveled his head around and saw that Rodlox was ascending. Dybo got up and walked along the wall's top edge—it was barely wide enough for that—until he was about five paces from the top of the ladder.

Rodlox reached the top and instead of walking five paces in the opposite direction, thereby putting the traditional territorial buffer between himself and Dybo, he simply sat directly down. Everything about the governor of Edz'toolar bespoke challenge.

The movement on the top of the wall caught the blackdeath's eye. It let out a thunderous roar. Dybo took some pleasure in noting that, just for an instant, Rodlox's fingerclaws danced out into the light of day in response. He was not as fearless as he liked to appear. Dybo was a gifted mimic—in his younger days, he'd been known for his humorous impressions of the voices of the palace staff. He thought about copying the blackdeath's roar to see again the sight of Rodlox frightened, but prudence got the better of him. Instead, he simply said nothing.

"You spend much time up here, looking at that beast," said Rodlox. "It must be frightening for you, to see the creature that will cause your death."

Dybo's tone was lackadaisical. "Whatever you say, Rodlox." He went back to looking at the dumb brute. *The other dumb brute, that is.*

Suddenly Rodlox was pointing at Dybo's right hand. "What happened to you?"

Dybo lifted his arm. Two of his fingers were missing. "This, you mean?"

Rodlox's teeth clicked together nastily. "Does the Emperor stuff his face so quickly that even his own fingers get chomped off?"

There was an ancient gesture that Dybo thought briefly about making, but this hand lacked the key digit needed for it. "No, Rodlox, nothing like that. I lost these fingers while practicing."

Rodlox apparently didn't really care about Dybo's injury; the digits, after all, would grow back soon enough anyway. He looked down at the blackdeath, slowly pacing the length of its pen. "I can beat that creature with one arm tied behind my back," Rodlox said defiantly.

Dybo's expression was inscrutable as he also looked down at the caged beast. "I can do better than that," he said at last.

Chapter 36

Fra'toolar

At last, the *Dasheter* set sail again, traveling along the southern coast of Capital province, past the shore of Kev'toolar, and finally across the Bay of Vatasor, to the windy, rocky coast of Fra'toolar, where it deposited Toroca and his team back at the same beach it had picked them up from all those days ago.

Toroca was pleased to be back at work. Pack Derrilo was now well established in the buildings overlooking part of the cliff face, and the Pack members seemed pleased to have once again visitors from Capital City—especially since Toroca had brought along many fine wares from the Capital as gifts for Jodor and her people.

As soon as they were settled in, Toroca ordered a major excavation, hoping to find another one of the strange blue artifacts. His team worked every daylight moment just below the chalk seam of the Bookmark layer, the bottommost rock stratum containing fossils, but nothing turned up. Toroca began to fear the strange thing he'd found was a one-of-a-kind fluke. Finally, frustrated, he ordered the use of explosives, the kind of blackpowder used to clear out rocks when building roads. It seemed a safe move: Toroca was pretty sure that even such blasts wouldn't damage artifacts built of the blue material, although, of course, he had to move far enough along the cliff face that the explosion wouldn't put at risk the buildings that Pack Derrilo was occupying.

Blasting was always dangerous; road builders lost many people in accidents with explosives—either blown up by mounds of powder that went off prematurely or buried under rock slides caused by the explosions. Indeed, it was not uncommon to see a road worker with one or both hands in the process of regeneration, stubby yellow fingers sprouting from a tiny palm.

Delplas was the team's explosives expert. She poured black powder into six funnels made of paper, each of which had a fuse of twine sticking out of its apex, and stuck them in cracks just below the Bookmark layer. Delplas's hands were her originals; they showed none of the mottling or discoloration associated with parts regenerated in adulthood. This inspired some degree of confidence, but the pheromones wafting on the wind made clear how nervous everyone was.

Six of the seven team members would have to act as fuse lighters. Toroca, of course, was going to be one of those. It wouldn't do to order others to perform a task he was reluctant to undertake himself.

From his vantage point, some hundred and thirty paces up the cliff face, he could see two of the other fuse lighters. But three more were hidden amongst the rocks. The only way to do it was to shout off a countdown.

"Five," yelled Delplas.

Toroca fumbled with the wooden match.

"Four."

He stuck the match against a rock. It didn't take.

"Three."

He tried again and this time it spluttered to life.

"Two."

The wind was stronger than he'd thought. It blew out the match. He scrambled for another—

"One."

—struck it, shielded the flame, and—

"Zero."

—touched it to the fuse, which began to burn with an acrid smell. He watched long enough to be sure the fuse wouldn't blow out, then, as fast as he could, scrambled down the steep rock face, climbing ropes providing handholds where the rock itself would not. Once on level ground, he ran, tipping forward, his thick tail flying out behind, his back parallel to the dirt. To his left, two others were likewise running with all their strength; to his right, three more. Toroca was counting in his head; the fuse should burn for twenty more beats.

Delplas had used a lot of powder; they'd have to run as fast as they—

Toroca tripped, his toeclaws having caught in a small crevice in the ground. His body slammed into the hard, cracked dirt, his chest riblets pressing in.

Dazed, he tried to make it to his feet, then realized there was no time.

He rolled on his side, looked back. Delplas was the only one behind him still, but now by only a body length or two. Her face was a mask of concern.

And then the powder ignited, like thunder, each cone exploding at almost, but not quite, the same instant. The face of the cliff seemed to shatter like an eggshell, then hang, suspended for a half a beat, and then, and then, and then—

—tumbling and falling down, thousands of slabs of gray shale, a massive cloud of dust blowing off to the west, a hail of pebbles raining out of the sky, even this far away—

—wingfingers startled into flight—

—and to Toroca's shock, a previously unseen herd of wild running-beasts stampeding away from the cliff's base.

Toroca brushed himself off and got to his feet. Delplas, mouth open in a loose grin, held up both hands, her badge of office, intact.

The dust cloud was incredible, and the stench of black powder filled the air. When it finally cleared, Toroca's jaw dropped wide open.

Half the embankment had been reduced to rubble. Protruding from what was left of the cliff face was a vast rounded structure, the size of a very large building, made of the enigmatic blue material.

Chapter 37

Capital City

Out on the street, Afsan couldn't see the crowd, but he knew it was there nonetheless. He could smell it, smell the pheromones of every single one of the passersby. How many? He couldn't say. Hundreds, perhaps even thousands. The pheromones weren't just the normal bodily scents, either. He was used to the occasional whiff of a female in heat, or a female about to lay eggs, or an individual of either sex primed for the hunt, or the unmistakable signal of one torpid after a large meal.

But these pheromones were different.

Fear.

Claustrophobia.

A sense of being trapped.

They washed over him, chemical waves. And he—even he, the scholar's scholar, the palace's foremost intellectual—was not immune to their effects.

The tips of his fingers tingled, his claws itching in their sheaths, eager to pop out into the light of day. Whether those around him were showing the same restraint as he, keeping their claws hidden, he had no way to tell.

With each step, he felt his torso tipping forward, as if into the horizontal posture of territorial challenge. He pulled himself upright again and again, but the tipping was becoming more and more pronounced.

Muscles in his throat were contracted, held rigidly under conscious control. His dewlap felt as though it was ready, at any moment, to balloon up into a great ruby ball.

And there was a strange sensation, a working of muscles, inside his head. It finally came to him—his eyes would have been darting left and right, nervous, scanning . . . if he'd had any eyes, that is.

He knew he should get out of there, get away from the crowded streets, get back out into the countryside, to Rockscape, perhaps, where the steady breeze from off the water would blow fresh air onto him, air free of pheromones, free of tension.

The clicking of toeclaws on the paving stones was like hail: a constant *rat-a-tat*, an unending barrage. How many feet? How many Quintaglios? How big a crowd?

He tried to calm himself, to think soothing thoughts. He thought about the stars, the beautiful stars . . . the stars he had intended to devote his life to studying, until he'd lost his sight. Afsan shook his head, clearing his mind. *Try again.* He thought about Dybo, his oldest friend, his greatest supporter . . . who had allowed his blinding. *No.* He thought about Novato, lovely Novato, brilliant inventor of the far-seer, and that one magical time when their bodies had come together, that glorious night that led to the existence of his children, Haldan and Galpook, Kelboon and Toroca, Drawtood and Yabool, Dynax and little Helbark, who had succumbed early on to illness. Wonderful children, brilliant children, *so many children*, children everywhere, underfoot . . .

Afsan found his body tipping far forward again. He forced it erect, forced his tail to touch the ground—

—and someone stepped on it—

—and that was it—

Afsan felt the change in his body, felt instinct rising up, taking hold.

He swung around, his torso coming forward as he did so, his tail lifting, his body bobbing up and down, up and down, the challenge upon him, *dagamant* seizing him.

They had called him The One in his youth, the greatest hunter since the Original Five. Even blind, even in a fury, even getting on to middle age, he still had the moves, still had the timing. He could hear the breathing of the one nearest him, short, sharp intakes, as if that person, too, was fighting to retain self-control. It was a male, Afsan knew at once, the pheromone unmistakable.

"Good Afsan," said the voice, trying to sound soothing but the tone curdled by fear. It was a voice he recognized, a person he knew. Pod-Oro, aide to . . . to . . . Afsan's mind was fogging, his intellect ebbing . . . to governor Rodlox of Edz'toolar . . .

So much the better.

Afsan lunged forward, arms outstretched. His hands connected. A shoulder beneath his left, a haunch under his right. Oro was completely horizontal himself, in a pose of challenge. His head would be right about—

Afsan felt his own skin tearing, Oro's claws slicing through his upper arm. It didn't matter; the pain didn't really register. All that mattered now was the kill—

As long as he was in partial physical contact with Oro, as long as he could feel a limb or a bit of his torso, Afsan could extrapolate where the other's vulnerable parts would be.

The One.

Afsan's torso shot forward and down, bringing his head in low, jaws agape.

The crunch of neck bones.

Teeth popping from their sockets.

And the taste of blood, hot and surging . . .

Oro didn't even scream as he died. His body just fell to the stone roadway with a dull thud.

And then Afsan felt hands upon his back.

He wheeled again.

The madness had begun.

Chapter 38

Toroca had hoped at most to find a few more artifacts. He'd never expected anything like this. Whatever the vast structure was, it was still half-buried in the cliff face. It was big enough to be a large building or a temple or even a great sailing ship. Only one thing was clear at this point: the object was blue, the same cool blue as the small artifact Toroca had found earlier. Ignoring the stench of black powder, Toroca moved closer, the rest of his team following behind.

The structure was completely outside of Toroca's experience. He kept staring at it, trying to fathom what it was, but it just didn't fit anything he'd ever seen before. The thing was roughly ovoid, assuming the part still buried curved back the way the exposed part did, but it had many projections and its surface was corrugated in some places, fluted in others.

Just getting up the rock face was treacherous. So much new debris had been laid down, and it had had no time to settle. But he couldn't wait.

Toroca and his surveyors spent the rest of the afternoon clambering around, examining the exterior of the vast blue structure. There was no direct way to associate such a massive object—some thirty paces high—with a single rock layer, but it was made out of the same blue stuff as the original six-fingered artifact, and that had been excavated from the layer immediately below the Bookmark layer, so it seemed likely this vast structure dated from the same period.

Finally, a shout went up. "Over here!"

It echoed badly against the cliff face and had to compete with the sound of crashing waves from the beach below. At last Toroca located the source. Delplas was gesticulating wildly. She was perched at the edge of the visible part of the object, where the blue material jutted out of the cliff. Toroca scrambled across the rock to join her, almost tumbling down the embankment in his eagerness to get there.

She was pointing at an inlaid rectangle in the blue material. The rectangle was twice as high as it was wide—or twice as wide as it was high; no one was yet sure which way was up for this vast object. A prominent series of geometric markings appeared in a line embossed across the short dimension of the panel. Beneath it was an incised rectangle where, perhaps, a sign or note had once gone. "It's a door," said Delplas.

Toroca was elated. It did indeed look like a door. But his elation was short-lived. "Where are the hinges?" he said.

"I think it's a sliding door," said Delplas. Such doors were common on cabinets: two sliding panels could be staggered to cover the entire interior, or both pushed to the same side to leave the other half of the inside exposed.

"Perhaps," said Toroca. "But how do we slide it aside? There's no handle."

Delplas's face fell, too. "Hmm. That does pose a problem, doesn't it?"

"We can't blast through that material," said Toroca. He drummed his fingertips on the hard blue surface, so solid, so unrelenting . . .

Something gave.

Just a little, a slight movement, as he tapped against the incised rectangle in the center of the door panel. There was a hollow behind it. The rectangle wasn't inlaid in the door material. Rather, it was tacked overtop of it, held in place with the same clever little gray clips that had sealed the two halves of the original hemispherical artifact Toroca had found.

"Help me with this," said Toroca.

Delplas stood there, not understanding.

"Come here," snapped Toroca. "Help me open this panel."

"There's not enough room for both of us . . . ," she said.

"Don't worry about that, for God's sake. It will only take a moment to try. Come here."

She seemed dazed.

"Here! Come on. You can go hunt afterward, but this will take more than two hands." At last she moved closer. "Thank you," said Toroca. "Now, pry your fingerclaws in there, and there. No, like this. That's right. Now pull."

"Nothing's happening, Toroca."

"Keep trying. Pull!"

"It's stuck—"

"*Pull!*"

"My claws are going to tear out—"

But at that moment that panel did pop forward, revealing a rectangular hollow within the door. It was filled with crumbling bits of corroded metal, at least some of which had been iron, or an iron alloy, judging by the orange color.

"Was that a lock of some sort?" asked Delplas.

"Whatever it was," said Toroca, "it's rusted away. Maybe it was some sort of recessed handle."

Toroca placed his fingers on the lip of the depression and, bracing himself against the rocky slope, pulled to the left with all his might. Nothing.

"Maybe it slides the other way," said Delplas.

Toroca tried pulling to the right. "I think—"

"It didn't move," said Delplas.

"I *felt* it move," said Toroca. "It shifted, ever so slightly. But it did shift."

There wasn't room enough in the indentation for two pairs of hands. Toroca stepped aside and Delplas gave a healthy yank. "Maybe," she said doubtfully. "Maybe it moved a little."

Toroca leaned in close, examined the remnants of whatever metal device had been hidden behind the little panel. "Maybe the door's jammed on the metalwork. Get Greeblo."

Greeblo was the oldest member of the survey crew, and, therefore, the largest and strongest. Delplas returned with her a short time later.

"It's seized up," said Toroca. "Perhaps with your strength . . ."

Greeblo, about twice Toroca's bulk, bent in low to examine the mechanism. The lip was fairly thin—no need for thick structures when building out of this fantastic material. "I'll slice my hand off if I pull with all my strength against that edge," she said. She fished a calibrated tape out of one of the pockets on her geologist's sash and made some measurements of the little declivity, the lip, and so on. Then, without a word, she turned to leave.

"Where are you going?" demanded Toroca.

"I'll be back," said the oldster.

And she was, about half a daytenth later. She had with her a little wooden block, rather hastily carved. Greeblo fitted it over the lip, giving her a decent handhold. She then gestured for Toroca and Delplas to stand well clear. Greeblo dug in her heels and yanked against her handgrip with all her might. The door did shift slightly. She yanked again. Toroca could hear a sound of groaning metal. Another pull. And then a loud snap. Toroca thought for a moment that Greeblo had broken her arm, but, no, the snap had come from within the wall of the object. The door panel was shifting slowly, until, at last, at long last, a tiny sliver of darkness appeared along the left edge. Toroca let out a whoop of victory. Greeblo gave one more giant yank. About a hand span's worth of darkness was exposed now. Greeblo collapsed, exhausted. "You'll have to get others to do the rest," she said.

Toroca did just that. Now that there was a gap down the entire long dimension of the door, he was able to get six hardy Quintaglios to move in and yank in unison. The territorial instinct would be flying high in such close proximity to others, but the anger could be taken out on the physical task at hand.

The door moved. Not quickly, and not far, but it did move, until, at last, it seized up again and no amount of pulling would shift it any farther. It was about halfway open, enough for a Quintaglio of Toroca's age, and maybe others a few kilodays older, to slip through, but poor Greeblo would never be able to make it.

The sun had already slipped below the top of the cliff—opening the door had taken most of the afternoon. Toroca managed to squeeze sideways into the dark chamber, bending his tail painfully as he did so. The floor was tipped at an angle, but it was still quite acceptable for standing.

"Well?" called Delplas.

"It's dark in here," said Toroca, his voice echoing. "I can't see a thing. Someone get me a lamp, please."

A few moments later a lit oil lamp was passed through to Toroca. Delplas craned to see in the half-open door. "Well? Well?"

Toroca's voice, still echoing, was heavy with disappointment. "It's an empty room. Nothing more than that. Just an empty room. Big enough for maybe two people, assuming they could stand to be this close to each other."

"There's no door? No hallway?"

"Nothing, except some grillwork on the walls," said Toroca. "It's just a cubicle; maybe a closet or storage locker."

"Nobody," rumbled Greeblo, "puts closets on the outside of buildings."

Toroca was quiet for a moment. Then: "You're right, Greeblo! The far wall isn't a wall at all; it's another sliding door, just like the first one." A pause. "I wonder why anyone would put two doors so close together. It's got a similar rectangular panel in its center, but this one's covered with some orange paint and bold markings. This panel's smaller than the one on the outside; the clips are closer together. I think I can get it off myself. Let me—there, it's off. So *that's* what the metal thing is supposed to look like!"

"Do you want me to come in as well?" asked Delplas.

It was an unusual question. There wasn't enough room to observe proper territoriality with them both in there. Delplas must be mightily excited indeed.

"No, that's all right. It's pretty straightforward, really—just an articulated handle of some sort. I'm opening the door now."

There was a soft scraping sound, then a strange musty odor.

"It's—"

Not another word from Toroca.

The flame from the lamp went out.

"Toroca! Toroca!"

Toroca slumped against the wall.

Chapter 39

Capital City

There were only a few ways to quell *dagamant*. The first was simply to let it run its course, but that would mean many, many dead. The second was to terrify those who were aroused, for fear made different instincts come into play; it was the panic caused by a landquake that had put an end to the great battle in Capital City's central square sixteen kilodays ago, after all. And the third way, which sometimes worked and sometimes did not, was to shift the individual bloodlust of the territorial fever into the collective, cooperative bloodlust of the hunt.

Dagamant spread on the wind, pheromones touching it off in one Quintaglio after another. Dybo had ordered his imperial staff to prepare for the eventual riots the population surge would cause. The question now was whether anyone who had been part of those briefings was still in enough control to actually enact the plan.

Pal-Cadool had survived a mass *dagamant* once before; he'd been in the central square, then, as now, an aide to Afsan, when the imperial forces and the Lubalites had skirmished all those kilodays ago. Cadool had seen the signs leading up to the current explosion and had taken pains to keep himself stuffed with food, the torpor that follows eating helping both to curb the hunting reflex and to make one less irritable, less territorial. He had no idea where Afsan was. His first thought was to try to find the savant, but he realized that heading into the mob would be a fatal mistake—if not fatal for himself, fatal for those he would encounter: the euphoria of a filled stomach could counteract only so much external stimulus. He ran for the stockyards, his giant stride—Novato did not call him Cadly without good reason—covering the many blocks quickly.

The stockyards, at the southern edge of Capital City, near places of business but away from any residential quarters, corralled a small herd of shovelmouths. Shovelers spent most of their time on all fours, but could rise up and even walk around on their hind legs if the mood struck them. They all had the wide, flat prows covered with bony sheaths that gave these animals their name. On the tops of their skulls, most kinds of shovelmouth had a different, distinctive hollow crest of bone.

Many types were present in the stockyard, milling about, eating cones from the thick stands of trees that lined the yard's periphery, nipping the grasses, or just sunning themselves beneath the purple sky.

The entire stockyard was surrounded by stone fencing, except for one wide, wrought-iron gate. Cadool lifted the bolt that held the gate shut and pushed his shoulder against the rusting metal bars to open it. They left a flaking orange mark on his sash.

The shovelers gave no sign of interest. Cadool shouted out to them, "Come on, come on!" But shovelers made deafening calls by pumping air through their head crests. The comparatively quiet shouting of Cadool wasn't enough to get their attention.

Cadool had been a butcher before he'd become Afsan's assistant. Indeed, he'd apprenticed here, at this very stockyard, before being assigned to the smaller imperial yard adjacent to the palace. He entered the yard, placed his palms flat against the sides of his muzzle to restrict the airflow, and whistled twice, while stomping his long legs into the ground.

Still no response from the beasts.

Cadool hurried far into the stockyard, approaching a shoveler with a semicircular crest. The creature, standing passively on all fours, was about three times as long as Cadool was tall, with a rough hide covered with a matrix of little conical bumps. Cadool slapped its rump as hard as he could. The creature didn't budge, but it did swing its supple neck around to look at him sideways.

"Come on!" said Cadool. "The gate's open. Go!"

He whacked it again on the rump. The shoveler's belly expanded as it took in breath, then its wide-brimmed mouth opened, and Cadool was blasted by a call like thunder and a rock slide and giant waves slapping against a ship's hull all rolled into one. Cadool staggered back, covering his earholes. Nearby, another shoveler, this one with a tubular crest sticking out of the back of its skull, lifted its head from the grass and also regarded Cadool.

He was trained in the art of animal handling, but it *was* a hot day, the tiny, white sun beating down. This beast seemed completely uninterested in heeding Cadool's wishes. But perhaps that other one . . .

Cadool hurried over to the tube-crested shoveler and gave it a slap on the flank. This one seemed a little less recalcitrant. It turned halfway around and was now facing toward the open gate—

—which, Cadool suddenly realized, meant it couldn't see the gate at all, since the beast's eyes faced to the side. Cadool danced to the left and the head tracked him, the long cylindrical crest cutting a swath through the air as it did so.

And, finally, the stupid animal caught sight of the open gate. This one, at least, was interested in escaping. It began a slow march toward the opening. Time was of the essence, and Cadool couldn't countenance such an indolent pace. He shouted at the creature and pounded it again and again on its flank. Finally it began to gallop, and, a moment later, it made a different, deeper, more resonant call than the one the other shoveler had pumped out earlier.

Another shoveler reared up on its hind legs to see what was going on, then, almost at once, it dropped back to a quadruped stance and began to charge after the tube-head. Two more quickly joined in, each making its resounding call. Three adults and a juvenile, all with double-spiked crests, began to run for the gate, too.

Cadool suddenly realized he was very much in trouble.

The shovelmouths were stampeding. Clouds of dust were swirling into the sky.

It was, more or less, what he'd wanted, but he hadn't planned on being in the way. They would trample him as though he were a shrub. He moved quickly, his long gait coming to his aid again, and with a smooth motion, hauled himself up on the back of the shovelmouth with the semicircular crest that he'd originally approached. The creature seemed startled, but Cadool moved his hands quickly to the sides of its neck, soothing it in the traditional way employed by animal handlers. Even over the pounding of feet around him, Cadool could hear a faint whistling with each of his shovelmouth's breaths as air moved through the curving passages of its crest. He pushed his feet against the shoveler's hide, taking care that the bony spurs on his heels did not pierce the rough skin. This shoveler, at last, was goaded into motion, galloping toward the open gate, Cadool holding on to the base of its neck tightly.

The ride was rough, and Cadool's full stomach threatened to heave, but soon he and his impromptu mount were out of the stockyard and heading down the streets of Capital City.

Pandemonium. Quintaglios shouting, individuals running back and forth, tails flying. Over there, two females locked in a death struggle, muzzles bright red with blood. To Cadool's right, a male's corpse, the neck ripped wide open, a vast puddle of blood spilling away from the wound. Ahead, a juvenile, still many kilodays shy of his first hunt, leaping through the air, claws extended, landing on the back of an older fellow in a merchant's sash, the force of the impact driving them both down onto the paving stones.

He heard no voices, only guttural screams, animal wails, and the ululations of the stampeding shovelmouths, five or six beasts in front of Cadool's own, several tens more bringing up the rear.

"*Kalahatch!*" shouted Cadool, as loud as he could, again and again, desperate to be heard over the din. "*Kalahatch! Kalahatch!*" It was an ancient cry, a traditional call to the hunt. The animal beneath him bucked, as if it knew what the word meant. Cadool moved his hands *so* and the beast's back stopped snapping up and down.

The pounding of shoveler feet and their deafening calls were enough to break a few of the Quintaglios out of the blood rage. In front of a shop he was passing, one fellow pushed aside the female he'd been grappling with and looked up. Cadool turned to him and shouted imploringly, "*Kalahatch!*"

The fellow looked indecisive for an instant, then charged toward the nearest shovelmouth, one of the rare ones with a crest like two crescent moons. He leapt onto the shoveler's side and brought his jaws together in a great scooping bite.

The female he'd been fighting charged after him, as if to tear him apart, but then with a visible effort of will at the last instant she changed her course and also leapt onto the shoveler, chomping into its meaty rump.

Cadool was carried farther down the street. He continued his hunting cry. Ahead, right in the middle of the road, was a ball of green arms and legs and tails—perhaps six or seven Quintaglios locked in mortal combat.

Cadool jabbed his feet into his shoveler's side, this time toes in, deliberately piercing the hide. The tube-crester pumped out an anguished cry, splitting the air like all the thunder of a storm discharged with a single blast. Heads appeared from the ball of limbs, slick all over with blood.

"*Kalahatch!*" shouted Cadool.

Three individuals disentangled themselves from the ball; the rest, dead, dying, or dazed, didn't get out of the way in time and were trampled by the stampede. But the ones who had escaped ran to the sides of the road, ensconcing themselves in recessed doorways, letting part of the shovelmouth herd thunder by. Cadool looked back long enough to see two of them leap onto shovelers. The third, a male apparently more injured than Cadool had first thought, collapsed slowly to the paving stones as the rest of the herbivores pounded on.

Cadool continued into the center of town. He was having about a three-quarters success rate at getting the crazed Quintaglios to switch from killing each other to hunting the shovelers. As for the rest, there was nothing he could do.

Suddenly the street widened into a large square, dotted with the red-spattered bodies of the dead or dying.

Entering the square from the opposite direction was another cluster of shovelmouths. Quintaglios were attacking them, purging their rage through the hunt, coming together in the hunt, cooperating for the hunt—

But how? Where were these other shovelers coming from?

And then Cadool saw. Dybo, the Emperor himself, riding atop a shovelmouth with an orange-and-blue-striped hide, one of the imported Arj'-toolar beasts kept in the private imperial stockyard. Dybo, unaggressive to the point of docility, thought to be the weakest of his mother's hatchlings, all but immune, apparently, to the clouds of pheromones drenching every corner of the Capital. Dybo, risking his life to quell the madness in his people.

Cadool saluted the Emperor, and Dybo waved back. The tide was turning, the madness abating, the population releasing its bloodlust. Shovelers fell to the paving, and Quintaglios feasted together, their mode shifting from violence to the torpor brought by full bellies.

Many had died, but most had survived—this time. But Cadool knew this was only a temporary reprieve.

Next time, they might not be so lucky.

Chapter 40

Fra'toolar

The first thing Toroca heard was a voice.

"What happened?" It was Delplas.

Toroca tried to rise, but made a small groan instead. "My head hurts."

"You banged it when you collapsed," said Delplas. "What happened?"

Toroca opened his eyes. It was dark; eight moons moved overhead. "When that inner door opened, I got this gush of air in my face. It was stale, musty. It smelled wrong. Then I collapsed."

"Something funny about the air," said Greeblo. "Your lamp went out, too."

"How long have I been unconscious?"

"Not too long," said Delplas. "About a daytenth."

Toroca sighed. "It's night. Let's wait until morning to let some decent air get into that thing, then head back inside."

"Aye," said Delplas. "You're probably right."

It was even-night, the night most people didn't sleep—everyone was back on normal schedules. Toroca lay on his belly, eyes turned up, watching the stars career across the bowl of the sky.

As soon as the sun was up, Toroca squeezed into the tiny room with doors at either end. The outer door was still jammed half open; the inner wasn't yet quite open all the way. Toroca had succumbed to the bad air before he'd slid the panel all the way to the left side. He sniffed warily. Everything smelled fine now. He pulled the inner door all the way aside and stepped through, into the interior of the object, whatever it was, the spluttering flame from a handheld lantern illuminating his way.

He was in a long gently curving corridor, running parallel to the outer wall of the object. Toroca was immediately startled by how straight the corridor was. Most Quintaglio corridors twisted and turned so as to keep other users of them out of sight. There was a standard walking pace for corridors: as long as you moved along at that pace, you could walk the length of most hallways without ever seeing another individual, even if the hallway was actually in heavy use.

"Well?" called Delplas from outside.

"It seems all right," replied Toroca, his voice echoing a bit. "Come along."

Toroca stepped about ten paces down the corridor. He could hear Delplas making her way through the strange double-doored room.

The light from two lanterns—Toroca's and Delplas's—cast weird shadows on the blue walls. The object, like everything on Land, had been rocked over time by landquakes, and its floors were canted at an angle. Thick black dust had accumulated along the downslope side of the corridors. Toroca thought perhaps it was the remnant of some fabric covering that had decayed over time, although why one would put tapestries on the floor was beyond him.

They passed their first room. It contained blobs of corroded metal; perhaps once they had been furniture. None of the rooms seemed to have doors, just open archways. That made even more peculiar the strange double-doored room they had first come through. Littering the floor were artifacts similar to the one Toroca had originally found and clumps of rusted material, presumably artifacts made of less-stern stuff that had corroded.

Toroca and Delplas continued along, ten or so paces between them. The next room they passed also contained corroded metal, and the one after that, nothing at all, except intricate metal panels—perhaps art of some kind?—embedded in the walls. Toroca leaned in to examine one of the panels. It was perforated with many tiny holes in regular patterns, and most of the holes were covered with bits of colored glass or crystal. Little geometric shapes were etched into parts of the panels.

It took a while, but Toroca finally noticed the roofs. The ceilings of the corridor and rooms weren't made of the same blue material. Rather, they seemed to be covered over with translucent glass. In several places, the glass was broken. Looking closely at a large piece that had fallen to the floor, Toroca saw that it wasn't really glass. It was a softer material, waxier, and when he looked at it edge-on, it was white, rather than the dark green or blue of glass seen thus. He also found he could flex the material slightly.

Toroca looked up to where the piece of milky material had fallen from. Recessed in the roof were long orange tubes, and these, mostly cracked and shattered, did look as though they were made from real glass.

It was one of those sudden flashes of insight. Toroca suddenly realized what was missing from the walls—hooks to hang lanterns on, candle holders, anything to hold a light source. The translucent roof, and the strange tubes behind, must have provided light, somehow. Perhaps the tubes were optical conduits, something like Novato's far-seers, channeling light from outside. Perhaps.

The next room they came upon was a complete surprise. Toroca motioned for Delplas to come stand relatively near him.

"What do you make of that?" said Toroca.

Jutting from the walls of the room were pallets, each one about twice as long as it was wide, covered with a pile of decayed material that might at one time have been fabric. There were a total of twelve pallets, three at about Toroca's knee level on each side of the room, and three more above these at his shoulder level. The upper pallets had strange ladder-like affairs leading up to them, except that the ladders were really two narrow ladders paired side by side, with a hand span's gap between them. Toroca couldn't fathom what the use of such ladders would be; they were almost what one might imagine for a Quintaglio who wanted to climb backward and needed a slot for his or her tail.

"They're beds," said Delplas at last, gesturing at the pallets.

Beds. Most Quintaglios slept on the floor, but such things were used in hospitals or in the homes of the very old to bring bodies up to a comfortable level for doctors to work on. But in all his life, Toroca had never seen a room with more than one bed in it.

"That would mean twelve people slept in this room at once," said Toroca. "That's not possible. No one could stand such close quarters for any length of time." And, when the words were out, Toroca realized how true they were—even for him, even free of territoriality, the idea of sleeping with eleven others was completely beyond his ken.

"They do look like beds, though, don't they?" persisted Delplas.

Toroca thought about that. "Yes. Yes, they do." He shuddered as a thought occurred to him. Yes, this vast object was miraculous, but he'd still retained the thought, the six-fingered handgrip of the original artifact not withstanding, that it was of Quintaglio manufacture. After all, who else could have possibly built it? But this room—this room was no room a Quintaglio would ever use. And those straight corridors— hallways no Quintaglio would feel comfortable walking in except when completely alone. Someone else—some*thing* else—had built this.

What, wondered Toroca, did the builders look like?

———

With the outer door jammed partially closed, poor Greeblo still couldn't get inside the great blue structure. Her job became cataloging the markings on its vast curving surface. Meanwhile, Toroca organized the other six surveyors into three interior-exploration teams. Because of the poor air circulation within the massive structure, each team had only a single lamp.

Toroca and Delplas constituted one such team. It was hard on Delplas, since Toroca carried the lamp and territoriality tended to make her lag behind in the dark. The blue structure was huge, and it was frustrating not to be able to get a really good look at its interior. Toroca's lamp flame lit only a small area. The rest faded away into eerie darkness.

The inner walls were all made of the same blue material as the outer shell. Toroca tried to find seams indicating where two sheets of the blue stuff had been joined, but he couldn't. It was almost as if the whole vast structure was one continuous piece, like blown glass.

Suddenly something occurred to Toroca. "It's not a sailing ship," he said, turning around to face Delplas, who cast a giant dancing shadow on the wall behind her in the swaying light of Toroca's lamp.

"Oh?" she replied, crossing her arms in front of her chest. "I agree it doesn't look like any ship I've ever seen before, but, well, it is streamlined on the outside, and it has a ship-like quality about it."

"Think about the *Dasheter*," he said. "Do you remember the doorways?"

"They had nice scenes carved into them," said Delplas.

"Yes, yes. But they also didn't go all the way to the floor, I'm sure. There was a lip, a hand span or greater in height, that you had to step over at each doorway."

"Now that you mention it, I do remember that."

"It was to keep water from sloshing from compartment to compartment," said Toroca. "As Var-Keenir once said to me, all ships leak."

Delplas nodded in understanding. "But here the doorways go right to the floor, and in most cases there are no actual doors at all, just open archways."

"Exactly," said Toroca. "Whatever this thing was used for, it wasn't a sailing ship."

"But it can't have been a building, either. It has a rounded floor. I mean, here, inside, the floors are flat, but the bottom of the—of the hull, call it—the bottom of the hull, as seen from outside, is rounded."

"Yes. And no one would build an edifice that didn't have a flat bottom."

"So it *is* a ship," said Delplas.

"Perhaps."

"But not a sailing ship."

"No, not a sailing ship."

"Then what kind of ship is it?"

"I don't—"

"Toroca!"

The shout came from deep in the interior of the structure. Toroca broke into a dead run, Delplas following. His lantern made mad shadows run along with them as they bounded down the strange, straight corridors.

"Toroca!" went the shout again, echoing off the hard blue walls.

Ahead, Gan-Spalton was standing by an open doorway. "It had been closed," he said, pointing. "One of the few I've seen that actually had a door. I operated the latch, and—"

The corpse was desiccated. If it had been at one time covered with skin, that skin was long since gone. The body was about the same bulk as Toroca, but that was the only characteristic they had in common. The dome-shaped head had five eyes. A long trunk dangled from the face. It ended in a pair of convex, shell-shaped manipulators, each with six little fingers within, just right for handling the strange artifact Toroca had found all those days ago.

The body was slumped over, a bowl-shaped structure visible beneath it that might have been a chair. The creature's torso was made up of a series of disks, shining like opals in the torchlight. At the end of the torso was a cup-shaped brace supporting three pairs of legs. The first pair was long, the second and third pairs much shorter, and looked as though they wouldn't have reached the ground if the creature had been standing.

Toroca staggered back on his tail. What manner of creature was this? It was unlike a Quintaglio, or anything else he was familiar with. Even the bizarre life-forms of the south pole had shared a fundamental body plan that he recognized, but this, this was like nothing he'd ever seen before, nothing he'd even imagined before.

And then it hit him, and his jaw dropped.

This ship, this giant blue vessel, must have traveled very far indeed.

Chapter 41

Two down, four to go.

Perhaps I should have done Toroca when I last saw him. It will be a long time before he returns to the Capital, I'm sure. Still, the fact that he is away so much of the time makes his existence tolerable . . . to a degree. Absence makes the heart grow calmer.

That mass dagamant *was a release for me, and for many others, I'm sure. Perhaps I'll wait awhile until I do number three.*

Or perhaps not.

Capital City

After the collective *dagamant*, Cadool searched and searched for Afsan. At last he found him, disoriented, unsure of where he was, slumped in an alley beside a building, exhausted, bruised, bloodied, but not severely injured.

They retired to Rockscape for three days, recovering, and waiting for Gathgol, now the busiest of all workers in the province, to collect all the bodies that littered the streets.

But, at last, Afsan and Cadool came back into the city to deal with the task at hand.

"Let's rest here," said Cadool. They'd been walking all afternoon, going from one side of the Capital to the other, the streets still a mess, blood splatters on the paving stones and adobe walls, broken tree branches and discarded sashes skittering along the avenues, propelled by the wind.

Here, in a small plaza, a marble likeness of the astrologer Tak-Saleed had been erected. Unlike many of the monuments in the Capital, this one was still standing despite the riots. Cadool helped Afsan find a seat on a bench, sitting him in the shadow of the statue.

"There is no sign that bloodpriest Maliden is in Capital City," said Cadool, easing himself onto another bench. "Dy-Dybo's guards have searched everywhere."

Afsan nodded. "I always thought that was a long shot. Maliden would do well to be on the run; he'd be a fool to have remained here."

"Indeed."

"And Rodlox is telling the truth when he says he didn't do it."

"I've not heard such invective in my whole life," said Afsan. "He took great offense that we should even ask."

"But he did not commit the murders."

"No."

"It's difficult to really fathom a motive for Dy-Dybo's other siblings," said Cadool. "Even so, only Dedprod and Spenress were already in town at the time of the first murder, and neither of them did it."

"That's right, neither of them."

"So that excuses all members of The Family."

"Yes."

"But not all members of *your* family."

Afsan's tail swished. "No."

"Toroca was away on his Antarctic voyage during the first murder," said Cadool.

Afsan nodded. "It pleases me that I didn't have to speak to him about this."

"And your daughter Dynax, although from Chu'toolar, where the mirror was made, told us the truth when asked if she was involved."

"Yes."

"Kelboon and hunt leader Galpook told us the truth, too; they're innocent," said Cadool, holding up a hand, ticking off fingers.

"A process of elimination," said Afsan.

"Yes," said Cadool. "Both what we're doing, and, in a way, what *he* is doing." There was no clicking of teeth accompanying the words.

"It was distasteful asking those questions of people I know," said Afsan.

"They will forgive you."

"I suppose."

"There's no doubt who the murderer is," said Cadool.

Afsan spoke quickly. "There's *little* doubt, yes. But until I confront him, I will assume his innocence."

"As you wish." Cadool paused. "Does it hurt?"

"What? Losing two children? Or being about to lose a third? In any event, yes, it hurts."

"I'll never know what it's like to have a family," said Cadool softly.

"Apparently," said Afsan, "different individuals react in different ways to the concept."

Cadool nodded. "Apparently."

They were quiet for a time, Cadool knowing that Afsan was composing himself, preparing for what must come. At last Afsan said, "Let's go."

"To see him?"

"Not yet. We must go to my office in the palace first. There are some things I need. And we should have an escort, I think."

They got to their feet and walked toward the setting sun.

Fra'toolar

It turned out that the part of the ship they'd been exploring wasn't the major part at all. Only a tiny fraction of the ship's bulk had been exposed by blasting away a portion of the cliff face. Much, much more of it was still buried in the rock. To get to the other section, one had to pass through another one of those rooms with doors at either end.

Everyone stood well back as Toroca, having taken a deep breath, operated the second door. But this time the air that spilled out, having been locked in for who knows how long, didn't choke them, although it did have a musty smell about it. Toroca walked in and found an aisle as tall as ten old Quintaglios and so long that it would take a daytenth to walk its length.

Lining the corridor were rectangular chambers. Some were tiny, others huge. They were packed tightly together like a quilt, with each opening a different size, but all interlocking so that no space was wasted. Each chamber was fronted with glass—or perhaps it was that strange transparent material used to cover the lighting tubes.

And within—

Within were animals.

All dead. Some had decayed completely to dust, others were just piles of bones, others still retained their skin intact.

Toroca recognized some of them. Sort of, that is. Turtles and lizards and snakes looked just like, or very similar to, the ones he knew. But others were, well, wrong. Here, in one of the biggest chambers, was a shovelmouth, lying on its side, its head crest unlike any Toroca had ever seen before, with a large blade-like front part and a short spike pointing to the rear.

And here, a hornface with down-turned horns, like melted wax, unlike any hornface Toroca had ever heard of.

And here, the bones of another hornface, but this one with the frill of bone over the neck simply outlined, with huge hollow spaces in the middle.

And here, an armorback. A—it came to him, staggering him back on his tail—an armorback like one of those whose fossils are found only in the oldest rocks.

But most of the specimens were birds.

Birds!

Known only from the fossil record, and even there, only exceedingly rarely. Indeed, Toroca had to stare at the gaudily colored specimens for what seemed an eternity before he realized what they were. Some of the fossils of them showed a frayed body covering, and these specimens were wrapped in things that looked a bit like fern leaves, densely packed with branches.

Some of the birds had long toothy beaks, like those of many wingfingers, and some had thick beaks with no teeth at all, and some had rounded bodies and wide, flat prows, like the prows of shovelmouths.

But they were all birds.

Completely unknown in the world today.

Birds.

At last, Wab-Babnol returned to join the Geological Survey team in Fra'toolar. She had come via boat—one not nearly as large or famous as the *Dasheter*, though. Toroca ordered the same boat loaded up with bird specimens to be taken back to Novato in the Capital.

As soon as he got close enough to Babnol to smell her pheromones, Toroca knew it was over. Her mating time had passed; barring unusual circumstances, she would be free of the urge until another full year had elapsed, another eighteen kilodays, another quarter of her lifetime.

"Welcome back," said Toroca, both sad and glad at the same time.

Babnol bowed deeply. "Thank you."

"How are you feeling?" he asked.

"Better," she said, and, a moment later, again: "Better."

Toroca nodded. "It's good to see you again." He wanted to close the distance between them, to reach out, to—

And then Babnol did the incredible. *She* stepped toward him, closing the gap, and, with what was clearly a great deal of effort, reached up with her left hand and clasped his arm. "Thank you," she said, still squeezing warmly, "thank you very much."

Toroca's heart soared. "It's wonderful to have you back, my friend," he said.

"And it's wonderful to be back with you," she said.

She held the position for five whole beats more, then stepped back three paces.

Toroca beamed.

Chapter 42

The room was dark. A leather curtain undulated gently like a wingfinger's flapping wing in the cool breeze from the half-open window. It was odd-night, the night on which most adults slept, but Afsan had always been out of synch with the mainstream.

The hinges of the door were well-oiled, and Afsan's entrance had done nothing to disturb the apartment's sleeping occupant. Afsan had only been here once or twice, but he knew the room's layout well enough and had no trouble making his way across the living area and into the sleep chamber. As he entered the latter, he placed his leather carrying case in the open doorway.

Afsan knew there would be a candleholder on a small stand next to the part of the floor upon which the occupant was sleeping. He could hear the gentle hissing of open-mouth breathing. Afsan bent down and, after a moment, found the holder and picked it up.

Then he crossed the room, found the stool he'd been looking for, swung his leg and tail over it, and made himself comfortable. At last he spoke, not loudly, but with a firm tone. "Drawtood."

There was no response. Afsan tried again. "Drawtood."

This time he heard the sound of a body stirring on the floor, followed by a sharp intake of breath as Drawtood apparently suddenly woke and realized he was not alone.

"Who's there?" Drawtood said, his voice thick and dry. Afsan heard sounds of exertion as Drawtood pushed himself up off the floor.

"It's me, Afsan."

Suddenly there was a note of concern in the voice. "Afsan? Are you all right? What's happened?"

"Easy, my son. Easy. Lie back down. I just want to talk."

"What time is it?"

"It's the middle of the night. The eighth daytenth."

There was a sound of rummaging. "I can't seem to find my candle," said Drawtood.

"I have it. You won't need it. Lie down and talk to your father."

"What's wrong?" said Drawtood.

"That's what I'm hoping to learn from you."

"What do you mean?" The voice was wary. Afsan could tell that the speaker was still standing.

"Things are not going well, are they, Drawtood?"

"I want my candle."

"No," said Afsan softly. "We'll talk on an even footing, both in darkness. Tell me your problems, son."

"I don't have any problems."

Afsan was silent, waiting to see if Drawtood would volunteer anything further. A great length of time passed in silence, save for the whispering breeze. At last, Drawtood did speak again. "Why don't you go, now?"

"I know about Haldan. And Yabool."

"Their deaths have upset us all, I'm sure."

"I know that you killed them, Drawtood."

"You're distraught, Afsan." The voice had risen slightly in pitch. "Please, let me take you back to your home."

"You killed them."

Claw-ticks across the bare part of the floor.

"I wouldn't try to leave if I were you," said Afsan. "Pal-Cadool and five imperial guards are waiting outside your front door."

Claw-ticks going in the opposite direction. "And other guards are waiting outside your windows, of course." Afsan said it calmly, as if making an offhand comment about the weather.

"Let me leave."

"No. You have to talk to me."

"I—I don't want to."

"You have no choice. Why did you kill them?"

"I admit nothing."

"I am blind, Drawtood. My testimony would never stand. Admitting it to me is no confession, for I could never assert that your muzzle didn't change color when you said it." Afsan paused to let that sink in. Then: "Tell me why you killed them."

"I didn't kill them."

"We both know that you did. A scientist should never make assumptions, Drawtood. I did—I assumed none of my children could be responsible. I was wrong."

"Wrong," repeated Drawtood softly.

"You killed your sister Haldan and your brother Yabool."

"You don't know what it's like to have siblings," said Drawtood.

"No, I don't," said Afsan. "Tell me."

"It's like having to face yourself every day. Except it's not you. It's someone who looks like you and thinks like you, but not exactly like you."

Afsan nodded in the darkness. "Broken mirrors. Of course. I understand the choice of implement now."

"Implement?"

"The device used for the murders."

"I did not commit the murders, Afsan."

"I can't see your muzzle, Drawtood, but others will ask you that same question, and they will be able to see it. Do you wish to lie to me?"

"I did not—"

"Do you wish to lie to your father?"

Drawtood was silent for a time, and when he spoke again his voice was very small. "Only one of us children should have lived, anyway."

"Is that what you believe?"

"I didn't do anything wrong," said Drawtood.

"Didn't you?" said Afsan.

"I—I was just putting things back the way they should have been."

"It's not for any of us to say who should live and who should die. The bloodpriests alone may choose that."

"But they made a mistake. They let your eight offspring live because they thought you were The One, the hunter foretold by Lubal. But you aren't."

"No, I'm not."

"So don't you see?" There was a note of pleading in the voice now. "They made a mistake. I was just putting things right."

"Would you have killed all of them, then?"

"It had to be done. Brothers and sisters—they're demons. Shades of yourself, but twisted, mocking."

"And you would have been the only one left alive?"

"If they hadn't gotten me first."

"Pardon?"

"They were thinking the same thing. I know they were. Dynax and Galpook, Kelboon and Toroca, Haldan and Yabool. They were all thinking the same thing. If it wasn't me doing the killing it would have been one of them."

"No, it wouldn't."

"You don't know, Afsan. You don't have brothers or sisters. But look at

Dybo! Look at how his sibling turned on him. It preys on your mind, knowing there's someone out there who is you, but not quite, who thinks like you, whom people mistake for you."

"Did any of them make an attempt on your life? Threaten you in any way?"

"Of course not. But I could tell what they were thinking. I could see it in their faces. They wanted me dead. Self-defense! It was just self-defense."

"So you would have left yourself the only one alive."

"No. Maybe. I don't know. Toroca, maybe. Maybe I would have let him be the one. He was always kind to me. Maybe I'd have killed the other five, then taken my own life." He was quiet for several beats. "Maybe."

"You've committed a crime," said Afsan. "What do we do now?"

"It was not a crime."

"You must receive justice."

"You, of all people, shouldn't believe in justice. You were blinded by imperial order! Was that justice?"

Afsan's turn to be silent for a time. "No."

"I won't submit to them."

"You must. You must come with me."

"You can't stop me."

A hard edge came into Afsan's tone. "Yes, I can, Drawtood. If need be. You are alive because sixteen kilodays ago, they mistook me for The One. I was the greatest hunter of modern times. You can't get past me."

"You are blind."

"I hear your breathing, Drawtood. I can smell you. I know exactly where you are standing, exactly what you are doing. You don't have a chance against me here in the dark."

"You're blind . . ."

"Not a chance."

Silence, save for the wind.

"I don't want to hurt you, Afsan."

"You have hurt me already. You've killed two of my children."

"They had to die."

"And now you must face the consequences of your actions."

Another lengthy quiet. "What will they do to me?"

"There are no laws governing murder, and so no modern penalties are prescribed. But there were penalties in ancient times for taking another's life outside of *dagamant*." A pause. "I will urge compassion," Afsan said at last.

"Compassion," repeated Drawtood. "Have I no alternatives?"

"You tell me."

"I could take my own life."

"I would be honor-bound to try to stop you."

"If you knew what I was doing."

"Yes. If I knew."

"But if I were to kill myself quietly, while we were talking . . ."

"I might not realize it until too late."

"How does one kill oneself quietly?"

"Poison might be effective."

"I have none."

"No, of course not. On another matter, there are some documents in my carrying case that you might find interesting. I've left it by the doorway. Can you see it?"

"It's very dark."

"Tell me about it," said Afsan, but there was no clicking of teeth.

"Yes," said Drawtood, "I see it."

"Please go get them."

Ticking claws. "Which compartment are they in?"

"The main one. Oh, but be careful. There's a vial of *haltardark* liquid in there, too. It's a cleaning compound for far-seer lenses. Your mother asked me to get some for her; it's quite deadly. You'd do well not to touch it."

A long silence. "Yes," said Drawtood. Silence again. Then: "The vial has a symbol on it. It's hard to see in this light . . . a drop shape, and the outline of some animal laying on its side."

"That's the chemist's symbol for poison."

"I didn't know that."

"You do now."

"Afsan . . . ?"

"Yes."

"I'm sorry."

"Yes."

And that was followed by the longest silence of all.

Chapter 43

Musings of the Watcher

I watched it happen, helpless to intervene.

Everything had gone flawlessly so far. The final Jijaki ark, the *Ditikali-ot*, had traversed the light-years to the target without incident. It had been timed to arrive a few Crucible centuries after the previous arks, bringing fauna specimens that would do better after the rest of the animals had been established.

Sliding down the star's gravity well had gone as planned, and a double-loop maneuver braked the craft first by swinging around the gas-giant fifth planet, then around the target moon. The *Ditikali-ot* settled into a stationary orbit around the moon, holding position directly above the great watery rift that separated the two landmasses, landmasses that would eventually jam together into one as convective heat drove their respective plates closer and closer.

The *Ditikali-ot* consisted of a habitat module made of super-strong blue *kiit* held by a metal superstructure between the funnel-shaped ramscoop at one end and the fusion exhaust cone at the other. Restraining clips retracted, allowing the habitat to separate from the stardrive portion of the ship. The precious cargo from the Crucible, and the entire Jijaki crew—the last survivors of that race, now that war and old age had taken all their kin—began to enter the atmosphere.

Everything went fine until the explosion. The habitat careened wildly, spinning around its long axis, and plummeted to the ground.

One Jijaki did survive the crash, although she was badly injured. She made it out onto the ground, along with her handheld computer, an expensive model also made of *kiit*. The area was too moist for fossilization: her space suit, then her body, rotted away, but the indestructible artifact eventually came to be buried, as did the massive ark.

The habitat module had crashed not far inland on the western shore of the eastern landmass. If it had hit just a little farther to the west, in the water between the two continents, it would have eventually been subducted as the tectonic plates drove together. But where it did fall, it would probably remain for a very long time.

I had hoped to leave no trace of my handiwork, but the *Ditikali-ot* was indeed the final ark. I had no way to remove its wreckage, and every last Jijaki was now dead, so none of them could be summoned to clean up the mess.

Fra'toolar

Toroca looked up at the night sky.

He reflected that he was a child of the new universe, conceived by Afsan and Novato in the very moment at which the two of them, pooling what they had learned through her far-seers, came to realize the shape of space, the structure of the cosmos.

Before then, the Face of God was an object of veneration, not merely a planet, and the other planets were just points in the night, not distinct spheres. Before then, the moons were something unto themselves, instead of more examples of what the world was—globes spinning around the Face of God. Before then, the rings around the planets Kevpel and Bripel were unknown. Before then, the sky river was thought to be the reflection of the great body of water that Land was said to float upon, instead of, as Toroca himself had seen through lenses, countless stars.

Before then, too, the world was simpler, for it was Afsan's work, and the work of his master, the great Tak-Saleed, that had demonstrated that the world was doomed, its orbit about the Face too close to be stable.

But now the universe was even more complex, for other beings apparently lived on one of the objects in the night sky, strangers who had visited this world once, long ago, leaving behind one of their ships and, apparently, their cargo of plants and animals.

Did the strangers live on one of the other moons of the Face of God? On Swift Runner? Slowpoke? The Guardian? The thirteen other moons had been observed now for kilodays through the finest far-seers from the tops of the tallest mountains. None seemed to have liquid seas or fertile land.

Could the strangers have come from another planet? It seemed clear that the closer one moved toward the sun, that brilliant white point that lit the world, the hotter it would be. Likewise, moving farther away would plunge a world into cold, more bitter than even that of the ice caps. No, the inner planets, Carpel, Patpel, and Davpel, were surely barren and scorched, and distant Gefpel, seeming almost unmoving in the night sky, must be chilled beyond all imagining. Perhaps Kevpel, next closest to the sun from here. Or perhaps Bripel, one planet farther out. Or perhaps one of their moons, those tiny points that could be seen to accompany them through a far-seer.

Or perhaps from somewhere else, somewhere much farther away.

The sun was tiny but hot, showing a barely perceptible disk.

There were those who said the other stars were also suns, just farther away.

And if those suns had planets—

And if those planets had moons—

The strangers could have come from any one of them.

From one with a longer day—

A longer day! Quintaglios slept every other day because they'd originated on a world with a day perhaps twice as long, and, despite all the time that they'd been on this world, they'd somehow been unable to acclimatize to sleeping more frequently . . .

And yet . . . the once-a-year mating cycle *had* adapted to the rhythms of this world, apparently.

They'd been here long enough to become attuned to this world in most ways, but still, deep within their beings, there were ties to whatever crucible they'd originally formed in.

Toroca stared up at the firmament, at the wide awe and wonder of the night.

One of those points of light, perhaps, was that crucible.

He wondered if they would ever discover which one.

Chapter 44

The Arena

The compartments in Capital City's stadium had been designed to each hold a single spectator. But one compartment had had its dayslab removed so that it could accommodate both Afsan and his assistant, Pal-Cadool, sitting on small stools. Cadool's territoriality was not aroused by Afsan; the blind Quintaglio had always been a special case to him.

"Describe everything for me, please," said Afsan.

Cadool craned his neck to look up and out of the compartment's opening. "There are a few clouds in the sky—the tubular, twisty kind that look like spilled entrails." Cadool paused, clicked his teeth. "Say, that's appropriate, isn't it?" His words were drawn out, protracted along the same stretched lines as his whole wiry frame. "The sky itself is bright mauve today. The sun is still rising, of course. It's passing behind a cloud just now. There are three, no, four moons visible in the sky, two showing crescent faces, the other two gibbous."

Afsan nodded. "That would be Big One, Gray Orb, Dancer, and Slowpoke."

"Yes."

"What about the crowd?"

"Because of the way the compartments are laid out, no one else is directly visible from here. But I'm told every compartment is filled today."

"Good. What's about to happen must be widely seen if it is to have any meaning."

"Don't worry. I understand every newsrider from Capital province is in attendance, as well as many from the outlying areas."

"How does the field look?" asked Afsan.

"The grass covering it is a mixture of brown and green, but it's quite even—they've done a good job of fixing it up for this event. There aren't any exposed patches of dirt anymore. You know the field is diamond shaped? Orange powder has been laid down, marking the east-west and

north-south axes, so the diamond is split into four triangular quadrants."
Cadool was quiet for a moment, then: "Afsan, will Dybo win?"

"I'm not an astrologer anymore, Cadool. Never really was one. My
master died before he taught me the interpretation of omens."

"But you have a plan?"

"Even a plan requires much luck."

A steady drumbeat began from down below. "Ah," said Cadool, "here
come the contestants."

"Describe them, please."

"They're entering from almost directly beneath us—there's a door
into the arena at ground level there, right at the midpoint of the diamond.
Dybo is leading the procession. He's got on a very thick red belt, but no
sash. I guess sashes would be too dangerous. Anyway, the belt makes it
easy to tell it's him. The other seven are following him, each about five
paces behind. Each one's wearing a similar belt, with the color of his or
her home province."

Cheers went up, spectators from each province rooting for their cham-
pion. The cheers for Dybo were the loudest.

"It's been kilodays since I've had to worry about things such as
memorizing provincial colors," said Afsan above the hubbub. "I don't
remember the scheme."

"Of course," said Cadool. "Dybo is wearing imperial red. Kroy, from
Arj'toolar, is wearing white. Spenress, from Chu'toolar, has donned light
green. Wendest, from Fra'toolar, sports black—or maybe it's dark blue,
hard to tell. Dedprod, from Kev'toolar, is wearing light blue. Emteem—
he's from Jam'toolar—has a belt of gold. The belt of Nesster, from Mar'-
toolar, is pink. And Rodlox, from Edz'toolar, who started all this, wears
brown." Cadool had one of Novato's best handheld far-seers with him.
He brought it up to his left eye. "Dybo looks nervous, Afsan."

"I'm glad to hear that," said Afsan. "A great hunter once said to me,
'Fear is the counselor.' Cockiness will get him killed. He's wise to be
afraid."

"The blackdeath will be hungry," said Cadool. "They've starved it for
twenty days. It may eat every one of them as it is."

"Perhaps," said Afsan softly.

A gong sounded below. Everyone turned their heads toward the
entrance at the north end of the playing field, except for Afsan, who
turned his head perpendicular to the noise, the better to hear it.

"They're opening the beast gate now," said Cadool. This door led directly to the stone-walled pen the great hunter had been kept in for several hundred days, awaiting the arrival of all the challengers.

Afsan nodded. "I can hear the ratcheting of the mechanism."

"And here comes the blackdeath—"

A hush fell over the arena, except for some wingfingers who had been circling, wondering what was going on. They shrieked at the sight of the great carnivore coming slowly through the gateway.

Even though he was terrified of it, Cadool had to admit the blackdeath was beautiful. An amazing hunter, all curving teeth and claws, blacker than even those rare nights when only a couple of moons were visible.

Through the far-seer, the creature showed some signs of its ordeal. In many places, the skin on its muzzle was light gray instead of black; the great ball of resin hadn't come off as cleanly as had been planned, and much flesh had been torn off as well. And the beast's belly was caved in—it was clearly hungry.

Suddenly it began. The blackdeath surged ahead, its great strides propelling it forward across the grass. The eight contestants scattered at once.

The monster had already focused on a target: Dedprod from Kev'-toolar, wearing the blue belt. Dedprod ran to the left, but the blackdeath's stride was so many times greater than hers that she had no hope of outdistancing it.

The blackdeath's back was straight, parallel to the ground as it ran, its tail flying out behind. Except for its puny forearms and dull-witted boxy head, it looked remarkably like a Quintaglio in this posture . . . a jet-black Quintaglio, a Quintaglio covered in soot.

Dedprod ran valiantly, with astonishing speed, but she was doomed from the moment the blackdeath cast its obsidian eyes on her. The beast quickly closed the distance between them. It tipped forward, its giant head coming down, its jaws gaping wide, wider still, the blue membranes at the corners of its gaping red maw stretched tight like drumheads. The blackdeath seized her, chomping down on her back. The crack of splintering spine was clearly audible in Afsan and Cadool's compartment. Dedprod let out a scream that was cut short in midblast as her torso split open under the closing of the blackdeath's jaws, the air that fueled the scream finding an easier escape through the great bloody rent in her hide.

There were seven others to deal with, of course, but the blackdeath was famished. The crowd watched from the safe elevation of the stands as the great carnivore dropped Dedprod's body to the ground. It fixed her torso in place with a massive three-toed foot, then bent low, tearing off one of Dedprod's legs with a yanking motion of its jaws.

Quintaglios were too small and bony to make a good meal for a black-death, but this one was famished. Dedprod's leg fit most of the way into its maw, the giant teeth tearing the muscle from it. The blackdeath used its tiny hands to maneuver the severed limb around, the way an eggling might play with a teething rod, then at last it dropped the remains— bones slick with blood, tendons and remnants of flesh dangling from them. They fell to the ground, still articulated.

The beast continued to work over the carcass, tearing entrails from Dedprod's body cavity.

On the field, Emteem, the male from Jam'toolar, was panicking. His screams were plaintive as he begged to be released from the arena. He clawed and clawed at the arena's stone walls, trying to get purchase, try-ing to climb out, but the crowd jeered him, shouted that he was a coward, a disgrace. Cadool described the scene to Afsan. "My heart goes out to him," Afsan said softly.

This screaming, this desperate bid for salvation, was Emteem's undo-ing. As soon as it had finished with Dedprod, the blackdeath rose up and surveyed the field. Seven tasty morsels to choose from, all trying to keep as far away from it as possible. The blackdeath focused its attention on Emteem, apparently irritated by the noise and deciding to put an end to it.

Twenty massive strides took the blackdeath from what was left of Dedprod—not much—to Emteem, who foolishly allowed himself to be backed up against one of the stone walls. The blackdeath's head darted out. Emteem, still screaming, feinted to the right. The blackdeath responded by darting out again and this time it connected, its jaws clos-ing around Emteem's head, that being the part from which the offensive noise had been emanating. It closed its mouth, the massive jaw muscles bunching together, shearing Emteem's head from his body and then, moments later, it spit out the crushed bones of the Quintaglio's skull.

The blackdeath evidently decided that its previous methodology had been satisfactory. It set about devouring Emteem's carcass by tearing off the limbs one at a time, then dipping its now blood-slicked muzzle into the torso, enjoying the organs and entrails for dessert.

Two down, six to go.

There was a chance that the beast's appetite might become satiated before all the siblings had faced its direct challenge. But it was unlikely— even eight Quintaglios would constitute a small meal compared to the blackdeath's usual fare of thunderbeast or adult shovelmouth.

While the blackdeath had been picking over Emteem's remains, Kroy from Arj'toolar, wearing a white belt, had decided to sneak behind the creature, assuming that by being out of its sight, she would also be out of harm's way.

The strategy failed. No moving object escaped those giant ink-pool eyes. As soon as it had cleaned Emteem's carcass to its satisfaction, the blackdeath wheeled around and made a direct path for Kroy. The governor-apprentice of Arj'toolar was full of strategies. She tried to weave left and right, but soon realized that this was simply allowing the blackdeath to close the distance between her and it more quickly. She ran in a straight line, back toward the north end of the stadium, toward the great wooden gate, now firmly closed, from which the blackdeath had emerged.

The predator closed the distance rapidly, and she realized finally that there was no escape. But Kroy was not one to go without a fight. She turned and ran *toward* the blackdeath. The monster was startled and faltered in its charge for an instant. Kroy leapt, claws out, arms extended, and slammed into the thing's left thigh. Her claws pierced the black hide, and rivulets of blood ran down. She chomped her jaws together, taking out a bite of blackdeath. The creature made a rumbling grunt and tried futilely to swat at Kroy with its tiny forearms. Kroy tore out another hunk, but rather than swallowing, she spit it aside, then ripped out a third piece. The blackdeath tried to swing its head around to get at the Quintaglio, but couldn't contort its body in that way. Finally, with a hiss that sounded like a sigh, it simply fell on its left side, crushing Kroy beneath it. The blackdeath immediately rolled onto its belly and, using its forearms to keep it from sliding forward, pushed with its hind legs until it was back on its feet. Kroy, limbs askew in an unnatural fashion, was still alive, but dazed. The blackdeath stomped a foot onto the Arj'toolarian, the great three-toed appendage all but covering her chest. The toe-claws tore into her flesh, and she died.

The blackdeath feasted once more. When it was done with Kroy, it rose again to an erect posture and surveyed the playing field. Here it was, back at the north end of the diamond. The five remaining Quintaglios had made their way down to the southern vertex. The beast seemed to be thinking that it was a long distance to that end, and that Quintaglios really were too puny to pursue. It turned its back, as if to go, but then stopped, its massive head swinging left and right. Now that it had had something to eat, it seemed to be realizing for the first time that it was trapped again, that there was no way out of this arena.

The beast threw back its ebony head and let out a massive, rumbling roar. It turned toward the spectator stands, two angled banks of compartments high up, out of reach. It could surely see the Quintaglios, each in its compartment, almost like a gift box of candy *raloodoos*. Hundreds of morsels, each good for a few bites, but maddeningly inaccessible. It roared again, sweeping its head in an arc as it did so, as if to make sure that each and every spectator understood that it was personally an object of the blackdeath's anger.

But then it caught sight again of the five remaining contestants, milling around at the far end. They, at least, could feel its wrath directly. It began to march toward them.

The beast took the shortest course, its massive legs pounding straight along the line of orange powder that marked the major axis of the stadium. The powder rose in little clouds with each divot kicked up by its footfalls.

As it closed the distance, Cadool continued to speak to Afsan, trying to make the spectacle as clear as possible. "Nesster, Spenress, Wendest, Rodlox, and Dybo are left," he said. "It's hard to say which one the blackdeath is going to go for next. I think it's Nesster—yes. Nesster, from Mar'toolar. His belt is pink. God, that thing can move! Nesster is running now, as fast as he can, I'm sure, but he's no match—he's tripped! He's down, muzzle-first in the grass. The blackdeath is almost upon him, jaws gaping. The blackdeath's head is coming in. Nesster is scrambling to get to his feet. The blackdeath's got him—no, wait! It chomped down on Nesster's tail, just above the rump. The tail sheared clean off. Nesster is scrambling again. He's on his feet, but his balance is all off without his tail. He's leaning too far forward in his run; he should be more vertical. The blackdeath's throat is distending; it's swallowing the tail whole. It's lunging after Nesster again. Roots! I knew that was going to happen. Nesster has tumbled over onto his face again. The blackdeath—the blackdeath's got him. Jaws digging into Nesster's shoulders, a giant foot pinning his lower back, and—and—Afsan, it's arched Nesster's back, yanking up with its jaws. I've never seen a back bent that far backward. It's ripping, God—the thing's torn Nesster clean in two. And there goes the upper half—head and shoulders—right into the mouth."

Silence for a moment, throughout the stadium. Afsan could hear the wet sounds of flesh being torn. Finally he said: "That leaves four. Dybo's halfway there."

"Maybe," said Cadool. "Maybe not. The blackdeath isn't spending much time on Nesster's remains. It's looking for another target, and I'm afraid—yes, it's Dybo. The beast is charging toward Dybo." Cadool shouted, despite himself. "Come on, Dybo! Run!"

"He won't run," said Afsan.

"But he is," said Cadool. "He's running for his life. No, wait. He's— he's *stopped*, Afsan. He's just standing there, absolutely motionless, about twenty paces from the blackdeath."

Afsan made a soft hissing sound that might have been the word for "good."

Dybo froze completely, even his breath held. The blackdeath stopped charging and swung its giant head left and right, as if momentarily lost.

"I don't understand," said Cadool.

"You were once an animal handler," said Afsan. "I think you do."

"I don't see—I *do* see! But *it* does not! The blackdeath can't see him unless he's moving! Its tiny brain doesn't register stationary objects."

"Exactly."

"But how does Dybo know this?"

"He knows everything there is to know about blackdeaths now. I made him study every source, every scientific paper, every popular account. I made him spend days just watching the blackdeath in its pen."

"But he can't stand still forever. And even if he does, the blackdeath can smell him, and hear him—"

"But something else will attract its attention—"

"You're right! There goes Wendest now, trying to make it back to the north end. The fool! The blackdeath has seen her and is leaving Dybo behind. It's on her tail!"

Wendest was short work for the blackdeath. It tore her limbs off, ripped the meat from them, and disemboweled the torso. There were now five bloody corpses spotted around the great diamond field, and three contenders left—Spenress, Rodlox, and Dybo.

Rodlox was targeted next: Rodlox, the governor of isolated Edz'toolar, the one whose challenge of Dybo had caused all this. His belt was brown, the color of his province, the color of barren soil like that which covered much of his land. The blackdeath barreled toward him. Rodlox was strong, strongest of all the contestants. He did not run away from the blackdeath. He preferred to meet it on his own terms. Instead, his muscular legs propelled him *toward* the creature. The ground shook as the two of them ran together, closer, closer still, a collision imminent . . .

Suddenly Rodlox feinted to the right, running now in a circle, around and around the blackdeath. The great carnivore couldn't turn with the facility Rodlox could, and although it tried to bring its jaws to bear on him several times, Rodlox managed to keep out of its reach, running and running and running in circles, around and around, dizzyingly . . .

The blackdeath continued to circle, too stupid to know that if it simply stopped for a moment, Rodlox would come rushing around into its reach.

The strategy was brilliant—disorient the monster. And what a definitive win it would be! Not just surviving the culling of the blackdeath, but actually defeating the creature. Rodlox would secure his position firmly.

The blackdeath was weaving now, tottering back and forth as it rotated, dizziness taking hold. Rodlox's strength and stamina were incredible, to keep up the game for so long. At last the great dark beast staggered and dropped to its knees. Rodlox seized the moment and launched himself onto the creature's back, his toeclaws making red scratches in the ebony hide as he scrambled higher and higher, the bony ridges down the monster's spine like tiny stairs in profile.

The blackdeath yelled. Rodlox positioned himself firmly between the beast's shoulders and opened his mouth wide, preparing to chomp into its neck—

But then the blackdeath rose to its feet, higher and higher, Rodlox himself now temporarily disoriented—

And then it did something that no one had ever seen before—

It tipped forward, way, way forward, the upper tip of its muzzle pressing against the ground, then it pushed with its hind legs, its spine curving, and it rolled forward, somersaulting, head over heels, its shoulders taking the brunt of the roll, Rodlox expiring with a loud wet splat between the blackdeath's shoulder blades and the hard ground of the playing field. The blackdeath completed the revolution, the stiff tail flexing around, and rose back to its feet, shrugging its giant shoulders, as if to dislodge Rodlox's remains. But the bulk of them were stuck there, a flattened bloody mess. After a couple more futile shrugs, the blackdeath seemed to resign itself to carrying around the residue. Perhaps it would let wingfingers pick at its back later, cleaning away what was left of Rodlox.

Just Spenress and Dybo remained now. Spenress, watching, stunned by what she had just seen, made a mistake. A potentially fatal mistake. She backed into the angle of the diamond, trapped, with no way out. Easy pickings.

Too easy, apparently, for the blackdeath. It ignored her, turning its attention to Dybo. It started to stomp toward him. Dybo stood his ground. The blackdeath let out its characteristic roar, low, rumbling, reverberating deep in the chest, like thunder before a storm . . .

And Dybo did the same thing. The exact same thing. Roared just like the blackdeath, in an uncanny imitation of its territorial cry.

The creature stopped advancing and tilted its massive head to the left. After a moment, it roared again. Dybo replied in kind.

"Dybo's turned his back on the blackdeath!" shouted Cadool, the excitement too much for him. "Afsan, he'll be killed—"

"He's facing the spectators?" asked Afsan.

"Yes."

"Perfect."

"He's—oh, my God, Afsan! Dybo's—he's—"

"Yes?"

"He's *chomping* off his own left arm! He's—he's brought his jaws down on it—"

"Where? Exactly where is he biting it?"

—between his shoulder and his elbow. He's biting right through the bone . . . he's done it . . . his arm is falling to the ground in front of him."

The air split as the blackdeath let out its thunderous call again. Dybo replied in kind, but whether in agony or imitation Cadool couldn't say. "You hear him screaming?" he said to Afsan.

"Pain can be controlled by a strong enough mind," said Afsan. "At least, for a short time."

"I suppose, but—oh, God, he's doing it again! God, how that must hurt! He's chewing off his own right arm now! There it goes . . . that arm has fallen to the ground, too. The blood is soaking the soil. He's just got two stumps now, coming off his shoulders. He looks—he looks—"

"Just like God," said Afsan.

Cadool was staggered. "Yes! From the first sacred scroll! After She sacrificed Her arms to make the five original hunters and the five original mates! Just like God!"

There were murmurs throughout the stands, as other spectators realized the resemblance. An Emperor who was as a God! How could they have doubted him?

It was well past noon now. Dybo had maneuvered carefully. He'd positioned himself to the west of the blackdeath, the sun behind him. He turned his body in a three-quarters view, and tipped low from the waist, the short stubs of his arms dangling in front of his torso. He bowed low, lower still, his tail lifting from the ground, matching the posture of the blackdeath. Dybo roared again, precisely mimicking the blackdeath's sound. The blackdeath roared in return, but then the incredible, the miraculous, happened. The blackdeath took a step *backward*, moving away from Dybo.

Dybo roared once more, stepping forward. He dipped from the waist, bobbing, up and down, up and down, a territorial challenge, a gesture shared by both Quintaglio and blackdeath, a gesture unmistakable to the spectators and to the great ebony monster. Dybo was challenging the blackdeath . . . and the blackdeath was retreating.

"I don't understand," said Cadool.

"He may look like God to us," said Afsan, "but silhouetted against the sun behind him, with his arms only tiny stumps, and assuming the proper posture, to his mighty opponent he looks like a blackdeath—like a juvenile blackdeath."

The blackdeath roared halfheartedly at Dybo, but continued to retreat, step by step, pace by pace, back farther and farther toward the spectator stands, toward the door through which the challengers had come . . .

"But why, Afsan? Why is it retreating?"

"A blackdeath is no different from other animals, Cadool, or from us, for that matter. A mature male is often challenged by young bucks. The male endures such challenges—they're a rite of passage for the juveniles, a growth experience. Among animals, true territorial battles are only ever fought between approximately equally matched opponents. A male that size would never actually fight a juvenile as apparently young as Dybo."

The blackdeath continued to fall back. About halfway across the field, it turned around and, slumped forward, head down, it simply walked across the rest of the arena's short axis, in full retreat from Dy-Dybo.

Spenress, the only other survivor, was clearly amazed—and clearly delighted that it appeared to be over. She bowed in territorial concession to Dybo.

The crowd was stunned for a moment, then a voice, thinned by distance and the constant east-west breeze, went up: "Long live Emperor Dybo!"

Afsan remembered the day, half his life ago, when he and Dybo came ashore after their long pilgrimage voyage. They had encountered a hunting party from Pack Gelbo. Kaden, leader of the party, had told them that Dybo was now the Emperor. Then, as now, the shout was soon going up from every throat: "Long live Emperor Dybo!"

Dybo, fully back in command, ordered the gate opened, and imperial guards hastened to comply. The air was split by a ratcheting sound as the wooden barrier jerked aside. It was an athlete's gate, small for the black-death, but the retreating beast shouldered its way through, spying the daylight at the end of the tunnel. The creature was let go; it had performed with honor and great skill. Once outside the stadium, it seemed as eager to leave Capital City as the citizens were to have it gone, heading back toward the foothills of the Ch'mar volcanoes.

Cadool cupped Afsan's elbow and the two made their way to find Dybo. By the time they'd arrived on the playing field, Dybo's physician, who had been waiting nearby as planned, was already attending to him, cleaning his arm stumps so that the limbs would regenerate properly, without infection or deformity. Dybo, leaning back on his tail for support—it was important that the Emperor be seen to walk from the arena—seemed dazed or in shock, but when he saw Afsan and Cadool approaching, he apparently recognized them and tipped his head in greeting.

"He sees us," said Cadool.

Afsan bowed concession toward Dybo and waited quietly for the doctor to finish his work, all the time glowing with pride in his friend.

Chapter 45

"Afsan!"

Afsan was lying on his boulder at Rockscape, snoozing. Gork was pacing quietly back and forth.

"Afsan!" Dybo shouted again, running through the field to the ancient arrangement of boulders, the stubs of his arms ending in bright yellow rings—the first signs of new growth.

The blind advisor woke up and lifted his head from the rock. Gork, moving with a side-to-side motion, waddled out to meet Dybo, its forked tongue slipping in and out of its mouth. Dybo bent to pet the lizard, then sighed when he realized he didn't have anything to pet it with. Gork didn't seem to mind. It nuzzled Dybo's legs.

Afsan pushed himself off his rock and stood, leaning back on his tail. "What is it?"

"They've found Maliden."

Afsan threw back his muzzle in a yawn, still not completely awake. "Who?"

"The imperial bloodpriest! The one who was there at my hatching! They've found him. He was brought here under guard from northernmost Chu'toolar."

"Have you spoken to him yet?"

"No," said Dybo. "I wanted you to be with me."

Afsan groped for the harness that Gork wore, and he and Dybo headed back to Capital City, the warm afternoon sun beating down on them from the mauve sky.

"Maliden is badly hurt," said Dybo as they walked back. "He, ah, resisted arrest."

"And your agents were overly zealous?"

"It came close to being a territorial challenge, I'm afraid. His injuries are severe for one as old as he. They say he won't live long."

"It must have been a hard ride for him, severely injured, all the way back from Chu'toolar."

Dybo nodded. "Hard indeed."

There was no specific place for holding prisoners, since so rarely was someone accused of a crime. They entered the new palace office building, Dybo leading the way, Gork helping Afsan to avoid obstacles. Afsan looked somewhat pained as it became apparent they were heading down a ramp into the basement.

"What's wrong?" said Dybo.

"Nothing."

"Your muzzle shows blue, friend."

"It's—I'm sorry, I'm just remembering my own time held prisoner in a basement, charged with heresy. My apologies; I didn't mean to bring it up."

Dybo said nothing. There was nothing to say. They continued down the ramp and rounded out onto the stone floor, their toeclaws and Gork's making little scraping sounds as they continued along.

Two imperial guards stood outside a wooden door. Dybo dismissed them—there were too many people in this confined space as it was. He, Afsan, and Gork entered the musty room, and Dybo quickly moved to the far side, maximizing the space between them. The room contained a couple of wooden crates; it was obviously simply a storage area. Looking old and haggard, flopped on his belly in the center of the floor, was Maliden, the imperial bloodpriest.

"Maliden," said Dybo.

The oldster lifted his muzzle slightly. "Your Luminance," he said. "And Afsan. *Hahat dan.*"

"You have no territorial permission to give," said Dybo. "You are a prisoner."

Maliden's voice was a wheeze. "I committed no crime."

Afsan's tail swished. "Yes, you did."

Maliden looked at Afsan, then grunted as though the mere effort of lifting his muzzle again had caused him great pain. "You're wrong, Afsan."

"Wrong?" Afsan crossed his arms in front of his chest. "Do you deny that you tampered with the selection of the Emperor-to-be?"

Maliden wheezed softly. "I have done nothing that was criminal," he said at last.

"You're evading the question," said Afsan. "Tell me—"

Maliden's breath sounded like paper tearing. "I will say nothing in front of Dybo."

"I am Emperor," Dybo said. "You are accountable to me."

Maliden shook his head, then moaned. That, too, had hurt. "I don't doubt your authority, Dybo. Indeed, I honor you for it. But I will be dead soon—within the daytenth, I'd warrant. Leave me, and I'll make my final statement to Afsan. Stay, and I'll say no more." He paused, catching his ragged breath. "You can't force me to speak. Any physical coercion would finish me off right now, I'm sure." A long, protracted wheeze, then: "Leave, Dybo. Please."

Dybo looked at Afsan, who, of course, did not look back. At last, his tone ripe with frustration, the Emperor said, "Very well." He stomped from the room. Without arms there was no way for Dybo to slam the door, but he glared at it as if that were his wish.

Afsan pushed down gently on Gork's head, and the lizard flopped onto its belly, limbs sprawled out at its side. He then let go of the harness and moved nearer to Maliden, crouching down.

"Now," said Afsan quietly, "tell me about your crimes."

"Crimes?" Maliden clicked his teeth, ever so softly. "Ah, Afsan, you are as they said. You believe there's a fundamental conflict between you who are scholars and we who are priests." Maliden's wheezing punctuated his speech. "But it's not true, Afsan. We both want the same thing for the people—we want them to prosper and be happy and well."

Afsan shook his head. "You wanted control, you wanted to be able to steer society in the direction you wished it to go."

With a grunt, Maliden forced his muzzle off the ground again. "No," he said at last. "You're wrong. Look at Dybo! A finer leader we've never had. He's strong enough to exert his authority when it's required, but calm enough to let others bring forth good ideas. You yourself, Afsan, with your goal of getting us off this world. Would Len-Lends have listened to you? No, of course not. She was too forceful, too determined to defend her own territory, to lead according to her vision, no matter what."

"So you chose someone who would be more malleable, someone whose views you could shape."

"We chose someone who might be more *moderate*, Afsan. Only that. I've been told about what happened here in the streets while I was gone. Violence, death, blood spilling everywhere. It's a never-ending cycle. You, Afsan, even you, killed then."

"To dispatch one in *dagamant* is not killing."

"Semantics. Polite beliefs that let us live with ourselves afterward. Don't talk to me about such things. In my time, I have swallowed whole more than a thousand Quintaglio children. I shudder to say I even came to like the taste of meat so young, so tender. We use euphemisms to describe it, and pretend that we're not killers, but we are, to the very core, killers not only of animals for food but of our own kind. *Murderers*."

"I don't understand," said Afsan.

Maliden's breathing was becoming more ragged, as if the effort of speaking so much was robbing him of his last remaining strength. "You mean you don't want to understand. The newsriders are all abuzz with Toroca's theory of evolution, of the survival of the fittest, and how that process changes species. Toroca thinks this is a new idea. He's wrong. My order has understood it since ancient times, understood it because we practiced it. We were the agent of selection. Every generation, we made sure only the strongest survived. And that did change us, changed us as a race. With each passing generation, we became more territorial, not less. We grew increasingly violent. Yes, we became hardier, too, but at a terrible cost. We're crippled as a people, unable to work together. It became apparent during the reign of Dybo's mother that it was only a matter of time before we were driven to war. To war, Afsan! To killing and killing and killing until there was no one left to kill."

"A Quintaglio does not kill other Quintaglios," said Afsan.

Maliden coughed. "So teach the scrolls. And yet we are killers. What happened here was echoed throughout Land: *dagamant*, the streets flowing with blood. We are poised at the edge of a cliff, Afsan—on the verge of a massive, worldwide territorial frenzy that will go on and on and on." He paused, catching his breath. "Aggression reigns over us; it's the trait we've bred for. And Lends was too aggressive a leader." He paused again. "You met her; do you not agree?"

Afsan thought back to the first and only time he had met Len-Lends. He had gone to seek permission to have young prince Dybo accompany him on the rites of passage, both the ritual first hunt and the pilgrimage. Alone in Lends's ruling room, she had held up her left hand, the three metal bracelets of her office clinking together as she did so. "I will allow him to go with you, but"—she unsheathed her first claw—"you will"— and then her second—"be"—the third—"responsible"—the fourth—"for his"—the fifth—"safe return."

She had let the light in the room glint off her polished claws for several heartbeats as she flexed her fingers. *A threat.* A threat of physical violence; the very leader of all the people deliberately striking fear into the heart of a child.

"Yes," said Afsan at last. "She was aggressive."

Maliden took in breath, a long, shuddery sound. "When she laid her first clutch, the clutch from which the new Emperor would be drawn, I saw a chance to try to change that. I selected the strongest male—it was indeed Rodlox—and sent him far away. The others, in descending order of strength, were sent to the remaining provinces. And Dybo, smallest and weakest of them all, did indeed remain here."

"But why did you do this with the imperial children? Why not with the general population?"

Maliden winced; he was in great pain. "If it had worked, perhaps we would have. But remember, although I am head bloodpriest, I have my opponents, even within my order. It would have been difficult to keep such a change from becoming public. This was easier. Although a closely guarded secret, all eight imperial children always got to live ever since the days of Larsk; I made no change in that. I could not be sure of the results of my—my *experiment*, to use one of your words—if I'd done it differently."

"A breeding experiment."

"Yes."

"And it was a success."

"In most ways," said Maliden, his voice now much fainter than when he'd begun speaking. "Dybo is the best ruler we've ever had; you know that to be true. Without an equitable person such as him on the throne slab, you'd never have gotten your exodus project off the ground, so to speak. Indeed, you'd be dead—long since executed." He paused.

Afsan, uncomfortable in the prolonged crouch, rose to his feet and rocked back on his tail. "Incredible."

"Every word is true, Afsan." Maliden's attenuated voice was all but lost in the room.

"Incredible," Afsan said again.

"You see the priesthood as your enemy; as the opponent of science. I can understand that, I suppose, for it was a priest, Det-Yenalb, who put a knife point into each of your eyes. But that was Yenalb alone, and even he thought what he was doing was for the good of the people."

Afsan nodded slowly. "I know that."

"And I know that what you are doing is also for the good of the people," said Maliden.

"Thank you."

"But, now, please accept that what *I* did was likewise for the common good."

Afsan was quiet for a time. "I accept it."

Maliden let his breath out. It took a long time, as though his lungs were so congested that the air was stymied in its attempts to escape. "I'm coming to an interesting moment, Afsan," Maliden said at last. "I've been a priest for a long time. I've told others what to believe about God, about life after death. Soon, I'll find out for myself if I've been right."

Afsan nodded. "It's something we all wonder about."

"But I'm supposed to *know*. And, here, when it counts most of all, I find that I don't. I really, down deep, don't know what's about to happen to me."

"I don't know, either, Maliden." A pause. "Are you afraid?"

A voice almost nonexistent: "Yes."

"Would you like me to stay with you?"

"It is much to ask."

"I was with my master, Saleed, when he passed on. I was with my son, Drawtood, when he passed on, too."

"What was it like?"

"I didn't see Drawtood, of course, but Saleed was . . . calm. He seemed *ready*."

"I'm not sure I am."

"I'm not sure I'll ever be, either."

"But, yes, Afsan, I would like you to stay."

"I will."

"When I'm gone, will you tell Dybo that he was indeed the weakest?"

"He's my friend."

Maliden sighed. "Of course."

"And I would never hurt my friend."

"Thank you," Maliden said.

They waited quietly together.

Musings of the Watcher

I, too, waited quietly, waited for millions of years.

I missed the Jijaki. None of the other worlds I had seeded had yet borne sapient life, although I had hopes for some of them. But my best prospects, I was sure, were the mammal planet and the dinosaur moon. I watched anxiously while this galaxy completed a quarter-revolution, desperately afraid that I had miscalculated, that because of my interference, no intelligent life would evolve on either world.

But on the reptiles' new home, despite the shock of transplantation, the slow and steady increase in brain-body ratios continued unabated. Likewise, the mammals, now that all niches were open to them on the Crucible, continued to climb up the same curve.

And, at last, intelligent life appeared, nearly simultaneously, on both worlds.

The dominant land life on the Crucible eventually came to call itself *Humanity* and to call their world *Earth*. In a place that came to be known as Canada, human geologists found the Burgess shale, fine-grained fossil-rich stones dating right from what they called the Cambrian explosion, a vast diversification of life, with dozens of new, fundamentally different body plans appearing virtually simultaneously.

Almost all of these body plans died out quickly on the Crucible, although I transplanted specimens of them to many worlds. One of those, the five-eyed, longtrunked *Opabinia*, was the ancestor of the Jijaki, those long-gone cousins the humans would never know.

For their part, on the moon I'd moved them to, the intelligent beings descended from Earth's dinosaurs—in particular, from a dwarf tyrannosaur called *Nanotyrannus*—named themselves *Quintaglios*, "the People of Land."

I thought I had succeeded. I thought I had allowed both sentient forms to flourish. But it eventually became horribly apparent that there was another factor I had failed to consider.

This universe differs from the one I evolved in. Here chaos reigns: sensitivity to initial conditions drives all systems. I thought I had done well, picking the third moon of a gas-giant world. But there were thirteen other moons, moons whose orbits and masses I could measure only approximately. I hadn't been able to reliably plot orbits more than a few thousand years into the future. Nor could I accurately gauge the minuscule but not irrelevant pulls of the other planets in that system.

The tugs of all these masses produce a chaotic dance to which even the dancers can't predict the outcome. The orbits of the moons changed over time, and eventually the third become the first, growing closer, and closer still, and at last, too close, to the planet it orbited. The Quintaglio world—now the innermost moon—continued to be tidally locked, so its day matched the length of its orbit, but now its days, days that are numbered, lasted slightly less than half the length of those on the Crucible.

I can nudge a comet ever so slightly, can attract hydrogen gas if conditions are favorable, even spin corkscrews of dark matter, but I can't move worlds.

The Quintaglios have a myth about a God who had lost her hands. Without my Jijaki, I have lost mine.

But I watch.

And I hope.

Chapter 46

Rockscape

Dybo's authority was no longer in doubt. He ruled the eight provinces and the Fifty Packs unchallenged.

Spenress, the only other surviving child of Len-Lends, had given up her claim to eventual power in Chu'toolar, and, instead, had accepted a minor position in Capital City. The thirst for blood was slaked, and no one was calling for further sanctions against her.

In six of the outlying provinces, siblings of Len-Lends still ruled, but they were slowly agreeing with the will of the people: their eventual successors would be appointed on the basis of merit, not bloodline.

And in Edz'toolar, the only province in which one of Dybo's generation had already been ruling, instead of just apprenticing, there was currently no one serving as governor, for no one had been groomed to replace Rodlox. That problem would have to be solved soon, and perhaps it could provide a model for the subsequent successions in the other provinces and—the thought still startled Dybo somewhat, although he was learning to accept it—here in the Capital itself.

Dybo could live with all that, but there was one more issue in the aftermath of Rodlox's challenge that gnawed at him, keeping him from sleeping. He wished it were not his responsibility, but knew, though it saddened him to the very core of his being, that he must deal with it quickly.

He had come to Rockscape many times of late, seeking the sage counsel of his friend Afsan, and now, slimmed down, he no longer found the trek to the ancient stones uncomfortable. He hoped Afsan would have a solution for him once more. With six of his own siblings dead, plus hundreds of others killed in the mass *dagamant*, the last thing Dybo wanted to contemplate was more death.

He saw the blind one up ahead, straddling his rock, his muzzle tipped up, enjoying the warmth of the sun. As Dybo drew nearer, Afsan turned to face him. "Who's there?" he called out.

"Dybo."

Afsan nodded. "Welcome, my friend, and *hahat dan*."

Gork was nowhere to be seen. Off hunting, perhaps. Dybo was silent.

"The garrulous Dybo at a loss for words?" said Afsan, gentle teasing in his tone. "What troubles you?"

Dybo's voice was heavy. "The children."

Afsan at once grew serious. "Yes," he said softly.

"There are thousands of them," said Dybo. He shook his head. "A census is not yet complete, but so far it seems that in at least two hundred and seventeen clutches, every hatchling got to live."

"Seventeen hundred and thirty-six children, then," said Afsan automatically. "Assuming no abnormally sized clutches."

"Yes," said Dybo. "Something has to be done soon. The overcrowding is far too dangerous. Every Pack is on the verge of another mass *dagamant*."

Afsan pushed himself up off his rock. Startled, a blue and yellow snake slithered away from the base of the boulder. "I understand for the first time, I think, the burden borne by the bloodpriests," he said.

"No other choice is possible, is it?" said Dybo.

"Than to eliminate the excess children?" Afsan exhaled noisily. "I am blind, but rarely do I feel helpless. And yet, in this instance, that's precisely how I do feel. No, I can conceive of no other solution." There was a long silence as each of them digested his own thoughts. "What is the status of the bloodpriests now?" said Afsan at last.

"They've been reinstated in just about every Pack, as far as we can tell, although word from the more distant provinces is still coming in. You were right, though, as usual: as the envoys return from here, having watched the spectacle in the arena, the news that no one, not even The Family, is exempt from the bloodpriests' culling is making the reinstatement easy. And, frankly, it seems that just about everyone is irritated by all the youngsters underfoot. They're calling out for population controls."

Afsan nodded. "Have you appointed a new imperial bloodpriest yet?"

"To replace Maliden? No. His body lies at Prath, and the palace is still mourning his passing."

"But is it not the imperial bloodpriest who leads the entire order?"

"Yes."

"Then a replacement must be appointed soon," said Afsan.

"Granted. But who? Maliden had no apprentice."

"Toroca."

"I beg your pardon?"

"Kee-Toroca. My son. Make him the new imperial bloodpriest—or, at least, assign him the task of determining which should live."

"But he's a geologist."

"Yes."

"Why him?"

"Toroca is special. He has no sense of territoriality."

Dybo nodded. "I've noticed he has a tendency to stand too close to people."

"It's more than that. He doesn't feel territoriality at all. He thinks it's a secret, but, even blind, I am more observant than he knows."

"No territoriality," repeated Dybo. "Amazing."

"You and he have much in common, really," said Afsan. "I heard from Cadool about how you helped quell the frenzy in the streets."

Dybo clicked his teeth. "I have my good days and my bad. I'm certainly not free of territoriality."

"No, but yours is subdued compared to most people's."

Dybo grunted. "Perhaps. But you think Toroca, because of his lack of territoriality, should be the new imperial bloodpriest?"

"Exactly," said Afsan. "It's a sad fact that almost all of those seventeen hundred children will have to be killed. Someday, perhaps, when we do finally get off this world, there will be room for all our children to live, but until then we must have population controls. Most of the hatchlings in question are old enough now to reveal more than just how fast they are. Let Toroca devise a way to select among them. He knows what to look for, I'm sure. I guarantee he won't simply choose the fastest or strongest."

Dybo sounded worried. "But that will change—"

"Change the entire character of a generation of Quintaglios," said Afsan. "Maybe not by much, but it will be a step in the right direction."

"A whole generation chosen for something other than aggressiveness," said Dybo. "It's a daring thought."

"But a productive one. We all need to be able to work together, Dybo. You know that. The old saying is true: time crawls for a child, walks for an adolescent, and runs for an adult. Well, our civilization is now past its childhood, and time is indeed running now—running out, for this entire world."

"I had exactly the same thought myself many days ago," said Dybo. "I agree, a reduction in territoriality would be a useful thing."

Afsan's tail swished. "And remember the giant blue structure Toroca has found in Fra'toolar. When we do at last leave this world, we may be entering someone else's territory. I have a feeling that, whatever's out there, we might do well *not* to challenge it."

Dybo nodded. "Very well. I shall appoint Toroca. He won't want the job, I'm sure . . ."

"The fact that he won't want it is perhaps his best qualification for it," said Afsan. "Once the current overpopulation problem is solved, he can step down."

Dybo bowed at his friend. "You are wise, Afsan. We need more people like you."

Afsan dipped his muzzle, seemingly accepting the compliment. He said nothing, keeping his promise to Maliden, but held on to a single thought: *No, Dybo, we need more people like you.*

Chapter 47

Just north of Capital City, not far from Rockscape, there were some wide plains ending in a cliff face overlooking the vast body of water that, for want of a better name, people still called the Great River. The plains were covered with grass, kept short by shovelmouths and other plant eaters. The east-west wind blew across its level surface.

A small crowd—the only kind possible—had gathered here, gathered around what some were calling Novato's folly.

It was a bizarre contraption, made of thin wooden struts and sheets of leather and pieces of light metal. It seemed fragile, almost as if the wind would blow it away.

"My friends," said Novato, standing on an upended crate so that everyone could see her, "I present the *Tak-Saleed*."

There were murmurs of recognition from some in the crowd, but many were too young to remember the person after whom the strange machine was named.

The *Tak-Saleed* had a wide triangular canopy and a small hollow undercarriage. Its front end was articulated, with a double-headed prow that pointed both forward and back. It resembled more than anything a crude child's model of a wingfinger made from odds and ends, and yet, that wasn't quite right either, for it had a tail that fanned out behind it and its wings were reinforced with struts.

In these particulars, it looked not like a wingfinger, but like the strange gift from the giant blue egg found in Fra'toolar—like a *bird*.

Novato moved behind the undercarriage and crawled in on her belly, lying flat within. Her tail, thick and flattened from side to side, rose up through a slit that ran down the rear of the hull. Once she was in position, two assistants stepped close, strapping the protruding part of her tail into a harness that swiveled the articulated prow.

At last, the ropes holding the *Tak-Saleed* in place were cut. The steady wind blew under its great triangular wing and . . . and . . . and . . .

—*lifted it into the air.*

The crowd gasped. The *Tak-Saleed* skimmed across the plain, barely clearing the grass at times, occasionally lifting to the height of a middle-ager's shoulder.

All too soon, it skidded to a stop, having traveled perhaps twenty paces. Tails thumped the ground in glee. Novato let out a whoop of joy—

—and then a gust of wind blew across the plain and suddenly she was airborne again. Unprepared, she yanked her tail, the pointed head of the craft turned, and the *Tak-Saleed* banked to the right, into the wind, toward the cliff face.

Members of Novato's team ran toward the runaway craft, hoping to grab hold of it, but just as they got close, the glider lifted higher, higher still, sailing over their heads, sailing over the precipice—

The entire crowd ran to the edge of the cliff, mouths agape. The *Tak-Saleed* was spiraling down, lower and lower. If it hit the cliff face, Novato would be killed. She was frantically moving her tail, trying to steer.

The craft rose slightly again, but only for a moment, and then continued its downward course. Below was rocky shore.

There was nothing to be done. It would take a daytenth to get down to the water. There were no easy paths from here.

They watched, horrified, as the fragile-looking craft continued to spiral in. A real wingfinger flew into view, apparently wondering what this thing was. The hairy flyer looked so much more elegant, more in control—

The *Tak-Saleed* touched the waves—just touched them—and seemed to break apart.

Novato was strapped in, her tail hooked up to the steering contraption. If she couldn't free herself, and quickly, she would drown.

Waves crashed against rocks.

The *Tak-Saleed* looked like a dead thing, broken on the water.

Wingfingers squawked.

And then—

Something moving through the waves—

Something green.

Novato! Her thick tail was swinging side to side, propelling her toward the shore. Closer, closer still. At last she stood, waves rolling against her legs. She gestured, a great, expansive arcing of her arm, at the crowd above.

And every single one of them cheered.

The first small step had been taken.

The first Quintaglio had flown.

Epilogue

A young Quintaglio used to go through two rites of passage at childhood's end. One was the first hunt—the first truly cooperative effort—coming together and feeling the camaraderie of the pack. The other was a pilgrimage by sailing ship to the far side of the world to gaze upon the spectacle of the Face of God, covering one-quarter of the sky.

That particular journey had lost its religious significance, thanks to Afsan, but still was something that everyone did at least once in his or her lifetime. Toroca was sure that a third rite of passage—a third thing everyone did at least once—would be added to that list. Everyone would journey to the cliffs along the coast of Fra'toolar to see the great blue structure, projecting out like a giant, half-buried egg. Toroca's surveyors, and teams of bridge and road builders, had removed much more rock than the original blackpowder blasts had, but the great hull, made of that strange indestructible material, was still mostly encased in layer after layer of stone.

Once conditions settled down in the Capital, Dybo insisted on going to see the structure himself. He summoned the *Dasheter*, and he, along with Novato and Afsan and gruff old Captain Keenir, made their way to the site of the discovery, joining Toroca and Babnol there. They all stood on the beach, chill winds whipping over them, and stared up at the structure: curving blue surface against beige rock, the sky purple overhead, the sun, near the zenith, brilliantly white.

"Incredible," said Dybo softly. His arms were back to about half their normal length, the new skin bright yellow.

"Aye," said Keenir, "that it is."

"But what is it?" asked Dybo.

Toroca spoke with some hesitation. "It's a ship."

"But surely not a sailing ship," said Keenir at once.

"No," said Toroca. "Not a sailing ship."

Novato looked at her son. "What other kind of ship is there?"

Toroca turned to face her. "Exactly. What other kind, indeed?" Then, back to Keenir: "You're right, of course, it's not a sailing vessel. But I do think it's a ship. It's self-contained, having its own sleeping areas, food storage areas, and so on—one could live within it for extraordinary lengths of time. And it is streamlined, like a boat's hull."

"Then it *is* a boat," said Dybo.

"No, it's not," said Keenir, his voice like gravel grinding together. "First, it has no sails or rudder or keel. Second, its design makes no precautions against water leakage; Toroca tells me it has doors that go all the way to the floor. And third, it's too heavy."

"Too heavy?" said the still-slim Dybo, the subject perhaps near and dear to his heart.

"Exactly," said Toroca. "The blue material the ship's hull is made of is very, very dense—no doubt part of the reason it's so incredibly strong. If you were to drop the ship into water, it would sink faster than a lead weight. Even with all the hollow spaces within, it's still much too heavy to be a sailing ship."

"A ship for what medium, then?" asked Dybo.

"For space," said Toroca.

"What is 'space'?" asked Keenir.

"In this context," said Toroca, "the intervening volume between celestial objects."

"You mean the air?" asked the sailor.

"Perhaps."

"But if the ship is too heavy to float," said Dybo, "surely it's too heavy to fly through the air."

"Novato's flying machine, the *Tak-Saleed*, was heavier than air, and it flew."

Dybo nodded. "A ship of the air. A ship of—of space."

"That is what I believe, yes."

"And this ship's purpose?" asked Afsan.

"To bring life here from wherever life really originated," said Toroca. He saw jaws drop around the circle and inner eyelids flutter in astonishment.

"What do you mean?" said Dybo.

Toroca gestured expansively, taking in the entire cliff face. "Those layers of rock are like the pages of a book," he said. "But they're not a complete book. Most of the early pages are blank. It's as though we've come in in the middle of the story. This rock book is—call it volume two in a series. Volume one is somewhere else, and that book, if only we could see it and read its pages, would show us our true origins."

"We did not originate here?" said Keenir.

"Does that shock you, old friend?" said Toroca.

Keenir shook his head. "I was with Afsan when he changed the world. I'm old, and if that has one advantage, it's perspective: I've seen so much change during my lifetime. No, Toroca, it does not shock me."

"Evolution accounts for all the diversity of life," said Toroca. "Of that I'm sure. You see that lowest of the white layers in the rocks near the top of the cliff? The one we've called the Bookmark layer? That name is more apt than we knew: it marks the beginning of our story here, on this world, but by no means the real beginning of the saga of the Quintaglios. That book, as I've said, is elsewhere. We used to think the Bookmark marked the point of creation, but it does nothing of the kind. It merely marks the point of *arrival*. Life originated elsewhere, evolved elsewhere."

They all looked up at the cliff face, awe on their faces.

At last, Toroca pointed at the great blue ark. "And that, and doubtless others like it that did not fail, is how we got here." He shrugged. "Who knows? Maybe it was indeed one of eight ships." He glanced at Babnol. "Maybe, in that metaphorical sense, the story of the eggs of creation is correct."

He looked at them each in turn. "But, in any event, a huge time ago by our own standards, although quite recently in terms of the overall age of this world, our ancestors were—were—*deposited* here, transplanted by those astonishing beings who built this ship."

Dybo leaned back on his tail. "A ship of space," he said again. Everyone was quiet for a time, until Dybo spoke once more. "This gives the exodus new meaning." The Emperor tipped his head up, up, past layer after layer of rock, past the vast blue ark, past the Bookmark layer, past it all, all the way to the sky, far overhead. "We're not just going to the stars," he said, his voice full of wonder. And then he tipped his muzzle down and nodded at his friends. "We're going home."

ABOUT THE AUTHOR

Robert J. Sawyer is probably best known these days for his Neanderthal Parallax trilogy (*Hominids*, *Humans*, and *Hybrids*), but his fascination with ancient creatures goes back much further, both in his own life and in geologic time. Indeed, even before he entered kindergarten, Rob knew he wanted to be a dinosaurian paleontologist; his father—a university professor—used to read science books to him every night before bed.

It was only the sad realization that there are very few jobs for dinosaurian paleontologists that led Rob to fall back on what he'd *thought* had been an impractical dream: being a full-time science-fiction writer. Still, one of the greatest joys of doing that for a living is getting to know real scientists, and when the Quintaglio novels were first published in the early 1990s, they became Rob's entrée to ongoing friendships with the people whose jobs he coveted, including dinosaur experts Michael K. Brett-Surman of the Smithsonian Institution and Phil Currie of the Royal Tyrrell Museum of Paleontology.

Rob is a top-ten national mainstream bestselling writer in his native Canada, and his books have hit number one on the bestsellers' list published by *Locus*, the trade journal of the science-fiction field. He has won both the Hugo Award (for *Hominids*) and the Nebula Award (for *The Terminal Experiment*). He's also won Canada's top SF award, the Aurora, seven times; Japan's top SF award, the Seiun, three times, and Spain's top SF award, the Premio UPC de Ciencia Ficción, twice. He lives just west of Toronto with his wife, Carolyn Clink, and lots of plastic dinosaurs. Visit his Web site, which contains over a million words of material, at www.sfwriter.com.